ROSE GARDEN REQUEST

AN EAMON MARTINI THRILLER

P.M HERON

PROLOGUE

Belfast, Northern Ireland, January 8th

NIAMH SHEERAN, a twenty-nine-year-old New Yorker, had just clocked her fifth year since moving to Belfast to begin her research at Queens University. Eighty thousand words of neatly organised study, research, and analysis had finally culminated in her thesis: *Twenty Years Post Good Friday Agreement*. Her study looked at the link between political theory, political economy and conflict resolution; how – whether or not – it had helped Belfast move from a city stained by thirty years of civil conflict to the modern-day vibrant city on par with the likes of London, Dublin or even her native Manhattan.

Brimming with a sense of pride and accomplishment, Niamh stood outside the two-hundred-year-old main building of Queen's University, breathing in the crisp air of freedom she now felt after all her hard work. Her thick black over-coat was wrapped tightly around her six-foot-tall slim figure, providing cover from the minus two degrees winter bite, her sunglasses shielding her pale blue eyes, blocking out the blinding sun that bore down on the city from the cloudless sky above.

It was coming up to one in the afternoon and she had some time to kill before picking up her son from school.

Eight-year-old Enda Sheeran was currently on the register of Sacred Heart Christian Brother's Primary in the north of the city and would be there for another two years before going on to Saint Malachy's Grammar School just a few hundred yards away.

Despite the world-class facilities offered by Queens, Niamh had spent a lot of her time on the third floor of Belfast Central Library, and now that it was all said and done, newly-appointed Dr. Sheeran, Ph.D., felt like one last pot of Barry's Tea and a "Belfast Bap" sandwich before the school run.

After a relaxed twenty-minute stroll from the university, her chest tightened as she ascended the steps and entered through the revolving door.

God she loved this place.

Built by H&P Tully Builders, the library had opened in 1888 and was, at the time, one of Ireland's first major public buildings. The place had an historic feel to it – like walking into one of the Roman Empire's amphitheatres.

As she stepped inside, Niamh felt the same sense of serenity that she had only ever felt inside a chapel. Being raised Catholic, she spent the majority of her Sundays at Saint Patrick's chapel on 34th Street in Manhattan's Hell's Kitchen, a notoriously violent district inhabited by Irish and Italian immigrants.

To Niamh, Belfast Central Library would always feel like home, a beautiful reminder of how she felt as a kid.

She felt safe here.

Anonymous.

The hollow echo of her leather boots, clapping off the white tiled floor sent a soothing wash over her, a stark contrast to the bustling city outside. The smell of wood and old books was something she had come to love. She stopped for a moment, closed her eyes and took in the aroma. It would forever remind her of the time she had spent here.

To the right of the foyer, beneath the spiralling staircase that led to the first floor, was the tearoom. She sat in her usual corner table beside the window that offered views of the equally historic building housing the Belfast Telegraph. The table was also strategically positioned beside the cluster of vendors that offered hot and cold drinks, and an assortment of snacks. She melted into the familiar wooden chair and fished her mobile phone out of her coat pocket, reading through the flood of congratulatory messages that had taken over her Facebook page. Each meant the world to her, but none more than the message from her father, who to the rest of the world was the current President of the United States (POTUS). But to her, he was simply 'daddy'.

Her eyes began to fill with tears as she read his message. She pulled a packet of tissues out of her handbag and dabbed her cheeks.

'You okay, love?' A middle-aged lady asked, looking at her with a slight tilt of the head. She was wearing a purple woollen hat and matching gloves, her hands busy fastening a white scarf around her neck.

Niamh offered her a smile, dabbing her cheeks again. 'I'm fine, thanks.' She dabbed at her eyes, trying not to smudge her make-up. 'Bit of an emotional day, that's all.'

'You're American?'

She wiped her nose and nodded. 'Been here a few years now.'

'Studying?'

She nodded again. 'Just finished my Ph.D. It's been a lot of work, but it's finally paid off.' She dabbed her eyes again. 'Hence the emotion.'

'Well, congratulations, love.'

She smiled. 'Thanks.'

'Best of luck.'

'Thank you.'

She watched as the lady made her way across the tearoom, weaving through the scattered tables and chairs, towards the two Secret Service agents who stood at either side of the door.

One of the agents, thirty-eight-year-old Bradley Hawkins, offered the lady a nod as she passed through the set of eight-foot oak double doors and out into the main study area, the clap of her heels off the floor fading into the distance. Hawkins looked across the room at Niamh, tapping the face of his watch, a subtle reminder that they were on the clock.

Born and raised in Antonio, Texas, Hawkins was a career Marine. Being one of the 170,000 US troops to enter Iraq in March 2003, he was attached to the 173rd Airborne Brigade, parachuting into Bashur Airfield in Northern Iraq. He had received an Expeditionary Medal for his part in the war, before joining the 1st Special Forces Operational Detachment – otherwise known as Delta. It was his performance during a covert operation in Iraq to rescue a mixture of British and US troops that had supported his application into the Secret Service.

Joining the Secret Service in 2013, Hawkins spent the first two years protecting various US heads of state before eventually being assigned to protect the president's daughter while she was in Belfast.

He was the head of her six-man close protection unit.

Niamh offered him a smile and a thumbs-up before reading through the rest of her messages while finishing her tea. Once finished, she stood up, collected her things and approached the door.

Alongside Hawkins was a thirty-nine-year-old Bostonian named Mason Torres. He had followed Hawkins from the 173rd into Delta, and then into the Secret Service. Despite not sharing the same blood, they had always treated each other like brothers. There was nothing that they wouldn't do for each other. Both stood around six and a half feet tall, and even though they always dressed in unassuming grey suits, their build was still intimidating to most. They had an edge to them that tended to make others feel uncomfortable. It had always made Niamh feel secure – which was why POTUS had assigned them.

'Time to pick Enda up, ma'am?' Hawkins said.

'Yes, thank you.'

As per usual, the traffic outside the Sacred Heart was bumper-to-bumper. The car park was full, but Niamh managed to find a space along the kerb on the Antrim Road, just a couple of hundred yards down from the school.

Hawkins parked his black Range Rover on the opposite side of the street.

Niamh put her matching Range Rover in park and switched off the engine, then grabbed her phone from the passenger seat. She got out and locked the car, zipping up her coat and made her way towards the school, seeing Hawkins and Torres in her peripheral, shadowing her from across the road.

Her phone rang.

Seeing who it was, she answered it with a small smile, 'Hi, Daddy, I just read your message.'

'How's Dr. Sheeran?' POTUS asked, pride and love evident in his tone.

She laughed, brushing a loose strand of her mousy brown hair out of her eyes.

'Congratulations, sweetie.'

'Thanks.'

'How's my favourite grandson?'

'Your *only* grandson is fine. I'm picking him up from school as we speak.'

'Good. Just checking that you'll be home this weekend?'

She nodded. 'I'll be home this weekend, Dad, of course. We're looking forward to it.'

'Can't wait to see you, sweetheart.' The murmur of a female voice could be heard in the background. The president sighed. 'Okay, I've got to go. Give Enda a big hug from me, and I'll see you in a few days.'

She ended the call and entered the school, Hawkins and Torres close behind. Enda was standing laughing with a group of five other kids outside room thirteen, all still waiting for their parents. She looked into the classroom and waved to Enda's teacher, Mrs. Henderson, then helped Enda with his coat. She lifted his school bag and lunchbox.

'How was your day, sweetie?'

'I scored three goals in football today,' he said enthusiastically. He looked at Hawkins, 'Three goals, Bradley.'

Hawkins smiled, 'Well done, champ!'

'Where to now, ma'am?' Hawkins asked, as they exited the building.

'Straight home, Bradley.'

As they approached the car, Niamh spotted the lady she had spoken to at the library. She was sitting at the bus stop just a few metres away from where Niamh's car was parked.

She shrugged it off as coincidental.

She opened the rear door for Enda, made sure he put his belt on, then set his stuff on the seat next to him.

Removing her coat, she set it on the front passenger seat, then got behind the wheel.

She started the engine and indicated to pull away from the kerb, then slowly edged the car out into the steady stream of traffic, appreciating the good graces of a fellow road user, who flashed their headlights and slowed to allow her out in front of them. She pressed the accelerator and took off, indicating her gratitude with the rear lights, and made her way further north of the city. They passed Belfast City Zoo on the left and the Bellevue Arms pub on the right before turning left at the lights. She followed the Collinbridge Road for half a mile, then took the next right onto the more residential Vaddegan Drive where number eighteen had been their home for the past three years.

The street sat high up the Cave Hill mountain, looking out over the Irish Sea.

They approached the gated driveway, passing a white Sprinter van with *Tierney's Electrical* sprawled across its side.

Niamh shut the engine off and helped Enda out of the car.

'Don't forget your stuff, love.' She pointed at his bag and lunch box.

He reached across and grabbed them. 'Can we have Chicken Dippers for dinner tonight, Mummy?'

'I was thinking we could get a takeaway as a treat, since it's Mummy's last day of study?'

His face lit up; his blue eyes wide. 'Can we have KFC?'

She laughed, nodding her head. 'We can have KFC.'

'Yay! You should pass courses more often, Mummy.'

She shook her head and laughed as they approached the front door. A flicker of movement in the reflection of the window caught her attention just as she was about to insert the key into the lock. A masked figure rounded the gate's pillar and charged up the driveway. Niamh's heart leaped out of her chest and into her throat. She pulled Enda in front of her and began struggling desperately with the key. The whine of a vehicle in reverse grew increasingly louder the longer she fumbled. She finally got the door open and pushed him inside.

She wheeled around to slam the door shut and came face-to-face with the intruder. She saw nothing but their eyes: black and emotionless. She grabbed Enda and took a hesitant step back.

'Get the fuck out of my house, now!'

The intruder didn't reply.

'Mummy?' Enda cried, his voice full of terror.

'Get the fuck away from us now!' She shouted. She felt a blow to the back of the head, then Enda being pulled from her grip. Disorientation washed over her. What happened next played out in slow motion. She fell backwards, smashing her head off the wooden floor. The masked figure in front of her had a claw hammer in their hand. Niamh reached out desperately for Enda, but she could not feel him anywhere. The attacker stood over her, crouched down, and raised their arm over her again. They took swing with the hammer, knocking her out cold.

1

Eamon Martini had just finished his double espresso whilst looking out the window of Marine One as it prepared to land on the lawn of the White House. The Sikorsky VH-6oN White Hawk was one of a fleet of eight presidential choppers whose sole purpose was the secure air-taxi of the commander-in-chief. On this particular flight, the president was not onboard. Instead, Martini was accompanied by Teresa Goodall, Director of the Central Intelligence Agency.

The flight from New York to Washington DC lasted exactly ninety-four minutes. The constant hum of the chopper's propellors extinguished what would have otherwise been an awkward silence, filled with throat clearing and uncomfortable shuffling.

Goodall and Martini had never gotten along. Despite him being one of their best, she never stopped him from leaving the CIA to work alongside POTUS as head of security. The CIA director disapproved of Martini's past and was even more opposed to the way he had, more recently, dealt with matters relating to US national security. She was a strait-laced, by the book type. She was great at her job – by far the best candidate – and she believed that everything should be done within the boundaries of the law. Martini had other ideas, often doing whatever was necessary to keep the country safe. And so, they both struggled to see eye to eye. Both were still young and equally successful. They were more alike than either would admit. Both had the same intentions, just different ways of getting there. Until last year, Martini had led POTUS's Secret Service detail, going everywhere he went, until deciding to take some time off and travel the world. He was the current president's go to guy, not just an employee, but a friend.

Like family.

He had known POTUS most of his life: a family friend, growing up in the same neighbourhood in New York, before becoming an integral part of his close protection during most of POTUS's walk through the timeline of the US order of precedence.

From New York Mayor to Governor, to Secretary of State for Defence and then all the way up to his current seat in the Oval Office as the most powerful man in the world – Martini had been by POTUS's side for the majority of the journey, taking only a few years leave to fight for his country.

In the wake of the death of one of his cousins on September 11th, 2001, who had worked for the New York Fire Department, Martini had been one of the first boots on the ground in Afghanistan, attached to the 15th Marine Expeditionary Unit. During what became known as Operation Enduring Freedom, he was involved in the Fall of Kabul, the Fall of Kandahar, and the Siege of Kunduz. After this, Martini spent a few years in Delta before joining the CIA's Special Activities Centre, a unit responsible for covert and paramilitary operations.

The chopper was new, which meant the ride had been comfortable and smooth. Despite the company, Martini felt relaxed.

As the chopper landed and the door of their cabin opened, Director Goodall was quick to disembark. He quickly followed. A crowded ceremony in the Rose Garden was still underway, with President Bill Sheeran announcing Melissa Bergman as the Supreme Court nominee.

Goodall marched through the grounds with purpose, completely oblivious to him behind her. Martini believed the hostility that she displayed towards him wasn't personal. Of course, she would say that his over-inflated ego was what had led him to believe such a lie. She was five-foot-ten-inches tall in flats, always wore a business suit, and was thirty-eight years of age. Many speculated that her big breasts, slim figure, bright brown eyes, and black, shoulder-length hair had gotten her the job. But she'd long gotten used to being one of the only females in a testosterone-fuelled world.

She had joined the CIA in 1999 at the age of nineteen, just shy of her twentieth birthday. She started as a reports officer and then moved into several overseas undercover posts in various parts of the world, mainly Africa. Following September 11th, she became one of an eight-man team of CIA operatives that successfully led the US army into Iraq.

As they approached the Rose Garden, Martini kept up with her fast pace, maintaining a ten-foot distance from her. They entered the garden to find a couple of dozen suits – mostly members of POTUS's cabinet and some press. Goodall cut through the crowd, offering no more than a civil nod to those she recognised. Martini did the same.

The president sat at the head of a long table. Beside him was his wife, Irish American Katherine Mary Veronica,

Melissa Bergman, and Frank Dott – the 26th Director of the United States Secret Service.

The president spotted them and rose to his feet. He was a fit man, standing just shy of six feet tall, with an athletic build. Now aged fifty-five, his thick black hair had gained a few more strands of grey since the last time Martini had seen him, giving the sides of his head a distinct salt and pepper look. His face was still relatively youthful, but again, different from the last time Martini had been in his company. Like every other commander-in-chief before him, the pressure of the job could be seen clearly in his face. The deep lines at the corners of his eyes and mouth had not been there before.

As they got closer, Martini noticed the president's eyes were rimmed in red, his pale blue eyes glazed – like a man who had been on an all-night whiskey binge.

'Eamon, thank you for coming on such short notice.' He offered Martini his hand, then looked at Goodall. 'Anything?'

She cleared her throat. 'Nothing, sir.'

Martini looked at Goodall, then at POTUS, his confusion growing. 'Mr President, what's going on?'

The president turned, making his way towards the white and grey marquee that occupied the edge of the garden. Two Secret Service agents stood on either side of the entrance. POTUS passed between them, Martini and Goodall followed. The marquee was empty, apart from a table with an open laptop sat in the middle.

The laptop displayed a grainy video on pause. At first, Martini could not make out what was on the screen, but as he got closer, it became evident: Enda Sheeran was tightly bound to a chair. The room around him was indistinguishable. The walls were a faded grey, cast mostly in darkness. A dim yellow light cast shadows over the boy's face, but Martini could still recognise him. The boy's eyes were puffy and red as if he had spent the last few hours crying. He was wearing a stretched-out navy jumper with the Sacred Heart crest on the left breast.

Martini's gaze jumped wildly between Goodall and the president, completely speechless. He could see the tears begin to pool in the president's eyes.

'Sir, shall I play the video?'

The president nodded.

She crouched over the table, took the mouse, and guided the cursor over the play button.

The video began.

Voice MoD software had been applied, and the speaker's words were spoken with the Deep Satanic facility.

'Your country has terrorised parts of the world it had no right to be in. Many people have suffered due to your western policies and alliances. The greed of the Americans and the British has ruined the lives of millions of people. And now you will feel the pain which you have brought onto others.' A person wearing a military-type green and black shemagh, dressed in Afghan Police uniform, moved into the picture, stepping up behind Enda. A blood-stained machete was clasped tightly in his left hand; with the right, he grabbed Enda by the hair, pulling his head back and exposing the bare skin of his neck. Enda's agonising cries could be heard echoing throughout the bare room. The kidnapper brought the weapon up to the boy's throat and held it against his skin. Enda's tears began to pool around the blade, dripping down the side of his neck and disappearing under his jumper.

The kidnapper spoke again.

'If you don't want us to post your grandson's head back to Washington, you will do exactly as we tell you...'

'Stop the video!' POTUS shouted, his voice cracking.

Goodall did as she was told and closed the laptop.

'What does he want?' Martini asked.

The president cleared his throat. 'They want us to kill the British Prime Minister.'

'What? Why us?'

'Because they know we can get close to her.' Goodall interrupted. She ignored Martini, turning her body away from him, towards the president. 'Sir, I think it's time we called Prime Minister Pears and...'

'No!' POTUS slammed his fist down on the table, causing the laptop to rattle. 'I've already told you, I don't want anyone else to know about this.' He looked at Martini, his expression vulnerable.

Martini was speechless. He had to remind himself who he was looking at. Despite POTUS's esteemed position, at that moment, he was nothing more than a terrified grandfather.

Martini folded his arms and sighed, 'Where's Niamh?'

'She's inside. Doesn't want to see anyone.'

'She was still studying in Belfast?'

POTUS nodded. 'Just finished.'

'And where the fuck was her security? Hawkins, Torres and the others?'

POTUS shook his head. 'Gone.'

'I'd selected those men myself before leaving. I'd left Niamh with the best security she could have. How the fuck do they just disappear?' He looked at Goodall, his brow pinched in confusion. She shook her head. He looked at POTUS. 'How do a team of our highest trained Secret

Service agents just disappear off the streets of Belfast without a trace?'

'It has to be someone on the inside,' Goodall said, 'Someone who must have something against the president.'

Martini gestured towards the laptop. 'Who's the guy in the video?'

'We don't know who the person with the machete is, but the attack's come from Ludwig Schuster, a German billionaire. He lives in Berlin.'

'Did you trace the video back to where it came from?'

'The sender cloned their ID, we've got spots all around Europe.'

Martini shook his head. 'I don't get it, a German?'

'Mr. Schuster is half Afghan, on his mother's side. Schuster's cousin, Ahmad Jaleel, was one of the only survivors of a US drone strike which took out his entire family during his wedding.'

'When was this?'

'Two years ago, during the last administration.'

'And his wife to be?'

'Dead.'

'Jesus.' He looked back at the president. 'Do we know where Enda's being held?'

POTUS shook his head, his shoulders sagging.

'I've contacted an off-the-books tech specialist, a hacker,' Goodall said, 'They're going to help us find out who's responsible for this. Some fucker close to the White House is responsible. But with Schuster's demands, we can't exactly go to anyone about it, including the Irish or British authorities.'

'Well, Schuster and Jaleel aren't going to wait around forever. You'll need to find out who the traitor is. Only a select few had access to Niamh's whereabouts and the security she was assigned.' Martini looked at the laptop again, trying to think. 'I'll go to Berlin. Meet Schuster. I'll tell him I'm there to discuss the job. Knowing my background, he'll believe I'll be only too happy to take out the British Prime Minister.' He looked at Goodall. 'It'll give your guy a chance to find out where Enda is.'

'What if we don't find him in time?' POTUS asked. 'They'll expect you to carry out the job. If this gets out, we'll start a fucking war.'

'Let me worry about that. I'll think of something along the way.' He turned to Goodall. 'Do you have any agents in Berlin?'

She smiled thinly. 'After our Station Chief was expelled from the country in 2014, US and German intelligence relations have been a little fragile, to say the least.'

'Well, tell nobody I'm there. Not yet.'

'Excuse me, *Martini*,' Goodall said, her expression hardening. 'I am in charge here, you've simply…'

'Eamon's here because he's the best man for the job,' POTUS interrupted. 'He's the only person I trust to get Enda back.' She didn't respond. He gave them both a stern look. 'You two are the only people I trust right now. I want you both to put aside your differences and work together. I don't want this going any further. Eamon, you go to Berlin. Teresa, you and your tech guy are moving into the White House until we get Enda back, I'll have you set up with a room in the Executive Residence. Niamh will be there, maybe she has something that can help us.'

'Sir, my guy won't pass vetting, we haven't enough time.'

'Fuck vetting him, just get him here. If you trust him, that's good enough for me. You will be Eamon's aide for anything he needs while he's in Europe.' He looked at Martini. 'The Germans can't know about this. As Teresa said, US and German relations haven't been good since they kicked Station Chief Murdock out of the country.'

Goodall frowned heavily, glaring at Martini, then turned to the president where her gaze softened significantly. She took a steadying breath, squared her shoulders, and turned back to Martini. 'Eamon, my guy's managed to hack into the German intelligence database to see if we can find anyone who could be involved in the attack in Belfast. We didn't know what we were looking for, but we knew when it popped out at us. The BFV – the German domestic security agency – has carried out recent checks on an Irishman and his wife; they do this will all new German residents. Seamus and Mary O'Toole have, just last week, received a wire transfer of one million euros into their Deutsche Bank account.'

Martini frowned. 'Friends of my father,' he shook his head, 'I've known them for a long time. I wouldn't like to think they'd be capable of something like this. But someone else who knows them; who's also living in Germany: James Greer. He'd sell his grandmother for some cash.'

'Funny you should mention him. Greer's been working in Berlin for the last couple of years. We've pulled off photographs of him with Schuster and an unknown male who fits the description of Ahmad Jaleel.'

'Send me everything you have.' Martini looked at the president. 'We'll get him back.'

'Arrange a flight for him to Berlin, Teresa.' POTUS looked at Martini and sighed heavily, the weight of the world on his shoulders. 'And for God's sake, Eamon, don't get caught.'

2

Berlin, Germany, February 2nd

EAMON MARTINI FOUND himself in a country that he had not
set foot in for more than ten years. Unlike his last visit, this
was more business than pleasure. The time was six forty-
three in the evening. The sun had set some time ago and the
star-studded black canvas above was, despite its beauty, an
unwelcome sight. The lack of cloud cover let whatever heat
provided by the sun disappear as quickly as the rays themselves, leaving a frigid cold to linger in the streets.

Martini stood in the doorway of number seventy-two
Bermannstre Street, shielding from the freezing wind. The
Deutsche Post had closed shop at six-thirty. The low
mumbles of postal staff members could be heard inside,
finishing off their post-closure duties before heading
home. He was looking across the street at an Irish pub
toting a bright green shamrock above its door. A football
match was due to get underway in just over an hour, and
the enthusiastic cheer from the patrons suggested that

there would be plenty of craic, regardless of the game's outcome.

Martini fished his Android out of his back pocket. Unlocking the device, he spotted a message from CIA Director Goodall.

POTUS has made contact with Schuster. He will be accompanied by Greer and Jaleel, expecting you at the Arthur Guinness Irish pub, 88 Bermannstre Street, Berlin. Greer's mobile number is: +497598366999. Watch your back, Eamon.

Martini activated silent mode and shoved the device back into his pocket.

Stepping in front of the post office window, he glanced at his reflection. His bright white trainers, dark slim-fitting jeans, and navy polar neck beneath a hooded leather jacket was meant to make him look younger than his thirty-nine years. He was six-foot-tall, with an athletic figure. His thick black hair cast a slight wave to the right on the top and was shaved around the back and sides. His eyes were icy blue and piercing; calculating and as cold as the ice on the road.

He shoved his hands inside the jacket pockets and carefully made his way across the slippery road towards the Arthur Guinness, the sound of Christy Moore singing traditional Irish folk music growing louder with every step.

A WHITE MERCEDES S Class was parked outside the Arthur Guinness with the engine running. A well-built man in his late twenties wearing a black jumper, with a shaved head was in the driver's seat. His left hand was clasped tightly around the steering wheel, with the letters K I L L R tattooed in red ink on the knuckles. He was accompanied by another two men of the same age occupying the back seat. They were all hidden behind the window's black tints.

'That's him,' one of the men in the back said in German. He was thin, with scruffy hair and wore glasses, 'He's dressed like a fucking twenty-one-year-old student; looks like he just stepped out of the Freie Universitat.' He removed a black Beretta from its holster beneath his jacket.

'Wait. Let him go inside. He'll have nowhere to run in there,' the second passenger said. He was built like the driver and also had a shaved head. 'He doesn't know we're here. Let's keep it that way. Besides we want people to witness us at work.'

'What are we supposed to do inside?' the driver said. 'He looks like a pussy.'

'Mr Schuster said to pick a fight with him then to go from there,' the one with the glasses and pistol said.

'With the amount that Mr. Schuster is paying us, and the possibility of full-time work, I'll gladly slit the bastard's throat right here.' The driver made a fist with the left, looking at the letters across the knuckles.

The one with the pistol laughed. 'As great as that sounds, you need to stay in the car and keep the engine running.' He looked at the bald one beside him, 'Let's go.'

Martini was not looking directly at the Merc, but he knew that there were eyes on him. He had to. His life depended on it. And with years of looking over his shoulder and sleeping with one eye open, he was used to being alert at all times. It was the only reason he'd lived so long.

Opening the door to the Arthur Guinness, he was hit with a wave of heat and the distinct smell of lager. A sea of green, white, and orange almost fooled him into thinking he was in his second home city. Belfast was his father's native city, and Martini considered it home as much as the Big Apple.

The lady behind the bar looked no older than twenty; her slim figure was curvaceous, and complemented her fitted Irish jersey. She stood with her arms folded, watching the widescreen TV behind the bar, the sports commentary blaring out louder than all the other noise. Her line of sight fell to Martini the moment he closed the door behind him. She watched him closely as he crossed the pub, weaving through the occupied wooden tables that seated the overly enthusiastic Irish football supporters.

He unzipped his jacket. The heat of the room, in contrast to outside, had turned his face an uncomfortable-looking shade of pink. The bartender smiled brightly at him, her deep brown eyes sparkling under the pub's fluorescent lighting. He responded with one of his own.

She spoke in German. 'What can I get you?'

'Just a cup of tea, please.' He answered in the same. 'It's freezing outside, need something to warm me up.'

She smiled, brushing a strand of her black hair out of her eyes. 'Have a seat and I'll bring it over.'

'Thanks.'

Much to his appreciation, the best seat in the pub – the one with a view of all exits – was without a good view of the television, and therefore blissfully empty. He did not care much for football, or Soccer as it was called in the States. He was a baseball man, a die-hard Yankees fan.

But all sports aside, he was more concerned about the patrons who were coming and going. He took his seat and surveyed the crowd. The attention of most of the patrons remained glued to one of the many screens strategically placed around the room, watching the commentators give their analysis of the teams warming up on the pitch. Football was the biggest sport in Germany, like the rest of Europe. Although Martini had never taken much of an interest in the sport before, he greatly appreciated it at times like these. Nothing provided more anonymity than being in a crowd of rowdy football supporters during a much-anticipated game.

The bartender brought his attention back to the table. 'Here you go.' She set a tray down on the table with a stainless-steel teapot and a cup and saucer. 'Sugar, milk?'

'Just milk, please.'

She smiled at him. He smiled back. Had he been fifteen years younger, and had she not been wearing an engagement ring, he would have asked her to join him. She was beautiful, but in a workplace where people indulged in liquid "Dutch courage" she would have heard it many times.

Martini busied himself with the contents of the tray while, out of the corner of his eye, he tracked the movements of the three men who had just entered the pub and seated themselves at a corner table. One of them sat cross-legged in a slim fit grey suit, looking like he would be better suited at a posh gentleman's club than at a pub filled with rowdy football supporters. Martini knew that he was, in fact Irish, and perhaps the biggest supporter in the pub. James Greer, an Irish republican to the core. Next to Greer sat a man of Middle Eastern origin who appeared to have not yet adjusted to the local weather, fully decked in a heavy fur coat, matching woollen hat, and gloves. From the intel Martini had received from Goodall, this was Ahmad Jaleel. The third man wore a navy suit with an open-neck white shirt underneath. His expression was serious, a stark contrast to the jovial faces that filled the room. He gave the impression that he was the one in control, the other two whispering in his ear while he just nodded and watched the TV. He was the one who wouldn't do much talking in public, but silently directed. He was the bastard responsible for kidnapping Enda Sheeran.

Ludwig Schuster.

The pub's front door opened, and two men stepped inside. The one at the rear was a few inches shorter than the door, thin, and wore a blue suit. He had chin-length scruffy brown hair and thick-rimmed glasses that sat perched on the end of his pointed nose. His accomplice stood a few inches shorter, dressed in a dark hoodie and baggy stonewash jeans. His black boots and shaved head reminded Martini of the Combat Eighteen knuckle-draggers that used to roam the streets of England.

The C18 lookalike met Martini's gaze and held his stare.

Martini knew straight away the pair were not there to watch the football.

The thin one walked with a slower gait than his thuggish mate.

They both weaved through the tables, nudging patrons in passing. Neither of them acknowledged the attractive bartender who was watching them closely from behind the bar. From her pinched expression, Martini could tell that she either knew them, or had the same gut instinct that he was getting. Perhaps they had a reputation, but with the image of Enda and Niamh Sheeran at the front of Martini's mind, he wasn't in the mood, and would gladly display an example of his own reputation.

Approaching Martini's table, the thuggish one continued to play the staring game from behind heavy brows, right up until the table rested against his legs. He crouched over the table, resting his fingertips on the edge. Martini could smell stale cigarette smoke.

'This is my table. You're going to have to move some-where else.'

Martini ignored him and poured himself a cup of tea, steam curling out of the cup.

'Are you deaf?'

Martini lifted the jug of milk and poured slowly.

'Maybe he can't speak German,' the thin one said.

'This is my seat,' the bald one repeated, this time in broken English.

Martini looked up at the pair. 'I don't see your name on it.' He spoke in German. He glanced at the slim one. 'And for the record, I speak German well.'

The thug turned and looked at his mate, switching back to German. 'Cocky bastard, isn't he?' He reached under his hoodie.

Martini calmly took a sip of the tea, twisted his wrist, and threw the rest of the cup's contents at C18's face. The guy raised his hands to his face and staggered back, screaming in agony. Martini jumped up off his seat as the thin one reached into his pocket. Martini launched the cup at him, hitting him between the eyes, sending him to the ground along with his glasses that bounced across the floor. He lifted the teapot and drove it into the side of C18's head, sending him to the ground next to his mate. He stood over the pair, realising all eyes were now on him, then knelt next to them and reached under C18's hoodie, pulling out a meat cleaver.

He stood up and studied the cleaver intently, various nicks and dents along the blade, then looked down at C18 and kicked him solidly in the balls.

He stepped over him and towards his mate, who was bleeding profusely from a deep laceration across his fore-head. He side-kicked the inside of the guy's knee as he attempted to get to his feet. The sound of bone snapping was followed by agonising cries as the guy fell to the ground again, clutching his leg.

Martini crouched down and reached inside the man's jacket, removing a Beretta from its holster. He stood up again, and removed the magazine and bullet from the chamber, putting them in his pocket.

A couple of patrons came over to offer help to the wounded men. Martini left them to it and walked over to the bar and set the weapons down next to the Guinness pump, looking at the lady. 'I'd get rid of these if I were you.'

She eyed him, speechless, then looked over his shoulder across the room. He followed her line of sight to the table Greer sat at. Her gaze fell back to Martini. 'These are dangerous men, sir. I don't know who you are, but I suggest that you leave before more trouble comes.'

'Thank you.'

He made his way towards the door, spotting Greer get up from his seat. Greer called out to Martini. He stopped at the door. The other patrons averted their eyes and continued to watch the TV as the audio came back. It was almost as if the last few minutes hadn't even happened, as if nobody had been left scalded and bleeding on the floor.

Martini remained where he was. Greer pursed his lips in irritation, but turned and said something to the other two at his table, then joined Martini at the door.

'Nice suit, Jim,' Martini said sarcastically. 'Why'd you pick this place to meet?'

Greer offered him his hand. 'Eamon Martini.' He spoke as if he were greeting an old friend, but Martini's reluctance to shake his hand showed that the feeling was not entirely mutual. 'How've you been, kid? It's been a long time.'

Martini turned and nodded in the direction of the two

thugs who were both having first aid administered to them by the bartender. 'What was that stunt all about?'

Greer looked over Martini's shoulder, smirking. 'Those clowns were after a job from Mr. Schuster. They're known to be quite ruthless in Germany. Killers. They came looking to fill a post as Shuster's problem solvers.' He laughed. 'I told him to give them a task, see how well they can handle them-selves – after all, they were applying for an important job. And knowing you were in town, you were to be their target.'

Martini cast another glance back at them, shaking his head, before turning back to Greer. His voice hardened. 'What the fuck are you doing, Jim? Getting involved in something like this. The president's grandson – are you stupid?'

Greer's smile dropped, as he glanced in the direction of his table. 'You don't know everything, kid. This crazy bastard's got money to burn, and he's got some very influ-ential people in his pocket. Either we join him, or we're all fucked.' He cleared his throat. 'I know you were sent here to get Sheeran's grandson back, but if you saw the way that poor bastard's family was wiped out on his wedding day...'

'So target the person responsible, don't kidnap a bloody eight-year-old.'

Greer swallowed. 'I'm not happy about this either, but when Schuster found out Niamh Sheeran was studying in Belfast, we didn't have a choice. He may be a lunatic, but he's a fucking intelligent one. And his cousin's even worse. Talk about a loose cannon. And Schuster's connections.' He shook his head and whistled, 'I'm talking Taliban.'

Martini sighed. 'Fuck the Taliban! I've fought them before, and I'll go after them again if I have to.'

Greer smiled, 'I know you would, you're fearless.'

'Don't blow smoke up my ass. I need to see the kid before we go any further.'

He shook his head. 'No can do, Eamon. The president's already requested that. Schuster's refused. POTUS gets nothing until the job's done.'

'If he wants me to do the job, I need to make sure the kid hasn't been harmed first.'

'Sorry, Eamon. The kid's not close by, anyway.'

'Get the kid here. I want to be in the same room as him before we go any further. For all I know he could be in a Taliban infested cave right now.'

'We can get you a photo, or even a video, but that's about as far as we can go.'

He shook his head. 'You've got my number. Get the kid here, and call me when he is.'

Anything he could scavenge on the boy's location would immediately be fed back to Goodall. He stepped around Greer towards the door. 'Don't waste my time, Jim. No matter the circumstances, if this kid dies, I'll be taking your head as well.'

'You've no idea what'll happen to that kid if you mess these people around, Eamon. They *will* send him over to Afghanistan. You know what they'd do to him if they found out who he is.'

'For all I know he's already over there.'

Greer turned and pointed at his table. 'Just sit down with him first and then we can go from there.'

Martini cast a quick glance at the table, both Schuster and Jaleel were looking at him, Jaleel was speaking, Schuster nodding. Martini turned back to Greer, looking him square in the eye. 'Tell Schuster I'm his best option. The president wants this done quietly to get his grandson back. The other option won't be good for anyone.' He turned his back to Greer and exited the pub. Once he was outside and far enough away from the pub, he pulled his phone out and called Goodall.

She answered almost immediately. 'Martini, what have you got?'

'I've told them I'm not talking business until I see the kid.'

'Now's not the time to be playing games with them, Eamon.'

'I know. Have you managed to get anything on the kid's location?'

'Not yet. We've just set up our workstation in the White House. I'm going to speak with Niamh, see if she has anything she can give us.'

'Get anything you can. He could be on a jet over the mountains of Afghanistan right now.'

'Let's hope he isn't.'

He ended the call and crossed the street in the direction he came. The driver of the Merc had the window down, and was blowing smoke out of the car. He frowned at Martini as he passed, his expression curious.

3

Greer returned to his seat, cursing Martini under his breath. He sat down and looked at Jaleel. 'It's a good thing you've wrapped yourself up nice and warm because you're going after him, now get going before you lose him.' Jaleel stood up. 'Ahmad.' Greer grabbed him by the arm. '*Don't* lose him.'

The Afghan nodded and rushed towards the door, disappearing outside.

'Martini doesn't look like much,' Schuster said over the rim of his glass before taking a drink.

Greer gestured across the room where the bartender was assisting paramedics who'd just arrived. He smiled. 'Would you like to tell them that?'

He took a sip of his drink, eyeing the down-trodden pair. 'You told me that this guy was not only tough, but smart. I want to see it for myself. And those goons over there are two of the most dangerous men in Germany.'

'And Eamon didn't even give them a second thought.'

'Impressive. But is he really President Sheeran's best man for the job?'

'He's the most valuable asset that the US President has,' Greer stated simply.

'Tell me more about him.'

Greer took a sip from his glass and sucked through his teeth, admiring the liquid in silent appreciation. 'Martini is an interesting guy. His father was from Belfast, one of the Provisional IRA's rising stars in the seventies. Damien Cleary Jnr. pretty much walked onto the movement's army council when Damien Snr. sat on the council as Chief of Northern Command. It was a crazy time – Catholics all across the north of Ireland were being burned out of their homes by the police and loyalist paramilitaries.' He shook his head, allowing himself to ponder for a moment, before continuing. 'That was a time when the Catholic community had nobody but the IRA to protect them.' He took another drink. 'Martini's mother was from New York, daughter and heir to the throne of the Martini family – one of the five families that made up La Cosa Nostra. Cleary Jnr. met Maria Martini whilst in America raising funds for the republican movement. They met at a NORAID function, fell in love...'

'NORAID?'

'Its official name was the Irish Northern Aid Committee. It was an Irish American aid committee set up in 1969 at the beginning of the Troubles. Its founder, Michael Flannery, who'd fought in the Irish War of Independence and the subsequent Civil War following the partition of the country in 1921, believed it was his duty to use his influence in America to seek funding to support the republican movement. It provided funds to support the armed struggle. And after Bloody Sunday, many Irish Americans believed the British should leave Northern Ireland and allow it to re-join the rest of the free state.' He paused to take another sip of his drink. 'Nine months after Cleary Jnr. and Maria Martini met at the fundraiser, baby Eamon popped out. Cleary Jnr. was his son's hero, a real hard-ass, but smart as well – a tactical genius when it came to urban warfare. But Eamon spent his childhood in New York while his father and grandfather fought the war on the other side of the Atlantic. His mother wouldn't allow her son to go over there and get caught up in it all.' He cleared his throat. 'But at seventeen, Eamon heard of a conspiracy to assassinate his father. A couple of members of MI5 and Army Intelligence were colluding with the UDA and UVF, passing on intel to target IRA volunteers, and members of Sinn Fein. Eamon, being an unknown face in Belfast, went and got involved. He unmasked an IRA double-agent involved in the plot. After preventing the assassination, and pissing off a few people in the British security services, he went back to New York to be with his mother. He loved her, Christ he worshipped that woman.' He took a shuddering breath. 'She was murdered protecting him. He witnessed an execution in Queens, something that would have incriminated the heads of two of the other five families and they decided he had to be eliminated. She died for him. Her dying wish was for him to move away from the mafia life, for him to do something good with the time he had been given in this world. She died in his arms. Apparently she told him she was dying happy because she was in her baby's arms.'

'Jesus,' Schuster said. 'Poor bastard.'

'Something interesting happened to Martini after that. He lost the one person that truly loved him, apart from his father. He didn't want to live anymore. His father, busy trying to fight the war in Ireland, a conflict that seemed to be going on forever, was furious when he found out that the killers of Maria Martini got off clean. The killers had the right people in their pockets. The death of Maria Martini was the last straw. Cleary Jnr. took a young and angry Eamon under his wing. He knew his son's mentality, he was the apple of his eye, stubborn as a mule. Cleary had to do something about it. He gave his son a focus, a discipline. Kept him at a secret location in Ireland where Cleary began training him in everything he knew.'

'What about the killers of Maria Martini?'

'They'd disappeared shortly after the trial.'

'Cleary got them?'

Greer nodded. 'Apparently one of them was Martini's first kill. Cleary killed the other.'

'You speak highly of them.'

'I understand that you want to avenge your family. I respect that. I'd do the same. But remember this, Ludwig, if you give Eamon Martini a reason to kill you, he'll snatch the life right out of you and not give you a second thought.' He smiled and shook his head. 'I was impressed when I heard you wanted to take Sheeran's grandson. That takes balls.'

'How much is Martini worth?'

'He's not for sale.' Greer took a sip from his glass, finishing off the drink. His phone buzzed. He pulled the Android out of the inside pocket of his jacket. It was a message from Jaleel:

He's just jumped into a taxi. I'm following him now. I won't lose him. I'll call you when we stop. Ahmad.

A thin smile spread across Greer's face as he read the message.

'What?' Schuster asked, as he finished his drink. 'Share the joke.'

'If Martini picks up on his tail, Ahmad's going to get the fright of his life.' He stood up and buttoned his jacket closed. 'Let's get out of here. These football fans are about to get a little too rowdy.'

Schuster led the way out of the pub.

The freezing air had a sharpness to it that cut right to the bone.

Greer wished the bartender, who was sweeping up broken glass from the smoking area, a good night and followed Schuster towards the blue BMW 6 Series that was parked across the street.

Bermannstre Street's nightlife was coming alive.

4

Ahmad Jaleel stopped his car fifty yards behind the taxi. They were at another Irish pub, just a few streets away from the Arthur Guinness. He shook his head and sniggered, thinking to himself that Martini must have a strong liking for Irish pubs. He shut the engine off and quickly killed the lights as he watched Martini get out of the taxi and make his way inside the Green, White, and Orange. He watched the taxi pull away, then hopped out of the car and rushed across the street. As he approached the pub, he noticed that these patrons were watching the same football match as the ones in the Arthur Guinness. He removed his gloves and scarf as he stepped inside. Martini was sitting quietly at a corner table, his eyes glued to his phone. There were only twenty minutes before the game got underway; soon the bar would be over-crowded.

Jaleel's nerves were on high alert, experiencing palpitations caused by the two cups of black coffee he'd ingested at the Arthur Guinness. He made his way to the bar, trying not to look in Martini's direction.

'Could you tell me where the toilets are, please?' he asked.

The barman was around his age, forty-five, maybe fifty, and was fully decked in the Ireland football jersey and hat. 'Just around the corner; past those three booths.' He pointed to the far end of the bar.

'Thanks.'

He quickened his pace, his legs feeling like rubber sticks underneath him.

He rushed into the males, holding the door open for two rowdy fans that exited past him. The place reeked of piss. He entered the only cubicle and closed the door, engaging the lock. He pulled his phone out. As he was typing a message for Greer, he heard the door open. It closed, followed by a small click. He ignored it, assuming someone simply wanted to take a leak in private. He was continuing with the update when Greer phoned him.

'James, I was just in the middle of texting you, he's in-'

Before Jaleel had a chance to say another word, his door splintered open. Martini stood in front of him, a Dessert Eagle .50 pointed straight at his head, with a suppressor fitted to it.

'Give me the phone, Mr. Jaleel.'

Jaleel's trembling hand reached towards Martini, handing the phone to him.

'We need to talk,' Martini said, dragging him out of the cubicle by the knot of his tie. Martini put the phone on loudspeaker 'Since this guy's following me, Jim, can I assume that Enda's in the city already?'

'Ludwig isn't willing to give away the kid's location just yet,' Greer said. 'You have to understand, Eamon, that poor bastard lost his entire family in one day. Ahmad, who you've clearly apprehended, is a man with very little to live for. The president's grandson is not going to be harmed. All he wants is someone to answer for what happened on his wedding day.'

'And how much is this worth to our German friend?'

'I told him to be prepared to pay a hefty price for your services, Eamon. He knows your story. Come on, you'll be taking out the British Prime Minister. That was once a dream for everyone in the republican movement, especially your father and grandfather.'

Martini sighed, turning to a terrified Jaleel. 'I'm not doing this for money, but I'll need help to get the job done, and a job like this will require a lot of financial rewards for whoever I choose. Meet us at the Green, White, and Orange on Schiffbauerdamm Street. My Afghan buddy and I are going to have a chat in the meantime.' He ended the call and tossed the phone back to Jaleel, then holstered his pistol. 'I hope you've got money on you because you're buying.'

5

Dorian Chance, a thirty-five-year-old from Silicon Valley in the southern San Francisco Bay area of California, began his career in hacking at the age of fifteen when he'd used a distributed-denial-of-service (DDoS) to bring down Dell, eBay, CNN and Amazon, overwhelming their corporate servers and causing their websites to crash. Chance, nicknamed "Chancer" had, at the time, opened the eyes of government authorities to the severity of cybercrime, something that costs companies trillions of dollars every year and was a tinder that sparked the evolution of global cybersecurity.

He'd just fired up his computer, when Goodall stepped into the room.

'Welcome to the White House,' she said in mock humour. 'Have you managed to find anymore on the German database?'

He re-positioned his glasses on the end of his pointed nose and cleared his throat. 'Nothing, yet. But I've some files I want to decrypt, see what's in there.'

'You wanted to see me?' Niamh Sheeran said, standing at the doorway. Her right eye was bruised, swollen and completely shut. Her left arm was in a sling. Her left eye was red and full of mascara smudge. She wiped her nose with a tissue and stepped further into the room.

'Niamh, I know this is hard,' Goodall said, walking across the room to her, 'But can you remember anything? Any tiny detail that might help?'

Niamh sat down on the sofa in the middle of the room, below a painting of President Lincoln. 'The lady.'

'What lady?'

'In Belfast Central Library, I was crying in the tearoom – tears of joy, not like these,' she wiped her nose again, 'She approached me and asked if I was okay. An hour later, when I was picking Enda up from school, I saw her sitting at the bus stop on the Antrim Road.'

'Can you describe her?'

'Middle-aged, around five-six. She was wearing a purple hat and gloves, with a white scarf and a heavy coat. I'm sorry, I can't describe any more than that.'

Goodall sat down beside her, 'Any memorable cars, vans, bikes – anything with a registration plate? Anything that made you look twice at it?'

She wiped her nose again, shaking her head. 'I'm sorry...' then she paused. 'Tierney's.'

'Tierney's?'

'Tierney's Electrical. It was a van parked close to my house. It was the only van on the street, the last thing I read before...' she broke down.

Goodall placed her hand on Niamh's knee. 'I'm sorry, I know this is hard.'

'I just want my baby back. Why are they doing this?'

POTUS walked into the room, his face red with anger. He looked at Chance then at Goodall, 'Anything?'

Goodall stood up, 'Dorian, I want you to hack into Her Majesty's Revenue and Customs. Look for Tierney's Electrical. I want to know who owns that company. Profiles and bank activity.'

6

Greer grinned at the phone, then looked across at Schuster who was in the passenger seat of the car, thumbing something into his phone. The vehicle was idling at the gates to his private estate on the outskirts of the city.

'Well?' Schuster asked impatiently.

'Ahmad's with him now. He's waiting for us at the Green, White, and Orange. I think we've got him onboard. We've got him ready to listen, at least. I'm know how close he is to the president, but he's always been Damien Cleary's son first and foremost. He should be happy to have the chance to assassinate the British Prime Minister.'

Schuster nodded. His expression was hard and cold, his piercing blue eyes devoid of any emotion. 'Let's hope so.' He glanced down at the expensive watch on his wrist, 'I have a meeting with a contact in Kabul soon.'

'Can't it wait? It would be better if you're there to meet him, too.'

Schuster shook his head, 'I'm sorry.'

'This is your operation, not mine. I only agreed to make the introduction.'

'This can't wait, James. You go and negotiate on my behalf.' He unbuckled his seat belt and opened the door. 'Tell Martini that I'll pay him whatever he asks if he'll come and work for me.'

'The only problem is that Eamon's spent his entire life working with President Sheeran. He may agree to assassinate the British Prime Minister, but I don't think he'll ever work for you.'

Schuster slammed the door shut and peered through the half open passenger window, glaring at Greer. 'Everyone can be bought. I want Eamon Martini. You know what my family is worth. Tell him that he can choose a number.'

He turned away from the car and approached the gate. After fishing a remote control out of his jacket pocket, he pointed the device at the black wooden gates. The sound of the gate's mechanics kicked in and they slowly began to part, revealing a driveway that ascended towards a modern style building with a stout garage block to the right. He waved Greer away as he walked through the gates. As he pressed the second button on the control, the gates drew to a close. Directly to his right was a large twenty-four-hour security hut. The door opened and a man dressed in black trousers, a black shirt, and a suit jacket stepped outside.

'Evening, Mr. Schuster. Do you need anything?'

'I'm fine, thank you, Hans. You have a good evening.'

'And you, sir.'

Hans Weber was a discharged member of the Kommando Spezialkrafte, the German Special Forces, that was recently disbanded. Plans to dismantle KSK's 2nd Company followed the discovery that the company had a culture that leaned towards far-right extremism. After 500 active soldiers were investigated by German counterintelligence, it was put to the German Minister of Defence that many of its members were still in support of illegal groups, including neo-Nazi organisations. And with many of the country's highest trained soldiers out of work, Schuster had employed a team of twelve to work for him on a twenty-four-hour basis, acting as his close protection and his property's security.

The estate was essentially a fortress. It was surrounded by a ten-foot-high perimeter wall, painted in a bright white with thick black slabs across the top. Factoring in the KSK members prowling the premises, Schuster slept well at night knowing nobody was getting onto his property without permission.

Schuster walked up the driveway, pulled his phone out of his pocket, and opened the app that he used to control the electronics in the house. After pressing a few buttons, the alarms were de-activated, the lights came on, and the electronic mechanism on the front door was released. He had even put the coffee machine on in the kitchen.

Schuster was not just a wealthy man, he was one of the richest men in the world. It was estimated that his family's net worth was sitting around twenty-three billion, but it was rumoured that they were worth much more. When he had told Greer to give Martini whatever was asked, he was being very literal. He would not bat an eyelid at most amounts. One thing Schuster knew for a fact was that President Sheeran would only put his faith in the best to get his grandson back. Now that Schuster knew who that person was, he desperately wanted him on his payroll.

As he stepped inside the house, he hung his overcoat and suit jacket over the coat rack next to the door. He kicked off his shoes and pulled off his socks. It was an unfortunate fact that his feet sweated a lot when he was nervous, and right now, he was very nervous. Schuster rarely found himself in situations where he felt out of control, but Martini's decision to come work for him was beyond even his influence.

The heated tiled floors that ran throughout the house were a pleasant sensation for his bare feet. He stopped and looked at the selection of family photos on the wall beneath the stairway that snaked up the left side of the entrance. He lifted one. It was a photo of him and Jaleel when they were younger. Jaleel was not only his cousin, but his best friend.

Schuster kissed his index fingertip and pressed it to the glass of the photo. 'My family, my heart,' he said in Arabic.

Schuster was born to a German father and an Afghan mother. Quite an unusual match, but when it came to love, culture and the colour of a person's skin didn't matter. A powerful message that Schuster's father had preached to his son, and the rest of the family. Schuster's mother had to leave her home in Afghanistan. Falling in love with a white Christian Catholic was not something that would have gone down well with the Shia Muslim community, and so Asal left to pursue a new life with her husband.

Schuster's father was from a long line of cigar merchants that had moved into the diamond trade in the early part of the twentieth century, building an empire that would become one of the world's leading precious stone corporations.

Ernest Schuster had become sick with lung cancer when Ludwig was just fifteen years old. A young Ludwig became the man of the house and the family business long before his time. His father's illness taught him to never waste a moment in life and to always strive for the best. All Ludwig had ever wanted to do was to make his father proud.

Naturally, without his father, his mother had become the closest person to him before her passing. Her dying wish was for her son to never turn his back on his family. Including her blood family in Afghanistan. So, when Ahmad Jaleel came crying at the door of Schuster's estate late one night, there was only one thing he could do: whatever it took.

Hanging the photo back up on the wall, Schuster walked through the hall and stepped into the kitchen. His espresso was ready. He made his way to the patio, mug in hand.

He relaxed on a lounger next to the pool, looking at the black and white helicopter that rested on the landing pad just fifty yards down the garden, like an overgrown child's toy – a rich man's toy.

He sipped his coffee and thought about the man he'd just watched in action at the pub in the city centre. He didn't look like much, a normal looking man. But then, those were usually the ones capable of doing the most damage – the average joes, not bulky bodybuilder types who stood out in a crowd. It was the people who blended in who often inflicted the most damage. Mr. Martini was the man who could help ease his cousin's pain and suffering. He hoped he would agree to do so. If not, he might require convincing in other ways. But from all the stories that Greer had spewed about Martini, Schuster had gathered that methods of a forceful nature were best avoided.

He received an alert on his phone. A news report. More suicide bombings in Afghanistan, targeting the heart of the country. A nation in turmoil and mourning. He felt himself heat up, his face and neck reddening. He was a man with so much power and influence. Something had to be done. The Great Satan had to learn.

A text message came through from a family friend: the former Afghan Finance Minister, recently voted in as the President of the Islamic State of Afghanistan.

My dear Ludwig, the Western powers have all but turned their backs on the Afghan people. This peace agreement with the Taliban is a joke. In order to win votes, the president of the United States and the British prime minister, will be pulling their troops out of our war-torn country. This will not be forgotten. I fear for the future of our nation, of our brothers and sisters. Many more people will suffer at the hands of the Taliban. I may need to call on your influence one day, my dear friend. May Allah be with us all.

Schuster sighed and made his way back into the kitchen. He grabbed a bottle of whiskey and a shot glass, then returned to the lounger. He poured himself a shot and downed it. He poured himself a second and held the glass up to his face, examining the amber liquid. He took a sniff of it, the sharp smell burning his nostrils, then downed it.

7

Martini sat in one of the seven booths that ran along the window of the Green, White, and Orange. Jaleel sat opposite him, struggling to maintain eye contact. Martini found some amusement in the fact that the Afghan had been sent to follow him, but ended up having the tables turned and now sat opposite him looking like a fish out of water. Jaleel was sent because Greer couldn't be arsed following Martini himself. And Schuster certainly was not going to be the one chasing people around in the cold. Perhaps it was just a prank. From what Martini remembered, Greer had a twisted sense of humour. He should've known that Jaleel would be caught. Had Martini been followed without realising it, they would not have wanted him for the job. But as it stood, he was the best and that left him wondering: why send the Afghan? Perhaps Greer was trying to get Jaleel killed, which Martini had considered, but then he thought about Enda. It had been many years since Martini had spoken to Greer, and people change. Some for the better, and others not so much. It was unclear to Martini which way Greer had gone. But he certainly wasn't the man he once knew.

Martini cast a glance around the room, then back at Jaleel. 'I'll have a coffee, when you're ready to go up. I don't drink alcohol, so don't even think of trying to come back with something cliché like Irish whiskey.'

'Alcohol is bad for your health, Mr Martini.'

Martini nodded. 'A lot of things are bad for your health, like following a man you know nothing about.' Jaleel was about to rise, but Martini stopped him. 'I'll get the drinks, in fact. Don't want something falling into my cup now, do I?' He stood up, slid out of the booth, and made his way to the bar. He spotted Greer entering through the front door and pointed towards the booth.

'What can I get you?' the bartender asked.

'Three cups of coffee, please.'

The barman nodded. 'Take your seat, I'll bring them over.'

Martini glanced at the pair at his table and made his way for the door. He stepped outside and made a quick call to the president.

POTUS answered immediately. 'Eamon, what have you got?'

'I'm just about to sit down with Greer and Jaleel. I've told them that I'm not talking about the job until I've had a visual of Enda. But they're not playing ball.'

The sound of the president swearing under his breath could be heard through the phone. 'Okay, Eamon. I don't want these fuckers doing something to him. Just play ball. Pretend you're going to carry out the hit. At least it'll buy us some time. Teresa's doing a search of HMRC for an electrical company that was at the scene of the kidnapping. If she finds anything, I'll let you know. Until we have a location on Enda, you're going ahead with the job.'

'Yes, sir.'

Martini ended the call and went back inside. He approached the booth, looking at Greer admiring the shiny Rolex and the gleaming bracelet on his wrist. 'Business good, then?'

Greer nodded. 'It can be good for you, too.'

'I'm not the flashy type. Couldn't see myself wearing pretty jewellery like that.' He smirked and slid back into the seat, his legs rubbing against the underside of the table. 'I do like the suit, though.'

'With the amount of money our German friend is willing to offer you to come work for him on a more permanent basis, you can buy one of these suits every day for the rest of your life.'

'Tell your billionaire friend to stick his money up his ass. If the kid comes back unharmed, then I'll maybe let him live.'

'Ludwig is ready to die for this, Mr Martini,' Jaleel said, 'As am I.'

'You better be ready for that, if something goes wrong.'

Greer's eyes shot over Martini's shoulder. The barman approached with a wooden tray, carrying the drinks. He whipped a stained tea towel off his shoulder, dried up wet rings on the table, then set the cups down.

Martini offered him a polite nod. 'Thank you.'

Jaleel lifted his cup and sipped on it with obvious pleasure. Greer looked at his drink as if something were about to jump out and bite him.

'Don't worry, I haven't poisoned you.' Martini took a sip, peering at Greer over the rim. 'Just drink the bloody thing, Jim. If I wanted to kill you, you'd be dead already.'

'You could have at least poisoned it with a few percentages of alcohol,' Greer replied, then took a sip. He nodded his head in appreciation. 'Not bad, though.'

'Mr. Martini,' Jaleel spoke up, apparently coming out of the shell he had been cocooned in since staring down the barrel of Martini's pistol. Perhaps his confidence had grown with Greer by his side. 'I want to talk to you about the state my country is in and explain to you why we've resorted to such measures.'

Martini took a drink, his steely eyes fixed on Jaleel then quickly jumping to Greer and back again. 'Go on.'

'I have lost most of my family in a recent drone attack...'

'The president told me about the airstrike.'

'On the poor bastard's wedding day,' Greer threw in.

Jaleel looked at Greer, then back at Martini. 'I am no poor bastard, Mr. Martini.' He cleared his throat. 'But yes, on my wedding day.'

'You're acting like the first person that's ever lost someone.' Martini set his cup down. 'Let me tell you something, you're not.'

'I know many others have been scarred by the bombs and bullets of the world's superpowers, not less your own family – in Ireland, am I right?'

Martini shifted, wanting to re-direct the subject. 'For what it's worth, I'm sorry. But you have kidnapped a young boy. An innocent. He's got nothing to do with the decisions made by the government of his country. He's become yet another innocent casualty - just like your family.'

'Yes,' Jaleel said, 'I agree with you. I am sorry that we had to resort to such measures, but it is the only way we can get justice. The British government has as much innocent blood on its hands as your commander-in-chief. You are someone, Mr. Greer tells me, who would take great pleasure in killing the British Prime Minister. The enemy of my enemy is my friend. That is you, Mr. Martini.'

'Eamon,' Greer interjected, 'the Americans have turned

their back on the people of Afghanistan. They've had their little peace talks with the Taliban and now President Sheeran's agreed to pull out. Thirteen thousand American troops will be going back to the US. The Afghan people will be ill-equipped to fight against the Taliban. Every Shia in the country will be butchered the moment the Yanks leave.'

Martini shook his head. 'I'm only here to get the president's grandson back. And not because he is my commander-in-chief, but because an innocent boy needs my help. I will take the job, just for him. Not for some political cause, and not to avenge your family.'

Jaleel cleared his throat, his eyes glazing over. 'You will need help carrying out the job. Do you have anyone in mind?'

'I do, but they'll require paying. And you will cover the cost.' Martini finished his coffee.

'How much?' Jaleel said.

'Ten million,' Greer said, finishing his coffee. 'Ten million, Eamon, will that cover the costs?'

'Give me ten million to sell the idea. But don't be surprised if I need more.'

'What about the British?' Jaleel said.

'What *about* the British?'

'How protected are they?'

'Not enough to stop me from getting the job done.'

'So, then, you will attack?' Jaleel exclaimed, his eyes wide.

'You realise that an attack on Prime Minister Pears won't bring your family back?'

'I want the western world to know the pain my people have felt. And still feel.' Jaleel rubbed his watery eyes, then his posture straightened up as if every muscle in his body had seized.

Martini looked at Greer. 'Do you know of anyone in Germany who might be aware of this planned attack?'

'Why do you ask?'

'I don't want to be left standing with my dick in my hand, surrounded by Germans and Brits. Not even the president could get me out of that if it goes wrong.'

'Ludwig has German police in his pocket, Eamon. I don't see there being a problem,' Greer said. 'This guy has eyes and ears in places you wouldn't think possible.'

'Germans, British and Americans,' Jaleel added.

Martini looked at him in deep consideration. The words registered, but he put them away for later. Jaleel had put his foot in his mouth, but Martini acted like the comment had been overlooked. 'He's a powerful man.' He took his phone out of his pocket and looked at Greer. 'I'm going to text you my bank details. I'll expect the money by midnight tonight.' He sent the text and waited. Greer's phone vibrated on the table.

Greer glanced down at his phone. 'Got it.'

'We can supply you with everything you'll need,' Jaleel said.

'I'd rather get everything I need myself. I haven't confirmed yet that the people I have in mind will take the job. But I'll know in the next twelve hours.'

'The fewer people that know about this operation, the better,' Greer added.

'Let me worry about that. You only need to worry about the money being in my account.'

Martini got up and slid out of the booth.

'Eamon,' Greer said, 'Why don't you come and spend the night at the Schuster estate?'

'I'm just making a call, then I'll be with you,' he said, then swiftly exited the pub.

A thin blanket of frost had covered everything. The ground sparkled. Steam rose from his mouth with every breath. He pulled his phone out and called Goodall.

'Eamon?'

'I've taken the job. I'm going to pay Seamus O'Toole a visit and offer him the chance to help me carry out the assassination. If the O'Tooles are involved with the group, then according to Greer, Schuster may have forced them into the kidnapping in Belfast. I suspect that they may have done it out of fear. If they have, then they might be willing to bend and give up Enda's location. Have you got anything?'

'The O'Tooles have recently had one million euros wired into their bank account, Eamon. They're involved.'

'Bastards,' he clenched his jaws, 'What about Enda?'

'It's as if he's just disappeared.'

'It's beginning to seem that way.' He sighed. 'When I asked Jaleel and Greer whether there was a chance the Germans might know what's going on, Greer assured me that there wasn't anything to worry about. But Jaleel let something slip. He said Schuster's got Germans, British, *and* Americans in his pocket. He's got someone helping him on the inside, Teresa. Some bastard within the US government has been feeding information to Schuster.'

'It has to be someone close to the president. And someone within the Secret Service. I do not believe for a minute that Niamh's bodyguards were just set upon. Nobody knew she was in Belfast except for the Secret Service and a handful of others.'

'I've been offered a room at the Schuster estate. I've accepted. I'll call you once I've spoken to O'Toole.'

'Before you go – Prime Minister Pears is at a UN meeting in Vienna. She's not in London. And she usually goes to her holiday home in Switzerland while she's in that part of the world. This might buy you some time so you can continue with the pretence that you're going to take her out.'

'Thanks. I'll call you once I've spoken to the O'Tooles.'

'Watch your back over there, Eamon.'

8

Frank Dott, forty-three-year-old from Kenton Town in the small, mid-Atlantic US state of Delaware, came from a family of teachers and university lecturers. His father, two uncles and grandfather had all held esteemed positions at the IV League University of Pennsylvania. Instead of following in their footsteps, Dott decided to pursue a career in law enforcement. He began his career in nineteen ninety-nine as a Special Agent in the New York Field Office, conducting investigations into cyber-enabled financial crimes for the joint FBI-NYPD taskforce. After nine years, he moved to the Presidential Protective Division and served as the Secret Service's liaison to congress, and all other bodies on Capitol Hill. In twenty-twenty, he was appointed Assistant Director of Protective Operations, where he oversaw the presidential campaign, and subsequent transition and inauguration of President Sheeran into his first term in office.

Dott had just arrived at the White House to go over the plan for his trip to the UK where he would meet with the British Prime Minister, the heads of MI6, MI5 and GCHQ.

POTUS had spoken to him on the phone just before he left the house, saying he was pulling out of the trip and wanted Dott to be there to ensure the British knew they had full US support in tackling the growing threat from Islamic extremism in the UK.

He stood looking at himself in the bathroom mirror, straightening the knot of his red tie and brushing the creases out of his navy suit jacket. He was six-three and two hundred pounds. He was built like a soldier and walked with the same gait as the scores of Secret Service agents protecting their commander-in-chief. His eyes were blue and intelligent. His hair was ginger and cropped. He was an average looking man. Not overly good or bad looking. A symmetrical face, with plain features.

His phone buzzed in his pocket. It was a text from the lady he'd taken to dinner last night before taking her back home and spending the night with her. She was gone by the time he woke up this morning, just the way he liked it. The text read:

Thanks for last night. Enjoy your trip to London and hopefully we can see each other when you get back.

He sent her a smiley face and pocketed the phone, then left the room and went to kill thirty minutes before his meet with POTUS.

9

Dorian Chance was playing on his phone when he received an alert from the computer. It had spotted something which caused his eyes to pop out of his head. He jumped up from his seat and rushed across the room to the door, Goodall and POTUS where just on the other side. He opened it. 'I've got something.' He turned and hurried back to his station, dropping himself into his seat. POTUS and Goodall followed him.

'What is it?' POTUS said.

'I pulled off the data from HMRC. Tierney's Electrical is owned by a Mark Tierney from Belfast. His wife, Danielle, is registered as the company accountant.' He opened another page. 'I performed a search of the two for any photographic imagery. Facebook pages, Instagram, Twitter.' He opened Facebook. 'Look at Danielle Tierney's profile picture. A middle-aged lady posing in a snowstorm with what looks like Belfast's Titanic Quarter in the background; what is she wearing?'

Goodall crouched over taking a closer look. 'Purple hat and gloves with a white scarf.' She looked at POTUS. 'I think this is the woman Niamh spotted at both Belfast Central Library and then at Enda's school.'

'I'll go and get her.' POTUS turned and left the room.

'There's more,' Chance said, 'Tierney's Electrical has a business account with the Bank of Ireland. This account has recently received two million British pounds from an account I can now confirm is owned by Ludwig Schuster.'

'Good work, Dorian.'

'There's more. I hacked into Schuster's account and took note of all other large transactions made recently. One I think you will be particularly interested in. Five million dollars was wired into the account of your current head of Secret Service.'

'Frank Dott?'

'Yes, ma'am.'

'Son of a bitch.' She looked around at the door as Niamh and POTUS arrived. 'Sir,' she pulled him aside, 'Where's Dott?'

POTUS' expression said he knew where this was leading to. 'He's here, I've a meeting with him soon before he leaves for London.'

'Well, sir, his bank account is linked to Schuster's, and is now five million dollars better off.'

POTUS' nostrils flared, 'I'll fucking kill him.'

'As much as I would like to help you with that, sir, he'll be more use to us if we let him carry on thinking we don't know about him.'

'What do you suggest, Teresa?'

'If you can somehow separate him from his phone, I can insert an I X chip and download his phone, it'll give us access to everything on it. Calls, text messages, emails, what porn sites he searches.'

'Something that might lead us to Enda's location.'

'That's the only thing we care about, sir. Let the son of a bitch go to London, pretend like everything's fine. He'll slip up, they always do. Once we have Enda, we take him down.'

'We better hope this leads us to Enda's location. As it's stands, Eamon's about to assassinate Prime Minister Pears and start a war.' He massaged his temples. 'You'll join me in the meeting with Dott. We'll have it in the Rose Garden. I'll take him for a walk. How long do you need his phone?'

'Should download in forty-five seconds, sir.'

They joined Niamh and Dorian back at the workstation.

'That's her,' Niamh said, 'That's the woman that approached me in the library.'

POTUS clenched his jaws. 'Get this sent over to Eamon. Teresa, I'll see you in the Rose Garden in one hour.'

10

Martini returned to the Hilton Hotel to collect his things. Being offered a room at Schuster's estate was the perfect opportunity for him to get close to the enemy. He collected his belongings and quickly exited the hotel, accompanied by Jaleel and Greer. He knew that the offer was a way for Schuster to keep an eye on him, but that worked well for him, too, as he would use the opportunity to get into the estate and familiarise himself with the layout, turn over a few rocks, see what was beneath. While unlikely, there was always a chance that he may find something useful to feed back to Goodall.

Pulling up at the gates in matching BMWs – Jaleel's being black instead of blue like Greer's – Martini had chosen to travel in the car with the Afghan, preferring not to ride along with Greer and run the risk of listening to him reminisce on the old days with Cleary Jnr. and Snr.

Jaleel fished a remote control out of the door's side pocket and sent a message to the security system to grant them access. The estate was quiet. Eerily quiet. The constant hum of traffic that could be heard throughout the city had fallen silent a few kilometres out. The stillness created an absence, and tension in the air caused an uncomfortable tingle to ripple down Martini's spine. Perhaps that was why Schuster had chosen to build there. It was like they were entering a completely different world.

The 6 Series ascended the driveway, passing the security hut where a security guard watched them with shrewd, dark eyes. The twin headlights beamed out in front of them, piercing the darkness.

As they got out of the vehicle, Martini could hear a radio blaring from one of the garages – the one on the far left. Then came a repeated sharp clink of a hammer striking metal.

'I see he likes to play around with cars,' Martini remarked, as he strolled towards the open garage. A black Ford Mustang was up on the ramp with Schuster standing beneath it, catching oil in a container.

'I still don't understand why you don't just pay a mechanic to work on your cars,' Jaleel shouted over the radio.

'You just don't appreciate a good invention like the automobile. Us Germans pride ourselves on being around these magnificent machines.'

'You mind if I borrow one?' Martini asked, stepping into the garage, inspecting the Ford. 'Just to get into the city – something reliable.'

Schuster set the container down and wiped his hands on his stained overalls. He stepped out from beneath the vehicle, offering Martini his hand. He accepted. 'You're a wise man, Mr. Martini.'

'Eamon needs some funds to support him in the job – some cash persuasion for hired help,' Greer said, approaching from his car.

'How much?'

'Ten million,' Greer stated simply.

'In pounds,' Martini added.

Schuster nodded. 'Who's your help?'

'I'll worry about them.' Martini eyed the wide range of expensive cars lined up in the garage. 'Just let me have a quick shower and freshen up. Give me the keys to one of these cars and I'll be on my way.'

'You are planning to assassinate the British prime minister, Mr. Martini. I would like to know who you're bringing in to this job with you.'

'Call me Eamon, please. Mr. Martini sounds too official.' He reached out to stroke the gleaming back bonnet of the Mustang. 'Two of my old friends are living in Berlin. Seamus O'Toole and his wife.' He looked for any kind of reaction from Schuster. There was none. The man was hard to read.

'Eamon, then.' Schuster smiled shrewdly. 'Is this O'Toole trustworthy?'

If the O'Tooles were involved, then why was Schuster disassociating himself from them? Perhaps they knew more about Enda's location.

'Seamus O'Toole and his wife were old friends of my father and,' he looked pointedly at Greer, 'of Jim here, too. They'll have no problem taking out a British Prime Minister.' Martini glanced at Greer then back at Schuster. 'And this is a fortuitous time.'

'Why?'

'Prime Minister Pears has a holiday home just south of the German border – Switzerland.'

'What makes you think she's going to be there?'

'Because she's recently been to a UN meeting in Vienna and she always stops there for a few days on her return trip to the UK.' He eyed the three.

Schuster looked sceptically at Martini. 'What makes you so sure?'

'CIA intelligence.'

'Okay then,' Schuster said, turning back to the Mustang. 'If you need any other assistance...'

'I'll let you know.' Martini turned and studied the house. Six windows along the bottom floor and six along the top. Two forty-foot-tall pillars stood at the entrance, leading up to a grand balcony that overlooked the estate. 'Nice way for a billionaire to spend their money, I suppose.'

'Come with me,' Jaleel said, 'I will show you to the guest quarters.'

'Give Eamon the key to whatever vehicle he likes,' Schuster called from beneath the Ford, staring intently up into the engine.

Jaleel started towards the front entrance. 'That's a dangerous game to play, cousin. What if he sees the chopper?'

Martini followed Jaleel up the marble steps to the black oak door and through the foyer that looked like something from a classically styled hotel. High ceilings, with ten-foot-tall paintings decorating every wall, and a brass lift sparkling beneath the chandeliers in the right corner, its glass tube stretching up to the next floor.

At the lift door, Jaleel pressed the button, calling it down. Martini hung his bag over his shoulder.

Jaleel smiled at him. 'Thank you for helping us.'

'I haven't done anything yet.'

They stepped into the lift. Soft classical music played inside. Jaleel pressed the button for the first floor, the doors gliding closed with the same smooth grace as everything else in the building.

Martini laughed.

Jaleel looked at him curiously. 'What do you so find amusing?'

'I have just never seen such a perfect waste of money in my life.'

'Ludwig gives millions to charity every year.'

A bell sounded and the lift stopped. The door opened. They both stepped out and Jaleel pointed down the long expanse of the corridor. 'The guest suite is down there. There's a wardrobe if you need to change. I will be in the kitchen.'

Martini offered Jaleel a civil nod and made his way down the corridor, studying the artwork displayed on the white marble walls. He'd always admired creative work – the most human form of expression and it was one thing that, in a world full of ever-advancing technology, would never be replaced by machines. Despite his roots, first in New York and then later in the Catholic areas of Belfast, he had always found himself particularly impressed by centuries-old works of art.

He entered the guest room, which was more like the executive suite in a five-star hotel. A four-poster bed sat in the centre, and a leather sofa was only feet away from a blazing fire. The wardrobe could have easily been on the gent's floor of a high street retailer. Clothes of every size imaginable filled the racks.

He set his bag down, grabbed his mobile, and brought it into the en-suite with him, typing a text to POTUS and Goodall.

I'm trying to buy us time, but we need to locate Enda soon before they know I'm bluffing. I will approach O'Toole and offer him money to help with the assassination. I've told Schuster the job will take place at the PM's home in Switzerland when security will be at its most vulnerable. I'll botch the job if I don't hear any more about Enda's location. But Teresa, the ball's in your court regarding his whereabouts. One more thing – Schuster didn't mention knowing the O'Tooles when I told him I'd be approaching them about the job. So, he may be keeping something from me. Will be in touch.

He sent the message then flushed the toilet. He went back into the bedroom, tossed the phone onto the bed, and went for a shower.

After freshening up, he chose a pair of dark jeans, a navy hoodie, and a long leather coat. The black boots were light and narrow at the toe. Once he was dressed, he grabbed his phone again and made his way down to the kitchen.

Jaleel, Greer, and Schuster were all sitting at the marble island in the centre of the room.

'How much input do you need from us, Eamon?' Greer asked. 'I know you like to work alone, but if there's anything we can help you with, just say the word.'

Martini shook his head. 'Just make sure the president's grandson remains unharmed.' He eyed them, warning in his gaze. 'Or else I'll be back here for all three of you.'

Jaleel shifted uncomfortably in his seat.

'How are you getting to Switzerland?' Schuster asked.

'I need to talk to O'Toole. Then I'll go from there.'

Jaleel reached down to his side and grabbed a grey gym bag, handing it to Martini. 'There's one hundred thousand euros in there. A little spending money to help with the job.'

'Check your account, ten million British pounds should be there,' Schuster added, sliding a key across the island. 'You seem like a man that likes to be high up. A black Audi Q7 is parked close to the gate.'

Martini took the bag and the key. 'Coffee to go?' He gestured towards the coffee machine.

'Absolutely,' Greer said.

The smell of freshly brewed coffee still lingered in the air as the three men escorted him out the door.

'Good luck.' Jaleel offered Martini his hand. 'And thank you again.'

Martini nodded and smiled wryly. 'Just pray that the president doesn't send me after you three.' He headed to the car, giving the speechless trio his back. He deposited his bag onto the rear seat and got behind the wheel, feeling as if he were test driving a brand-new vehicle. As the engine rumbled to life, he read only one thousand and five hundred miles on the clock. The vehicle had barely been touched. He selected the sat nav on the dashboard screen and thumbed in the address to the Green, White, and Orange.

He studied the impressive security guard who stood to attention beside the gates as he passed. He could tell that the man would be a handful. The gates slowly parted, revealing the outside world once again. Turning left, he made his way back to Berlin.

11

President Sheeran sat at the table in the Rose Garden, waiting on Goodall and Dott to arrive. He was looking at a photograph on his phone: Niamh and Enda standing outside Queens University in Belfast. It had been their first Christmas in Ireland. Enda was only five years old. A mix of anger and confusion left him shaking. He'd been unable to sleep; furious at himself. The most powerful man in the world; how could he not have kept them safe? Catching Goodall in the reflection of his phone screen, he turned and watched her approach the table. She sat down next to him.

'I want to strangle the bastard, Teresa.'

'Sir, we'll get Enda back, and after that, you can do whatever you want. Just keep it together. All I need is forty-five seconds to download his phone, then you'll not have to deal with him again until this is over,' she looked to her right, 'Speak of the devil.'

Dott approached. The afternoon sun, despite being the middle of winter, was blinding. Dott had a pair of sunglasses on, a brown leather bag clasped in his left hand. 'Good afternoon, Mr President,' he said, offering POTUS his hand.

POTUS could feel Goodall's eyes burning a hole into the side of his face; she needed him to stay calm, and it took every ounce of his self-control to do so. He stood up and shook Dott's hand, it was clammy. 'Are you all set for your trip to London?'

'Yes, sir.' Dott set his bag down on the table. 'What's keeping you both from attending the meeting?' He looked at Goodall, then back at POTUS.

'Let's take a walk, Frank,' POTUS said, leading the way along the garden, passing the vegetable patch his wife Katherine had been working hard to maintain during the cold months. 'This goes no further, Frank, okay?' POTUS kept him walking.

Dott looked at him, confused, 'Of course, sir.'

'I need to keep Teresa close; need to keep an eye on her.'

'Why?'

'I can't tell you more at this moment, but I believe she's become a security risk, and until I'm certain, you understand, I can't go into any more detail than that. But I need you to make sure Prime Minister Pears knows she has our full support with the Jihadist threat. They're our closest ally.'

'What shall I tell her when she asks why you're not there?'

'Just tell her a personal matter has come up, offer her my sincere apologies, and ensure her I will call her soon. Can you do that for me, Frank?'

'Of course, sir.'

They made their way back to the table. Goodall was watching them.

'Have a safe trip, Frank.' POTUS stopped at his seat and put his hand out to Dott as a sign that their meeting was over. Dott accepted. 'I'll expect a full brief when you get back.'

'Yes, sir.' Dott lifted his bag and nodded to Goodall before making his way back towards the West Wing.

POTUS sat down, looking at Goodall. 'You get it?'

She nodded, 'Got it, sir. And well done, that mustn't have been easy.'

12

Arriving back at the Green, White, and Orange, Martini reversed the car into the last vacant parking bay on the street. He could hear the jovial cheers of the fans inside the pub. A couple had spilled out onto the street for a smoke and a chat with the door security. He had been listening to the football on the radio since he left the estate, less out of interest and more to judge the atmosphere he'd be walking into. Ireland had won four goals to three. He pulled out his phone and scrolled through his contacts list, selecting Seamus O'Toole. He made the call.

It was answered almost immediately.

'Jesus, I wasn't expecting to see your name flash across the screen of my phone, Eamon. I heard about your little situation in the pub tonight. Thought you'd have left the city.'

'We both know that was a setup, Seamus.'

'You just like causing a scene. You always did, kid.'

Martini grunted. 'It's good to hear your voice, buddy.'

'So, what can I do for you?'

'You hear much from Jim Greer these days?'

'Christ. Jim Greer. No, Eamon, we lost touch a while back. I know he's been in Germany for a wee while, but I've not had a peep out of him. Why, what's happening?'

'He's working with a local billionaire. A Ludwig Schuster. They have offered me a job. Paying a lot of money.'

'How much money?'

'Ten million. You want to earn yourself a bit of cash?'

'Who do I have to kill, Eamon?'

Martini smiled. 'Nobody. It's just a drive from here to Switzerland.'

'Do I want to know what the job is?'

A sly grin slowly stretched across Martini's face. 'You should know better than that; the less you know the better.'

'Suppose you're right, kid. It was the first thing we were told when we joined the republican movement. And the Provisional IRA's leadership weren't people you crossed. Remember the nutting squad?'

'We were both there when that piece of shit Bianco was brought in.'

'How he managed to get away with being a double agent for so long is beyond me. An agent for the Provos and for the other side.' His voice had a hint humour. 'And then a young lad like you comes along and brings him to the surface. Us older lads had a good laugh about that one, kid. Including your da'.'

Martini didn't want to talk about his past with someone involved in the kidnapping of a kid, let alone the grandson of a man with an Irish Catholic background who was always supportive of the republican movement. He cleared his throat abruptly. 'Yeah.'

'You heard from your da'?'

'Still missing in action.'

'He's out there somewhere, I'm sure.' O'Toole sighed heavily. 'Where are you now?'

'Sitting in a car just outside the Green, White and Orange. Judging from the sound of it, and the end score of the Ireland game, it's going to be some craic in there tonight. I heard you're in the area.'

'Aye. We have a wee ice-cream and coffee parlour in the street just behind where you are now. We're closing up, but we can still offer you a drink and something to eat. Where are you staying? We can put you up for the night if you want?'

'I'm at the Hilton,' he lied. 'But I'll come around. See you in a few minutes.'

'It's only me and Mary here.'

'Okay.'

The next street was essentially the same as the previous one. Grocery shops, jewellers, a bank, a library, and a pub. Martini laughed silently to himself as he pulled up outside the parlour with the sign "Brain Freeze" scrawled upon its top. He remembered how O'Toole had always eaten ice-cream, even on the coldest days of the year, and if he'd been in a rush, he'd shovel the ice-cream in his mouth and spend the next twenty minutes complaining of headache.

He shut the engine off, got out and locked the Q7. Feeling the cold air touch his skin, he zipped his jacket closed. 'Christ, I don't want any ice-cream tonight,' he mumbled, as he approached the shop. Mary O'Toole was outside putting rubbish in the bin. 'Well, Mary, it's been a while.'

'God in heaven, Eamon,' she gasped. 'How the hell are you, love?' She walked towards him with her arms outstretched and pulled him into a hug. 'It's good to see you, son.'

Martini looked at her. She was short, around five-five, and as thin as a rake. She had a long bony face that looked sunken and weathered, most likely as a result of her two box a day smoking habit. He admired her shop uniform. White trousers with a matching shirt and cap, making her look half her age. 'You, too, Mary.' He wrapped his arms around her, lifting her off the ground, then lowered her slowly again. 'It's good to see you're both doing well.'

'What has you in Berlin?'

'I've got something I want to talk to you both about. A job, lots of money.'

She looked at him, her smile dropping into a frown. 'No offence, love. But this isn't going to mess everything up for us, is it?'

'I just need to talk to you both if that's okay?'

'Come on inside, love.' She turned and led the way in.

Seamus O'Toole was sweeping in the corner of the shop. He glanced up at them and then back down at the ground. 'Close the door, Mary, and make a round of coffee.'

He was the polar opposite of Mary. His hair was dark and he had bushy eyebrows. He still had the thick handlebar moustache that Martini had first seen when he turned up in Belfast to save his father. He was the same height as Martini and just as broad, although the years had softened him up a little.

A click echoed across the room as Mary closed the door and locked it.

'I'll make the coffee,' Martini offered, walking around the back of the counter. He switched on the coffee machine. 'Cappuccinos?'

'Can't live without them!' Seamus exclaimed, brushing the dirt into a dustpan.

Mary rounded the counter, affectionately shoving Martini away from the machine. 'Take a seat, love. You're the guest.'

Martini stepped back, his hands in the air in mock submission. 'You're the boss.' He returned to the customer side of the counter and sat himself down on one of the stools, watching as she cleaned around the area while making the drinks, taking pride in her work. She took her time with it, reminding Martini of how his father used to clean his beloved Ford Shelby Mustang – or as Cleary Jnr. would have called it, the best set of wheels in Belfast.

'How long have you guys been here now?'

'Two years,' Seamus said, sitting down on the stool next to him. 'So, Eamon, what have you been up to since we last spoke?'

'Just drifting around. Didn't really want to stay anywhere too long, so thought I'd see a bit of the world before I leave it.' He smiled. 'God knows we've all come awfully close to leaving it earlier than nature intended.'

'The Troubles claimed many people before their time, kid,' Seamus replied.

Mary set the drinks down.

'It's been a long road, my friend.' Seamus placed his hand on Martini's shoulder. 'We're incredibly lucky to still be here.'

Martini took a sip of his cappuccino. Mary sat next to her husband. They toasted.

'Slainte.' Martini toasted them in Irish.

'So, what's the craic?' Seamus asked.

'How would you two like to earn a little bit of money?'

'Go on...' Seamus said, looking at Martini over the rim of his cup.

'I've been hired to do a job for a very wealthy, very anti-Western man. I don't trust anyone else.' He looked at Mary then at Seamus. 'I'm going to Switzerland to assassinate Prime Minister Michelle Pears. And there's a hefty payday for you both.'

Seamus was speechless, his blue eyes almost popping out of their sockets. He glanced incredulously across at Mary. 'How much are we talking?'

'I've negotiated ten million for you both. You'll get half now, and half after the job's done.'

Seamus's eyes gleamed with something that Martini recognised instantly: greed. 'That's quite a bit of money.'

'It's a lot of risk, too,' Mary added. She didn't seem to share in the excitement displayed by her husband.

Martini studied the space around him. The shop had a brand-new feel to it, in both smell and appearance. White and pink tiles covered the walls, and the tables and chairs gave the space the feel of a nineteen sixties American diner. It was cute and probably attracted hordes of locals and tourists. If the shop was bringing in plenty of honest money for them, they'd already be comfortable. But not in the millions. And the chance at making a lot more money didn't appeal to her.

'What's your plan, Eamon?' Seamus said.

'I've just taken the job, but it won't be hard.'

Mary grabbed Martini's hand. She studied him closely. 'And who's funding this?'

'A half German, half Afghan billionaire. A man who wants to let the West know that not even their leaders are safe.'

Mary glanced at Seamus for a heartbeat before looking

back at Martini. He was quick to notice the anxious under-current in her gaze as she had peeked at her husband. They both shifted uncomfortably in their seats. They were keeping something from him.

'Is this political or personal?' Her questions were breeding anxiety, and anxiety was breeding suspicion.

'Christ, you sound like a peeler,' Martini said, casually taking another drink of his coffee, as if all they were talking about was stealing a loaf from the local supermarket.

Mary sighed, rubbing her neck. 'Eamon, you come walking into our lives, telling us you have this dream job, and expect us to just jump on the band wagon with you and take out one of the most powerful people in the world?'

He shook his head and sighed heavily, looking around the shop. 'Was this all worth it?'

'Was what worth it?' Seamus asked, sounding defensive.

'Where's the kid?'

'What kid?' Mary asked, her brow drawn in confusion.

'CIA analysts have linked you both to the kidnapping of President Sheeran's grandson in Belfast. A job that James Greer organised, who is working for Ludwig Schuster and his cousin, Ahmad Jaleel.' He looked around the shop again. 'I'm guessing all this has been paid for by Mr. Schuster?'

'What the fuck are you talking about, Eamon?' Seamus exclaimed, jumping off his stool. 'No, I swear, we've not been involved in anything like that.'

'When was the last time you spoke to Greer?'

'He comes in the odd time, you know what Jim's like, Eamon.' Mary had replied too fast for someone telling the truth, then she quickly changed the subject. 'But what is this all about? President Sheeran's grandson has been kidnapped?'

Martini nodded. 'He has. And Schuster has said that he's

going to mail the kid back to Washington in pieces if I don't carry out the hit.'

'Jesus Christ, Eamon. You know us.' Mary's voice trembled. 'It wasn't us. And whoever's telling you that shite is feeding you a bunch of lies.'

He didn't know what to say. They'd received a lot of money from Schuster. But did they know what they were getting involved in? Was he being cruel for suspecting his old friends? Or would it be naive for him believe them when they were acting so out of character? He had known them for a long time. He didn't want to believe that they could be involved in something like that. He stood up, setting his cup down. 'I love you both. We've had a long history together, but now I think that you're both lying to me. If I leave here now without you telling me the truth, then I won't be able help you.'

Seamus and Mary studied Martini silently. He got the hint. They weren't going to talk. He offered his hand to Seamus, then Mary. She took his hand and pulled him in for a hug, almost cutting off the circulation to his head, her arms wrapped around his neck like a boa constrictor. She released her hold and gazed intently into his eyes.

He smiled dismally. 'Maybe I'll see you both again sometime.' He looked at them both, committing them to memory. 'It was good seeing you both.'

He pecked Mary on the cheek one last time and left.

Stepping back into the cold, he shoved his hands into his pockets and swore.

'Fuck.'

He made his way back to the Audi and got in. He pulled his phone out and called POTUS. He started the engine and got the heating system started while it rang. He connected the call through the vehicle's sound system and then sped off.

'Eamon, what have you got?' POTUS said.

'I've been to the Schuster estate and I don't think that Enda's here. They wouldn't have left me unsupervised if he had been on the property. I've just met with Seamus and Mary O'Toole. I'm not completely sure they know about Enda. But they're definitely lying about something. They sure as shit know more than they're letting on. Kidnapping isn't in their nature. Greer's – absolutely. But not them. I don't know what their part is.'

POTUS' voice deepened. 'Frank Dott's involved.'

'What?'

'He's received five million dollars from Schuster.'

'Did you bring him in?'

'Goodall suggested we play dumb. She's hacked his phone. Every communication he receives, we'll receive. We're hoping it'll lead us to Enda's whereabouts. So, for now, nothing changes until she finds something.'

'I have a feeling that Schuster will have someone else to help me with the job. But I will make him aware that I'll be choosing the help, not him.' The president was about to speak when Martini interrupted. 'Don't worry, sir. I'm not going to take anybody out. I need the job in Switzerland to go sideways so that I can have more time to find Enda.'

'Just get my grandson back for me, Eamon. Please. He's innocent. He's done nothing wrong. I'll fucking hand myself over to them if I have to.' His voice trembled on the last few words.

'I'm not going to fail you, sir. Just keep it together. I'll call you when I have more.'

'Do you need any more support?'

'With all due respect, Mr. President, you can't trust

anyone in your entire cabinet at the moment. We don't know if Dott's the only one; and if there are more, they will feed our plan back to Schuster and we'll risk losing Enda.'

'Christ, the bastards really have us by the balls.'

Martini nodded. 'They really do, sir.'

'Good luck, Eamon.'

'Thank you, Mr. President.'

13

Martini knew that Seamus and Mary O'Toole had not been honest with him. He could feel it in the pit of his stomach. Despite their demeanour – on the surface they seemed the same – he could tell that they had both changed. He'd become a good reader of people, a skill he'd been forced to develop throughout the years. It was one of the reasons he was still alive. Despite his reluctance to believe it, he was starting to believe they were involved in the kidnapping.

Seeing his old friends again had caused a wave of nostalgia to wash over him. He began to miss his old life in Belfast. His Irish family.

He returned to the Green, White, and Orange and spent the rest of the evening as a nameless face in the crowd, blending in with the football fans.

He was briefly tempted to contact his family in Belfast, but quickly scrubbed the idea, remembering why it had been years since he'd spoken to any of them. Damien Cleary Jnr., along with his two older brothers, had been leaders of the North and West Belfast brigades of the Provisional IRA. Martini's father sat on the ruling army council of Northern

Command, while his two uncles had commanded several twelve-man Active Service Units or ASUs, throughout the conflict. Martini's grandfather, Damien Cleary Snr., was the Chief of Staff who also sat on the ruling army council.

During his youth, Martini had not been aware of what his Irish family was involved in. His mother had been opposed to her "baby boy" being exposed to the war in Ireland, which was understandable given the increased intensity during the late nineteen eighties and early nineties. The war just seemed to get dirtier and dirtier as it went on. The southern Irish government was known to have been secretly supporting the Provos, while the Westminster suits turned a blind eye to certain figures within MI5 and Army Intelligence who'd been colluding with the UDA and other loyalist militias, assassinating key members of the republican movement. Loyalists believed killing Catholic civilians would weaken Catholic support for the PIRA. A dirty war, where mainly the innocent suffered – British and Irish. Maria Martini argued that her son was safe as long as he remained on the other side of the Atlantic, despite the criminality her own family was involved in.

Maria Martini had become known as the "Queen of New York" when she had taken over from her father as the boss of the Martini crime family. She had a face like butter wouldn't melt, and had worked hard to keep her throne. She had always known that the one person she would be able to rely on was her only son. So she had not been prepared to risk losing him to a war three thousand miles east across the ocean separating America and Ireland.

Martini missed his mother. And his father. It was why he couldn't settle anywhere, and why he avoided making contact with the Italian or Irish sides of his family. New York brought back memories of her. Belfast brought back memories of him.

His thoughts were dragged back to the present by the buzz of his phone. It was a text message from Seamus O'Toole.

Sorry about Mary, Eamon. She's just nervous. We've both reached a ripe old age, both of us relatively unscathed, and we want nothing more than to live the rest of our lives in peace. I think we've all earned that. Where are you? I might come and see you without her knowing.

He read the message twice. Why was he asking for Martini's location? Seamus knew for a fact that asking someone who did not trust you for their location wasn't done in their world. You came to them, or you met at a neutral location. Could it be possible that Seamus would send someone to bring him in? For all he knew, their conversation could have been recorded. He struggled to accept that they would rat on him. But traitors had been a huge issue that had tarnished the republican movement his family had been so heavily involved in. The freedom fighters that worked as a collective mind, a body of people who wanted nothing more than the occupied six counties of Northern Ireland to be united with the twenty-six free state counties, tarnished by traitors.

He sighed and shook his head, feeling like he'd been punched in the gut. He sat alone and took some solace in the honest craic that was being had around him.

It was shortly after eleven. He had decided sometime during his drink that to ease his worries, he would have to find out the truth. And the only way to do that was to test the O'Tooles. He needed to find out if they were trustworthy or not.

He sent O'Toole a reply, giving him the address of the

Hilton, but with a different room number. Martini had booked a room on the ground floor – closer to the exit in an emergency – but told Seamus he was staying in room forty-four on the third. He had a sickening suspicion that the moment the text was sent, the German police would be on their way, hoping to catch someone in the act of plotting an assassination. He hoped, for O'Toole's sake, that this would not be the case.

After sending the text, Martini got up from his seat, left the pub and headed towards the Hilton. A late-night coffee shop sat directly across the street from the hotel; he could sit back and watch the show unfold.

14

Seamus and Mary closed the shop and, in a sombre mood, made their way to the car park. Seamus unlocked their silver Lexus and approached the driver's side. He caught Mary glaring at him from the other side just as he was about to get in.

'What?' he asked, looking at her across the roof.

'Stop looking so goddamn miserable. We've built a good life for ourselves here. I know you love Eamon like a son, Christ, so do I, but he's getting involved in something that'll ruin everything for us. I hate that we've been dragged into something like this, but we have to see it through.'

'I know, Mary, but Eamon...'

'But nothing, Seamus. We helped James Greer move someone from Belfast to Berlin. We didn't know who it was. We didn't ask any questions, and for that, we were able to clear our mortgage, develop the shop, and have plenty left over. I also don't want to get on the wrong side of Eamon, but we have to think about our future.'

He pulled the door open and sagged into his seat, gripping the steering wheel as if the situation had a throat, and he had his hands wrapped around it. 'Let's just pretend we didn't see him.'

She got in and fastened her belt.

He started the engine just as his phone buzzed in his pocket. Opening a message, he read it and looked across at his wife. 'He's just sent us his room number at the Hilton – forty-four.'

'For Christ's sake,' she complained, reaching for the heating. 'We'll go to prison just for knowing what he's planning to do.'

Seamus dropped the phone down into the cup holder in the central console. 'I'll call him once we get home. Tell him thanks, but no thanks.'

'That's not enough, Seamus.'

He looked across at her, shaking his head. 'I'm not calling the police, love. No fucking way. MI6 will butcher him if they get their hands on him. Eamon Martini? After the way he left Falkner's unit looking? They'll not only want to bring him in and jail him. They'll send their best hitman to put a bullet in his head.' He shook his head. 'I won't do it.' He put the car in drive and took off, repeating, 'I won't fucking do it, Mary.'

'We're already involved, Seamus,' she spat.

He didn't reply. Instead, he led the car out of the car park and drove at a crawl past their little shop. He shook his head sadly. 'We've worked too hard to lose what we have.'

'Well, if Eamon goes ahead with what he's planning and our names get brought into it, you can sure as shit wave goodbye to all of it.'

Again, he was unresponsive.

'I'll make the call, for God's sake.' She sighed. 'You don't have to be the one to rat him out.'

15

Inspector Moritz Becker was an old school German police officer who had devoted his entire life to the badge and uniform. He had lost his youth and two marriages to the job. He was relentless in his pursuit of the "big fish". He was fascinated by Ireland and its history – both recent and further back – so he hadn't wasted any time in visiting the O'Toole's parlour when it had first begun its trade. Knowing their place of birth, and always the investigator, he had done a little digging, wanting to know who exactly had just opened up shop in a place he thought of as *his* city. He had gotten wind from the PSNI and Scotland Yard that Seamus O'Toole had been released from the Maze Prison in 1999 under the terms of the Good Friday Agreement. One of many active members of the Provisional IRA, O'Toole had been in the middle of a forty-year sentence for shooting dead three British soldiers in a gun battle on Belfast's Antrim Road. Mary O'Toole had also been released from prison. She had barely begun serving a fifteen-year sentence for her part in an arms deal with a Boston based supplier that had resulted in two undercover officers being killed.

Becker knew that everyone had a past. The Irish couple were simply two people caught up in the dealings of an organisation they had been born into. He held no grudge. And they were free to earn a living just like anyone else. But he had made them well aware that there would be eyes on them, and that any involvement in dodgy dealings would result in him coming down on them like a ton of bricks. He had even informed them that their phones would be monitored and that he had listening devices fitted in places they frequented.

Midway through the second day of the AT&T Pebble Beach Pro-Am golf tournament in California, he heard his phone go off. He would have let it go to voicemail had it been anyone but an O'Toole. 'Mary, my dear,' he spoke in English with a thick German accent. 'This better be good. My guy's just about to make a putt that will put him in first place.'

She was quick to respond. 'This is much bigger than some golf tournament.' She cleared her throat. 'The British prime minister is about to be assassinated at her holiday home in Switzerland. Thought I'd give you the opportunity to stop it before it happens.'

Becker froze. He grabbed the remote and paused his golf. 'Where'd you get this intel? How do I know it's worth my time?'

'Seamus and I were asked to help carry out the hit.'

'By whom?'

'Eamon Martini.'

Becker stood up from his sofa. A small grin stretched across his face. 'Say that again?'

'You heard me right.'

'Eamon Martini has resurfaced?'

'If I were you, I'd get on the phone with the British.' She ended the call.

Becker sank back down again, taking a deep breath. He was brimming with enough excitement to make his hands quiver. He gazed at the photo of him and his late wife displayed on the coffee table. 'I haven't sacrificed it all for nothing, Annie.' He turned sightless eyes back to the TV. His previous interest in the golf now seemed foolish. He had the chance to catch the biggest fish of his career. He grabbed his keys and sauntered towards the door. 'You may be smart, Eamon Martini, but you're not too smart for me.'

16

Commander James Falkner, a decorated British soldier and counter-insurgency operative, was one of the men who had set up and led the Force Research Unit in Northern Ireland. It had operated out of Aldergrove in Belfast during the early nineteen eighties until being shut down ten years after the Good Friday Agreement. Following the Steven's Enquiry in 2007, the unit had been shut down after being found to be neck-deep in collusion with loyalist paramilitaries, not just the UDA, but the other, smaller groups. The inquiry had found that FRU had supported the UDA in procuring arms from South Africa. Just the way the Irish government had supported the PIRA in building its arsenal.

Damien Cleary Jnr. was known as the thinking man within the republican movement, and he was the one Falkner wanted the most. Intelligence, not force, was how the war would be won – or lost. Falkner knew that. And he knew Cleary Jnr. knew that. On one drizzly September evening in Belfast in 1997, Cleary had set up the men who'd been tasked to set him up, leaving FRU red-faced and wondering just what the hell had happened.

Commander Falkner had, at the time, been directing an operative within the PIRA: an Irish Italian by the name of James Bianco, who'd been acting as a double agent for the PIRA and MI5. Falkner had believed this man would be the one to beat the IRA, tear it up from within. What Falkner and nobody else knew was that Cleary's seventeen-year-old son, Eamon Martini, had been raised by his mother in New York by the Martini family, who had long-standing ties to the Bianco family in the Big Apple.

Bianco was clever, but he was only human, and humans make mistakes. His, unfortunately for him, had cost him his life. Maintaining his links with the family in America, he'd often have conversations on the phone, which had eventually landed on the discussion table of the Martini crime family – including the plot against Cleary Jnr. Young Eamon Martini heard of FRU's plans to assassinate his father, and had immediately nominated himself to go to Belfast.

Falkner, following the shutdown of FRU, had taken on the more global role of leading a group of highly skilled assassins that operated in the shadows. A deniable group of killers with a Westminster stamped license to kill. Whenever diplomatic channels failed, a red stamped folder would fall on Falkner's desk and he'd assign the target to one of the agents – always a clandestine operation. It didn't exist, because they didn't exist. These agents were thought of as the ghosts that cleared up the mess which MI5 and MI6 couldn't.

Now aged fifty-nine and semi-retired, Falkner acted as an advisor to British SIS until they could find someone more permanent to fill the role. He lived in a cosy, one-bedroom apartment on the top floor of Baileys House on Charles Clowes Walk. A mere stone's throw away from St George Wharf Pier, and a little further from Vauxhall Cross House, he was never too far away from HQ. He was tall – around six foot six – and thin, with receding grey hair. He spent most of his time in his black leather armchair that overlooked the street below, watching the world go by. He had always said that his greatest regret was not catching the man who had brought unprecedented shame to him and his unit. A young man who had dared to take on one of the most sophisticated intelligence groups in the world. Martini was both loathed and respected by the British, especially Falkner.

He sat at the dinner table, swiping through the pages of the Daily Telegraph, trying to enjoy the digital version on his iPad, when Becker's name flashed across the screen of his mobile. He set the device down and grabbed the phone. 'Have you called to gloat about the fact that your guy has gone to the top of the leader board?' He lifted his coffee pot and topped up his cup. 'There's still another two days before our little wager is sealed.'

Becker chuckled. 'As much as I can't wait to gloat when I win and you wire me fifty euros, I've something of much more value to us both. I've heard from a legitimate source that Cleary Jnr's son has approached former comrades to carry out a hit.'

The cup froze at Falkner's lips. 'Martini?' He spoke in a whisper as if he were afraid to say his name out loud. 'Can't be.'

'I thought the same, but my source has no reason to lie.'

'What's he doing?'

'Apparently, he's going for a hit. A big hit. Your Prime Minister.'

'Christ.'

'Don't panic, I'm sending people after him.'

'Don't be stupid and go in there all guns blazing.'

Falkner stood up and walked towards the window, looking down onto the street below. Just after midnight and London still had a handful of pedestrians and drivers keeping the city alive. 'I'm going to finish this little prick.'

'I want to share in the glory.'

'I'll set up a Zoom call tomorrow. Can you jump into it once I've got a few others who need to hear?'

'Of course.' Becker cleared his throat. 'Are you going to inform the PM?'

Falkner made his way back to his seat. 'Not yet. I'm scared that we might lose him if the PM changes her plans. Martini could be watching her as we speak, and he'll know if something's off, he's got eyes in the back of his head.' He lifted the coffee, a smile stretching across his face. 'I'm going to scrub out the only blemish of my otherwise spotless career.'

'I'll wait for the invite.'

'Thanks for your call, my old friend. This might just change both our lives.'

Falkner ended the call then sent a text to his former #1 assassin. Victoria Greenwood had stepped away from the killing and had taken over from him as head of SIS when he'd retired, and she was the only one with whom he would share his information, because despite the more administerial route she was headed down, she was first and foremost a cold-blooded killer. And great at her job. From Falkner's recollection, she'd killed between eighty and one hundred people in various locations around the world and would be the best chance at getting Martini.

He called her, and as expected, she was still up. 'Let me guess, you're in the gym or somewhere equally damaging to one's health.'

She laughed, 'What's wrong? Fed up with retirement already?'

'Semi-retired. But I think I may have just won the lottery.'

'I don't understand.'

'The one regret of my career has resurfaced and I'm itching to right that wrong.'

'Eamon Martini?'

'I knew that name would liven you up.'

'I'll come around to yours first thing in the morning.'

'Can you bring some bagels? I'm all out.'

'I'll see you in the morning.'

17

It was shortly after eight the next morning and Falkner sat watching three of his goldfish fight over the food he'd just dropped into the tank when he heard Greenwood's heels clapping off the wooden flooring of the communal hallway.

'The door's open, Victoria,' he called out.

She strode into the living room. She stood just short of six-foot-tall, her navy pantsuit clinging to her slender body. Straight, black hair cascaded down both sides of her face like a pair of silk drapes, curling inwards around her chin. Her bright, emerald-green eyes were set in a pretty, oval face. She was beautiful in the classical sense, with no need to go overboard with make-up. It had always baffled Falkner as to why she was still single.

With her laptop case in her left hand and a plastic shopping bag in the right, she walked through the room with purpose, passing him towards the kitchen. 'Bagels are warm. Cinnamon, right?'

He got up off his seat and joined her in the kitchen. 'Very take charge,' he said humorously, 'I always knew you were the perfect replacement for me when I stepped away, thought you'd done enough killing for Queen and country.'

She smiled, lifting the kettle. 'Go and have a seat, I know my way around your kitchen.'

He raised his hands in mock surrender and returned to where he'd been seated. 'I swear if I were twenty years younger, I'd have asked you to marry me.' He sat back down. She ignored the comment and opened her laptop on the kitchen counter. 'Still single, I guess?'

She typed on the keyboard and nodded. 'Comes with the job.'

'Beautiful lady like you should have a family, some kids.'

'Haven't time to think about kids, sir.'

'Sir? No need for formalities. I'm no longer your superior. In our position, we only have one boss.'

'The Prime Minister.' She chimed, preparing the coffee. She brought a tray with two cups and plates over to the coffee table. 'So, Martini has re-surfaced and you're staging a comeback tour?' She cut one of the bagels open and smothered it with butter. 'You sure you want to re-open that wound?'

'That wound has never healed, Victoria,' Falkner stated sourly, lifting one of the bagels. 'Martini brought my unit an insurmountable amount of shame. It's time for me to get my own back. Even the score.' He watched as the butter melted. 'At my age, it's the small things in life that mean the most – like eating a butter-soaked bagel with a beautiful young lady.'

The comment barely resonated with her. 'So, we don't alert the PM of this threat yet?'

He shook his head. 'We leave it for now. Let's see what the hell his game is. This is not Martini's style. He doesn't need the money. If it's a hit for someone else, then we could benefit from finding out who it's coming from.'

'The prime minister's at her home in Switzerland.'

He nodded. A slow smile stretched across his face. 'And Martini knows that.'

18

Verbier: a picturesque Alpine Swiss village, as beautiful in the summer as it is in the freezing winter. And it was here, in the Valais Canton, where Prime Minister Pears had purchased her intimate chalet, complete with open fires, balconies boasting jaw-dropping mountain views, and seclusion that was perfect for both a quiet getaway and a contracted hit on one of the world's leaders. The home was still under construction. The refurbishment was to bring it into the twenty-first century, with a wing finished to serve her when she was in the country.

At Geneve Airport, Martini went to the AVIS customer service desk and collected the keys for his pre-ordered rental as soon as his flight touched down. A silver Land Rover Defender. On the way to Valais Canton, he stopped off at a building site he had researched before the flight. It was closed for the day due to an accident resulting in health and safety inspectors being brought in.

Leaving his rental there, he hot-wired a white transit van with *A.M. Elettrica* emblazoned on its side then typed the chalet's address into the satellite navigation.

Two miles away.

Arriving at the property, he was almost tempted to go in and ask for a room. But as it stood, he wasn't going to be there for very long. A failed attempt on the PM's life to buy himself more time was the reason he was there. *And*, of course, to see how much they'd talked. It would give him a good indication as to how trustworthy they were. He'd left Seamus instructions that he was going to scope the house out, pretend to be an Italian electrician, get a look around inside, and then go from there.

He drove fifty yards past the property and parked on the deserted country road. He abandoned the van, and went to retrieve the rental. The prime minister had good taste. He had to give credit where credit was due.

After a fifteen-minute jog, he was back at the SUV he'd left at the building site. He sat in the driver's seat, waiting until ten - twenty minutes before the time he'd told Seamus he was going to move in on the property. Three police cars, two marked and one unmarked, flew past him in the direction of the chalet. He put the Land Rover in gear and followed at normal speed. As he approached the property, he noticed that the van was boxed in by three vehicles. The doors were open. He continued past. This will be on the news in the next hour. More time to find Enda.

A few miles down the road, he pulled into a parking place behind an LGV and called the president.

'Eamon?'

'I'm in Switzerland. The attempt to take out the PM has been foiled. I've bought us some more time.'

'So, what now?'

'Prime Minister Pears' security will be increased. We won't be able to hit her, or at least not without more planning, which is the information that I'm going to bring back to Berlin. That'll buy us some time. Has Teresa got anything from Dott's phone?'

'Nothing yet.'

'I think I may have an idea. I will need your help, but this will only go ahead if we can't find Enda.'

'What?'

'Former Prime Minister Churchman – you've always had a good relationship with him, am I right?'

'Yes, but I don't understand?'

'You have faith in my marksman skills?'

'Yes, why?'

'If I can sell the idea of assassinating the ex-British prime minister, the man who'd supported your predecessor, sending troops over to the Middle-East in the first place, then you could ask him to play along.'

'Christ, Eamon, if it goes wrong...'

'You trust me to get Enda back, Bill?'

'You know I do.'

'Our backs are against the wall, sir. We don't know who or if anyone else within your cabinet has betrayed you. Goodall is going to struggle to do anything without arising suspicion. I'm not willing to risk Enda's life. The only way I can get my hands on him, is if Schuster believes I've completed the job.'

The president remained silent.

'Unless you can think of a better way?'

There was a pause. 'Christ.' He sighed heavily.

'Time's running out, sir.'

'Okay, talk to Schuster. Give him your plan. Then call me the moment you've spoken to him.'

'Yes, sir.'

19

Martini arrived back at the Schuster estate shortly after eight the next evening. Jaleel, Greer, and Schuster all sat around the outside table by the pool. Martini wasn't bringing news they'd be hoping for, but they already knew that. Had he been successful, they would have heard about it on the news. He cleared his throat as he walked across the perfectly manicured garden and over a small putting green. He wasn't much of a golfer, but he often found such greens to be both entertaining and therapeutic.

In sync, they all turned around to look at him.

'Any more coffee left in that pot?' he asked Jaleel in Arabic. Jaleel lifted the pot's lid and nodded.

Martini sat down next to Schuster, facing Greer. 'I've got good news and bad news.'

'Bad news first, Mr. Martini.' Schuster spoke through a sigh.

'The bad news is the people I'd hoped would support me have turned their backs on me.'

'So, undoubtedly the wrong people now know what you have planned,' Greer chimed.

Martini shook his head and took the coffee from Jaleel, continuing to spin the web of deceit. 'You know Seamus and Mary, Jim. There's not a chance in hell that they'd say anything. It's more a case of thanks, but no thanks.'

Schuster eyed Martini while grabbing the coffee pot from his cousin. 'Okay then. What's the good news?'

'The good news is that you've still got me for the job.' He blew into his cup, then took a sip.

Schuster mumbled in German. 'All I've heard is talk.'

Martini responded in German. 'Just a setback.'

Schuster switched back to English, smirking. 'I like a smart man, Mr. Martini. But a smart-ass, not so much.'

Greer intervened. 'Ludwig, Eamon may be a cocky bastard.' He spoke out of the side of his mouth while looking across the table at Martini. 'But he's got a right to be. And I can vouch for him that when he says he's going to do something, he'll deliver.' He lifted his drink. 'That's one thing I'm willing to bet on.'

'So, what is next?' Jaleel asked. 'If the heat is on, the prime minister will have security up to her back-side and you won't get near her.'

'Mr. Jaleel, there's a reason why President Sheeran sent me. You think he would send someone who couldn't pull this job off? Risk his grandson's life?' He looked at Greer, then back at Jaleel. 'I feel your pain, Ahmad. But you've gone about your revenge completely the wrong way...'

Schuster sniggered. 'Still, all I hear is talk.'

'I've got a better proposition for you.'

Schuster's mouth tightened slightly. 'Go on.'

'Former Prime Minister Churchman.'

'He will burn in hell for what he's done to my country,' Jaleel spat.

'You're right,' Martini said. 'It was he who sent troops over there. He should be the one to pay.'

'You can get him, Eamon?' Greer asked.

Martini took a sip of his coffee, looking at Schuster over the rim of his cup. 'I can.'

Greer looked at Schuster, then at Jaleel. Jaleel was smiling from ear to ear, nodding his head.

'Don't mess up this time, Mr. Martini,' Schuster said. 'You said the president sent the best to do the job, well, don't disappoint him.'

Martini looked over his shoulder at the pool. 'You mind if I take a dip before getting some rest? It's been a busy couple of days.'

'The house is yours,' Schuster said. 'Do as you wish.'

20

Paddy Lyttle was an Irish American scholar. A man who'd spent a lot of his life inside a book. Many people who'd come across him would describe him as being socially awkward. A loner. Others thought of him as being strange, a bit alien. But what everyone who'd ever had the pleasure or misfortune of spending time with him agreed on, was that he was perhaps the smartest person they'd ever came across. Nicknamed "Rain Man", he had more degrees than most people had digits in their mobile phone number.

An honorary lecturer at Princeton University in the United States and Cambridge University in England, he spent the first half of his life studying, trying to understand the psychology of the paramilitaries involved in the Irish conflict. On a research trip to Belfast in 1988, his assistant was abducted and murdered by the UDA for venturing out onto the Shankill Road with a local lady. He'd made the mistake of saying he was an Irish American, and a Catholic. Irish Americans were widely supportive of a united Ireland, which made him an enemy of the people on the Shankill. Lyttle had never forgiven himself. He held himself responsible for what had happened and being the eccentric he was, even back then, he had joined the republican movement, simply wanting to take out as many loyalist paramilitaries as he could.

It wasn't long before he got his hands bloody and quickly concluded that murder wasn't in his nature. He did, however, learn a lot about the motivation behind the republican movement and could at least understand, if not completely agree with, their struggle. The provisional movement realised his potential and offered him higher ranking positions, directing a handful of Active Service Units within Belfast and Derry.

Being one who the movement's leadership came to for advice on operations, he had learned who the informers were within the movement and had tasked James Bianco to lead the group known as the Nutting Squad. Bianco and Lyttle grew close. Started as friends, comrades, and then one night, Lyttle had stared down the barrel of a loyalist revolver and Bianco had saved his life. Lyttle was forever indebted to Bianco. When someone saves your life, it creates a bond – an intimate connection, felt by soldiers and freedom fighters the world over. And as Lyttle saw it, there wasn't anything you wouldn't do for someone like that.

Lyttle had found out too late that his smarts were not enough when seventeen-year-old Eamon Martini had outsmarted Bianco and delivered him to the republican movement. There was nothing Lyttle could do about it. And the man who was believed to be the most intelligent in the IRA had been outsmarted by a young Martini. Lyttle was left mourning Bianco. But he eventually learned to live with it.

Now, in his early sixties, most of Lyttle's time was spent

on the west coast of Ireland, walking his red setter – Scarlett – along the beach of Bundoran, County Donegal.

It was a cold night. He returned to his home after an evening walk beneath the stars, entering the kitchen with a bowl of warm tomato soup in mind. His mobile phone rang in the pocket of his raincoat. Falkner's name flashed across the screen.

'Well, well, well, if it isn't Commander Falkner,' he said humorously. 'I didn't think I'd ever hear from you again.' He pulled a chair out and sat at the end of the kitchen table.

'How's life over on the west coast?' Falkner asked.

'Windy, but great for surfing.'

'Don't tell me you've taken up water sports. I think golf might be a better option for a man your age.'

'Speak for yourself.' Lyttle sat back, Scarlett at his feet looking up at him lovingly, her tongue dangling from her mouth, slobbering all over his feet. 'What can I do for you, Commander?'

'I think we have an opportunity to scratch an itch we've both had for twenty years.'

Lyttle paused, his left hand stopping mid-stroke on the back of the dog's head. He stood up and walked towards the back door, looking out across the long narrow garden, fringed by a four-foot white wall. 'You've found him? Dead or alive?'

'I love how you know I'm talking about Martini without even using his name.'

'Well, he made the both of us look like fools.'

'He made the entire British establishment look like fools, Paddy. He took a lot of people down. Incriminated us all. I still remember the look of disappointment the prime minister at the time gave me when it all became public.'

'So, he's turned up?'

'He's gone to a couple of his father's old comrades about one last job.'

'Who's the target?'

'Prime Minister Pears.'

'And has the PM been informed that there's going to be an attempt on her life?'

'Well, I thought we could...'

'Jesus Christ, James, you need to tell her. This is not just any clown. If Martini's planning something, he's going to be pretty hard to stop.'

'That's why I'm calling you.'

'I'm not getting involved. I've laid the past to rest. I'm sorry.'

'What about Bianco?'

There was a pause.

'Fuck you.'

'He saved your life, didn't he?' Another silence. 'And it's because of Martini that Bianco met the horrific end that he did.'

Lyttle didn't reply.

'Anyway, I'm having a Zoom meeting with people in Germany that have seen him recently. You're more than welcome to jump into the meet if you want to know more.'

Lyttle sighed. 'What time?'

'We'll call around ten tomorrow morning.'

'If I'm around, I'll answer the call. But James, you need to inform the prime minister.' Lyttle ended the call, feeling more on edge than he'd felt in a long time. His urge to go after Martini had been put to bed a long time ago.

He cursed himself for answering the call; and he cursed himself for how he was feeling. Temptation. Feeling like he was being pulled back into the life he'd gladly left behind.

He stood up and grabbed Scarlett's lead from the table.

She barked at him excitedly, thrashing her long tail from side to side. 'Come on, Scarlett, your lucky day – two walkies.'

He stepped out the back door, zipping his jacket up to the neck and watched as the dog ran ahead of him.

21

The next morning, after a third walk in twenty-four hours, Lyttle sat on the beach, staring out to sea, looking for an answer that the Atlantic Ocean wasn't going to give him. Had it not been for Scarlett, moaning at him to move, he would have sat there until sunset. But he'd finally conceded to his curiosity. He needed to know what Martini was up to.

He rose and made his way home. The time was shortly after ten and, having been up all night, his cognitive processing was beginning to slow.

He could hear the call coming in from his laptop as he entered the kitchen. That Zoom call ringing, a noise that he'd now associate with Martini.

He answered it and sat down. 'So, who am I talking to?'

'You're on with Seamus and Mary O'Toole, now residents of Berlin,' Falkner replied. 'Also on the line is Ms. Victoria Greenwood, who is my successor for the British Secret Intelligence Services...'

'Temporarily,' Greenwood cut in.

'Only until the Secretary of State for Foreign Affairs

makes it official, Victoria,' Falkner replied. 'And last but not least, Inspector Becker of the Berlin Police Department.'

'So, what do we all know about Martini?' Lyttle asked, massaging his temples with his eyes closed, feeling the night of tossing and turning taking its toll.

'Apart from the fact he's taken a job that's paying quite handsomely,' Becker said, 'nothing – yet.'

'Seamus, Mary, what can you tell me about him? How'd he come across when he approached you?' Lyttle asked. Awkwardness lingered between them. Seamus and Mary were both ex-comrades of Lyttle during his stint within the Provisional IRA.

'The same as he's always been,' Seamus said. 'You remember the way he was, Paddy. Calm, emotionless. Always with that glint in his eye as if his mind was processing every little detail of his surroundings. As if he was planning something.'

'But he was there seeing you as old friends?' Lyttle asked. 'Mary, what did you think of him? How was his state of mind?'

'I don't know what you mean,' she replied, 'As Seamus said, same as always.'

'What are you getting at with these questions, Paddy?' Falkner asked.

'He's trying to assess why Martini has surfaced.' Greenwood answered before Lyttle had the chance. 'Martini doesn't need the money, he's set for life – ten times over. Whoever's hired him must have a ton of cash. Enough to convince him to take the job. But if it's not money, then why?'

'Victoria's right,' Lyttle said. 'Find out who's hired Martini, and you might have a chance of stopping whatever he has planned next.'

'What makes you think he's going to try again?' Becker asked.

'Come on?' Lyttle laughed. 'Eamon Martini didn't go to Seamus and Mary to ask for help without knowing that there'd be a slight chance they'd grass on him.'

A pregnant silence followed his statement.

He continued. 'And if you think he didn't expect the police to get wind of his proposition, then you don't know him at all.' He paused. 'Mr. Becker, have you spoken with anyone at the Federal Intelligence Service in Berlin?'

'Of course, this was the first place I went to for answers, Mr. Lyttle,' Becker replied, 'I've spoken with my friends in the Chancellor's Office and paid a visit to the BND head-quarters. They have no intelligence on Martini. It's as if he's a ghost.'

'Bit like his father,' Falkner mumbled.

'What was that?' Becker sounded confused.

'Damien Cleary Jnr. was known as "The Ghost".'

'Can we remain focused, please?' Greenwood jumped in. 'Mr. Becker, you mean to tell me that German Intelligence, one of the largest intelligence groups in the world, doesn't know anything about Mr. Martini?'

'Nothing new.' Becker sighed. 'Nothing that I'm sure you don't already know.'

'What we know is that he's been missing for years.' Falkner added. 'I'd hoped the bastard was dead.'

'Seamus, Mary – he must have given you something else?' Lyttle asked, a tinge of desperation in his tone.

'Eamon came to us because we're two of the few people he can trust,' Mary said, sounding defensive.

'And look how well that turned out for him,' Lyttle was quick to respond.

'What do you recommend we do, Paddy?' Falkner asked.

'There's nothing you can do other than go back to the last location he was sighted and hope that he's left clues as to where he plans on going next. And more importantly, find out who the hell's hired him for the work.' Scarlett could be heard barking at Lyttle in the background. 'I've got to go. I'm sorry I couldn't be any more help.' He dropped out of the conversation.

22

British Prime Minister Michelle Pears sat at her desk at Number 10 Downing Street, sipping her first coffee of the day. She was scanning through her emails, deleting more than she opened. The temperature in the room was a comfortable twenty degrees, but she still felt the need to wear her navy suit jacket, buttoned closed. She wasn't sure whether she was coming down with something, or if she just needed warming up. She felt a shiver running up her spine. She got up and walked across the office, checking if the radiator was on. It was.

Now in her early sixties, she had to use hair dye to remove the grey streaks from her shoulder-length, black hair. Her eyes were brown and intelligent. She was still a regular at the gym, a strong believer that an active lifestyle was important and promoted self-confidence. She never drank or smoked. She had been in the Prime Minister's seat for just over one year, but was still one of a handful of ministers known as "chasing Churchill". She was the fourth longest-serving minister, racking up 38 years. Having first stepped into the political world in 1982 at the age of twenty-four, she'd filled various roles as education secretary, justice secretary, chancellor, and home secretary until taking the highest seat in the land. She was short, just five-four, and thin. A northerner, her early career had been spent opposing the conservative government's policies. Although she didn't agree with the Iron Lady, she did respect her work ethic and how she'd clawed her way to the seat that, she herself now sat in.

Having just opened an email that came through from Agent Victoria Greenwood, which had Falkner's name mentioned in the subject heading, she feared that the car which had just gained access to Number 10 was likely to be them. She knew that if Greenwood was coming to see her, accompanied by Falkner, then it was related to something she'd rather not know about. Falkner's name had been tarnished during the Martini business all those years ago, but he'd still been kept in employment despite his wrongdoings. The PM was reluctant to use the methods of Falkner's last unit, and was aware that Greenwood had been the number one "fixer" in that group. But she had accepted that for the greater good, and for matters relating to national security, sometimes when you're left with only one option, elimination was better than dealing with the potential alternative.

Hearing the dull thud of two car doors shutting from below her office window, she got up walked over to see if her suspicions were true. She was right. Agent Greenwood was making her way towards the door of Number 10, Falkner close on her heels.

'For God's sake,' she mumbled below her breath, returning to her seat. She sat, rolling her pen back and forth on her notepad, listening to heels and Falkner's distinctive walk getting closer to her office door. A knock came. 'Come in,' she called.

The door opened. 'Good morning, Prime Minister,' Greenwood said, entering with Falkner following behind her.

Falkner took a thoughtful look around the room as he closed the door, as if reliving times past. 'I wish I could say I'm happy to be back in here again, but...'

'The feeling's mutual,' Pears cut in sharply. 'I've got a lot to do, so tell me, how bad is it?'

'Eamon Martini bad,' Falkner said, lowering himself into one of the leather chairs facing Pears.

'And according to your message last night, you believe that he's been tasked to assassinate me?' She leaned forward, resting her forearms on the desk, joining her hands.

'Ma'am, I think it would be wise for you to step up your security for a while, just until we find out what he's planning,' Greenwood said. 'I've got a call with the head of the Canton of Valais in Switzerland this afternoon. Inspector Christian Verrone was one of the first officers at the scene of the foiled attempt on your life at your house in Verbier. He's got forensics running the vehicle for prints and CCTV is being studied. Facial recognition has confirmed that it was him at the house. He parked the vehicle outside and left it there.'

The PM sighed. 'Was it rigged?'

'No, ma'am.'

'Strange. Who's he working for?'

'We don't know yet.' Greenwood sat in the chair next to Falkner, crossing her legs. 'I've come to you for permission to make him disappear. I'll take the bastard out at first sight. Shoot to kill.'

Pears studied her, then looked at Falkner. 'She will be a good replacement for you.'

'I haven't accepted the job yet. I'm only filling in.' She was quick to respond. 'Not sure I'm cut out for a desk job yet. I like to be more involved. But thank you.'

'So, how do you suggest we deal with this threat?'

'I'm on my way to HQ now to run some checks, see if we can find anything on his movements. I didn't want to worry you, Ma'am, until we had more info, but decided you should know.'

'Thank you, Victoria. It's not every day you find out someone has been hired to kill you.' She felt her heart rate increase slightly.

'Not least one of the best government assassins in the world,' Falkner added. 'This guy's not just smart, ma'am, but he's as dangerous as they come. You remember what he did in Afghanistan.'

She nodded, 'Yes, he performed quite well over there, didn't he?'

'Quite well? The Yanks decorated him as a war hero, before he moved into CIA blacks ops. He's saved a lot of lives, but he's taken just as many.'

'Are you trying to frighten me, James?'

'No, ma'am, just highlighting the severity of the situation.'

'When did he leave his post at the White House?'

'Stepped away from Secret Service duties a year or two ago.'

'Perhaps I should contact President Sheeran.'

'No, ma'am,' Falkner said, 'POTUS is like a second father to Martini, if he finds out we're coming after him, and Martini turns up dead, you don't need a personal vendetta with him.' He laughed sarcastically. 'He thinks the sun shines out of Martini's ass. POTUS would want you to bring him in, we need him dead.'

Greenwood's phone vibrated. 'We should get moving.' She stood up. 'Ma'am, I will keep you informed on every development.' She made her way to the door.

Falkner followed.

Pears stood up, 'I'll walk you both out.'

As they walked down the narrow hallway outside the PM's office, Falkner briefly studied the images of Prime Ministers gone before. Both Tory and Labour leaders who'd all once sat in the big seat. 'What an awful job to have,' he said.

'Sometimes I'd be inclined to agree with you, James,' the PM said, looking at the display, deep in thought. She looked at Greenwood who was looking at her phone. 'What have you got?'

'Inspector Becker of the Berlin police has said that he's got officers in Berlin checking areas and following up leads on the possible location on Martini. But I'd imagine he's nowhere near Berlin now.'

'You think he'll attack here, in London?' The PM asked Greenwood but was looking at Falkner.

'I'm not sure, Ma'am. He is dangerous. I would certainly take this threat seriously.'

'What happened in Switzerland doesn't make sense. He just left the vehicle there, no bombs, nothing?'

'He must have known police would be tipped off,' Green-wood said.

'Bastard's playing games,' Falkner said, 'I'd pretty much bet my retirement fund that whatever the Germans are doing, they'll come up short.'

The door of number ten opened.

Greenwood and Falkner stepped out onto the street,

morning mist was rising off the road. A grey Jaguar XF sat idling.

The PM rubbed her hands together to generate some heat. 'Victoria, I want this mess cleaning up as quickly as possible.'

'Yes, ma'am.'

23

Seamus and Mary O'Toole were closing up for the night. Neither had spoken to the other the entire evening. Both had been grateful to have the shop's customers to converse with, slicing through the otherwise awkward silence. Mary was upset at Seamus for putting the responsibility on her to call Becker. Seamus was pissed off at her for ratting on Martini. They'd both had their lives saved by him during their younger years. Both had dodged bullets from UDA assassination attempts. And even though he never made them feel like they owed him, they still felt like they did. It was eating away at Seamus. He hummed as he wiped down the tabletops, then flipped the chairs upside down, setting them on top of the tables, clearing the floor to be swept and mopped. Mary was humming to herself, too, as she stripped down the coffee machine. It was as if neither of them wanted a silence but weren't willing to speak.

The last of the customers had left. The clatter of metal and glass was an obvious sign that the tension in the air was thickening.

'So, it is true. Couples stop talking when they're

married.' Ludwig Schuster stood at the doorway. His expensive navy suit clung to his athletic figure, a black overcoat draped over the crook of his left arm. He stepped further inside, the door slamming behind him. His face was emotionless. 'You're closing?'

'Christ, you catch on quick, don't you?' Mary said dryly.

Schuster smiled. Seamus was more curious about the visit.

'What can we do for you, Mr. Schuster?' Seamus asked.

'It seems that we have a mutual friend. A Mr. Martini.' He strolled across the room, stepping over the pile of broken glass and dirt that Seamus had collected. Sitting on one of the soft seats that ran along the wall, he said, 'You've made his job a little more difficult. A job that I've hired him to do.' He crossed his legs and took out his phone. 'Now – the little job you carried out for James Greer two weeks ago, driving the van from Belfast to Berlin. Did you look in the back?'

'We've already assured Jim that we didn't look in the back. He knows he can trust us,' Mary answered quickly. 'We go a long way back. He knows secrets about us, and we know secrets about him. We were all part of the same movement.' She brushed a loose strand of hair out of her eyes. 'He came to us offering us a job, paying a lot of money for a drive from Ireland to Germany. We followed our orders to the letter.'

'Why have you been in touch with a Mr. Becker of the Berlin Police?'

'Eamon came to us, offering us work,' Seamus said nervously. 'We turned him down. But Mr. Becker has had eyes on this shop ever since we arrived here. What Martini was planning would have been picked up by the local police. It would have came back on us.'

'I'm the man that employed Mr. Martini. I'm the man

that paid for this nicely refurbished shop. I'm the man who paid off your mortgage and...'

'I don't give a fuck who you are, mate,' Seamus exclaimed. He stepped closer to Schuster. 'You've got five seconds to get the...'

Schuster stood before Seamus could say another word, his eyes on the door. Two men wearing black balaclavas, navy overalls, and black boots stalked in. One of them was holding a Heckler & Koch VP9 pistol aimed at Mary, while the other had a Glock 46 pointed at Seamus's head.

'What the hell is this?' Mary shouted, reaching for her phone. The one with the VP9 fired a shot. The bullet sailed straight past her head, shattering one of the freezers containing ready-made tubs of ice-cream. He snatched her phone.

Seamus turned and swung the brush at the man with the Glock. The guy dodged it and fired two shots, one into each leg. Seamus fell to his knees.

Mary screamed, a trembling hand covering her mouth.

Seamus tried to get back up, but the man approached him, his weapon pointed directly at his head.

'You can thank Eamon Martini for this,' Schuster said blandly.

The guy lowered his aim a couple of inches and put three bullets in Seamus's chest. Motionless, Seamus fell forward, face first on the floor at the man's feet. The guy emptied his magazine into his back.

The guy with the VP9 approached Mary, she cried, looking down at her husband.

'You may as well kill me, too, because if you don't...'

The guy pulled the trigger, hitting her in the chest. She fell behind the counter. He rounded the counter and put another four into her back.

Hearing his phone ping, Schuster sat down on one of the seats and crossed his legs. He fished his phone out of his coat pocket. It was an alert. He opened it. 'Is that so?' he said in response to whatever it was he read. He made a call and pressed the device to his ear. 'Mr Dott? It appears some hackers have been snooping around my bank account. Looking at transactions...' He paused abruptly. 'Calm down. You've left Washinton for London?' He paused again. 'Okay, good. I'd advise you to change your phone so you can't be tracked. It's...' he was cut off again. 'Calm down, we're still in control, here, and President Sheeran knows it. Why else would he have let you leave? Because he wants to find his grandson's whereabouts. Now replace your phone and I'll see you at the location at the agreed time.'

24

Karl Page had not always been a driver for heads of the SIS. It was how he'd chosen to spend the second part of his working life. A step or two slower with age, he knew he'd move better behind the wheel of a car than on foot. Like Falkner, he'd gotten used to running around. It was what a career as an agent for Her Majesty's services entailed. Unlike Falkner, however, Page had developed a bad taste regarding his country's involvement in Ireland. He had witnessed first-hand the mayhem that had ensued during the invasions of the Catholic neighbourhoods which were seen as no-go areas for any British crown force, including the local police – Royal Ulster Constabulary.

On August 9th, 1987, the second day of severe unrest in West Belfast during an Internment commemoration, escalations had resulted in eleven civilians being killed. Internment without trial, named Operation Demetrius, was remembered every year since it was brought in on August 9th 1971, which saw over three hundred Catholics arrested and over 7000 displaced.

During an IRA ambush, Page had become separated

from the Ist Battalion Parachute Regiment whilst helping the
Royal Ulster Constabulary with a raid on a home on North
Belfast's Cliftonville Road. A search that had served to anger
the residents more than their operational goal of finding
IRA weapons.

Eighteen-year-old Page found himself alone and
without his weapon, being chased by the crowd that they'd
been trying to control. A narrow, red-bricked entry separating two rows of terrace houses had been where Page was
about to meet his end. He'd been caught by the crowd. Only
through the good graces of a sixteen-year-old, blue-eyed
Irish girl, Elizabeth Cleary, daughter of Damien Cleary Jnr.,
one of the PIRA's commanders in the north of the country,
had he survived.

She had dragged him into the back garden of the house,
taking him away from the hostile crowd and certain death.

Little did Page know that the young lady who had just
saved his life was the granddaughter of the Chief of Staff for
the Provo's Northern Command, and a member of the
ruling army council. This had been a turning point for both
Cleary and Page.

Damien Cleary Jnr. had secretly given Page back to the
British as a goodwill gesture. Proof that the IRA weren't just
a bunch of thugs, but a legitimate political movement,
supported by the Catholic people of Northern Ireland.
Page's life, and the gesture, was initially welcomed by the
British, but eventually became nothing but that. A gesture.

Page had never forgotten the risk Elizabeth had taken to
save his life. People spoke about love at first sight. He was
inclined to agree. Leaving the Regiment a year later, he had
gone back to Belfast to ask for the right to date her. She'd
accepted, much to the fury of her father and grandfather.
Page had assured them both that he would go back to

England with Elizabeth and build a life with her in a safer society than what she'd have if she remained in Belfast. After the initial reluctance, the Cleary family had accepted.

Eventually Page, with his history of serving in Northern Ireland and with the medals he'd received during his tour of duty, had gained employment working in the intelligence world. After a decade of sitting in an office for GCHQ, he had fancied a change. Applying for a job with the Metropolitan Police Royalty and Specialist Protection Branch, he had showcased his skills in protection convoy, anti-hijack and evasive driving. He had breezed through the recruitment process, landing on the comfortable leather seat of the ministerial Jaguar XJ. Retiring as a VIP chauffeur for the likes of Falkner and Greenwood, he'd quickly learned that many deals were discussed and struck on the back seat of a moving vehicle. But never before had Page come into such important information. His wife's half-brother, Eamon Martini, was about to go head-to-head again with the powers of British Intelligence. And their deadliest assassin – Greenwood – was going after him.

Once he'd dropped both Falkner and Greenwood off at HQ, he went for something to eat and made a phone call.

'Mr. Page, how's life in London?'

'Eamon, this is just a quick call. You need to watch your back. Falkner's retired, well, semi-retired. That's how he likes to be described. The agency is now run by a lady so ambitious that she would have made Thatcher look like a pussy cat. But until recently, she was the British government's number one killer.'

'And she's coming after me?'

'Hence the call. She's a nasty piece of work, and very smart. I'll try and get more information and send it across to you in an email.'

'Thanks, Karl. How's Lizzy?'

'Wants me to retire to the south of France with her.'

Martini grunted. 'You're like me, pal, you'd get bored too easily.'

'Take care, Eamon.'

'You, too. Say hello to my sister.'

25

Paddy Lyttle had taken a drive into the seaside village of Bundoran, just six miles away from his home. He sat in his car just outside O'Neill's bakery. His left hand gripped the steering wheel tightly. He studied the knife scar on his wrist and the bullet scar on his hand, feeling something brewing inside of him. Unable to control it, he knew deep down that he was slowly becoming the man he said he'd never become again. His line of sight moved from his hand towards the pebble-sized rain drops that had been assaulting the windscreen since he'd left the house. BBC Radio Ulster was on, delivering a news report about the families of those affected by the Troubles. Thousands killed, tens of thousands impacted. And more often than not, as with all war, too many civilian casualties. Combatants on all sides chose to get involved, but the civilians had to live among it all.

'I should be grateful that I'm alive.' He concluded, reaching over to the front passenger seat and grabbing a paper bag with *O'Neill's* scrawled on the side. He pulled out a salad stick and took a bite. The simple things in life, something that so many took for granted, but just as many had taken away from them.

His phone rang, a +44 mobile number flashed across the screen.

He set the bread roll down, swallowed his mouthful then lifted the device.

'Hello?'

'Mr. Lyttle, Victoria Greenwood speaking. Thank you for your time today. I wonder if I can send someone to escort you to London? I'd like to talk with you more about Eamon Martini.'

He laughed, shaking his head. 'You really want to add him to your list, don't you?'

'I think we both want him dead. Perhaps you've just lost confidence in your ability to do so.' She spoke frankly. 'How about it?'

'This is your personal number?'

'Yes, you can reach me directly on this. Save it to your phone.'

'I'll give you a call in a few hours.'

'Very well. I look forward to hearing from you.' She ended the call, and the radio came back on.

26

Martini sat at the edge of the indoor pool inside the separate leisure complex within Schuster's estate. He watched the ripples of water cause the logo of the estate – a black tree – to dance off the pool's floor, looking as if it had come alive. At thirty-nine, Martini was no spring chicken, but he'd made sure to keep his level of fitness high. His life could take a drastic turn at any time and he needed to keep his body *and* mind sharp. His exercise regime was as important as eating or washing.

'I'm glad you're taking full advantage of the estate,' Schuster said, entering through the patio doors that led in from the garden. Taking off his jacket, he draped it over the back of one of the five wooden loungers that bordered the pool, looking out through the transparent wall of glass out into the well-manicured garden.

'You've got quite a house here,' Martini replied, pulling his legs out of the water. He got up and grabbed his towel then stepped into his flip-flops, making his way towards the table where he'd left his phone and watch.

'You're welcome to stay for as long as you want.' Schuster

sat down, unbuttoning his top two shirt buttons. 'I'd like for you to come work for me, Mr. Martini. Name your price.'

Martini shook his head. 'Let's just get the first job done first.'

'I've done you a favour. Free of charge.'

'What?'

'Your old comrades won't be ratting on anyone ever again.'

Martini froze. 'They're dead?'

'Let's just say they've been removed from the equation. And my two new handymen, who you just happened to have a run in with the other night, were the ones who pulled the trigger. Well, the big one who you scalded. The other is nursing a broken leg.'

Calm as usual, Martini gave away none of his emotions. Schuster couldn't discern if he was happy, sad or indifferent about the news. He had the perfect poker face. He glanced at his phone. 'I guess thanks are in order,' he lied. An email came through.

It was from Page.

Victoria Greenwood, newly-appointed head of British MI6. People believe that if anyone's going to have a career as impressive as Falkner's, it'll be her. And we all know that the only blemish in the old commander's career was the fact that he couldn't put you down. The British government's sending their best after you, Eamon. So be careful. From what I've gathered, she's considering a flight to Berlin.

'Interesting novel?' Schuster asked sarcastically, dragging Martini's attention away from the phone.

'The novel that is my life.' He handed the phone over to Schuster, allowing him to read it. He took a drink from his bottle of water that was no longer cold.

'Is this guy trustworthy?' Schuster asked, passing the device back.

'I'd trust him with my life.' Martini responded in German.

'So, your plan to go after the former Prime Minister. How easy is he to get to?'

'You ask a lot of questions.'

'You haven't got a chance of getting near him, have you?' Schuster wiped away the idea, dismissively waving his hand across his face. 'You can't even get into the UK. The Brits will kill you on sight.'

'They've been after me since I was seventeen. They've sent their best after me before. Yet, here I stand.'

'How many of their so-called best have you taken out?'

'Doesn't matter. I'm the one still breathing.'

'I have an idea. Go shower and get dressed. We can go for a drive, somewhere quieter.'

'I think that if you're planning on taking any of those supercars, it won't be so quiet.' Martini stood up and grabbed his phone. 'I'll see you in half an hour.'

27

Twenty-five minutes later, Martini stepped out through the front door of the main house onto the porch, wearing a three-piece light grey suit, fitted to his athletic figure. The smell of flavoured smoke drew his attention towards the garage block on his right. Schuster stood in front of his black Lamborghini Aventador, staring absentmindedly into the front storage space.

Martini approached him, taking a mental note that his Dessert Eagle .50 pistol was holstered beneath the left side of his jacket. 'You'll not get much shopping in that.' He looked into the storage space that contained nothing but a folded raincoat. He buttoned his suit jacket closed, unappreciative of the freezing temperature. 'How much for the suit?'

Schuster, with an electronic cigarette in his left hand, closed the storage compartment and tossed the key to Martini. 'The day that somebody takes a car like this to the shops for some basics is the day that they should have it taken off them.' He pat Martini on the upper arm and walked past him towards the passenger side. 'You can drive. The suit's free. Glad you could find something that fits.'

Martini lifted the Lambo's scissor door and peered inside before getting in. All white leather interior, none of it cracked or worn. The black contrast stitching drew neat lines around the outline of the seats. The raging bull logo was stitched into the headrest in black. He shook his head and dropped himself into the sports bucket seat and started the engine. The 6 litre V12 roared to life. 'Where are we going?'

'Go out through the gates, then turn left.'

Martini pressed the accelerator only slightly and felt the full power of the mid-engine located directly behind their seats. He approached the gates, offering nothing more than a nod to the security guard who stood at the doorway to the security hut. He glared into the car, clasping a German manufactured Haenel MK 556 semi-automatic. The rifle acting as a visible reminder of the danger posed to anyone who tried to get in without invitation. 'What's his story?'

'He's an extremely dangerous man, Mr. Martini. One of a team of twelve German ex-Special Forces under my employ.' Schuster pressed a button on his phone and the gates parted.

Turning left, Martini slammed his foot down, sending them both back into their seats. 'Sounds like you've good security here at the estate.'

Schuster smiled. 'Yes, I do. That's why if anyone tried to enter, they'd be dead without realising it. Even you.'

Martini smirked but remained silent.

'How much extra would you charge if I were to ask you to go after a member of the royal family?' Schuster spoke loudly as the car slowed, negotiating a bend to the left.

'Targeting the royal family when they're not the ones making the decisions for the Brits isn't worth my time – or your money.'

'The royal family has the overall authority over the British Prime Minister and can stop her at any time. You know that.'

'Churchman's the best option, and only Churchman. He was the Prime Minister that sent the bombs over to Afghanistan in the first place.' He lowered the window, cold air hitting his skin instantly. He rounded another corner, this time to the right, finding a steep, almost vertical drop. He put his foot down again and flew, the wind whipping in through the cabin. He fit into the bucket seat like a hand in a glove.

'I own a deer park on the right just up this road. Two hundred yards. Pull in there and we'll have a drink. It's called the Rastplaz.'

He did as he was told. The carpark was covered in loose stones, not great if you visited in an expensive car and avoided stone chippings like the plague. He reversed into the free bay next to a grey van, shut the engine off and got out.

He followed Schuster inside.

Taking the seat in the corner, next to the window and directly facing the door, Martini scanned the shop. It was like a shack. Family-friendly. Cosy. A group of four, two males and two females, sat on the group of four leather armchairs around the blazing fire on the far wall. An elderly couple sat two tables away from the table Martini had selected, and a middle-aged guy who appeared to be the most likely candidate to own the lorry that was parked outside, sat at the far end of the shop, closest to the door. The driver looked as if he were about to fall asleep on the plate of pasta he was eating. The heat of the fire was obviously not helping to keep him awake.

Martini people-watched for a moment until Schuster brought over two cups of coffee and two buns.

'You're not on any weird diet, are you?' Schuster asked, nodding towards the buns.

He shook his head. 'As long as it's not poisoned.' A glimmer of a smirk stretched across his face. He lifted one of the buns and took a bite.

Schuster tipped two spoons of brown sugar into his coffee and stirred it in, scanning the shop the same way Martini had. 'What do you think of this place?'

'I don't think you've brought me all the way here to get my opinion on the quality of service.'

Schuster laughed and set the spoon down on the tray. 'You're right.' He took a sip from his cup and set it down. 'You know money can buy you a lot. Pretty much anything you want. It's a wonderful commodity.'

'From that house you live in, and that car I've just driven us here in, I'm inclined to agree.' He took a drink from his coffee. 'Get to the point.'

'My cousin, who I love dearly, is becoming a nervous wreck. Unstable to say the least. I need you to deliver something, quick. I may not be able to control him for much longer.'

'What do you mean?'

'He's got access to many resources, including intelligence. The intelligence of an attractive Irish lady by the name of Elizabeth Cleary.' Schuster's line of sight fell from Martini's eyes, a smile stretching across his face. 'You know the lady I'm talking about?'

'I'd be worried if I didn't, given the fact she's my sister.' He spoke calmly, fighting against the urge to grab Schuster by the throat and squeeze the life out of him.

'There are people out there that would pay handsomely

to get their hands on you, Mr. Martini.' Schuster took another drink of his coffee, this time glaring at him over the rim of his cup. 'If they can't find you, they'll draw you in.' He looked over his shoulder as the door opened. Martini followed his gaze. Greer was making his way towards them, signalling the barista to send another drink over.

'Eamon.' Greer greeted him, taking a seat and bringing with him a waft of cool air from outside. 'We have intelligence that someone who's studied you for a long time is on their way here.'

'Who?'

'Paddy Lyttle. And word has it, the Brits have sent their best assassin. You've got your work cut out for you.'

'I've got a job to do, and I'll get it done.' He cleared his throat. 'They've sent the best after me before.' He looked at Schuster. 'The job will get done.'

'You need to be fast, Eamon.' Greer repeated what Schuster had already said.

'I've heard,' Martini replied, taking a bite of the bun and washing it down with a mouthful of coffee. 'Ahmad's growing restless and has the whereabouts of my sister.' He spoke again with no sign of emotion, neither on his face nor the tone of his voice.

Greer pulled out his phone and handed it across the table.

Martini took the smartphone and watched the video. It was taken from outside George Best Belfast City Airport showing Paddy Lyttle getting out of a taxi, pulling his hood up, and rushing towards to doors of the departures lounge. 'Looks like Paddy's on his way.' He handed the phone back to Greer, but was told to watch the next video. The second recording was of Karl Page, kissing his wife, Martini's sister, on the lips before getting into his car. 'She looks well, my sister.' He handed the phone back over. 'You've got eyes everywhere.'

'Like I said, Mr. Martini. If you have enough money, you can buy whatever you want.'

'Can't buy loyalty.'

Greer set the phone down on the table. 'Ahmad's becoming a royal pain in the ass, Eamon. We need you to produce something for him.'

'I hope he knows that regardless of who's head I deliver; it won't bring his family back.'

'We are in agreement,' Schuster said. 'But you see, Mr. Martini, I made my dying mother a promise – that I would always help my family. Even illegitimate animals like her sister's son.'

Martini sat forward, resting his arms on the table. 'You know I made my mother a similar promise.' He finished his coffee and rose from his seat. 'I'm taking the car. You can ride back to your house with Jim here. Thanks for the drink.'

28

Bradley Hawkins woke with a pounding headache and a stiff neck. His jaw hurt to move, and he could taste blood when he swallowed. With his tongue swimming around his mouth, he could feel a gap at the front; he'd lost at least one tooth. His ears were ringing, reminding him that he'd taken a blow to the side of the head before he went out. His stomach muscles were tender, and he felt like a couple of ribs were broken, lucky none of them had punctured a lung. He knew little about what had happened in Belfast, and even less about where they were; but he knew they weren't on dry land. The room was rocking from side to side, making him feel nauseous. The cold burger and fries sitting just a few inches from him on the table made him want to expel the lining of his stomach. He was bound to a wooden chair, feeling plastic cable ties biting into the skin around his ankles and wrists. He was in what looked like a small staff room; a twelve-by-twelve square box with white walls, paint flaking in areas, stained in others. A fridge/Freezer had a magazine cut-out of a topless lady with something written in German across her chest, shielding her nipples. He looked around the room. To his right, Enda Sheeran was tied to a single bed that ran along the wall beneath a small window which was providing some sunlight. From what he could tell, the boy was unconscious, but alive, his chest rising with tiny breathes. Enda's nose had been bleeding, two crimson lines running down to his upper lip. Hawkins thought of his own son, seven-year-old Jason, and what he wanted to do to the people responsible for this. Mason Torres was in the corner, next to the sink and cupboards, beaten senseless and rope-tied to a hook from the ceiling, like a slab of beef ready to be carved up and distributed to the butcher. His body was limp, exhausted; the rope was the only reason his body hadn't collapsed to the ground.

Unless...

Unless

Hawkins thought. Unless Torres could use his weight to rock the hook, working it loose. He heard footsteps above, walking along the deck. Whoever was holding them would eventually come down. There were no cameras visible. They wouldn't know what was happening in the room until they came to check. And if Hawkins had anything to do with it – the bastards would be walking into their worst nightmare.

'Mason,' he whispered, not wanting to attract attention. 'Mason!' He hissed, this time with a little more volume. For his efforts, he got a groan in response. 'Mason, wake up.'

Torres rolled his head, 'What?'

'Break time's over, let's get out of here.'

Torres grunted, 'In case you haven't noticed, we're a little tired down at the moment.'

Hawkins considered manipulating his bodyweight to walk the chair closer to Torres, but he couldn't do it without attracting attention, alerting whoever was up on deck. He parked that idea. 'That hook you're dangling from, try swinging, see if it rocks any. Maybe we can work it loose.'

Torres didn't answer.

'Come on, Mason, work with me here.'

'Death must be better than this.'

'You don't get to choose when to check out, Mason. Not when there's an eight-year-old boy lying in the *fucking* corner wondering where his mom's gone.'

Torres remained silent for a moment, then he grunted. He swung himself, lifting his feet off the ground, allowing gravity and his bodyweight to deliver as much stress as possible on the hook.

Hawkins watched as the hook began to wobble, with each swing giving the fixing more travel.

Torres dropped his feet back to the ground, 'My arms are dead, Brad. I can't.'

Hawkins looked across at Enda, the boy lying still, looking at the ceiling, putting on a brave face; trying to be strong, to be man. His mother would be proud of him. Hawkins looked back at Torres. 'Well, you can tell Enda you've given up trying.'

Torres sighed, then swung again. The hook kept loosening.

'Keep going, I think it's coming.'

Hawkins realised he was clenching his fists so tight that his nails were beginning to dig into his skin. It was nail biting, he couldn't take his eyes off the hook, watching as wood chippings and cement began to fall out of the ceiling, clouds of dust decorating Torres's head and shoulders. Then, with a satisfying clunk, the rope pulled the hook out of the ceiling. Torres was free. He brought his hands down in front of him. He looked at Hawkins and smiled.

'That's the first time I've seen you smile since you were

accepted into the team,' Hawkins said. 'Now check for a knife, something that can get us free.' He looked at Enda, the boy was watching him. He offered him a smile and a wink.

Torres went to the sink, a tray of cutlery sat on the steel drainer. He retrieved a serrated knife, returned to Hawkins and began sawing through the ties. Once Hawkins was free, he took the knife off Torres and cut the rope from his wrists, then went to Enda.

'You okay, kid?'

'I just want to go home.'

Hawkins began cutting. Enda's left ankle was the last of the four limbs to be freed. Hawkins playfully messed the boy's hair. 'Let's see if we can make that a possibility.'

'I think someone's coming?' Torres hissed from the door. 'They must have heard the hook being pulling out of the ceiling.'

Hawkins slid the knife across the floor to him and went to get another from the sink. He pulled the drawer below the sink open and found a large butcher's knife.

Footsteps could be heard thundering down a flight of stairs.

'Mason, you stand behind the door; Enda, get back to your bed and pretend you're still tied up.' Hawkins slipped the knife down his sock then re-positioned his trousers over it, taking his seat again. Fast footsteps crossed the creaky wooden floorboards, stopping just outside the room. 'I need some help in here, please. Help!'

A set of keys rattled as one was inserted into the lock. The lock disengaged and the doorhandle lowered. A familiar face walked in. One of their own men. Thirty-three-year-old Edward Shaws. Recently recruited into the Secret Service.

'Eddie, what the fuck?' Hawkin's said, 'What's this all about?'

Shaws took one step into the room, 'I'm sorry you were dragged into this...' Torres forced the door closed and drove the knife into Shaws' throat, blood spewing everywhere. Shaws hit the ground, clutching his throat, desperately trying to stop the blood, while chocking. Torres searched him, finding a Glock 17 and a mobile phone. He pocketed the phone and checked the pistol was loaded. It was, with one in the chamber. He lifted the keys that lay next to Shaws. 'Let's get out of here.'

'You've got the gun, you go first. I heard radio static from the next room. We need to send out a distress call,' Hawkins said. He looked at Enda. 'You stay between the two of us, alright?'

Enda nodded.

The three exited the room into a narrow passageway. To their left were doors on either side. Female toilets on one side and the males on the other. To their right was a communications room, beyond that, was a flight of stairs, leading up to the deck.

'Mason,' Hawkins whispered, 'Comms room, go.'

They approached the room. Torres got to the door and listened for a moment, nothing coming from inside. He tried the door. It was open. He looked back at Hawkins and nodded. He pushed the door open, seeing a radio station in the corner. He rushed in. Two loud cracks came from behind the door. He took two bullets in the back and fell face first into the ground, but managed to toss the Glock back towards Hawkins.

Hawkins grabbed the pistol and fired three shots through the door. Hearing a dead weight hit the floor, he stepped in and looked around the door. Another of his men assigned to protect Niamh and Enda. 'Why Marko?' he said as the guy lay on the ground looking up at him.

'I'm sorry,' the guy mouthed, breathless, blood pooling around him.

'Masson?' Hawkins rolled Torres over to face him. He was dead. He closed his dead friend's eyes. 'Fuck!' He hissed. He ran over to the VHF radio mounted to the wall at the desk. He pressed the red button, held for five seconds, then called, 'Mayday, mayday, mayday – can anyone hear me out there?'

There was a moment of static, then came a voice, speaking accented English, 'What is your distress?'

'My name is Bradley Hawkins, United States Secret Service. I need an urgent message sent to Teresa Goodall of the CIA. I repeat – I have an urgent message for Teresa Goodall of the CIA. Do you copy?' A gunshot went off behind him, hitting him in the back.

He fell onto the table.

'Bradley?' Enda cried.

Hawkins reached for the pistol, but before he could turn around, he took another two shots in the back, then one in the head.

29

Greenwood sat in the living room of her Central London apartment, her laptop open and resting on the coffee table just inches away from her knees. A document was opened in front of her, a report from the Northern Ireland Independent Monitoring Committee. The IMC was formed in 2003 when political disaster was about to strike the already unstable six counties of Northern Ireland – the 1998 Good Friday Agreement in jeopardy. The province had experienced relative peace since the 1994 ceasefire between the IRA and the British army. The IRA, however, hadn't given up their weapons, which was a power-sharing deal-breaker for the largest loyalist political party – the Democratic Unionist Party.

Greenwood picked holes in the report, finding inconsistencies throughout, and knew it was as legit as the first handshake between the leaders of Sinn Fein and the DUP, who were forming the new government together. Greenwood couldn't put her finger on it, but she knew that whoever had written the report had, at the very least, put a slight fictional spin on it. She made a point to compile all available documents relating to Northern Ireland, paying particular attention to any with a mention of the Provisional IRA. Anything that could help her better understand Damien Cleary Jnr., might, in some way, allow her to better understand Eamon Martini. She knew she was up against the biggest name of her career – *if* she could put him down. She'd always looked up to her former commander and mentor, and she knew Falkner was not easily beaten. So when he'd given up on his battle of wits against Martini, she knew this big fish would not be easily caught. But that was a challenge she was more than ready to take on.

Just as she was skipping to the next page, her phone rang on the sofa next to her.

'Commander Falkner?'

'It's James, not commander anymore, Victoria. I keep telling you.'

'What can I do for you, sir?'

'Have you managed to look through those documents we pulled off the system today?'

'I'm going through them as we speak.' She lifted her coffee and took a sip. 'You're right about one thing, sir – the Irish Troubles was a messy affair. I can't believe it went on for such a long time.'

Falkner laughed softly. 'I spent my entire career in that place, and to this day I still don't understand it all. Who was working with who, who was supporting what – it rightly earned itself the nickname, "the dirty war".'

'Are you more concerned about the attack on the PM or catching Martini?'

'I think you already know the answer to that.'

'So, I'll expect you on the plane to Berlin?'

He cleared his throat and paused for a moment. 'What time should I be ready?'

30

Unable to sleep, Martini made himself a double espresso and a long coffee. Lifting his laptop along with his drinks, he went out into the back garden. The estate owned by Ludwig Schuster was impressive. He'd made himself very comfortable, and Martini could understand why a man who had all this would expect to get what he wanted. But on the other hand, Martini knew that it took brains to keep it all. Inheritance was not enough – any clown could be born into a billion euro empire and squander it all. But Schuster *was* smart, about everything, that is - until he'd uttered the words: Elizabeth Cleary. Martini was unlike anyone else. Which was the reason why Greer had recommended him for the job. Sooner or later, Schuster would witness first hand what exactly that meant.

Opening his laptop, he clicked on Google Chrome and searched for BBC News. Finding the website, he opened the home page. The top story was another public knife attack on the streets of London, Camden area. An Asian male in his mid-twenties screaming "Allahu Akbar", "God is great", before being gunned down by officers from West Hampstead Met. The journalist reported a worrying increase in attacks. Events like the one on London Bridge that had cast the English capital in a poor light again would, like many times before, lead back to the same old question: how were they going to combat Islamic extremism without alienating the good, honest members of the Muslim population in England?

He took a drink of his espresso. 'Decisions cost lives. Regardless of who's making them,' he mumbled to himself.

As he scrolled down the page, an image of Victoria Greenwood getting into her chauffeur-driven Jag outside Number 10 made him sit forward in his seat. Apart from the fact that his brother-in-law was the one driving the vehicle, his excitement grew as the next image of the story showed Falkner getting into the back after Greenwood.

He shut his eyes and closed the laptop. His mind cast back to when he was nothing but a teenager, collecting information on Bianco. The rat. The double agent. Bianco, gathering information on the Provisionals, whilst leading the IRA unit tasked to sniff out their internal rats and make examples of them.

Martini had been just seventeen years old when he'd played British Intelligence at their own game – and won. Young Eamon Martini became a living legend in Ireland, long before his time would have suggested it possible. But as President Bill Sheeran had recently said in a speech to university students in Paris: political change, political upheaval and social revolution often owed its gratitude to those of the younger generation. More often than not, it was the younger members of society demanding change – whether it be the black civil rights movement in America, the Catholic civil rights movement in Northern Ireland, or the anti-apartheid movement in South Africa. Most influential people in those movements were young people. Martini was a youngster just like the rest of them. This allowed him to accept he wasn't special, just like the rest of them: unwilling to settle for the status quo.

Then he thought about Paddy Lyttle. He'd never forgiven Martini for handing Bianco over to the PIRA hit squad. But what was he supposed to do? Let the British kill his father, with the smoking gun in the hands on a UDA or UVF man? An assassination on Damien Cleary Jnr. would have brought an end to the ceasefire and the war would have been back on, peace talks would have gone up in flames. Martini also believed that Lyttle hadn't forgiven himself for not equalling the score for Bianco. He knew Lyttle was on his way to Berlin, and the chances of them both coming face to face with each other was highly probable.

He caught a whiff of cigarette smoke and opened his eyes. Jaleel was approaching him, silently moving across the garden like a stealth soldier, but his glazed eyes and slight wobble in his gait was anything but stealth. The half-empty glass of whiskey in his right hand was obviously not his first of the evening.

'Mr. Martini,' he slurred, as he pulled a seat out and dropped himself onto it.

'Call me Eamon.'

Jaleel finished his drink and set the glass down on the table, harder than he'd perhaps meant to. He looked at Martini. 'Eamon...' He hiccupped. 'Tell me, Eamon, why haven't you managed to hand me the head of a British official yet?' He sniggered. 'I heard you were good. The best, even.'

'I am,' Martini was quick to reply. 'And if you want me to get my job done, you need to relax. Stop drinking that piss and let me get on with it.' He wanted to force the glass down Jaleel's throat, but he maintained his composure. 'Have a little faith, my friend,' he added in Arabic.

'Faith?' Jaleel spoke mockingly. 'My faith has pretty much run dry, Mr. Martini. A drunk Muslim is not a man of faith.' He spat on the ground next to Martini's foot. 'Now get to work, and get me what you're employed to do or...'

'Or what? You need to dry your eyes and quit feeling sorry for yourself.' Martini replied, switching back to English. A look of shock was evident on Jaleel's face. 'You think you're the only person who's lost someone they love?' He uncrossed his legs and sat forward, his forearms resting on the table, glaring across at him. 'Your loved ones would be turning in their graves if they saw the pathetic drunk you've become.' He looked at Jaleel's hands, both clenched tightly into fists. He gestured towards them, 'What are you going to do with those?' He sat back in his chair and waited for Jaleel to reply. He didn't. 'Now fuck off. I'll find you when the job's done.' He was reaching down for his coffee when he caught the glint of metal out of the corner of his eye. Jaleel had a Heckler & Koch in his hand, the VP9SK swaying towards Martini. He stepped up to Martini, the pistol pointed right at his forehead. Martini stood up, the gun pressed against his forehead now, the metal cold against his skin. He glared into Jaleel's eyes, pushed his head into the gun forcing the weapon back a little, then quickly moved his head to the side, both hands coming up to retrieve the pistol before Jaleel had a chance to react. He ploughed the handle of the gun into Jaleel's temple, sending him into the table.

'What the hell's going on?' Schuster shouted.

Martini removed the VP9's magazine from the bottom, retracted the slide to the rear, popped the 9mm round from the barrel then disassembled the weapon, tossing the pieces down on the table. He lifted his phone and turned to Schuster. 'Your cousin and I were just having a little chat.' He pocketed the phone. 'I'm going to bed.' He walked past Jaleel, towards Schuster. 'I think you should keep him on a tight leash.'

Jaleel jumped up from the table, grabbing a knife. Martini saw the shadow passing his line of sight, the arm arching down towards him. He spun around and caught Jaleel's wrist, applying pressure until the knife dropped. He snapped Jaleel's wrist and hyper-extended his arm, a cracking sound swiftly followed by the agonising screams. The Afghan fell to one knee.

Martini looked at Schuster. 'Perhaps you should lock him up until we're finished. Next time, I won't just break a couple of bones.' He fixed his jacket, grabbed the laptop, and made his way towards the house.

31

At Berlin's Gatow Airbase, the weather was much like that in London: freezing. Temperatures hovered around five during the day and dropped below zero at night. Normal for the time of the year. Greenwood led the way down the steps of "Vespina", the RAF voyager, quickly pulling her gloves on. The metallic handle of the aircraft's steps was covered in a thick blanket of ice.

She was quickly followed by Falkner. Both already missing the heating provided within the cabin of the VIP private jet. Greenwood paid particular attention to the ground as she took the last step onto the runway. The moment she felt her heels grip something, she carried on towards the terminal.

'I'm starting to wonder if catching Martini is worth all this effort,' Falkner complained, tagging along behind her. 'I could be tucked up in my nice warm bed right now.' He caught his scarf as it whipped in the wind.

'You can get back on and return to London if you prefer,' she said, stopping at the automatic doors, trying not to react to the slight delay and its painfully slow opening. 'Or you can sit tight in Becker's nice warm office and watch from the side-lines as I take this guy down.'

'You're confident,' he replied, 'that's good, you'll need to be.' He rubbed his hands as he stepped inside, unzipping his coat. 'I think I might spend more time in the company of Becker and his warm office instead of going out and trying to catch a man who's got more lives than a cat. Becker better make a good cup of tea, that's all I'm saying.'

'You can ask him,' she said, moving past the luggage collection zone towards the second set of automatic doors, a sign above saying in German: *No return beyond this point*.

Becker was pacing back and forth at the doors, his phone in his hand.

Catching Greenwood's eye on her approach, he froze on the spot and said something into his phone. He removed his earpods as he approached her, greeting her with a handshake and a peck on each cheek.

'Try kissing me and we're going to have a problem.' Falkner joked as Becker shook his hand.

'You're not my type, and certainly not as beautiful as the new head of British SIS.' Becker looked at Greenwood, dressed in a navy trousers, navy jacket, and white shirt. The diamond earrings made her look wealthier than someone working for the government, and the youthful good looks made her look like she shouldn't be facing off with a killer like Eamon Martini.

'Don't let her looks fool you,' Falkner said. 'If there's anyone who can give Martini a run for his money, it's Ms. Greenwood.'

'*Ms.* Greenwood?' Becker looked stunned.

'Work has taken precedence in my life,' she was quick to say.

'Very well,' Becker said thoughtfully, 'let's go.' He offered to take Greenwood's bag, but she refused. He led the way through the terminal towards the carpark. He gestured towards the Costa shop. 'Can I treat you both to a coffee and a cake?'

'If you don't have a full English breakfast, then I'll accept that as second best.' Falkner mumbled. 'I'll have a café latte and a croissant.'

'I'll have the same, please.' Greenwood sat down at the first table they came to and pulled her laptop out of its case. Falkner sat down facing her, crossing his legs. She entered the password and gained access to the computer then looked up at him. 'Commander Falkner, you know it's not polite to stare.'

He smirked. 'I know.'

'Then I have something on my face?'

He shook his head. 'No.'

'Then what?'

'I've lived my life. I'm an old man. If I were to die trying to stop Martini, I would at least have died living a good life. You on the other hand...'

'I'm not going to die at the hands of Mr. Martini,' she finished for him as Becker joined them. 'I might even give him the chance to come in peacefully and let him live.'

Falkner laughed. 'God, it would truly have been something else had you both been on the same side.'

'Who?' Becker asked, joining the conversation.

'Somehow I don't think Martini's a team player,' she said. 'And I don't think I could work with him, given that he's been on the top of our hitlist for so long.'

'I wouldn't make that decision until you get a chance to chat to him.' Falkner was quick to say. 'One thing to note about the young Eamon Martini is that he was born into a family and caught up in a world that he didn't choose.' The barista came over with their drinks. Falkner took his cup and blew into it before taking a sip. 'Christ, maybe I would have done the same thing.'

'My father was killed by an IRA sniper in Belfast in 1981,' she spat.

'Some of his family died at the hands of our forces. That bloody Parachute Regiment should never have been sent over there. Worst decision the British government ever made.'

'Sounds like you're defending him,' Becker was quick to say.

'Not at all, just stating what I saw. I've learned a lot from the Irish. My contribution to combatting the PIRA taught me a lot. It was a war. Eamon Martini should pay for the things he's done wrong, but so should the highest-ranking members of our previous governments. You can't punish one side without punishing the other.' He looked at the laptop as Greenwood's eyes fell back to the screen. 'What are you looking at?'

She quickly glanced at him before looking back down at the screen. 'Our collection of Troubles-related reports.' She looked at Falkner. 'You're right, our government has done many shady things to keep the truth from people. No wonder people like Martini hate the Brits so much.'

'Anything in particular that you're looking at?'

'The Brighton bombing was known beforehand by British intelligence.' She shook her head as she spoke. 'A decision was taken to let it go ahead because the person feeding the intel back to us was our most valued informant. The Irish Italian – James Bianco, and guess who happened to be the person responsible for Bianco's death?' She looked at Becker.

The German shrugged his shoulders. 'It can't have been Martini. He would have been...'

'Seventeen at the time he handed Bianco over to the Army council.' Falkner finished for him. 'He wasn't the only youngster involved in the IRA, but he always stood out from the crowd because he wasn't a native Irishman. He was raised in New York by his mother, Maria and his *Nonno*: the boss of the Martini crime family.'

Becker shook his head. 'Colourful life to say the least.'

'Kid never stood a chance,' Falkner concluded.

'We all have a chance,' Greenwood snapped, a potent sting of contempt in her words. 'I'll soon straighten the bastard out.'

'Just don't lose that cool of yours.' Falkner tapped her affectionately on the hand. 'It's why I'd recommended you as my replacement.'

'Aren't you thinking of coming out of retirement?' she asked, finishing her coffee.

He shook his head. 'I'm thinking of taking a leaf out of Lyttle's book and taking off to the coast somewhere, spending the rest of my days walking Coco up the beach.'

'Who's Coco?' Becker asked.

Greenwood looked at him, smiling. 'His dachshund.' She smirked casting a glance over to her old superior. 'Yappy little bastard.'

'Coco serves a purpose,' Falkner protested.

'What about our friend, Lyttle? Do you think he's going to be any use to us?' Becker asked. 'I was expecting him to accompany you on the flight.'

'He's booked a later one. Whether he shows or not is another question.' Falkner stood up. 'I need the loo. Then you can take us to Berlin. I want to see this Brain Freeze joint where the O'Tooles have made their home.'

32

Becker parked his silver Range Rover on the street directly outside Brain Freeze. The shop was closed and in complete darkness, but according to the opening times on the website, it should have been open. What the three didn't know was that its owners were now dead, gunned down, and left lying on the floor like two empty ice-cream cups. Only one person's name would be engraved on every casing that would rattle along the streets of Berlin – Eamon Martini. Regardless whether he was responsible or not. He was involved. That would be their conclusion, and he would be the one that would have to answer for it.

'Nice place,' Falkner said honestly. 'Looks like old Seamus and Mary O'Toole have made a real stab at an honest life. After all the crap we've been through, one can only respect them for it.' He opened the rear passenger side door and got out, buttoning his jacket closed.

Greenwood flicked her jacket collar up and followed him, disembarking from the rear driver's side. 'You think something's wrong? Perhaps their old buddy Martini has come to call on them again.'

Leaving the vehicle idling, Becker stepped out from behind the wheel and crossed the front of the car, stepping onto the pavement. He looked at the building, shaking his head. 'Something's not right here. Out of all the times I've visited this place, not once have I ever seen it closed during the hours it should be open. One thing that I've always respected the O'Toole's for is their work ethic and the effort they've put into this place.' He looked at Greenwood and then at Falkner. 'Something's wrong.'

'If something's happened to them, I don't think it'll have been him.' Falkner answered before Greenwood had a chance to.

'Neither do I,' she agreed. 'From what I've learned about him, it doesn't fit his description.'

Becker led them towards the entrance. He looked through the window and spotted two broken cups lying below one of the tables nearest the counter. The wooden shaft of a brush could just about be seen, lying next to the broken crockery and a blue plastic dustpan full of dirt. Someone had been about to scoop the fragments up before being interrupted. Becker grunted as if mentally taking note. Spotting the front door open a crack, he removed his weapon and indicated to the others that he was going in.

Greenwood looked at a laminated poster pinned to the notice board that was advertising a fundraising event due to be held on the weekend, the funds being donated to the local children's hospital. 'Looks like they were trying to do something good.' She pulled the sign off the board to study it more closely. 'Can't fault them for that.'

Becker looked at the poster. 'The event will have to be somewhere else if Martini's come after them.' His voice held a tinge of humour. He opened the door and led the way in. Switching the lights on, he could see the place was spotless.

In perfect order, except for the accident at the counter. The reason for the abrupt end to the clean-up job was right there in front of them. The bodies of Seamus and Mary O'Toole were behind the counter. Each with a number of bullet holes.

'Looks like whoever did this had the decency to drag them away from the view of the window,' Falkner said, casually strolling in, hands in his pockets.

'This wasn't Martini,' Greenwood said. She stepped up to the counter and peered over at the body. 'To leave someone like this, it's got to have been someone else.'

'Who else?' Falkner asked, as he followed Becker towards the counter. 'If not Martini, then who?'

'Perhaps the people that employed Martini to carry out the hit?' Greenwood suggested. 'Maybe the people wanting the PM dead sent someone to follow Martini. Realised that they were old comrades and concluded that Martini had tried to outsource the job. Leaving loose ends.'

Becker shook his head. 'I don't think he'd be that stupid. To lead people here and endanger them.'

'I wouldn't think so, either.' Falkner walked around the counter. 'Definitely a pro, whoever did this. They weren't afraid to be caught, perhaps someone with a lot of leverage. Like the same someone who could leverage a person like Martini to take on this kind of job.'

'If it wasn't Martini, then it has to be someone linked to him and what he's doing.'

'I'll call it in. Have the office stripped. We'll check the CCTV, documents, electronics and paper – we'll get it all removed for inspection.' Becker reached down to the fridge and grabbed himself a bottle of water. He offered one to Greenwood and Falkner.

'Very smart. Interrupt a crime scene,' Greenwood said.

Falkner sniggered. Becker didn't reply. 'We're not going to find anything here. You can go check CCTV but I'm fairly sure the killers would have thought about that.'

'Well as far as we know, this is one of the last places our friend set foot.' Becker walked back around to the customer side of the counter and made his way towards the door again. 'I'd be honoured if you would both accompany me to dinner tonight.'

'I wouldn't say no to some fine German grub,' Falkner said, seemingly more interested in feeding his hunger instead of the dead bodies on the ground.

'Thanks, but I think I'll just work from the hotel tonight,' Greenwood replied. She exited the building last. 'But you two can go out and talk about the old days. Pretend you're both the young men you once were. I'll do the work.'

Becker closed the door and locked it. 'She's such a charming lady, isn't she?'

33

Martini was in the pool house of the Schuster estate. He had a shower and selected a pair of grey jogging bottoms and a matching hoodie to lounge around in. His phone had been buzzing for the last few minutes as he dried and dressed. As he stepped out of the bedroom, the vibrating started again. He lifted it from the arm of the cream leather sofa next to the tropical fish tank.

'How's my favourite brother-in-law and driver to the head of British SIS?'

'Eamon, watch your back. Victoria Greenwood and James Falkner have arrived in Berlin today. Falkner is more there to tag along, getting bored in retirement and wanting some fun and excitement in his life again. But Greenwood – she's hellbent on getting you. The PM has issued a shoot to kill order on you.'

'Noted.'

'She's even skipped the cabinet meeting due to be held tomorrow.'

'What cabinet meeting?'

'The PM has called an emergency Cobra meeting

tomorrow to discuss the increase in Muslim attacks in England.'

'Where is this meeting being held?'

'I'll see if I can find out for you. I've got to go. But you watch your back, pal.'

'You, too.' He ended the call just as Greer appeared at the door. He tossed the phone down on the sofa.

Greer strolled in, focussing his attention on Martini's phone. 'Anyone interesting?'

'Paddy Lyttle, believe it or not,' he lied. 'No idea how he got hold of my number.'

'What did he have to say?'

'Wants me to walk away from whatever it is I'm planning.' He filled the kettle and put it on.

'Paddy Lyttle was once a likable man.' Greer shook his head, leaning against the kitchen top. He folded his arms. 'You sure about Churchman?'

Martini turned and met Greer's gaze. 'Remember Brighton?'

Greer smiled. 'Christ, do I remember it? I almost cried when I heard the news. To be so close to killing that old bitch, but not close enough.' His head tilted slightly to the side, looking at Martini quizzically. 'Why?'

'Just thinking about how much that war would have changed if she weren't in office.'

He made two cups of coffee and returned to the sitting area. Sitting down on the sofa, he picked up the remote control for the television and switched it on. Sky News was on, talking about tensions between the US and Iran. The story was coming to an end. The bottom of the sixty-inch plasma had a continuous strip of news running across the screen. According to one report, Jihadist extremism was something that the people in England were growing tired of and something had to be done about it.

Both Greer and Martini sat reading the stories.

'No innocents,' Martini said, as he lifted his cup to his mouth, blowing on his coffee.

Greer looked at him. 'What?'

'This attack can't have any innocents.'

'Collateral damage is always a possibility, but only you can control...'

'People who've been responsible for taking the lives of innocent people, I've no problem in taking out. But nobody innocent gets dragged into this.'

'Eamon, why'd you take this job?' Greer asked.

'I know if I don't take the job, that crazy bastard Ahmad will send an eight-year-old boy to an early grave. I can't sit back and watch that. The president knows he's a target. It comes with the job. But a child, Christ, if I have to die trying to save him, I will.'

Greer nodded his head, taking a drink of his coffee. 'Ahmad's very unstable. But the man just lost his family in a strike ordered by the Americans.'

'We've all lost loved ones,' Martini said, clearing his throat. 'That's why I understand his pain.'

'What about your mother's side of the family, you still have contact with them?'

'The Martini clan?' He shook his head.

Although most of the Martini crime family had gone legit, there were some members within the family who'd been drawn back into the dark world Maria Martini had told her son to move away from. Martini was a man of his word, and he kept that promise to his late mother, despite some of his cousins rummaging around in the dirt with the other drug dealers, launderers, pimps and human traffickers.

'Christ, your family was one of the most powerful crime organisations in New York.' Greer took another drink. 'You don't have *any* contact with them, nothing at all?'

He didn't reply.

They looked at the TV. The news was now showing the British prime minister getting into her grey Range Rover Sport outside Number Ten. The reporter mentioned how the former PM, who'd served in Northern Ireland as a member of the paras, had been employed to lead the Cobra meetings.

Martini zoned in on the story.

Greer stood up and sniggered. 'By the way, Ahmad's waiting on a doctor. You've fucked his hand up.'

'Maybe he'll think twice before pulling a weapon again.' Martini stood up and walked Greer to the door. 'What the hell are you doing working with this guy? Didn't think you were a man who'd be scared into working for someone.'

'I'm not doing this for me, Eamon. I already told you. Helping Schuster keeps my family safe.'

Martini grunted. 'Yes, I know. Well – let's see what happens.'

'Sleep well, kid.' Greer smacked Martini on the upper arm and exited the pool house.

Martini watched him walk away. He could act friendly, but part of him wanted to tear his throat out. What he'd done was unforgivable. Greer, like many, had sold his soul for a taste of the high life. He wasn't completely sold on the idea that he was doing this out of fear. He went back to the sofa and continued to watch the news, knowing Greer was right – he was going to be plastered all over the news again. He grabbed his phone and called the president.

'Eamon, what have you got?' POTUS was quick to answer.

'I'm in the Schuster estate now. I've told them my plans to take out Churchman.'

'They're onboard?'

'They love the idea.'

'Okay, good.'

'Since I've not heard anything from Teresa, I'm guessing she's no further in finding Enda's location?'

'Not yet.'

'I've been watching the news. The PM's holding a meeting to discuss the increase in Jihadist attacks in England. I'm still planning my attack...' he looked at the door, got up, and walked to the bathroom. Having just swept the pool house for bugs, he knew he was okay to talk. 'Mr. President, there's no sign of Enda. I'm running out of ideas, here. I think we have to go with a faked death. We'll need this to hit the news. Can you get Churchman to play along?'

The president sighed. 'I'll talk to him. But Eamon, we can't start a war with the British. They're our closest allies. We can't break that bond.'

'I know.' Martini scratched the back of his head. 'There's something else.'

'What is it?'

'Commander James Falkner, former head of MI6.'

'He's the one who led FRU in Northern Ireland? Colluded with the UDA and UVF?'

'Apparently he's come out of retirement and has just arrived in Berlin, hopeful to get his hands on me.'

'Christ, Eamon, if he's there, he'll be after your head.'

'He's brought his replacement. His number one assassin. Her name's Victoria Greenwood. The PM's ordered a shoot to kill. There's well and truly a target on my back.'

The president was silent for a moment before asking, 'You want out?'

'Sir, they've got your grandson. I'm not coming back without him.'

'You need some backup?'

'Just keep Goodall on standby. If she can use her resources within the CIA to try and locate Enda, that would be great. If she were to get that, then we could move in; but until then, it looks like I'll be working for Schuster.'

34

Paddy Lyttle took shelter from the rain beneath the doorway of a charity shop across from Brain Freeze, which was now a crime scene. The time was six twenty-five in the morning, and Berlin was starting to come alive for another day's trade. The drizzle made him feel like he hadn't left Ireland. The raincoat and umbrella were a welcome habit of people who'd become used to seeing rain. He had checked into the Premier Inn two streets away just before midnight and had tossed and turned for three hours before getting up and reading up on the story of how James Bianco met his end, further developing the bitter taste in his mouth at the points where Martini had been mentioned. The man who'd saved his life had consumed Lyttle's head-space since hearing Martini's name and wouldn't leave until he'd at least tried to settle the score. He hadn't spoken to Greenwood yet, nor Falkner. He wasn't sure whether or not he was going after Martini legally or if he was going to take the law into his own hands. The latter seemed more appealing, however, and he was wise enough to know that would be the method chosen by the British. He knew how dangerous Martini was, and so did the British government, they couldn't afford to keep him alive. If he was going to kill the British prime minister, it was highly likely he would be successful.

Two shops down, a breakfast bar was just beginning to open. Feeling his stomach rumble, he thought some warm food and a cup of tea would work wonders. As he went to move out into the rain, his smartphone buzzed in his pocket. Falkner flashed across the screen.

'You're up early, James.'

'Could say the same about you, Paddy.'

'What can I do for you, Commander?'

'Paddy, it's no longer commander.'

'Whatever. What do you want?' He was snappy, showing signs of stress, his mind doing loops, trying to figure out what he was doing. Impulse had brought him to Berlin, but it would take more than just impulse to see the job through.

'I was wondering if you were coming to Berlin?'

'Not sure yet. If you need me, I'll give it more considera-tion. But I think Victoria Greenwood is more than capable of doing the job. You should give her more credit.'

'I'm fully aware of what she's capable of.' Falkner cleared his throat. 'Enjoy the rest of your day, Paddy.'

'Give my best to the beautiful new face of MI6.' He ended the call and pulled his hood up, making his way towards the café. He ran along the footpath, splashing through puddles as the rain got heavier. His socks were soaked. He stepped inside the shop, unzipping his raincoat. He folded down his umbrella, shaking off the drops of rain, and left it against the wall at the door.

'Morning,' he said in German, 'Is the food being served yet?'

'Morning.' A lady in her mid-twenties said. She was a few inches shorter than Lyttle's six foot, and had an athletic figure. Her white t-shirt had "Grobes Fruhstuck", German for Big Breakfast, across the chest, matching the sign above the shop front. 'I've just put the machines on. Hot food will be ready in around thirty minutes. I can make you a drink while you wait? Will that be okay?'

A voice came from the door in German. 'That's fine, we can wait.'

Lyttle looked around, Martini was standing at the entrance, removing his overcoat.

Lyttle turned back to the lady, trying to compose himself. 'Perfect. Two coffees please.'

The lady brushed a loose strand of hair out of her bright blue eyes and smiled. 'Take a seat and I'll bring your drinks over.'

Martini made his way across the tabled area, taking a seat in the corner of the room, watching Lyttle in the reflection of the window as he followed him towards the table. Martini removed his suit jacket and hung it over his chair. He sat down and unbuttoned his shirt cuffs, then rolled up his sleeves.

Lyttle was slightly more uptight, not taking his eyes off Martini as he pulled the opposite seat out and sat down. His eyes glazed over as he looked across the table at Martini. He smirked and shook his head. 'You always were a cocky little bastard, Eamon, weren't you?'

'Wouldn't say that.' He shook his head. 'I'm just sure of myself.' He looked over Lyttle's shoulder at the lady bringing them their drinks. 'It's been a long time.'

'Here you go.' She set the cups down. She went to hand Martini one of the menus, but he refused. 'Two omelettes, please. With mushrooms.' He looked at Lyttle who was glaring at him across the table. 'Right?'

Lyttle nodded.

'Okay. I will bring them over as soon as they're ready. Should be in about twenty to thirty minutes.'

She left them both sitting there in silence. Neither of them appeared overly happy to be seated opposite the other.

'What are you doing here, Paddy?' Martini lifted his drink and blew into it before taking a sip, not taking his eyes of Lyttle.

Lyttle shifted uncomfortably and asked, 'Why'd you kill Seamus and Mary?'

'I didn't.'

'It's got something to do with you being here. So if not you, who then?'

'I'll deal with the killers when the time's right.' He set his cup back down. 'Mary and Seamus didn't deserve to die. I put them in a bad position, coming to them with what I had. The fault is on me. So, it'll be me that evens the score for them.' Martini still wasn't sure if Seamus and Mary O'Toole had been involved in kidnapping the child, not that he wanted Lyttle to know that.

Lyttle smirked, taking a drink from his coffee. 'You always did have your own justification for your actions. That's why you've aged well.' He took another drink then set the cup down. 'You probably sleep well at night, too, I'm sure.'

'Like a baby. My conscience is clear.'

Lyttle didn't respond.

'I know you loved Bianco,' Martini continued, 'he saved your life. But he was responsible for many more deaths than he saved.'

Lyttle remained silent. He took another drink. 'Nice coffee.'

'Why have you come, Paddy? You're not going to stop me from doing what I have to do.'

'Killing the British prime minister isn't going to make the world a better place,' Lyttle said.

A young couple, dressed like backpackers – wearing black hiking boots, rain proof trousers and jackets – ran inside, complaining loudly about the weather. Both spoke with English accents.

Shaking the rain out of his curly hair, the male unzipped his jacket, and pulled a Glock 17 from its side holster. He pointed it at Martini.

The female told the male that Martini was hers. Then turned to her target, 'Eamon Martini.' She produced her own Glock. 'A lot of people would like to get their hands on you.' She spoke with humour in her voice. 'Nice and slow.' She indicated for him to get up.

Martini looked across at Lyttle. 'Looks like you brought back-up, Paddy. Well done.'

Lyttle took another drink of his coffee, a smug grin stretching across his face. He stood up. 'Don't worry about the omelettes, we've got to go,' he called across to the girl who was now looking at them in sheer terror, not sure what was happening.

Martini rolled his sleeves back down and buttoned his cuffs. 'Actually, sweetheart,' he said, 'if they're ready now, I'll take mine to go.'

Lyttle looked around at Martini, shaking his head in confusion. Before he had a chance to speak, a shot came from outside, the male backpacker took a shot in the back. He fell face-first into the ground, his pistol sliding across the floor. A second shot hit the female in the chest, she went down next to her accomplice. Lyttle reached inside his jacket, Martini grabbed his wrist before he had a chance to produce whatever was concealed. They struggled. Martini over-powered him, charging him into the wall, then wrestled him to the ground. A gunshot went off beneath Martini and Lyttle stopped resisting; blood began to pool from his torso. Martini stood back.

'Fuck.' He rolled Lyttle around to face him, he was unconscious. He took a Dessert Eagle from Lyttle's hand and opened his jacket. He'd shot himself.

Greer ran in from the street. 'Let's go, Eamon, we can't be here when the police come. Move your ass, you can't help him.'

'Fuck!' Martini repeated. He pointed the pistol at the male backpacker, then took a good look at them. He clenched his jaw and pointed the gun at the female. He lowered his aim and shot into the ground in anger. He stepped over them and ran out the door, following Greer across the road towards a set of Ducati Multistrada bikes. They straddled one each, started the engines and flew off up the street, onto the main road that would take them out of the city. Three miles past the "Welcome to Berlin" sign, and they were out in the countryside.

Greer led them into the derelict grounds of an abandoned warehouse. They parked the bikes behind the main building, out of view from the road. Martini grabbed a green petrol can and doused the bikes as Greer ran over to the black Audi A5 that was parked fifty feet away, still out of sight. Martini grabbed a lighter and lit the bikes, then jumped into the front passenger seat, grateful that the car had tinted windows. Greer guided the vehicle slowly out of the grounds, swerving left and right to avoid the potholes. Turning right, he put his foot down and made use of the Audi's 3 litre Quattro beneath the bonnet.

Arriving at the Schuster estate, the gates parted before

the vehicle even stopped. Schuster, like a statue, stood at the front door.

Martini got out.

'I guess his plans were as you expected?' Schuster asked.

Martini and Greer made their way up the steps.

Martini entered the house, nodding his head solemnly. Noticing blood on his shirt cuff, he addressed Schuster, 'I'm going for a shower.' That was all he said before he made his way through the entrance, into the kitchen, and out into the back garden towards the pool house. The sun was just coming up for the day. The rain had stopped, the clouds had drifted on, leaving a chill in the air.

He stepped into the pool house and tore his shirt open, the buttons flying everywhere. He took off his watch, noticing a speck of blood on the metallic bracelet. He tossed it on the kitchen top, pulled the fridge open, and grabbed a bottle of water, finishing it in two gulps.

He kicked off his shoes and pulled his trousers off, stepping into the bathroom. He put the shower on, then turned and looked at himself in the mirror. Studying himself, his heart rate finally began to slow. Noticing the scar of what was a bullet hole on his left shoulder, he cast his mind back to when it happened. He was in New York once again, facing a man with a death wish and a desire to take out the Queen of New York. The closest Martini had come to being killed was when he'd been saved by the one person he loved most in the world. His mother.

He closed his eyes, seeing her face. 'Wish you were still around,' he spoke in Italian.

He stepped into the shower and closed his eyes. The shower not only washed away Lyttle's blood, but also thoughts of the morning's events.

35

Greenwood had just completed seven miles in under one hour on the treadmill. The hotel's gym was quiet, and the exercise allowed her to clear her head – her preferred way to unravel her tangled thoughts.

She was on her way back up to her room when Falkner sent her a text.

I'm in the restaurant, come and join me when you're finished assaulting your body.

She smirked as she dried sweat from her head and face, then quickly replied to his text, saying she'd be down in thirty minutes. She dropped her phone into her bag and pulled the room's key card out of her purse. She stepped into the room and sat on the edge of the bed. Her phone rang.

'I've just sent you a text.'

'Check the local news, Victoria.'

She did. A camera crew was outside a café across from Brain Freeze.

'It looks as if Lyttle *did* come to Berlin.'

She didn't reply, just continued to watch the news. 'I'll see you soon.' She ended the call and went for a shower.

36

Martini's alarm woke him at ten-thirty. He'd crashed on the bed in the pool house for two hours and woke feeling groggy. He deactivated the alarm and sat up. Looking across the room, he noticed that his shirt lay discarded on the floor, spots of Lyttle's blood on the cuffs, serving as a reminder of the life he'd tried to walk away from. The problem solver for the most powerful man in the world, only taking jobs because he was that good. Eamon Martini came with a guarantee. There would be no innocent casualties, but as he studied the blood, his heart sank. Just another needless casualty. Lyttle wasn't innocent. He was a grown man with his common sense intact. He knew what he was doing. Still, Martini didn't feel good about leaving him lying on the floor of the café.

'Why did you have to get involved, Paddy? For fuck sake.'

He swung his legs off the bed and lifted his phone. He stood up and trudged across the room to the kitchen area, grabbing a bottle of water out of the fridge. As he took a drink, his eyes caught a piece of art on the adjacent wall. It cast him back to his childhood once again.

His mother, Maria Martini – the Queen of New York and last acting boss of the Martini family – always had a keen love for artwork. Renaissance period art had been her favourite, with a particular love of any work that came from the Italian mainland. Her father was Sicilian. Her mother was from the Bologna region, a part of Italy where many famous pieces of art came from. It appeared Schuster shared the same taste.

'A fine piece, isn't it?' Schuster spoke from the door.

He looked around and nodded, setting the bottle down on the kitchen top.

'Events have been playing on the news non-stop since you got back this morning.'

Martini sat down on one of the stools at the breakfast bar. 'What are they saying?'

Schuster walked further into the room with an arrogant grin on his face. 'Not much. The lady who works in the café has developed amnesia. Just a couple of dead bodies and a traumatised girl. CCTV in the area just happened to go down for a couple of hours at the time. I told you, Mr. Martini, money is a very useful commodity.'

Martini looked at him. 'What do you mean a couple?'

Schuster turned his back on Martini and made his way back out of the pool house. 'I can't keep cleaning up after you, Mr. Martini. You need to get this job done. And fast. The president's grandson won't last much longer in his current location.'

Martini watched him exit the building then lifted the remote control off the coffee table. The news report was talking about increased crime. Businesses were beginning to take a hit. Martini knew security was about to be stepped up in the area and that Falkner would be gunning for him now.

Paddy Lyttle hadn't just come to Berlin out of the blue,

and there was only one person who would have requested his support in stopping Martini. Falkner. Lyttle and Falkner both shared a loathing for him.

He went to the wardrobe. Sliding the door open, he looked at the collection of suits. Tailored suits of all sizes. Schuster had no idea of Martini's fit, but he apparently didn't need to. It appeared that billionaires just brought the store home.

He dressed in a three-piece grey suit, and black shoes. He gathered the clothes he was wearing in the café, stuffing them into a bag, and burned them at the bottom of the garden in an old metal bin.

He made his way up the garden towards the house. Greer, Schuster, and Jaleel were all sitting at the garden table.

He fiddled with his shirt cuffs, pulling them out from beneath the jacket sleeves.

'Any coffee left in that pot?'

Schuster lifted the lid and looked at Jaleel, speaking in Arabic. Jaleel lifted the pot and made his way towards the kitchen, offering no more than a civil nod to Martini.

Martini took a seat.

Schuster looked at Martini. 'My people within the local police say they're looking for you and will have eyes on every airport and ferry terminal in the country.' He cleared his throat and took a drink of his coffee. 'I think it's important that you leave the country through a back door.'

'Eamon, have you decided on where you're going to carry out the hit?' Greer asked.

'I'll have Churchman's head for you in the next few days. I echo what I've already said – it'll be worth more to anyone impacted by the war in Afghanistan.' He took off his suit jacket and hung it over the back on his chair. 'He deserves it, so please, just be patient. I will deliver.' He unbuttoned his shirt cuffs and rolled his sleeves up, smiling falsely at Jaleel as he returned with another pot of coffee. He stood up and offered him his hand. 'Shall we put last night behind us?'

Jaleel set the tray down and accepted. 'Water under the bridge, as you say in English.'

Martini sat back down and filled his cup. He addressed Jaleel directly. 'Former Prime Minister Churchman is the reason your part of the world became the unstable hotbed for terrorism that it is today. I believe your people will relish the news of his execution, much more than the current PM.' He smirked as he took a drink of his coffee. 'We might even make a hero out of you.'

'Where and when?' Schuster repeated Greer's question.

'I've had an idea that's just come to light. The cabinet has begun holding meetings in more private locations. I've got someone on the inside who'll give me the location when it becomes known.'

'Who is this person?' Jaleel asked. 'Can they be trusted?'

'I'd trust them with my life.' He took another drink. 'Lovely coffee.' He raised his cup in salute and continued. 'All I need from you is time for me to get there and perform a little reconnaissance before the meet.'

'Do you need any help?' Schuster asked.

'I have a way into the UK undetected. Once I'm in England, I'll need to purchase some supplies. I need more cash.'

'We've already given you ten million to hire your help,' Schuster said.

'That money's going to the kids and grandkids of Seamus and Mary O'Toole.' He smiled at Schuster. 'You've just lost ten million for acting on impulse and trying to be helpful.'

'Don't fuck me around, Mr. Martini.'

'Half a million will be enough to make sure I get the job done.'

'Can we help you with weapons?' Jaleel asked.

'With all due respect, Ahmad, I didn't reach my ripe old age of thirty-nine by putting other people in control of the tools I need to carry out my job. All I need from you is the financing to purchase what I need. I'll do the rest.'

Greer nodded his head.

Schuster studied Martini. 'Very well.'

'I'll need a car. I have contacts in Italy. They can get me to England.' He took another drink of his coffee, then looked at Jaleel. 'As I said before, this is some great coffee.'

Jaleel shook his head. 'I wish I was so easily satisfied.'

Martini finished his coffee and filled the cup again, glancing at Jaleel as he poured. 'Will Churchman be enough to settle the score?' Jaleel didn't reply. 'This is the best offer you're going to get. You have the grandson of the US president. If I kill Churchman and if this gets out, it could start a war between the two western superpowers.' He paused. 'But if you kill the boy, there'll be no stopping him. He'll go to war with anyone involved in this.'

Jaleel froze for a moment, perhaps realising the gravity of the situation. He finally nodded his head.

'Are you sure? Because I don't want to come back looking for you.'

Jaleel narrowed his eyes at Martini, his mouth tightening. 'You're confident in yourself, Mr. Martini.'

'I can't afford not to be.'

'I assure you that once this job is done, I will go on with the rest of my life.'

'When are you leaving for Italy?' Schuster asked.

'When can you have a car ready?'

'What would you like?' Schuster said. 'Would any of the cars on the driveway suffice?'

Greer sniggered. 'He's a flashy bastard, this one. He'll want the Ferrari.'

Martini took another drink of his coffee. 'Well, if I'm going to Italy, I may as well travel in an Italian.' He finished the coffee and stood up. 'I'll take the Lamborghini.'

Schuster stood up with him. 'What's mine is yours.' He offered Martini his hand across the table. Martini accepted. He wanted to drag the German across the table and snap his neck, but the thought of the kid helped him keep his composure. 'You're sure you don't need any extra help?'

'More bodies will only slow me down. But on the day of the hit, I may call upon you for a quick exit out of the country. Like Germany today, after the job, all gates out of the country will be locked down tight. I'll have to disappear for a while, and I'd prefer to lie low in a warmer climate.'

'I'll have a chopper on standby, ready to airlift you to whatever location you prefer.'

'Once I've returned for the kid, we can say farewell.'

'The offer to join my payroll is still on the table.'

Martini clenched his jaw, thinking of how his old friend President Sheeran must be feeling right now, and took a steady breath. 'Let's get this job done first, then we'll talk more.'

'Of course.'

Martini unrolled his shirt sleeves and buttoned the cuffs. Putting his jacket on, he lifted his phone and dropped it into his jacket pocket. 'Well, I'll be in touch.'

Jaleel stood up and offered his hand to Martini. 'Good luck, Mr. Martini.'

Martini accepted and patted Jaleel on the upper arm. 'Call me Eamon.'

'I'll walk you out, Eamon,' Greer said.

Greer was deep in thought as they rounded the house.

'What's on your mind?' Martini stopped and eyed him suspiciously.

'Good luck, Eamon.' Greer gripped Martini on the bicep, a tiny spec of intimacy evident.

'You, too, old friend.' Martini clenched his fists behind his back and wished he could put a bullet in the bastard's head.

'Less of the old,' Greer joked. 'You may be twenty years my junior, but I can still kick your ass.'

Martini shook his head. 'You never could.' He smirked. 'Not even twenty years ago.' He lifted the driver's door of the Lambo and noticed the key left carelessly on the seat. 'You know you've got money to burn when you leave your Aventador unlocked with the key in it.'

He dropped himself into the seat and pressed the start button. The car roared to life. Pulling the door down, he lowered the window. 'I'll be in touch.'

'Let me know when you get to England.'

He put the car in drive and led it down the driveway towards the gate, updating the navigation system as the gate opened. The watchful eyes of the security guard followed him until he passed the gates.

37

Greenwood entered the restaurant on the hotel's ground floor, finding Falkner on his phone, looking bored. He looked up as she approached. 'Good gym session?' he asked through a sigh.

She didn't answer. She removed her jacket and hung it over the back of the seat, before pulling it out and sitting down. Pouring herself a glass of orange juice, she nodded towards his empty plate, 'You've already eaten, I see.'

'Martini's starting to get on my nerves.' He rubbed his temples.

'I'll stop him.' She sipped the juice just as the waitress came over. 'Can I have a full English breakfast?'

'Yes, of course,' the lady said in accented English. 'Anything else?'

'Just a pot of coffee, please.' She looked across the table at Falkner. 'You want anything else?'

He shook his head, looking at his phone again.

'That's it, thank you.'

'It will be ten minutes.' The lady lifted Falkner's plate and went back to the kitchen.

'What's got your attention?' she asked, taking another drink.

He handed her the phone.

An email from the PM saying that she was meeting with former Prime Minister Churchman, and the UK Secretary of State for Defence. The heads of MI6 and the CIA were due to attend. But CIA Director Teresa Goodall had cancelled her plans to come to the UK for personal reasons, sending instead the Director of the Secret Service – Frank Dott. The meeting would focus on security and the role of MI6 and the CIA in a joint effort to combat terrorism and other matters relating to national security. The meeting was due to take place at the end of the week.

Greenwood handed his phone back. 'Looks like our German holiday is being cut short,' she said. 'I'll need to be at that meeting.'

Falkner smirked. 'Rather you than me.'

'Why did you come along then...' Before she could finish, she remembered that it had nothing to do with saving anyone's life. It was about him, having one final shot at Martini. 'God knows where he is now. He won't get out of Germany. Becker has assured me that he will not leave.'

'But you know what Martini's like, he's got a job to do. He's a perfectionist. He won't hide away. He'll pop up somewhere. And when he does, we're going to castrate the bastard.' He smirked at her. 'Or at least you will. If you just keep that cool head of yours. It wasn't only your cut-throat determination that convinced me that you should step in as my replacement. You're smart. Hopefully clever enough to get him – with a cool head, not an angry, all-guns-blazing mentality. Listen to what I'm telling you, Victoria, and you might just be the person to finish him. I know in our old roles, you've put many people to sleep.

You were my number one. But Martini's not like the others.'

'He's still contracted to do the hit, so this isn't over. And if he's anything like me, he won't stop until someone stops him.'

'I think that if he's going to hit us, it will be on home soil. Besides, you've got that meeting to attend at the end of the week.'

She sipped from her glass. 'I'll arrange transport back to London.'

38

Schuster and Greer were sitting at the garden table. Jaleel had gone to pray. He'd begun to think Allah had forgotten him, leaving him without his family, but he still prayed. It was a welcome reprieve for both Greer and Schuster, as it gave them time to talk properly without Jaleel's unstable ears listening in. Despite Schuster's love for his cousin, and understanding the pain he was going through, it was becoming more and more difficult to control him.

'So, Ludwig, you've killed off poor Seamus and Mary, and now we've taken out Lyttle and the...'

Schuster put his hand up. 'Paddy Lyttle is alive.'

Greer looked at him, his eyebrows meeting in the middle. 'But the bodies...'

Schuster shook his head. 'The male and female who you shot were the ones disposed of.' He poured himself a cup of tea from the stainless-steel pot, then filled Greer's cup. 'If Mr. Lyttle is as smart as Martini, he could come in handy.' He stirred his tea and blew into the cup before taking a sip. 'Besides, it might be interesting to watch each one try to outsmart the other. We can enjoy it from the side-lines. It'll be fun to see which one of them comes out on top. As long as Mr. Martini does what we've tasked him to do, then the president's grandson will make his way back to the US alive, and in relatively good condition.' He cleared his throat and took another sip of his tea. 'Talking of which, we've had to bring the boy onto dry land earlier than planned. There was a situation on the boat.'

'Christ, what happened?'

'The boy's still alive, but Mr. Hawkins and Mr. Torres are not. Hawkins managed to get a distress call sent out on the radio before he was shot in the back.'

'Fuck, Ludwig,' Greer said, 'And you're just casually bringing this up now?'

'I've learned a long time ago, Mr. Greer, that a calm head can control the stormiest of waters.'

'What is that – sailor's jargon? So, the Yanks will know about the boat.'

'I've started a clean-up operation of everyone that can trace this back to us. Everyone who can link us to this act, is now dead or soon will be.'

Greer looked at him, shaking his head, 'You forget they know money came from your account?'

'The money that went to Seamus and Mary O'Tool was a business transaction. I am a silent partner in their company, assisting their plans to expand and open more shops in Germany.'

'And Tierney?'

'You know I bought a large plot of land in Ireland last year. Planning permission has recently been granted. Building work starts next year. One hundred houses. Tierney's Electrical won the contact to oversee electrical installations.'

'And Frank Dott?'

'Mr. Dott had expressed an interest in running for office. I simply offered a generous donation to assist him in a future campaign. Once President Sheeran has been removed from office for events in London, a man with Dott's credentials, his expertise in security, might be what the American people want when they learn their commander-in-chief has alienated their closest ally.'

'And Eamon?'

'I want Mr. Martini to work for me. His value is obvious. But if he refuses, then I can imagine the British will want to get their hands on him. Perhaps I can assist with that.'

Greer shook his head. 'The head of MI6 has sent scores of their best after him. All of them dead or MIA.'

'Which brings me back to Mr. Lyttle.'

'Paddy will eventually get killed if he goes after him.'

'Well from what I can tell, the English couple who accompanied him here is a painful reminder of how he felt when Martini handed James Bianco over to the IRA hit squad all those years ago. It appears Mr. Lyttle is suffering from the same guilt that he's been struggling with all these years, and with the same man to blame. That can be a very powerful motivator, especially in a man as cunning as Mr. Lyttle.'

'It's as if you're rooting for Lyttle. Like you want Eamon to lose.'

'I want Mr. Martini to be triumphant, of course. At least up until the job's done, but I want to make him sweat.'

Greer shook his head, then smirked. 'Doesn't matter how much you make the man sweat. He's too good.'

'Exactly why I hired him. To be honest, I wish that an innocent boy hadn't been brought into this, but it's the only way for us to get the most powerful man in the world to jump through a few hoops.'

39

Promenadenstrabe 3 – 5, 12207, Berlin, was entered into Google Maps from the hotel, which directed Greenwood and Falkner to Bethel Hospital where Lyttle had been taken. He was conscious. A nurse was just leaving the room as Greenwood and Falkner entered.

'How are you feeling?' Greenwood asked.

'Like I did in '96 when the bastard handed James Bianco over to the Provos.'

'How's the wound?' Falkner asked.

'I'll live.' He looked down at the bandaged area. 'What about the other two?'

'Grace and Chris are both dead.' Greenwood spoke fast and to the point. 'The lady who was working in the café is the only witness.'

'What has she said?'

'She said she didn't see a thing.'

'Bullshit,' Lyttle spat.

'That's her story,' Falkner said through a sigh.

'What the hell were you trying to do?' Greenwood said. 'Meeting him without telling us?'

'You're lucky to be alive,' Falkner added.

'It was Martini who approached me, and someone else fired the shot. We had him apprehended, at gunpoint. He had someone there with him.'

Greenwood looked at Falkner. Falkner shrugged his shoulders. 'Told you he was smart. It's like playing a bloody game of chess.'

Greenwood sat down on the chair next to the bedside cabinet. 'Did they say how long you were to be kept in for?'

He shook his head. 'They said that I've lost a lot of blood, so I'm guessing a day or two.'

'Well, we're going back to London,' she said. 'I have a meeting with the PM and a few others.'

'About him?'

'Among other things. There's a threat on her life by someone very capable, and it needs to be taken very seriously.'

'When do you leave?'

'This evening.' She stood up. 'We just wanted to check that you were okay before leaving.' She stepped closer to him. 'You should have told us you were here. What did you expect was going to happen?'

He cleared his throat. 'Don't worry about me, I'm fine. If he's planning on taking out the prime minister, it's going to be one hell of a job stopping him.' He coughed, then winced. It appeared that anything more than breathing and talking brought unbearable pain. 'But you need to stop him.'

Greenwood stroked his face with the back of her hand. 'That's what I plan to do.'

A middle-aged doctor came in; she excused herself, then asked Greenwood and Falkner to leave while she carried out some tests. They both said goodbye and told him that they'd keep him in the loop.

Becker was waiting by the door as they stepped outside. 'How is he?'

'He's alive,' Falkner replied.

'Anything on Martini?' Greenwood asked.

Becker shook his head. 'Nothing.'

'He's gone already, I'd say,' Falkner said. 'He left the city the moment this happened.'

'So, what does that mean?' Becker asked.

'We go back to London and report back to Number Ten,' Greenwood said. 'Any chance of a lift to the airport?'

40

After an eleven-hour drive south, Martini reached the northern suburb of Milan, Italy. Sesto San Giovanni was part of the world his grandmother on his mother's side originated from. The Martini family had not only been rulers in New York City's underworld for the greater part of the twentieth century, but had more recently moved away from criminality and involved themselves in some legit businesses in one of the world's fashion capitals.

Martini rolled into the city centre in his black Lamborghini Aventador, dressed in one of Saville Row's finest. He felt and looked right at home.

Café Americano was one of the businesses operated and owned by his cousins Pietro and Paolo. The two brothers were nicknamed the Apostles – but they were anything but holy. As he pulled up outside the coffee shop, the car attracted about as much attention as a fighter jet would have.

He got out and made his way in, spotting Paolo behind the counter, serving a young mother and her son. 'Buongiorno,' he said, taking his sunglasses off. Even though it was February, the cloudless sky still played host to the blinding sun. 'Come stai?' He asked his cousin how he was, as he approached the counter, making his way around to the serving side.

'Eamon, ciao.' Paolo smiled, showing his hand. He was an inch or two taller than Martini and about thirty pounds heavier. He had the same angular face and strong jawline as his cousin, and identical jet-black hair. The only difference was that where Martini had his Irish father's piercing blue eyes, Paolo's were a deep brown. He quickly served the lady and turned to him. 'Where have you been? And what have you done now?'

Martini smiled and went to the coffee machine, making himself a latte. 'A long story.' He scanned the shop. 'Where's the other Apostle?'

'He's in the kitchen.' He nodded towards the machine. 'Make me one of those, too, and let's go and sit down.' His tone turned a little more serious.

Martini wasn't there to have a pleasant chat about the old days, and he'd gathered Paolo knew that.

A tall female, around the same height as Martini's six-foot, with flawless olive skin, wide brown eyes, and waist-length jet-black hair approached the counter. She wore a black t-shirt with Café Americano in bold white, written across the chest. 'Ciao, Uncle Eamon, come stai?' She gave Martini a hug, and the usual peck on each cheek. 'I haven't seen you for a long time.'

Martini looked at her, pleasantly stunned. 'Francesca, you've grown into a beautiful young lady.'

She pushed a strand of hair out of her eyes and smiled, a full mouth of brilliant white teeth. 'Grazie.'

'You're working here now?' he asked. 'You're a smart girl, you should be at university getting yourself an education.'

'I work here only part-time. I'm studying medicine.'

He was pleased. 'That's good to hear.' He lifted his and Paolo's latte. 'I've got to go and talk with your pop.' He looked at Paolo across the shop floor, on his phone, his expression serious.

'You want any food?' she asked.

'No, grazie.' He stepped around the counter, and approached his cousin. He took a seat with his back to the rest of the room. Paolo had taken the seat that Martini would have preferred. 'It's a good thing I can trust you, Paolo, otherwise, I wouldn't be so comfortable sitting with my back to the room.' He took a sip of his coffee.

'The best coffee in Italy,' Paolo said. 'How's life? I'm glad you're staying away from trouble.'

'Trouble seems to find me.'

'What do you mean?'

'I need to get into England.'

Paolo crossed his legs and scratched the knife scar on his cheek, a daily reminder of the Martini Bianco family war that raged across New York at the turn of the millennium. The white gold watch and diamond earring, along with the navy Armani suit made him look like a model, a picturesque Hollywood depiction of a member of the Italian mafia. He loved the attention it gave him. He was a player. A lady's man. As was the other Apostle. He took a drink. 'When?'

'Tomorrow.' Martini glanced over his shoulder. 'I need a place to stay tonight, too.'

Paolo nodded. 'You ever hear from the ones in New York?'

He shook his head, dropping his line of sight momentarily, then raised it again, smiling at his cousin. 'It's really good to see you.'

'And you.' Paolo raised his cup. 'Salute.'

Martini raised his. 'Slainte.'

Paolo laughed. 'You half Irish prick.' He slapped Martini across the upper arm. 'I used to love listening to you speak Irish. Fucking smartass. English and Italian weren't enough.'

'You can thank your Aunt Maria for that.'

Paolo's face straightened again. 'A great woman, your mother. The Queen of New York.' His face stretched into a smirk. 'Falling in love with a leader of the IRA.'

He mulled over his coffee. 'Let's not talk politics.'

'Should I ask what's taking you back to England?'

'Probably best if you didn't.' He finished his drink. 'But keep an eye on the news, I'm sure you'll know why in the coming days.'

He looked at Martini more seriously. 'Do you need help?'

He didn't hesitate to answer. 'I work better alone.' He stood up and offered his hand to Paolo. 'But I could do with a shower and a bit of rest.'

Paolo stood up and took Martini's hand, pulling him in for a hug. 'Here.' He tossed Martini a key. 'I'll text you the address. It's not far. I'm helping Francesca for a few hours until it gets a bit quieter. Come back later and we can go somewhere else.' He looked through the window at the car. 'You can try the new drink that people in Milan are loving at the moment.'

'What is it?'

He tapped Martini on the shoulder. 'Flaming Lamborghini.'

Martini laughed. 'I'll see you later.' He stepped back outside, and got back into the car, making his way north of the city.

41

Paddy Lyttle woke up in the hospital bed later that evening. The nurse had just left his dinner on a tray, the plate inches from his face. The smell turned his stomach, bringing him close to a retch. He hadn't eaten, or at least been able to hold down a meal, since before that omelette he was meant to share in the company of Eamon Martini. His stomach was empty, and he needed food inside it. He was a man who loved his grub – food in abundance being the reason his gut hung over the waistline of his trousers. He was slowly being tortured by the smell. It was teasing him.

He sat up slowly, the wound feeling tender. Lifting the remote control from the bedside cabinet, he put the TV on. Skipping through channels – children's cartoons, football, and the poor acting of a German soap – he finally landed on the news. Despite the fact it was in German, he could understand. It was as if he and Martini were not the normal kind of smart. Genius in the traditional sense of the word. Both very gifted. The only difference being: Martini was twenty years younger, and a step or two faster. This gave the younger man the upper hand. But it certainly didn't put a dent in Lyttle's confidence.

As he sat there watching the news, the story he and Martini had brought to the headlines was right there in front of him. The reporter talked about it being linked to a gang war going on the area.

Lyttle laughed, but the sharp pain reminded him not to.

Martini was going to get away and would not be brought in unless someone who worked in the same world as he did went after him.

After indulging in a moment of self-glorification, he concluded that he would be the one to stop him. But he couldn't do anything from a hospital bed. He lifted the lid off the dinner plate, and watched the steam rise off the mashed potatoes and green veg. He lifted a chicken leg and took a bite, an infant-sized piece, mindful that he was still weak.

Eventually, he got the food down. Satisfied to have cleared the plate, he pushed the tray away. Swinging his legs over the edge of the bed, he moved as delicately as possible. Better to take it slow than to open the wound again. Subtlety would keep him moving. Slowly, he pressed his left foot down on the cold floor, followed by his right. His leg trembled, fighting to support his weight, but as long as he wasn't bleeding, he was going to get himself back to London. He was going to get the bastard.

42

After a three-hour nap, a shower, and a change of clothes, Martini returned to Café Americano, and met up with Pietro and Paolo. He wished Francesca the best of luck with her med studies and took the Apostles out for dinner. They visited another of the family's law-abiding establishments.

Eamon Martini's mother had been intelligent enough to realise if the family's wealth and comfortable lifestyle were to last, it would be a good idea to move at least half of its revenue streams away from criminality, getting law enforcement off their back and allowing the Martini money-making machine to continue to grow. During the time of John Gotti, the Dapper Don had taught the young Queen of New York a life-long lesson: those who fly below the radar last in the life, while those who try to be a celebrity would follow Gotti down to Southern Illinois, becoming a guest at the United States Penitentiary Marion.

They arrived at the nightclub and restaurant named Black and White, finding a queue of roughly sixty people waiting to get in. Leaving the car in the staff carpark to the rear, they entered in through the secure back door, avoiding the crowds. The VIP room sat next to the manager's office on the first floor. Martini and Pietro took advantage of the comfortable seating and privacy as the club got increasingly busier. Despite the floods of customers filtering in through the security, the CCTV monitors in the room showed the queue outside not getting shorter, but longer. The street cred and word of mouth was delivering for Black and White. Business was good, and as long as only the cleaner elements of society used the facilities, they'd continue to rake the euros in.

Paolo made it a point to check in on the manager to make sure everything was fine.

Martini sat down on the white sofa and gazed out through the one-way mirror that ran the length of the adjacent wall, looking out into the club's main entertainment area: two bars, one either side of the room, a dancefloor in the middle, and comfortable seating around the dark outer edges of the dancefloor.

He stood up and walked closer to the window. A young couple in their early twenties was growing intimate on the other side of the glass, completely oblivious to the fact that they were being watched.

'There's something nice about being able to watch people and to know they're not watching back.'

Pietro smiled, nodding his head to the beat of the drum and bass. 'We've all been on the other side of those mirrors, Eamon.'

Martini looked around the room. A log fire roared beneath a white marble and granite fireplace, two yellow downlights casting twin streams of glow down either side. 'You've all done very well over here.'

Pietro went to the minibar. 'We've done okay.' He looked back at his cousin. 'Can I offer you a Flaming Lamborghini?'

Martini shook his head. 'I try not to drink. Besides, I've just driven for nearly twelve hours in a flaming Lambo.' He pulled the key out of his pocket. 'Just a soft drink will do.' He walked towards the bar.

'We've heard a lot of stories about you, Eamon.' Pietro reached down into the fridge at his feet and pulled out a bottle of Pepsi. He popped the lid off and lifted a glass, scooping a couple of ice-cubes into it. He emptied the bottle, the fizz bubbling around the ice-cubes as they rose to the surface, then handed it over.

'All good, I hope.' Martini smirked, taking the drink.

'Some – but not all.' Pietro turned to him. He was his older brother's double. Despite the fact that there were two years between the two, people could be forgiven for thinking that the Apostles were twins. 'Salute.' He raised his glass.

'Slainte.'

Paolo walked in. 'You've got a private flight waiting for you. From Linate Airport to the North French border. A second flight will take you to whichever part of England you want.' He approached the bar. Pietro handed him a Flaming Lamborghini. He eyed Martini's glass sceptically. 'What the hell is that?'

'It's a man who doesn't see the need to pour poison into his body.' Martini took a sip, both Pietro and Paolo ogling their cousin as if he had grown three heads.

'You always were strange,' Paolo joked. 'But you were also the glue that held our family together in New York, so for that, you can do whatever the hell you want.'

'I better make a move. The more time I spend here, the more risk there is of me bringing trouble.'

'I know Paolo has already asked,' Pietro said, 'but are you sure you don't need any help?'

He finished his drink and set the glass down. 'I'm fine, but I'll come back and visit you sometime soon.'

'*If* you're still alive,' Paolo said.

'I'll be fine.'

'You never do anything small, Eamon. So, whatever you're doing in England, just be careful.' Paolo finished his drink and set the glass down. 'Don't be afraid to reach out if you need it.'

'I know.'

Pietro looked at Paolo. 'I'll hang around here for a few more hours. You can pick me up on the way back from dropping him off.' He pulled Martini in for a hug, then left the room.

'Pietro's always been a big softy,' Martini said as the door closed. 'Let's go.'

'We'll leave through the fire exit,' Paolo said, making his way across the room towards the corner, opposite to where they'd entered. He isolated and silenced that door's alarm, then pushed it open. They stepped out into the side passageway. 'Never create patterns.' He smirked as he closed the door behind Martini. 'Isn't that what the Queen of New York always drilled into us.' He led the way along the perimeter of the building, staying close to the outer wall and remaining in the shadows, following it around to the car park. 'What do you want me to do with that car of yours?'

'Whatever you want,' Martini said. 'Change the plate and give it to Francesca as a present.'

'I want her to earn her way in the world.' He unlocked a silver Audi Q7, and got behind the wheel.

'Then tell her it's a gift from me.' Martini got into the

front passenger seat. 'But tell her she needs to finish her studies first before she gets the key.' He flashed the key to Paolo, then dropped it down into the cup holder in the central console.

43

An hour later, after a quick detour to Paolo's house, they arrived at Milano Linate Airport, five miles east of the city. A 2006 Hawker 800XPi private jet was there, the engine running. The pilot stood a few feet away from the left wing, his phone glued to his ear.

'Who's this guy?' Martini looked across at Paolo.

'Remember Gino "Goodfella" Luciano?'

Martini nodded, a slight smirk on his face. 'I remember him strutting around Manhattan like he was Robert De Niro.'

The Audi crossed the airfield, swerving potholes and stopped just a few feet away from Luciano.

They both got out.

Luciano was short, hovering around five feet seven inches, and stood with his arms out at an angle, as if he were holding blocks under each arm. His suit was black with white pinstripes. The gold chain that hung over his black shirt made him look like an over-exaggeration of how the media portrayed someone involved in Italian organised crime. Hence the nickname.

'Gino, you remember Eamon?'

'How could I forget, the man who caught James Bianco – that dirty rat bastard.' He spoke with a broad New York accent.

'Good to see you again, Gino.' Martini shook his hand. Luciano's stocky build made his arms and hands overly broad, giving him an abnormally strong grip.

'And you, Eamon, and you.'

'You know where you're going?' Paolo asked.

'Si.' Gino nodded.

'Good. Call me when you land.' Paolo turned and looked at Martini. 'Last chance...'

'As I said, I work better on my own. More people will just slow me down.'

Paolo pulled Martini in for a hug. 'It was good to see you, Eamon.'

'And you, Paolo.'

'Ciao.' Paolo stood back and watched as they climbed into the plane. He shouted after Martini as he climbed the steps. 'Tell my little brothers that I said they better be keeping out of trouble in London.'

Martini smirked and waved back at him. He stepped inside and took one of the passenger seats, buckling himself in.

Luciano entered the cockpit and prepared for take-off.

As the aircraft taxied along the runway, preparing to turn and make its run to build up speed, Martini offered his cousin a thumbs-up through the window.

Before he knew it, they were in the air.

'How long have you had your pilot's licence?'

'Three years now. Love being up in the air.' He cast a glance over his shoulder at Martini. 'So, what have you done that warrants a private escort to England?'

Martini looked at his phone. No calls from anyone. That was good. He slipped it back into his pocket again and leaned his head back against the headrest. 'It's more about what I'm going to do than what I've already done.'

'Care to share?'

Martini smiled, his eyes closed, feeling himself relax for the first time since he'd arrived in Europe. 'Come on, Gino. You know the drill. It's safer for you not to know.'

44

Greenwood sat with her laptop open as their plane cut through the thick clouds that had blocked out the sun for the majority of their time in Berlin. With no internet, she was grateful to have downloaded the documents she was most interested in studying. It appeared she wasn't going to rest until she got Martini. Her work ethic was there. But would she manage to outsmart him?

Falkner sat watching her, like a proud father. A smile stretched across his face. 'You should get some rest.'

'I will when this guy's heart stops beating.' She glanced at the screen, the lens of her glasses reflecting the document she was reading.

'What have you got?'

'Two files. One: the Irish republicans who've settled in the London area. And two: the Italians who set up shop in Leicester City after the city's 2016 Premier League win.' He was looking at her, his bushy grey eyebrows meeting in the middle. He shook his head. 'You were out sick that time, remember? That hip replacement.'

He grunted. 'How could I forget.'

'Leicester's manager was an Italian. So, in the summer of 2016, there was an influx of Italians. Waves of supporters came to celebrate one of their own creating a moment in global sporting history. But it wasn't just the good, honest Italians that came over. An element of La Cosa Nostra and La Camorra visited our lovely country, too. And according to Harper Black – one of MI6's finest – a certain notorious Italian-American family has recently moved from New York to Milan, opening up a cluster of businesses in the north of Italy; with a few members of the immediate family setting up business in London.'

'The Martini family?' Falkner asked.

'And Martini's not going to trust anyone other than his own family when it comes to getting weapons. Whether the items in question are guns, bombs, even his ticket out of the country again – he'll use them.'

'Either that, or he'll seek support from his father's side of the family in Belfast.'

She nodded. 'Or there's that.' She looked back at the screen. 'So, I've got a list of locations where he's likely to visit. The Martini family has some legit businesses in London, and in the midlands area: Leicester, Nottingham and Derby.'

'Also, in Birmingham – if they're as smart as I think they are. Why wouldn't they try and get some of the money from the second biggest city in England?' He turned and looked through the window, thoughtfully. 'I think we should focus on the Italians. I don't think the IRA will have any part in this. It'd be too damaging for the Good Friday Agreement.'

'Don't forget, a lot of republicans didn't buy into the peace accord. Many of them labelled the ceasefire as a sell-out by Sinn Fein and the Provos.'

'Yes, but what side did Damien Cleary Snr. and Jnr. fall on?' He looked at her, she shook her head. 'That's a mystery,' he said, 'They went underground the moment word hit the streets that Damien Cleary Jnr. came to work for us.' He smirked. 'Or should I say *pretended* to work for us, then turned around and spat in our faces.' He shook his head.

'Can't blame him, can you? I mean, you did plot to have him assassinated, which was why Eamon Martini came over from New York in the first place.'

'You're right – I can't blame him. We'd framed him for murder just to bribe him onto our side. And I can't blame Martini either. I would have done the same thing, had it been my father. That doesn't mean I have to like the man though.'

'It was a risk,' she said. 'One that just didn't pay off.'

'I wonder where he is now.' Falkner thought out loud.

'He was working with the Americans the last time I heard. Of course, they'll never admit to it.'

'Anything Irish related was always kept hush-hush. People as high as the US speaker of the house, supportive of the Irish armed struggle. Even supporting the Provos.'

'Just like our government colluding with the loyalists.'

Falkner looked at her, his face reddening. 'You sound like you're on their bloody side.'

She shook her head. 'I'm not on anyone's side.'

He cleared his throat. 'As I said, it's a sensitive topic, and always will be.' He leaned his head back against the head-rest and closed his eyes. 'Perhaps that's why you're the best for the job. You have no emotion. Just pull the trigger and walk away.'

'I've got a job to do, and I take my work seriously.'

The flight attendants were making their way down through the plane with their trolley of beverages.

'Do you want a drink?' Greenwood asked him.

With his eyes still closed, he shook his head. 'I'm going to sleep.'

She got herself a black coffee and got back to reading through the documents.

45

Lamballe Poterie, a private airstrip just north of Rennes, on the northern tip of France, was quiet and deserted. Exactly what they needed. The owner of the strip, a Monsieur Arthur Caron, had closed the strip for public use two years ago around the time the Martini family had moved some of its business into London. The Apostles made Monsieur Caron an over generous offer to purchase the land. He couldn't refuse, and he wouldn't refuse. He was only too happy to accept the price they were offering. It provided them with a place to land and take off on occasion.

A second, identical aircraft was there, waiting to take Martini on the second leg of the journey across the English Channel.

Martini was pleasantly surprised at how well Gino landed the jet. As they taxied along the strip, he disengaged his seatbelt and stood up, putting on his jacket. He approached Gino as they came to a stop and offered him his hand. 'Arrivederci, Gino.'

'In boco a lupo,' Gino said, wishing Martini good luck in Italian.

Martini got out, immediately recognising the second pilot.

At thirty-two, Leonardo Martini was a younger brother of Paolo, who was the same age as Martini. All the Martinis looked the same, except for Leonardo, who had the same blue eyes as his cousin. But it wasn't just the physical appearance that they shared; an intellectual mind was something Leonardo possessed, too. Not the cunning street smarts of his older brothers, but he had the capability to be the brains that would successfully run the family's empire.

'God, it's like looking in the mirror.' Martini joked.

'How are you doing, Eamon?' Leonardo was dressed in a charcoal suit, a white gold watch gleaming under the fluorescent flood-lighting of the land. Like the Apostles, Leonardo was a few inches taller than his cousin, his face angular and his eyes intelligent. His hair was black and cropped around the sides. He shook Martini's hand.

'I'm good.' Martini took his hand and pulled him in for an affectionate hug. 'It's good to see you.'

'And you.'

'Let's get moving.' They got into the second aircraft and sat there, waiting for Gino to take off.

'How was the flight with Gino?' Leonardo looked across as Martini watched his previous taxi take off into the sky.

'You know Gino – fancies himself as a movie star gangster.'

He smiled, nodding his head. 'Si, si.'

'How's business been since you moved to England?'

He shuffled in his seat, breaking eye contact. 'It's becoming a little saturated in London. We're starting to tread on a few toes.'

'What do you mean?'

'We've recently had a few Russians come into a couple of our clubs, trying to flex their muscles.'

'The Russians have been in London for a long time, so of course they're going to get pissed off at someone coming in and taking some business away from them.'

'Fuck them,' Leonardo said in Italian. 'They'll have to get used to it.'

'Those are Antonio's words, not yours.'

Leonardo didn't reply.

'Just be careful,' he said, 'the last thing you want is to start a turf war with them. The Russians are nasty bastards. And you're a long way away from Milan and New York.'

Again, Leonardo didn't respond. He cleared his throat, and finally changed the subject. 'So, what are you planning on your trip?'

Martini sighed and took his suit jacket off. 'I'll tell you the same thing I told Gino: it's better if you don't know.'

'Do you need help?'

'Just help me get my hands on some weapons and a few other things. After that, I'll be on my way.'

'So, you're carrying out a hit?'

'You're no mug, are you?' he said sarcastically.

'Is it the Russians? The Apostles have sent you?' Leonardo pressed him.

'It's safer if you don't know.'

'But...'

'Leonardo!' Martini spoke more forcefully.

'We're family, Eamon. We stick together.'

'I know.' Martini slapped him affectionately on the arm. 'I know. If I need help, you'll be the first person I call.'

Leonardo studied him for a few seconds, then nodded his satisfaction. His mouth stretched into a sly grin. 'Antonio's excited to see you.'

'I'll bet he is.'

Nothing else was said. They both sat there, engrossed in the comfort of their own thoughts.

46

Antonio Martini was two years younger than Leonardo. He was the youngest of Martini's four cousins from the same family – the Apostles, then Leonardo, and finally Antonio. He was undoubtedly the most feared. He was ruthless. Martini's mother often remarked to young Eamon that a nasty streak ran through his cousin. In contrast to his three brothers, who were all businessmen first, perhaps resorting to violence if all else failed, Antonio simply loved violence. His brothers had to pull him out of more sticky situations than they'd have wanted. But like all Italians, blood was thicker than water, and they looked after their own, even those that needed punishing. Everything was done in-house. And Antonio had received numerous punishments from the family for putting them in difficult positions.

Eamon Martini and Antonio had never seen eye to eye. Martini saw him as a loose cannon. His ego was larger than his unjustifiably inflated bank balance. Antonio had almost caused a war between the New York mafia and the Provisional IRA, causing the bosses of the five families to increase their security and live under constant worry that any window they looked out of, or any car they got into would be pierced with bullets. Antonio had been approached by the LVF, the Loyalist Volunteer Force. The Protestant para-military group had offered him a substantially large sum of cash for their business. Antonio, thinking only about the money, had agreed to the deal without consulting the rest of the family, thinking he was making a good business choice.

Upon hearing this, Martini's grandfather, acting as the Chief of Staff for the republican movement, had arranged a sit down with the Queen of New York's father, who had then been the acting boss of the Martini family at the time. The mistake Roberto Martini had made was having Antonio there in the meeting with Cleary Snr. and Jnr. Antonio had challenged him, joked about the republican movement, and had finally made a comment about the ten men that had died on hunger strike. The room had fallen into silence, Roberto Martini dropping his head into his hands. The two Irishmen had simply excused themselves. A young Eamon had heard of this and had ended up in a punch-up with not only Antonio, but Leonardo, too. Antonio and Leonardo both came off worse in the altercation. The Apostles had simply laughed and congratulated Eamon, saying he was exactly right for doing so. New York's five families had been worried that Antonio's big mouth had just started a war with an organisation that was in its third decade of a guerrilla war.

There was a lot of respect between the Martini and Cleary families. And Antonio was lucky to be alive after what he'd said.

What bothered Martini the most was that Antonio was now running the family's arms business. The Apostles and Leonardo believed that they were better off looking after the legit business, and left Antonio to run the other side, with

Leonardo's intelligence and diplomatic head to keep him out of trouble while they were in London.

Martini had just replayed that memory in his head, just as the first bit of English land came into view below. 'How is Antonio?' he asked as they circled, preparing to land.

'He's changed, Eamon.'

'I hope so, for your sake,' he was quick to respond. He cleared his throat. 'As long as I can get what I need, I'll be out of your hair.'

'It might be useful to have you around. He's meeting with the Russians this afternoon.' Leonardo looked at his cousin, smirking. 'And you know how diplomatic he can be.'

'That's what you're there for,' Martini said in Italian. 'He should not be meeting with anyone alone.'

'What about your Irish family, your sister?' Leonardo appeared quick to steer them away from the topic.

'I'll make contact with her when we touch down.' He watched as the plane landed and taxied along the runway. 'Who owns this land?'

'We bought it off an old farmer. The guy had no family to leave it to. Sold it for just over three mil.'

Barrington Farm was situated just outside the village of Wisborough Green, West Sussex. Set on eighty acres, the land comprised a private landing strip and three separate buildings. A rusted hangar sat two hundred yards from the main house.

Leonardo guided the aircraft into the hangar, and shut it off.

They left the hangar and made their way to the garage. A sleek, black Maserati was parked inside.

Leonardo tossed the key to Martini. 'You can drive. I'm tired.'

'You're the boss.' Martini unlocked the car, approaching the driver's door.

'Not the boss yet, but one day.' Leonardo looked across the roof at his cousin, smiling.

'You don't want to be the boss,' Martini said as he dropped into the white leather seat. Starting the engine, he looked left at Leonardo. 'Live a long life, in peace.' He fastened his belt and regarded Leonardo. 'Trust me, we got out of that life once. Don't fucking drag us back into it.'

'And leave Antonio?' Leonardo said sarcastically. 'He wouldn't last a year.'

Martini shook his head. 'He's only the way he is because he thinks he can get away with it. Because of you and the Apostles. He will follow the three of you.'

47

The Borough of Islington, a segment of inner-city London's northeast, stretched from Highgate down to Hackney, hosting a population of a quarter-million over a ten square mile radius. It was notorious for being home to the most powerful crime syndicate in the UK. The Carney family was estimated to be worth around the region of half a billion pounds. A family of Irish Catholics who'd moved from Belfast to London in the early seventies, had quickly turned to crime. The Carneys were less than pleased when the Martini family had muscled in on the Islington area. But for the first time in their family's existence, the Martinis had clung to the Cleary name like an emigrating half-brother coming a thousand miles east. After a sit down with Eamon Martini, who was there to represent both his Italian and Irish family, the Carneys had agreed to allow Leonardo and Antonio to open up some business, as long as it didn't interfere with their own financial interests.

Antonio had quickly moved into the city with a thirst for power, money and sex. He was in his office on the ground floor of Club Mediterranean, the newest casino on Islington's Upper Street. He had just climbed off a twenty-three-year-old stripper and had thrown four twenty-pound notes onto her bare chest. Rebecca Sharp had started working for him to pay her way through university. 'Stay where you are.' He ordered her as he emptied a small pile of cocaine onto her left breast. Using a credit card, he arranged the coke into two thick lines. 'God, I love your tits.' He kissed her breast then rolled up a ten-pound note. One line went up his left nostril, then the second disappeared up his right. He snorted and wiped his nose, walking across the room and admiring himself in the mirror. Despite the fact he was the youngest of the four brothers, he looked the oldest. He was over-weight, with salt and pepper hair, receding into his crown.

A knock sounded at the door.

'What is it?' he shouted.

A youthful guy opened the door just enough to pop his head in. He was around the same age as Rebecca and was also there earning himself some cash to support his studies.

'The Russians are here, Mr. Martini.'

'Send them in.' Antonio made his way back to his desk. 'You can go now.' He looked at Rebecca lustfully as she pulled on a white t-shirt. She stepped into a pair of jeans and smiled at him. 'I'll give you a call later.'

'Hope the meeting goes well with the Russians.'

'Shut the fuck up about the Russians. You know nothing.'

She turned and made a beeline for the door just as it opened, her head dropped in shame.

Antonio fixed his shirt, stuffing it down the front of his trousers, then sat in his desk chair.

Two men walked in. One was around his age, early-thirties and about five foot seven inches tall and thin. The second was a few inches taller, and at least ten years younger. He appeared to be the hired muscle type, that lifeless expression pasted onto his face. His shoulders were as broad as the door.

'Antonio Martini,' the smaller of the two said. He strolled across the room, his black overcoat draped over the crook of his left forearm. He had a small, round head, with a flat nose that looked as if it had been broken on more than one occasion.

'Alek Sobolev.' Antonio stood up and offered his hand across the table. 'It's good to finally meet you.'

Sobolev accepted and sat down. 'Likewise.' His tone didn't match that of Antonio's, offering a civil response and no more.

Antonio sat back down again. 'What can I get you to drink? I'll have them brought in.'

The Russian put his hand up as if attempting to silence Antonio. 'We aren't staying.' He looked back at his accomplice who stood over him like a loyal guard dog. 'This is Bruno.'

Antonio looked up at the man. 'Lovely to meet you, Bruno.' The guy didn't respond. He just fixed his lifeless brown eyes on him. His skin was paper white, and his face bore many scars; one that stood out more than the rest was the inch-thick line that ran from his upper lip to his right nostril. His hair was well-kept and brown. He appeared to have a slight nervous tick, and the more you stared at him, the worse it got. Antonio smiled, his gaze falling back to Sobolev. 'Bruno doesn't talk much.'

'He is useful in other ways,' Sobolev said.

'Mr. Sobolev.' Antonio's tone lowered, matching the Russian's. 'Are you trying to frighten me?'

Sobolev sat forward in his seat. 'Not at all. I'm here to make you an offer.'

Antonio looked at Bruno, then back at Sobolev. 'Go on.'

'We get thirty percent of your profits, and we forget the fact that you've moved into our patch.'

Antonio laughed. 'You're a funny guy.'

Sobolev smiled. You won't think so if I walk out of here without an agreement to our demands.'

'Let me get this straight. You come into my office, refuse a drink, show zero respect, and then start barking orders like you own the fucking place?'

Sobolev smirked. 'We own these streets. You know that, Antonio.'

'The Carneys control these streets. And we've come to an arrangement with Mr. Carney.'

'Thirty percent.'

'Fuck you. You're not getting a penny.' He stood up, sending his seat crashing into the wall. 'Now get out of my office while you still can.'

Sobolev sat back in his chair, looking up at Antonio, a smug grin on his face. 'Are you sure that's the answer you want me to take back to the boss?'

'Fuck you. Bring him down here and I'll tell him myself.'

The Russian stood up. Putting his coat on, he buttoned it closed as his smirk fell, his expression emotionless. 'Enjoy the rest of your day.'

'And you.' Antonio spoke this time in Italian, sitting back down in his chair.

Just as they reached the door, it opened from the outside. Leonardo and Martini entered, both eyeing the Russians.

Sobolev stopped at the door and looked back. 'See you soon.' He looked at Leonardo and Martini, smiling one of those smiles that were usually followed by a knife in the back. He stepped around them. Bruno closed the door.

Martini turned to Antonio who was taking a seat on his throne again. 'Making friends, Antonio?' he asked sarcastically, approaching the desk.

'Not quite, Eamon,' he mumbled, lifting a bottle of whiskey out from the bottom drawer. 'Drink?'

Martini shook his head, walking behind the desk. He noticed some family photos of them all as kids.

'What did they want, Antonio?' Leonardo asked.

Antonio ignored the question and got up. Opening the top drawer of the filing cabinet next to the photos Martini was still reminiscing on, he lifted out two glasses.

'Antonio?' Leonardo shouted.

Antonio set the glasses down on the desk. 'They want a percentage of our profits.' He filled the glasses and handed one to Leonardo. 'Salute.'

Leonardo set the glass down without taking a drink. 'This isn't a time for a celebration. How much have you agreed to give them?'

'He's told them to fuck off,' Martini said. 'Am I right?' He walked around the other side of the desk and sat down on the chair previously occupied by Sobolev.

Antonio ignored Martini and sat down, sipping from his glass.

'Antonio, should we expect trouble?' Leonardo asked.

'They'll not do a damn thing.' He set his glass down hard, glaring across the desk at Martini. 'How's the golden boy of the family?'

'Shut up, Antonio,' Leonardo told him.

'I'm here for some weapons, then I'll be gone.'

'Helping the Provos again?' Antonio joked.

Martini sighed and crossed his legs. 'I'm working alone.

And you should be grateful the Provos let you live all those years ago.' Antonio didn't reply. 'You're welcome, by the way.'

'Fuck you, Mr. Above-It-All,' he spat.

'I'll let you know what I need within the next forty-eight hours,' Martini said dryly. 'I just wanted to come and say hello. It's been a long time.' He stood up and walked around the desk again. 'There are a lot of people out there that would like to do us all a lot of harm. The past is the past. We're still family.' He offered Antonio his hand.

Antonio accepted. 'You got somewhere to stay?'

'I'll get a hotel room.'

'Bullshit. You'll stay with us.' He stood up. 'I'm about to go for food, are you coming?'

'Lead the way.'

48

Martini had dinner that evening in the Pietra Preziosa – the Precious Stone – one of the new Italian restaurants opened by Leonardo and Antonio. It was a classy joint. Despite the fact the building was one of those Victorian-era builds, it had gone through a recent refurbishment. The inside had been completely ripped out and rebuilt, new wiring, joinery, fixtures and fittings, and brand-new furniture. A new paint job cast a creamy glow over the seating area, creating an elegant and relaxing mood. The entrance smelled of fresh emulsion, and the chandeliers sparkled blindingly above. The squeak of freshly polished marble gave the place an air of elegance with every step.

While Antonio and Leonardo went into the kitchen to meet with the staff, Martini sent a quick update to Greer, telling him he was in London and would be collecting the tools for the job within twenty-four hours. Greer was quick to respond, as if he'd been waiting for the communication. His response was short and sweet, simply asking for the updates to continue with every progression, and again, reminding him that there was help if it was needed.

Martini called Page, hopeful that everything was okay. He understood the hell Jaleel was going through. Martini, knew if he were in the same position, he too, would have been driven by the same rage as the Afghan. But threatening Martini's family was suicidal – perhaps the guy was.

Page answered after the second ring. 'Eamon, are you alright?'

'I am. I'm in London – just having dinner with Antonio and Leonardo.' He looked up at the bar which extended out from the corner, built with seven-tone grey brick styling with black marble across the top. His cousins were making their way down through the restaurant, weaving through the cluster of tables. 'Are you and Lizzy okay?'

'Of course we are, Eamon. Why wouldn't we be?'

'Never mind, just wondering. A habit of asking, that's all,' he lied. No point in scaring them. 'Any news about where this meeting is going to be held?'

'Greenwood usually tells me an hour before we're due to leave, giving me enough time to prepare the car. I can't be sure on this, Eamon, but I think it's going to be in one of the stately homes. I heard her talk to Falkner about blocking ticket sales for visitors to Strawberry Hill House at Twickenham.'

'Why there?'

'She joked about how the former PM would be revealing his first book and signing his first copy in the place designed by Horace Walpole, the son of Britain's first Prime Minister, and author of the world's first Gothic novel.'

Martini smirked at Leonardo as he sat down. 'Sounds like the perfect location.'

'If I hear anymore, I'll let you know.'

He ended the call and set his phone down.

'Good news?' Leonardo asked.

'Possibly.' He lifted the menu, not wanting to give away any more than he had to. 'What's the best meal in here?'

'It's all great, but my favourite is the spaghetti.'

Martini set the menu down. 'Order me that, then.' He pulled his phone out of his pocket and went through his contact list. Finding Raymond Geer, he pressed call. The phone rang twice before someone answered. 'Hello, Raymond.'

'Eamon? Where the hell have you been?'

'Long story. I'm in London on a quick visit. Are you still in the area?'

'Haven't left in twenty years. How's life?'

'Good. I'll swing by and say hello if I get a chance. Just wanted to make sure you're still there and still in the same place.'

'Still here.'

'Brilliant. I'll speak to you soon.' He ended the call, Leonardo smirking at him. 'What?' he asked his cousin, confused.

'Your accent always gets broader when you talk to someone from the Irish side of your family.'

'Suppose it's like when you go back to New York. Your accent does the same.'

The waitress came over. She looked like she'd just stepped off the catwalk of Milan's fashion week. Her bright brown eyes were captivating. Her tanned skin made her look more southern Italian than northern. 'You guys ready to order?'

'Si,' Martini replied.

49

Igor Basov Jnr, a forty-eight-year-old Russian, born in Moscow to mother Sofia, and father of the same name, had lost both of his parents to poisoning in 1992, one year after the fall of the Soviet Union. Both parents were agents within the KGB, and it was believed that their untimely deaths were the work of the old Russian government.

Basov found London more appealing than his native Russia, and began running errands for the Ivanov family in the British capital. Channelling his anger that had stemmed from the murder of his parents, Basov soon fought, stabbed, and shot his way to the top of the Ivanov gang, unleashing a brutality the city's underworld hadn't seen since the rise of the Krays.

Worth an estimated fifty million pounds, Basov owns a collection of nightclubs and restaurants, adding to his lengthy property portfolio. He'd developed a mutually beneficial relationship with the Carneys, and until the Martini family had moved in, few angry words had ever been exchanged.

Antonio Martini was only too happy to change that.

Sobolev and Bruno arrived at Basov's car garage, both knowing he'd not be happy with what the Italian American had said. Being a lover of cars and anything with an engine, Sobolev knew the boss would be exactly where they'd found him: under his red Mercedes.

From his position lying beneath the car, Basov recognised Sobolev's well-polished shoes, 'You spoke to him, then?' He had to shout over the sound of a wrench clicking repeatedly. Then came the banging.

Sobolev crouched down on his haunches, watching as the boss banged on the sump. Two more bangs and he quickly reached for the blue plastic container next to him, holding it under the stream of oil that was now gushing out. 'He was as we expected, boss.'

Basov swore under his breath and waited for the oil to completely drain, then pushed the container out. Sliding himself out from under the car, he reached an oily hand up for Sobolev to help him to his feet. 'These fucking Italians, coming over here with their fancy suits and slick hairstyles. They're as bad as those bloody Irish coming over here way back, blowing the city up, never a bloody ounce of consideration for the ordinary decent criminal.' He wiped his hand on his overalls.

'It's funny you should mention the Irish, Mr. Basov.' Sobolev glanced at Bruno, then back to the boss. 'Guess who walked past us as we were leaving?'

Basov eyed them suspiciously and shook his head.

'Eamon Martini.'

The boss's eyes widened. 'Really?' His mouth curled into a grin.

Sobolev nodded. 'Just casually strolled in with Leonardo Martini.'

'Interesting.'

'What do you want us to do?'

'Find out what Eamon Martini's doing here. I want to know if it's business-related or is he here on an IRA job. If he's here representing the IRA, then we leave him alone. If it's business – then it's in our world and we'll need to look into it more.'

50

After dinner, Martini borrowed Antonio's white Range Rover, and made his way to Antonio's place. His cousin would be staying out for the night, so he had full use of the property. The four bedroomed detached was located on Islington Place, a street where the house prices hovered around the two to five million mark – one of London's more affluent areas.

As he passed through the rustic gates that operated electronically, he fully understood why the lifestyle was so attractive. To say Antonio lived a flamboyant lifestyle was an understatement. Everything from his collection of luxury cars in the front driveway, to the expensive paintings that decorated the inside, said he'd spared no expense on kitting out the place that he'd brought an endless stream of women back to.

Walking through the front entrance, he shook his head as he spotted a piano in the corner of the room. He stepped into the kitchen, filled the Moka pot with water and Lavazza, then placed it on the hob. He checked his phone while waiting for the coffee to brew. Nothing. No messages. No missed calls. That was good. He was of the firm belief that the fewer people who knew about him being in England, the better. He planned on being in the country no longer than he had to. He made the coffee and went to sit out in the back garden by the pool.

The garden was shrouded in darkness, but the fibre optics in the pool caused a blue glow to stretch out across the tiles. He sat there for a moment, enjoying the quiet and the heater situated directly behind him. He connected his phone to the house's Wi-Fi and google searched the supposed location for the cabinet meeting.

Strawberry Hill House. The Gothic Revival-styled home had, following its restoration in twenty-twelve, a brilliant white exterior, blinding to look at on a sunny day. He bought himself a visitor's ticket and selected a time for the following morning. He closed his laptop back down again and sat there finishing his coffee.

51

Martini's alarm went off at eight-thirty the next morning. He rolled over and switched it off, then rolled back, looking at the ceiling. It took a moment for him to come around to full consciousness. Sitting up, he lifted his phone and swung his legs off the bed. He got up and sent a text to Leonardo, telling him that he was going out for the day, but would be around in the afternoon. He was hinting that he'd be around if, for any reason, those Russians were to come back for another *meeting*. He had a strong suspicion that they hadn't heard the last of them, and he'd prefer to be in the country if something were to kick off. Blood *was* thicker than water. And if blood were to spill in England, he wouldn't allow it to be his own, or that of his family. Unless, of course, it was him spilling Antonio's blood for bringing trouble to the family, yet again.

He sauntered across the room and opened the balcony door that looked out onto the back garden. The swimming pool was tempting, but the weather wasn't. He had long ago realised that the British weather was the same as the Irish weather: a pool in the garden was more for show than for actual use.

'Don't jump, life's not that bad,' a lady's voice came from behind him.

He jerked around. A tall lady in a red dress stood at the door. She stepped inside, closing the door behind her. Her brown hair was tied up in a bun, complimenting her oval-shaped face. Her full lips were coloured to match the dress. As she approached him, Martini couldn't help but notice where the tip of her stockings ended, and where the room's cool air touched her bare legs .

'Who are you?'

'A friend of Antonio's. Been out all night. Just arrived back. He mentioned you, and said that I should come up and wake you. But it seems you're already awake.' She approached him, about half an inch taller in her heels.

'You're a hooker?'

'Fuck off, cheeky bastard.'

He shrugged.

'I'm a friend. And when Antonio told me that his cousin, who was the only person in the world he wouldn't fuck with, had come to town, I just had to meet this guy. He thinks of himself as this godfather of London, the most feared guy since the Krays. So, when he finally admitted to being afraid of someone, I was understandably curious.'

'Well, look at what happened to the Krays.' He looked into her blue eyes. She was beautiful; and he found her soft English accent endearing. 'What do you do for him?'

She stepped around him and strolled towards the window. 'I manage one of the restaurants just a few streets away. You know the Pietra Preziosa?'

He nodded. 'We ate there last night. It's a nice place. Are you a local?'

'Born and bred in East London. Finished my degree in hospitality management then applied for my first job with Antonio last year. Been with him ever since.'

'So, you're not a hooker or dancer?'

She turned around, leaning against the bow window's four-foot wall that was lined with balustrades. 'You say that again, and you're going to get a good slap.'

He smiled. 'So, you won't join me in the shower?' He tested her.

'Piss off, you dirty bastard.' She stormed in from the balcony, making her way towards the door.

'I was only joking.' He grabbed her hand as she stalked past him. 'I'm sorry, but if you know my cousin as much as I do, then you can't be surprised that I'd think that.'

'Guess not.'

'Okay, what's your name?'

'Michelle.'

'Michelle, I'm Eamon. It's nice to meet you.'

She looked at him for a moment, her expression gradually softening. She shook his hand.

'Are you free this morning, Michelle?'

'Why?'

'How'd you like to spend the morning with me? I'm visiting Strawberry Hill House, and don't fancy wandering around on my own.'

She shrugged. 'Sure.'

'Great. I'll have a shower then I'll be ready. I'll even make you some breakfast.'

She laughed. 'You're not what I expected.'

'What did you expect?'

'A real hard-ass,' she said. 'Well, based on what Antonio has described.'

'Don't listen to everything my cousin tells you. I'll see you in the kitchen in half an hour.'

52

Michelle had no idea as to the real reason why Martini wanted to visit the estate, but a walk around Strawberry Hill House was far from what she'd expected from the infamous Eamon Martini. But her misconceptions were welcomed. She much preferred him over the man that Antonio had described.

'How long are you in England for?' she asked, as he reversed into one of the parking bays.

He shut the engine off, the roar of Antonio's Aston Martin fading into silence. He looked across at her. 'A couple of days, probably. But who knows.' He twiddled the key in his hand, offering her a soft smile, stunned by her beauty. 'So, you and Antonio aren't...'

'God no,' she gasped. 'No offence, but he isn't my type.'

He laughed as he got out. 'He isn't many people's type.' He buttoned his suit jacket closed and donned his coat.

She got out and closed the passenger door. 'You got the tickets?'

He pulled his phone out of his pocket. 'Electronic copies.'

He accessed his emails as they made their way in through a set of fourteen-feet-tall solid oak doors.

'You don't seem the type to be interested in artwork and stately homes,' she said. 'I'm not complaining, though. Most men in my life are knuckle draggers, bloody bruisers who appear to be the missing link between man and ape.'

He smiled, holding the door open for her. 'You need to find yourself a better circle of friends.'

They went to the reception desk. He handed the receptionist his phone. She looked at the tickets and scanned them into the system, logging them both into the building.

'And is there a Mrs. Martini?' Michelle asked.

He shook his head. 'What about you? Why's such a beautiful lady linking arms with a stranger in a stately home, instead of making plans with her significant other?'

She sniggered. 'As you said, I need to find myself a better circle.' She linked arms with him again as they walked along the corridor. 'Maybe you can buy me dinner and take me on a proper date sometime?'

He stopped and looked into her eyes. 'Maybe if...' He paused, looking over her shoulder. Commander Falkner had just stepped out of a room and into the corridor, his face pointed down towards the screen of his phone. Martini spun her around and quickly made for the foyer again, rushing through the turnstile, passed the reception, and through the front door towards the carpark.

'What the hell's going on, Eamon?'

'We need to get out of here,' he said, his voice hard for the first time.

'But we just got here,' she complained.

'Just get in the car.' He unlocked the vehicle, dropped himself in, and started the engine. He took off before she'd even closed the passenger door.

'Eamon, what the hell's going on?' she shouted, as he flew down the entrance, sending stones into the air.

'Just saw a face from my past.' He looked across at her, forcing a smile. 'I'm sorry we've had to cut this date short. How about I make it up to you another time?'

She fastened her seatbelt. 'So, it was a date now, was it?'

He smirked, turning his attention back to the road.

53

Prime Minister Michelle Pears sat in her office of Number Ten, Downing Street, looking at her never-ending list of engagements. The role of Prime Minister was something she, like most in British politics, aspired to. But there was a lot of work to do, and it had led to many sleepless nights. The morning sunlight reflected off the framed family photo that sat next to her coffee cup. Her husband and two young sons with smiles etched across their faces. Happy times. She knew the pressure of the job was felt as much by them, as it was her. She knew that they'd sacrificed a lot to support her. She knew they'd continue to support her. And she wasn't going to make them regret it. She wanted to make them proud.

There was a knock on the door. 'Come in,' she called, looking at her diary.

Brief with Greenwood was noted for nine o'clock.

'Morning, ma'am.' Greenwood stepped into the office and shut the door behind her.

'How was your trip?'

'Cold. Both weather-wise and case-wise.' She sat down

and crossed her legs, pulling her laptop out of her bag. Business as usual.

The PM laughed softly. 'Your enthusiasm is infectious, Victoria.'

'Thanks, ma'am, but we've got a big problem on our hands and we need to keep you safe.'

'I know the role I took on,' she said, 'Is my safety your number one priority, or is adding Eamon Martini to your list taking precedence?'

She opened a document. 'Both, ma'am.'

Pears laughed. 'At least you're honest.'

'I've been reading through this guy's profile. Everything he's done, it can't be true, is it?'

'Afraid so.' Pears got up and strolled towards the window. 'Clever bastard.'

'Looks like it,' she mumbled, reading through the documents, 'Did we ever find Bianco's body?'

Pears stood to attention, her arms straight and resting behind her back. 'James Bianco is out there somewhere. But he was never found. And what's most unnerving about the whole thing is that Bianco was in possession of a tremendous amount of information on the IRA, MI5 and Army Intelligence. He'd worked closely with your former mentor.'

'That's the reason why Falkner is so lit up by the sound of Martini's name.'

'A blemish on what was otherwise an impeccable career.' Pears returned to her desk. She sat down and looked across at her. 'And Lyttle?'

'Paddy Lyttle is lucky to be alive. He came to Berlin, had a run-in with Martini, and ended up the worse of the two.'

Pears grunted. 'Yes, he's reopened that old wound, too.'

Greenwood looked at her laptop. 'According to documents pulled off our database by Agent Black – I've compiled a list of things that jumped out at me – Bianco had saved Lyttle's life in an ambush by loyalist paramilitaries. The UDA was about to execute Lyttle when Bianco intervened. And after Martini handed Bianco over to his father, Damien Cleary Jnr., and his grandfather Damien Cleary Snr., who both sat on the IRA's ruling army council, Bianco was never seen again. Stories bounced around the republican world that Bianco did not meet a good end. And Lyttle was there, completely powerless to do anything about it.'

Pears nodded.

'Lyttle has been living with that ever since, and just like Falkner, is tormented by guilt and regret.'

'Sounds like a good book,' Pears joked. 'But absolutely true.'

Greenwood closed her laptop and set it on the PM's desk.

'Do we have any idea who's behind this?'

She shook her head. 'Nothing yet, ma'am.'

'I don't think he's acting politically.'

She looked at the PM, confused.

'What I mean is, I don't think there's an Irish agenda to it. I very much doubt this is coming from the IRA.'

'Not the Provisional IRA, but what about the New IRA?'

'I don't think it's in his best interests to bring the Good Friday Agreement into jeopardy. It doesn't make sense. Not after all the work that's been done since the ceasefire.'

'Intelligence has nothing on the bastard.'

'What about the Americans?'

'I've spoken to our friends in the CIA. They've got nothing either.'

'Do we know if he's in the country or not?'

Greenwood shook her head.

'Then we carry on as normal. I'm not going to hide away in here.'

'I'll assign one of our best agents, see if they can help shine a light on him. If he's in London, there are only a few people he'd trust enough to contact. We know who they are, so we'll be watching them, see if he turns up.' Greenwood stood up and slid her laptop into her bag. 'Good day, ma'am.'

'Victoria,' the PM leaned back in her chair.

'Ma'am?'

'If the Americans aren't releasing any information on him, that's a good indicator they're protecting him. If they're keeping us in the dark, then we keep them in the dark. Find the bastard and make him disappear. It'll be like we never saw him.'

'Yes, ma'am.'

Greenwood left the PM's office.

Page was standing at the front door. 'How'd the meeting go?' he asked, as she stepped outside.

'She wants Martini dead.'

He walked in front of her and opened the driver's side rear door, taking her laptop as she got in.

'You seem happy about that?'

She took the bag off him. 'I'll get him.'

He closed the door and got behind the wheel. 'You know, all the years I've worked in this job, I've never met someone with as much ambition and enthusiasm for their job as you have.'

'That's very kind of you.' She cleared her throat. 'Mr. Martini is known in the world of British Intelligence as the man who got away.' She fastened her belt. 'But he won't get away from me.'

54

After dropping Michelle back at Antonio's house, Martini made his way back to Club Mediterranean to meet with Leonardo. As he pulled up outside, he spotted a black Rolls Royce parked on the corner of the street, just outside the post office. Despite the fact they were parked on double yellow lines, the driver and front passenger gave the impression that either they shouldn't have been there, or they were there for the wrong reason. They just had that appearance. He recognised something dodgy when he saw it.

Before getting out, he called Leonardo.

'Eamon?'

'Where are you?'

'I'm in the club, in a meeting.' His words didn't give anything away, but the tone of his voice did. 'Where are you?'

'I'm coming in now.' He ended the call and got out of the car. As he closed the door, he glanced over at the Rolls. The driver quickly looked away as their eyes met. Buttoning his suit jacket closed, he approached the vehicle. He could see the driver's lips move, mumbling something to the passenger who got on his phone and made a call.

Spinning his index finger in a circular motion, Martini indicated for the driver to lower the window.

'Is there a problem?' the driver said in accented English.

Martini responded in Russian. 'Only if you make one. Otherwise, we should be fine.'

The driver sat in his seat looking like an undertaker. A black overcoat zipped up to neck. His hands were the size of shovels, gripping the steering wheel. A gold ring sparkled under the sunlight that shone in through the windscreen. He looked across at the passenger who'd abruptly ended the call he'd just made.

'Perhaps you shouldn't park on double yellow lines.' Martini indicated the markings on the kerb.

'Who are you, the fucking traffic police?' the passenger asked.

'Just offering some friendly advice. Unless you want to attract unnecessary attention to yourselves.' He straightened up and walked around the car to the footpath.

'Nice car,' the passenger shouted out the window.

Martini turned and walked over to him. He crouched down, almost putting his head right in through the window. 'It's not mine – belongs to my cousin. You know... the loud-mouthed Italian guy that just loves to annoy people.'

They both laughed.

'So, what's your name then?'

Martini straightened up again without answering the question. His eyes scanned the Rolls. 'I could say the same about this car.' He smiled at them both. 'Have a nice day.'

He made his way into the club. The smell of coffee immediately welcomed him as he stepped inside. A smell he'd never get tired of. He got to the manager's office. The door was closed. A sign on the door said *Do Not Disturb*. Blatantly ignoring the sign, he opened the door and walked in. Sobolev and Bruno had returned.

'Eamon,' Leonardo said. He looked at Sobolev. 'This is our cousin. Eamon Martini.' He looked back at Martini. 'Eamon, this is Mr. Sobolev. And this other guy is his associate – Bruno.'

A third man seated on the opposite side of Leonardo's desk uncrossed his legs and stood up, turning towards Martini. 'And my name is irrelevant.' He offered Martini his hand. 'I'm simply here to talk business.'

Martini shook his hand. 'You want to talk business, but you don't want to give your name?' he asked sarcastically, looking over the guy's shoulder at Leonardo. 'I don't know how you guys do business in Russia, but in the Western World, if we're doing business with someone, we need to know their name. Or do you not want people to know your name because you're in the Russian mafia? Mr. Basov?'

A tense silence descended over the room like a dark cloud.

Basov looked across at Sobolev and cocked his head in the direction of the door. 'Let's go.' He looked at Martini. 'Nice to meet you, Eamon Martini. Perhaps we can talk more someday.' He stepped around him and strolled towards the door.

'Perhaps,' Martini said.

After the three left, Martini approached Leonardo, whose face was red with fury. 'My brother is a *fucking* asshole. He never learns.'

Martini sat in the chair Basov had occupied. 'Don't panic.'

'What do you mean, don't panic?' he complained, dropping back into his chair. 'If Antonio starts a war with the

Russians, then we may as well close up shop and go back to Italy.' He pulled the top drawer open and lifted out a bottle of whiskey and two glasses.

'He's a businessman. You're a businessman. You can come to an arrangement.' He watched Leonardo pour two glasses of whiskey, a slight tremble in his hand. 'And that shite won't help.'

Leonardo offered one of the glasses to him.

He put his hand up and shook his head. 'What did he say?'

'That he's interested in learning more about our business. He knows we've been bringing weapons into the country and that we have a nice collection of all sorts.'

Martini massaged his temples. 'You haven't gone near your weapons dump?'

Leonardo shook his head. He downed the glass of whiskey, took the one Martini had refused, and did the same with it. 'I was planning on taking you this evening.'

'Okay, well, that's out the window now.'

'Why?'

'They'll be watching the place. And they've probably been watching you for a while. Get a message out to everyone who knows where you keep the weapons, tell them not to go anywhere near them. You'll need to get on the phone to the Apostles, keep them informed about what's been going on.' He stood up and headed for the door.

'Where are you going?'

'I'm going to see about getting my weapons elsewhere.' He stepped outside and called Greer.

'Eamon?' Greer said.

'Is the old Provo's arms dump in England still there?'

Greer paused for a moment. Martini listened. Shuffling around could be heard on the other end, then a door closing. 'You know we've never gotten rid of all the weapons. We both know the loyalists didn't give up their arms, so we sure as shit didn't give up ours.'

'Good.'

'Why?'

'I need access to them to get the job done.' Martini left the club. Rain was pelting down. He ran to the car and jumped in, noting the Rolls had gone.

'Our Raymond keeps an eye on the arms, works the land, and pretends he was never involved with the IRA.' Greer laughed.

'I spoke to him on the phone and told him I'd pay him a visit. I'll need him to show me where the weapons are, and I can do the rest.'

'Do you know where and when it's happening yet?'

'I'm almost certain I know the location. It won't be Number Ten. It'll be somewhere else. Not certain of the time. But I've got someone looking into it.'

'Keep me updated.'

Martini ended the call and took off, making his way back to Antonio's house.

55

Greenwood arrived home and offered Page some dinner. He kindly declined and wished her a lovely evening. As she climbed the six steps that led to the front door, she fumbled the key out of her bag. Being startled by the sudden buzzing of her phone, she quickly entered the house and answered as she rushed into the living room. 'Hello?' She put the heating on and kicked off her shoes.

'I want to help. I want to see him go down.'

She stopped what she was doing and stood still. 'Mr. Lyttle?'

'Hope you haven't given up on the idea of getting the bastard yet?'

'Where are you?'

'Just arrived in London.'

'How are you feeling?'

'I'll be better once we find him.'

'Which airport?'

'Heathrow.'

'Okay. Sit there. I'll send my driver to pick you up and bring you to my place.'

'Don't you think I'm too old for you? Surely there are strapping men your own age better suited.'

She smiled. 'I'll see you soon. Stay there.' She hung up and called Page.

'Ma'am?'

'Sorry to be a pain, Karl, but could you nip over to Heathrow and pick up a Mr. Lyttle, and bring him back to my house? I'll text you his number so you can call him when you're there.'

'Of course.'

'Thanks, Karl.'

She ended the call and texted the number. She went into the kitchen and put the kettle on. Putting a ready-made meal in the microwave, she returned to the living room and put the TV on for some background noise. She sat down on the cream leather sofa and looked at her phone as she received a message. A link was sent to her from her sister. It was of a man's profile from the online dating app she was logged into. She laughed and replied.

Like I have time for dating X.

She looked up at the news and noticed a news report of a terrorist attack in France. A lorry had been driven off the road, straight into a crowd of pedestrians.

'Bloody world's going to shit. Can't even walk down the street.'

56

Martini arrived at Raymond Greer's home shortly after three the next afternoon. Greer's Chicken Farm was situated on Rottingdean Road, Balsdean, Brighton. It was no more than a stone's throw from the eye-watering south English coast. A pair of white pebble-dashed pillars stood shoulder to shoulder at the end of the mile-long gravel-covered driveway that gave access to the house.

Unlike the rest of his family, Raymond had never been actively involved in the republican movement; he had never fired a bullet. His low-key existence, however, was perfect in other ways for the Provisional IRA. An off-the-radar location for them to hide their arms. The British didn't know he existed. But even though he'd never joined the armed wing of the republican movement, he was sympathetic to their cause, and just as trustworthy as his older brothers who'd all taken up arms.

Martini guided Antonio's Range Rover along the driveway. Reaching the house, he shut the engine off and got out. A dog's bark came from the back, quickly followed by a man shouting. The barking ceased, replaced by the sound of feet crunching on the gravel, coming from the side of the house, getting louder with every step.

Raymond Greer appeared. Standing at around six foot three inches tall, he was stick-thin. A man now in his late sixties, with chin-length messy grey hair and a matching beard, he repositioned his thick-rimmed glasses and squinted.

'Well, well, well.'

Martini smiled, approaching him.

Raymond laughed. 'Eamon, how are you not dead yet, kid?'

Martini laughed, shaking his hand. 'You know they say God only takes the good. He won't be calling me any time soon.'

'Yes, yes...so you must be unbelievably bad.' Raymond tapped Martini on the upper arm. 'What are you doing here?'

'I need access to the weapons.'

'The war's over, Eamon. Didn't you get the memo?'

'Still quick-witted, I see. You always were a smart-ass.'

'Look who's talking.' Raymond turned, and led the way towards the rear of the house. 'It's good to see you, kid.'

'So, you decided to spend the second half of your life in England. Never thought about going home?'

'I did once, especially now there's peace over there. But I chose to stay and live with the lovely English people. I've had a good life here since I came over.' He stopped as they reached the back garden. The dog started barking again. 'Besides, the Provos needed me to hold onto their weapons over here.'

'You've done very well to keep it a secret.'

'I'm the one nobody knows about. Not the guy all over the news like the Provos young Eamon Martini.'

'I'm no Che Guevara. I didn't do it to inspire a nation or a rebellion. The British government planned to kill my father.'

'Yes, that's right. And that scumbag Bianco had enough dirt on the movement to get a lot of people killed. Had the British gotten their hands on that information, everyone would have been sent away to either a prison or a watery grave. And the way the Brits were playing during the late eighties and early nineties, SAS hit-squads would have been the way everyone got dealt with.'

'It was a war, so dead IRA men had to be accepted as much as dead Brits.'

'I hear your involvement wasn't welcomed by your mother's side.'

'The Italians knew I was always going to be my father's son.'

'But you were also your mother's son. How is the Queen of New York?'

Martini ignored the question and turned his attention to the dog instead. 'What's his name?'

'Finn.'

Martini called the dog over. It charged at him, giving him a sniff.

'Finn, behave,' Raymond said. 'You don't want to mess up Eamon's nice suit.' He had always loved to poke fun at Martini's clothing. 'He probably thinks that you're part of the government, not many suits around these parts.'

He reached down and stroked the dog. It was a golden retriever, its coat glistening from the remainder of the day's sun.

'Come on inside, I'll make a cup of tea.'

'You live here alone?'

'No, Sharon's gone to the library. She usually spends the

day down there reading.' He held the back door open for Martini to go in first. 'Think she does it to get away from me for a while.'

Martini laughed. 'She's from here?'

'Aye.' Raymond shut the door. 'Think she fell in love with the accent. It definitely wasn't the face that won her over.' He strolled across the kitchen and filled the kettle. He pulled out a chair at the table and sat facing Martini. 'So, who's brought you back to this part of the world? Judging by the tan on your face, you've been spending more of your time in warmer climates.'

'A random phone call from your big brother.'

'James?'

Martini nodded.

'Is he still in Germany?'

'You don't talk?'

'Not much. Is he still working with that German billion-aire...what's his name?'

'Ludwig Schuster.' Martini cleared his throat. 'He's the one who's employed me. You know he's half Afghan?'

Raymond's eyebrows met in the middle. 'Strange mix.'

He nodded. 'That's what I thought. It is what it is.'

'What's the job?'

Martini smirked. 'Come on, old man. You know it's dangerous for you to know that kind of information. Keep an eye on the news over the next few days. You'll know it when it comes.'

Raymond got up and went to the cupboard. 'Tea or coffee?'

'Make a pot of tea. It's one thing I don't drink enough of – proper English tea.' Martini rose and walked towards the wall covered in a collection of photographs. Most of them were old family photos from an earlier life in Belfast. 'Kodac?' He shook his head. 'God, these are old photos.'

'Everything's digital now.' Raymond filled the teapot and dropped three teabags in. Carrying it to the table, he pointed at the most recent photo. 'That's the lady who's managed to put up with me all these years.'

Martini looked at the photo. Raymond was stood next to a lady around his age. Both wore raincoats zipped to the neck, laughing, an ice-cream cone in their hands, standing beneath a sign reading *North Pier*. 'Where was that taken?'

'Brighton. Last summer. We had a laugh,' Raymond smiled, looking at it adoringly. 'We always do.'

Martini smiled, feeling a sense of longing for the same. He returned to the table and sat down, placing his phone on the table and shrugging off his jacket. 'You seem happy.'

'I am.' Raymond studied him, tilting his head slightly and narrowing his eyes. 'But you don't.'

'I'm okay.'

'You've got to be happy in this life, Eamon. God, we're not here for long. And after what we were all involved in, you've got to count your blessings that you're still alive. Many others aren't. None of us are promised tomorrow. So, don't waste your life chasing down bad guys and equalling scores, or whatever the hell it is you're into now.'

Martini didn't reply.

'I know what you've been doing. You've become known as the guy who likes to sort out problems. No job too big.' Raymond lifted the lid of the teapot and dipped a spoon in, stirring it. 'And I guess this job you've taken will bring you more money, but won't bring you any sense of peace. Am I right?'

Martini dropped his gaze to the spoon, almost hypnotised by its rotation. 'Suppose you're right. But this job's not about money. I'm helping a friend. Just the same way I'd help you if you needed it.'

Raymond dropped the lid and poured the tea. He put a drop of milk in his, and the same for Martini. 'Still remember how you drink yours.' He handed Martini his cup, then pointed at the photos on the wall again. 'That lady is all I need to make me happy, Eamon. I suggest you find peace, and live the rest of your life creating good memories with someone.'

'God, I came here looking for some weapons, not for a pep talk.' He blew into his cup and took a sip, staring into the old man's grey eyes. 'But I get where you're coming from.' His phone buzzed on the table. A message from Page.

The cabinet meeting is to be held after lunch tomorrow afternoon at Strawberry Hill House. I overheard the PM on the phone.

'Looks like we're on for tomorrow.' Martini took another drink, then set his cup down. 'Take me to the weapons so I can see what there is.'

Raymond finished his tea and got up, leading the way back outside.

From the rear of the house, the land carried on for another two hundred yards. A narrow, poorly kept driveway that was dotted with potholes led down towards two large barns. One was stainless-steel and looked new, while the other was wooden and covered in years of rot. Both were large enough to act as small aircraft hangers. Plenty of room for Raymond to store his plant machinery.

They were accompanied by Finn as they approached the front of the wooden one. Raymond nodded his head towards the tractor parked at the barn's front doors that were slightly ajar.

He climbed in, started the engine, and reversed slowly. Martini watched as a steel chain rose from the ground, hidden beneath dried soil and hay. Cleverly hidden. Not too obvious. Attached to the end of the chain was a large steel cover, measuring about eight feet squared. The tractor dragged the cover along the ground, the metallic rumble sending Finn into a fit of barking until the hole beneath revealed a flight of stairs.

Raymond shut the engine off and disembarked. He led the way down into the bunker, both of them swatting airborne dust particles out of their eyes as they descended. As their vision cleared, they reached the bottom of the steps, and there it was: an arsenal. A collection of rifles, handguns, grenades, surface-to-air missiles, and RPGs. All organised in neat groups.

'Think you can find what you're looking for here?' Raymond asked.

Martini nodded. 'I think this will do it.' He turned and made his way to the exit. 'I'll be back for the stuff later.'

Martini called Leonardo as he ascended the stairs, emerging from the bunker to find that it had begun to rain, bringing with it a cold, wintery breeze.

He got back to the car and was just about to hang up when his cousin answered. 'Leonardo?'

'Eamon, where are you? Is everything okay?'

'Of course, I'm okay,' he said humorously. He got into the car. 'Why wouldn't I be?'

'Never mind.' Leonardo replied loudly over the sound of music in the background. 'Hang on.' The sound of a door closing suppressed the noise.

'Where are you?'

'At the club, why?'

'I'm coming to see you.' He ended the call and started the car. He put the heating on as high as it would go. Raymond waved him off as he made his way down the driveway, back out onto the road. As the vehicle built up speed, his phone rang. It was Goodall. 'Teresa?'

'Eamon, I've just received a call from authorities in Germany. They'd received a distress call from a boat in their waters. The message was from Bradley Hawkins, saying he had an urgent message for me.'

'Christ, so we know where they are?'

'Not exactly.'

'What do you mean, not exactly, Teresa? I'm planning an assassination on a fucking British prime minister. If that can be avoided, things would be a lot better.'

'The boat where the call came from has docked. Hawkins and Torres were found below deck, both dead. Enda's not there.'

Martini sighed, rubbing the two-day old stubble on his face. 'So, Brad died getting the message out to you.'

'Looks that way.'

'Well, this guy's giving me plenty of reasons to put a bullet in him.'

'Watch your back, Eamon.'

57

As he approached the club, Martini spotted both Leonardo and Antonio standing at the front door, talking to the door staff. He pulled up directly outside, all heads turning in his direction. When they realised that it was one of Antonio's cars, they continued with their discussion. Judging by the raised voices and body language of the door staff, it was becoming a debate.

Martini shut the engine off and got out. As he approached the door, Antonio stormed back inside.

Martini looked at Leonardo in confusion. 'What's happened?'

He shook his head, holding the door open. He gestured for Martini to go in first. 'What did you want to see me about?'

'Are you okay, or has Antonio started trouble with the Russians?'

'That depends on the Russians,' Leonardo replied.

'Look, Leonardo – I'm not going to be in the country very long,' Martini said, 'two days at the most, and I'm not sure when I'll be back. So, if there's a problem, I need to know before I leave.'

Leonardo looked at him, his eyes narrowed. 'What are you up to, Eamon?'

'Never mind.' He shook his head. 'I'll bring you up to speed soon, but not right now.'

58

Greenwood was in her office, scanning through her collection of intelligence documents pulled up by Agent Harper Black. Intel on the Cleary family, the Martini family, the republican movement, and the New York Italian mafia.

MI6, MI5, Army Intelligence, and the Police Service of Northern Ireland had all contributed to what was becoming an interesting read. Being the new Director of SIS (stand-in) at such a young age, many would argue that she was just as impressive as Martini. Her previous role meant she had the ability to put him down. And if anyone were to catch him, it should be her. She knew she was smart, and confident that she could catch him, but she had to take her hat off to him. Eamon Martini, the Cleary family in Belfast, and the Martini family in New York, had become known as people the government regretted ever trying to play with, and were given a pass. The British government's decision had simply boiled down to: we'll leave them alone if they leave us alone. Thanks to one person - Eamon Martini. They'd tried to silence him on numerous occasions – and failed, losing many of their top assassins. Up until now, with the threat against the PM, they'd let him go. But Greenwood now had that weight on her shoulders. Could she use her chosen weapon's stopping power to do what others hadn't? She had a feeling there was only a matter of days before she found out.

She'd gathered from her reading that Martini was able to shine a light on certain elements within Her Majesty's armed forces that would incriminate many people in power. According to what she read, during the Troubles the British conservatives were just as dirty and non-law-abiding as the Provisional IRA. The files implied that Martini knew a lot. Enough to put many people away. But why didn't he? She couldn't understand it. If Bianco had so much dirt on his handlers, information that Martini had intercepted when he had prevented his father's assassination, why had Martini never used it? Perhaps his goal was to make people sweat. One file from a person known only as Agent Eight of MI6, dated 24th October 2004, was stamped at the bottom across Martini's profile photograph. The stamp read: *Passed on to Commander Falkner for Execution.*

They wanted him dead.

They needed him dead.

She shook her head. Lifting her cup of tea and sipping from it, she lifted a file titled: *Damien Cleary Jnr. – AKA the Ghost*. The file on Martini's father would be just as interesting a read, she was sure of it.

'You haven't given up then?' Paddy Lyttle asked, standing at her door.

She looked up at him and shook her head. 'Not a chance.' He smiled, walking in. 'Are you feeling more rested?'

'That bed in your guest room was better than the hospital bed in Berlin. I wanted to get up early and make breakfast to thank you for letting me stay, but as soon as my head hit the pillow, it was lights out. I think it's the first time I've ever slept in until after eleven.'

'Well, you've just been shot, Paddy, you must have needed the rest.'

'Do you have any ideas about where he is yet?'

'No.'

'What about his contacts in Belfast?' Lyttle suggested.

'The Provos?'

'He's not acting on their behalf.'

'Are you sure about that?'

'One can never be sure, but why would they upset the peace agreement?'

'Well, if he's planning on carrying out an attack on the British Prime Minister he'll need the weapons. Maybe we should look at who'd be willing to hand over that kind of stuff?'

'Perhaps his Italian family.'

His eyes widened. 'You might be on to something. I heard the Martini family have set up a few businesses in London. Do you know where they're operating from?'

She paused for a moment. 'We don't want to give ourselves away. Maybe we should send someone over there to check the place out.'

Lyttle smirked. 'You want to catch Martini in the act or do you want to save this Prime Minister's life?'

'What do you mean?'

'Is this about saving someone or catching someone who's supposed to be uncatchable?'

She smiled dryly. 'Of course, the Prime Minister comes first.'

'I think it's important to find out who's put him up to it

and why. Whoever's hired him is willing to pay a lot for his services.'

'I don't think he's doing this for the money. There has to be another reason.'

'An ulterior motive? Or do you think he's just bored and toying with us? Let's not kid ourselves. We both know the job to target the PM's house in Switzerland was just a test to see how you guys would respond.'

'Well, it's a pretty big bloody game to play.' Her phone rang, the shrill sound piercing the otherwise tense silence. 'That's the Prime Minister. I'll get Agent Black to pay the Italians a visit. If he's going to attack Number Ten, then he'll need some heavy firepower to do it, and there's a limited number of people he'd trust to go to for that kind of stuff.' She lifted her phone and stood up. 'Please excuse me.'

59

Martini's half-sister on his Irish side was the closest thing to normal he'd ever known. How the government never clocked on to who she was, given the fact her husband was the personal driver to the British Prime Minister and other heads of state, was a mystery. But their father, Damien Cleary Jnr., had always believed that it was better to keep your enemies close. Before his disappearance, Cleary Jnr. had all of his kids set up with false identities. Governments never had any record of Elizabeth Cleary. And it was the safest place to be. Elizabeth lived under a different name, never went back to Belfast, and did not associate with any of her Irish family. She'd been reborn, in a sense, as a new person in England. To most she came into contact with on a daily basis, she was simply the wife of a former British soldier who had become one of the British government's drivers; to a select few, including her husband, she was the sister to one of the most wanted men in Britain, and daughter, granddaughter and niece to men that all had Westminster stamped approvals for execution at one point in time.

But like their father, Martini had always believed she'd be safer in London, away from Belfast.

Martini stood at the corner of Bloomsbury Street at the junction with Malet Street, the Victorian era road in Central London, watching as Elizabeth emerged from the library of the University of London where she was spending most of her time studying for her Ph.D. in Criminal Law and Politics.

She was making her way towards him.

As she passed, he called to her in Irish, 'Hey sis – you nearly finished studying yet?'

She turned around and, after the initial shock, transformed her gasp into a blinding smile. 'I'm a life-long learner, Eamon.' She replied in Irish. Her eyes scanned the area, as well as the crowds of people passing in both directions.

'Coffee?' He gestured to the front door of the coffee shop he stood beside.

Although initially reluctant, she nodded her head and followed him in.

'Grab a seat and I'll get us some coffee,' he said, but she quickly interrupted.

'No, you go and sit down, I'll get them. The fewer people you come into contact with the better.'

He always did respect his older sister, and was never one to argue with her. She may have looked soft – her spotless porcelain skin, bright blue eyes, and unruly brown hair made her look like an Irish doll – but that couldn't be further from the truth. She grew up in harsher conditions than he had, the family house constantly being raided by the RUC and British army, looking for IRA weapons. She'd become emotionally resilient at a young age. And her brother, to her, was simply that – her little brother.

He sat down beneath a picture of an old nineteen seventies Fiat Five Hundred, taken on one of the iconic cobbled side streets in Rome. He admired the picture for a moment, a feeling of nostalgia wash over him. It wasn't the car, but seeing his sister again that brought all the memories back. His eyes fell from the picture and crossed the shop to where she was making her way towards him. He smiled at her and she returned it. Her smile had always been able to make him instantly happy, wrapped in childlike innocence.

'So, Lizzy – how's it going?'

'I'm dead on, Eamon.' Her tone was more serious than one would normally offer a sibling. But given the circumstances, she'd every right to be uptight. 'How are you?' She crossed her legs and folded her arms.

'I'm alive. That's enough for me.' He sat forward, resting his forearms on the table, looking her in the eye. 'Why are you being defensive?'

She shook her head, her face tightening up as if she was shocked by the question. 'Let me see...how about the fact that you're one of the most wanted men in Britain, and that we're both sitting in public, just a few streets away from the heart of the government.'

He lifted his coffee and shifted in his seat, looking over her shoulder at the door, his eyes constantly scanning the area. He sighed, his gaze finally meeting hers again. 'I'm sorry, you're right. It's dangerous for me to come here, and it puts you in danger.'

She looked at him seriously. Then her expression softened, her mouth slowly stretching into a grin, the edges turning upwards. 'You should try not to be so bloody arrogant, *little brother*.' She lifted her cup, and took a drink of her coffee. She set the cup back down again, shaking her head. 'I mean, do you want to get caught by them or something?'

'Of course I don't. And I don't want to bring you any trouble either.'

She switched from English to Irish. 'I can handle myself.'

'That I don't doubt.'

She cleared her throat and took off her brown leather jacket, hanging it over the back of her chair. 'So, where've you been?'

'United States. Then central America. Then south America. Then eastern Europe. Then the middle-east.'

'I knew that tan didn't come from being here or in Belfast.' She smiled, brushing a loose strand of hair out of her eyes. 'Why'd you take on this new job?'

'Just helping a friend.'

She tutted. 'Everybody's best mate.'

'Piss off.' He sniggered.

'Who's the target?'

'Just keep an eye on the news.'

'Then you're away again?' She didn't seem too pleased with the question.

'Why don't you guys come over to America?'

'I can't just pull Eoghan and Lucy out of school, Eamon. Kids need stability. They've got a good life here.'

'What age are they now?'

'Eoghan's ten and Lucy's nine.'

He looked at her, thoughtfully, holding his thoughts for a moment. 'That's nice.'

'Have you paid your other cousins a visit?'

'The Italians?'

She nodded, sipping from her cup. 'They've set up shop in London. I hear they're making quite a name for themselves.'

'Well, if Antonio doesn't wise up, he's going to start a war with the Russians. I went to them for some supplies, but ended up having to go to old Raymond Greer for the Provo's stash.'

'Antonio needs a slap. He's always starting something with the wrong people. Remember when our family and theirs almost went to war just because he wanted to sell guns to the loyalists.' She set her cup down with a loud clatter.

'The New York families would not have gone to war with the Provisional IRA,' he said, 'As *untouchable* as those godfathers thought they were, they weren't stupid.'

'Stay away from them, Eamon.'

He didn't respond.

'Just get the hell away from them, find yourself a nice lady, and go and live your life in peace.' She cleared her throat. 'Isn't that what daddy always wanted for us?'

'I love how Irish adults still refer to their parents as mummy and daddy.'

'What would you call him?'

'Pop.'

'He's your daddy.'

'When I was eight.'

'Piss off. Prick.'

He looked at her and laughed.

'Am I getting through to you?'

He nodded slowly. 'You might be.' His phone started to vibrate. He lifted it out of his pocket. 'It's your husband.' He answered. 'I'm just having coffee with your wife right now.'

Page laughed. 'They're sending an agent over to Club Mediterranean to scope the place out, see if they can find or get any news on you. Agent Harper Black. Also, Paddy Lyttle turned up at her office a few hours ago. I think she's seeking his help to catch you.'

Martini looked across the table at Elizabeth. 'Good luck to them. Thanks for your help, pal.'

'Before you go - I think Churchman's doing a book signing in the gardens of Strawberry Hill House, lots of photos being taken, etc, nice, picturesque scenes for a moment in time, when he gives his documented take on the wars started by him and his US counterpart.'

'Okay, good. So, I've about twenty-four hours to get the job done and be out of here again.' He finished his coffee. 'I should get moving. Let me know if anything changes.' He ended the call.

Elizabeth looked distant. He tapped the table to get her attention.

'Why don't you just cancel the job and give it to someone else.'

He sighed. 'I didn't want to take the job, but the guy who has hired me is a bloody loose cannon. He's just lost his family in a drone strike. And he's using an innocent kid as the ransom. An eight-year-old child will die if I don't do something.'

'Who is this bastard?'

'His name's Ahmad Jaleel, an Afghan. He's pretty much lost everything he has to live for. If I don't do the job, I don't know what they'll do to that kid. But whatever it is, it won't be good.'

'And you're the only one that can do the job?'

He nodded his head. 'The Afghan's cousin is a German businessman. He's funded it. I've met with them. The Afghan's very unstable and will stop at nothing to see that someone pays for what happened. At least now I'll be in control of who does the paying.'

She frowned heavily, worry evident on her face. 'Eamon, do you need any help?'

He shook his head. 'I'm not involving any more people than necessary.'

'You sure?'

He smiled across at her.

She smiled back at him. 'I've got to go and pick the kids up from school.' They both rose and he walked around the table to her. She pulled him in for a hug and whispered in his ear. 'You take care, Eamon. Get the hell out of here.'

He watched her as she left, sitting back down again, thoughtful. She'd gotten to him.

He ordered himself another coffee and took his seat again. Checking his phone, he read a BBC News report about the Director of the United States Secret Service landing in the UK for talks with British SIS. The American president wasn't going to be at the meeting, but the British Prime Minister was in attendance. Ms. Greenwood, the newly appointed Director for British Secret Intelligence Service, would be leading the meeting, with former Prime Minister Churchman being brought in to act as the advisor on counter-terrorism. The reporter went on to say how Churchman was holding a book signing event on the estate the morning before the meeting. The reporter cut to the video feed showing the entrance to Strawberry Hill House. The grounds appeared to be getting some TLC from the maintenance staff. A lot of eyes would be on the estate during the event. The sound of lawnmowers could be heard in the distance. The reporter in the studio asked the reporter at the scene if the cold weather was going to have an impact on the grounds. The reporter responded by saying that there were quite a few people out on the ground, working to set up for the event.

'Looks like I'll be joining the maintenance crew today,

then.' Martini mumbled to himself, looking up from his phone, his eyes scanning the area.

He called Leonardo.

His cousin answered after a couple of rings. 'Eamon?'

'Leonardo, can you get a van I can use?'

'I should be able to.'

'In the next two hours?'

'Sure.'

'Great, get me a van. Throw some tools in there, too. And overalls and steel-toed boots. I'll meet you at Antonio's house in two hours.'

'Eamon, what's going on?'

He shook his head. 'I'll tell you when I know more about what's going on myself.'

'Okay, I'll see you soon.'

Martini ended the call and rang the US President.

'Eamon, I was just about to call you.'

'You've spoken to Churchman?'

'I have. He's now aware of the situation.'

'How does he feel about lending a hand to get Enda back?'

POTUS managed to let out a slightly sarcastic laugh. 'Is he happy to fake his own death? He's not overly enthusiastic, but I've sent him the video you watched in the Rose Garden. He's giving it some consideration. He would first like to meet with you to discuss it more.'

'Well, we're running out of time, Mr. President. This is the only way we get our hands on Enda. The world will need to believe that the former Prime Minister is dead for at least forty-eight hours.'

'Will that be enough time?'

'It has to be. The moment I pull the trigger, I'll be travelling back to Berlin.'

'I'll send you Churchman's contact details. Give him a call, Eamon. Arrange a meet and get him on board.'

'Send the number across. I'll call you when I've met with him.' Martini ended the call. Five seconds later, the text came through with Churchman's number.

Without haste, Martini made the call.

The call rang for ten seconds before being answered.

'Hello?'

'Prime Minister Churchman, this is Eamon Martini – I believe you've been expecting my call?'

'Mr. Martini, yes – this is quite a situation President Sheeran has brought to me.'

'We've run out of both options and time, sir.'

'You know Essex at all, Mr. Martini?'

'Not much, but enough to get around.'

'I'm going to send you a location to meet me. This evening at nine-thirty. A quiet little coffee shop just on the outskirts of Chelmsford.'

'I'll see you at nine-thirty.'

60

Greenwood walked into the prime minister's office. She was sitting in her armchair, sipping from a mug, a printed photograph of her family on the side.

'You have a moment, ma'am?'

'Victoria, please come in.'

Shutting the door behind her, she approached the desk. 'I've no more news on Martini since the last time, but I think we need to figure out if this has the backing from the Irish Republican Movement.'

'Why would they do that, Victoria? It doesn't make sense. So far into the peace process. To be in breach of the Good Friday Agreement would just push Northern Ireland back twenty years and do away with all the progress that has been made.'

She sat down in the armchair facing the PM. 'I know, ma'am, but why else would he be targeting you, or any member of the British government?'

'That's what your office has been tasked to find out.' Prime Minister Pears set her cup down and sat forward, resting her forearms on her knees. 'With the Americans coming here this week, do you think he's going to try something with them here?'

'It would take a lot of balls for him to try something with the Americans here.'

'We both know just how self-assured this guy is.'

'I'm going to talk with Sinn Fein and other members of the republican movement. Let's see if they know anything about what he's doing.'

'I don't think it'll do any good, but it's worth a shot if you've got nothing else to go on.'

'I'll call the deputy first minister.' Greenwood stood up. 'Would you like to be a part of the call?'

'No.'

Greenwood turned and made her way towards the door again. She paused with her hand on the door, wondering if the prime minister knew about the information that Martini supposedly held on the British government. She turned back and cleared her throat. 'Excuse me, ma'am?'

The PM looked up at her. 'Yes, Victoria, what is it?'

Greenwood sat back down again. 'How much do you know about Martini and his involvement with the IRA?'

The PM sat back in her chair. 'Victoria, I believe you're the one whose job it is to collect the intel. You direct MI6, then whatever you have, you bring to me.'

Greenwood sat forward. 'I've discovered that Martini's file was stamped – passed on to Commander Falkner for actioning.'

'Actioning?'

'Yes. Martini was too dangerous to keep alive, so his profile was passed to Commander Falkner for execution.'

'It's not just Martini's skill in combat and defence that's kept him alive, but he also has some enormously powerful friends across the water in America. It is my knowledge that his closest friend in the US is the current commander-in-chief. This is a very delicate situation, Victoria.'

'I've tried to contact my counterparts in the CIA again, but they've refused to comment or pass on any information about him.'

'They're protecting him,' the prime minister concluded. 'I'll give you a few more days. If you can't find out what Martini's up to, then I'll approach the president myself, and demand that he hands the bastard over. He cannot protect him if I show him evidence of his attempt on my life.'

Greenwood stood up. 'Thank you, ma'am.'

61

The Sinn Fein leader and Deputy First Minister for Northern Ireland, Declan Meehan, sat in the office of the devolved government alongside the Democratic Unionist Party leader Craig Johnson – First Minister for Northern Ireland.

At sixty-eight, Meehan had grown up in the thick of the country's civil unrest. Becoming one of the Provisional IRA's unit commanders, he had first been elected as a Sinn Fein representative in the late nineteen seventies, and had been at the forefront of Irish Republicanism ever since, his face plastered all over West Belfast on huge green and white posters, making him recognisable all around the world.

His phone rang suddenly, distracting him from his thoughts. He stopped what he was doing and answered. 'Meehan here.'

'Mr. Meehan, this is Agent Victoria Greenwood, stand-in Director of British Secret Intelligence Services. I wonder if you have a moment to talk?'

'How can I help you?'

'As you may know, Prime Minister Pears is holding a

meeting this week regarding the terrorist threats here in the UK. I wanted to talk to you about an Eamon Martini.'

'What about him?' Meehan was quick to respond, his tone defensive.

'We have reason to believe that Mr. Martini is planning an attack here in London. We've already prevented an attack on the Prime Minister's holiday home in Switzerland, but we think that first attempt may have just been a test to see how we'd react.'

'If Martini wanted to hit someone, then the chances are, you wouldn't know about it until the job was done and it was too late.' He spoke humorously. 'Unless he's let himself slip.'

'How likely do you think that is? For him to make a mistake, I mean.'

'Not likely.' His tone deepened. 'I'm sorry Agent Greenwood, but what does this have to do with me?'

'Is this attack the work of the IRA?'

His grip on the phone tightened, like he wanted to squeeze a stress ball. 'I can't speak for the New IRA or any other dissident group, but I can assure you that the republican movement has not sanctioned an attack on the British government.'

'You do realise that if something like this were to happen, Mr. Meehan, it would destroy the peace process.'

'And no doubt your troops would be back on Irish streets again. And our power-sharing executive would be down the toilet. So it's perhaps in all of our best interests that Martini, whoever he's working for, does not leave the blame lying at the door of the republican movement.'

'Do you have any idea who'd be behind it?'

'The British government has made enemies all around the world. It's got to be someone with a lot of financial backing. Martini doesn't need the money. Even when he was in Belfast, he always took work from his Italian family, and from what I can remember, he charged a hefty fee. But anybody that knows of his reputation wouldn't bat an eyelid at giving him whatever he asks for.'

'What about IRA weapons? Does he have access to any?'

Meehan chuckled. 'Come on now, Agent Greenwood. You know full well that the IRA has decommissioned its weapons.'

'Very well,' she said with a sigh. 'If he contacts you, or if you hear anything, can you please get in touch? This could be catastrophic for all of us. Especially the people of Ireland.'

'I certainly will, Agent Greenwood.'

'Have a lovely day, Mr. Meehan.'

'And you.' He ended the call and immediately went onto his computer. He Google searched Eamon Martini. The first item that came up was the Belfast Telegraph newspaper from 24 September 1993. The story titled *The Young Republican That Outsmarted Even the Highest Ranked Officials in the British Government.* 'Where are you, Eamon? What are you up to, kid?'

62

Martini arrived at Antonio's house before Leonardo. He parked the car in one of the garages and went into the house, hearing Antonio's voice coming from the kitchen.

'He's here now,' Antonio could be heard speaking loudly as Martini crossed the hallway towards the kitchen. 'Sneaky bastard's always popping up out of nowhere.'

Martini smirked and entered the kitchen.

Antonio was sat on one of the stools at the central island, his iPhone pressed against his right ear. 'I'll speak to you later. Ciao.' He ended the call and set the phone down. 'The brothers in Milan send their regards. Paolo told me to tell you that if you need help with whatever you're doing, not to be stupid and to just ask.'

'Looks like you have enough problems to deal with without taking on mine, too.' Martini sat down on a stool facing Antonio.

'Leonardo's just stopped off somewhere. He's on his way with your van and toolkit.' Antonio stood up, stretching. He stifled a yawn. 'Café?'

'Si.' Martini pulled his phone out of his pocket. He'd

received a message from Greer. He didn't bother opening it. It was only going to be a question that he couldn't answer yet. If it were important, he'd call. He set the phone down. 'So, what about these Russians?'

Antonio looked around as he filled the coffee machine with ground Intermezzo. 'They're all talk. Besides, we've made a deal with Mr. Carney.'

'Carney may be a businessman, but he's a nasty bastard, too. And he's a psychopath. Don't make enemies where you don't need to.'

'But he loves you, thanks to your pop and the Provos.'

'Carney was a wannabe IRA man.' Martini shook his head. 'But when it came down to it in the war, we didn't see him out on the Irish streets in the middle of gun battles with the British army and the UDA. Men like him want to use the name of the movement as some sort of street cred.'

Antonio regarded him for a moment. 'You feel strongly about that.'

'Talk to the Russians. Make a deal with them. All of you can earn money.'

'Is there an alternative?'

'You go to war with them. And you don't want to go to war.' He stood up and walked across the kitchen, studying the tropical fish tank built into the wall near the patio doors. 'The Russians are just like you, motivated by money. Work with them, and you can all make a lot of money.'

'Or I can tell them to fuck off and keep the money.'

Martini shook his head. 'You've moved in on their territory. Do you expect them to just bend over and take it up the ass?'

'Screw them. They don't want to fuck with us.'

Martini turned around and looked at him, shaking his head. 'You always were fucking stupid, weren't you?'

Antonio slammed the Moka down, glaring across the room. 'What did you say?'

'What? Have those drugs caused you to go deaf?' He shoved his hands in his pockets and casually made his way across the kitchen. 'You're stupid, Antonio. Thick as Irish stew. You think you can do whatever you want and to hell with everyone else.'

'You better watch that big mouth of yours, Eamon.'

'Please.' Martini laughed. 'You're not going to do a thing.' He sat back down on the stool. 'Remember the war you almost started when we were teenagers? Selling weapons to the so-called loyalist brigadiers of Belfast?' He shook his head. 'If it hadn't been for my mother, your aunt, allowing me to do a job for the Provos, Little Italy and the rest of Manhattan would have been painted with our blood.' Antonio glared at him, his face quickly changing from the Italian olive complexion to a more furious shade of red. 'My father, had he not been the man he was, could have sent two hundred heavily armed men to make an example of you. Don't forget that.'

'Why are you bringing this up?'

Martini laughed in astonishment. 'Because you're still a pain in the ass, after all these years. But you're family. We can't afford to go to war with these Russians.'

Antonio sat down on the opposite side of the island, his face full of fury. He poured two coffees and handed one across to Martini, his hand trembling. He held his cup up, 'Salute.'

'Slainte.' Martini took a drink of his coffee, looking directly into the eyes of his cousin. 'Don't be stupid, Antonio, come on. You're a Martini. We're smart.'

The sound of the front door opening and closing broke the silence. Leonardo entered the kitchen, oblivious to the tension. 'I've got what you need. The van's outside. I have a friend in the electrical business. He's filled the van with everything a spark would use on the job.' He slid the key to an Iveco across the island. 'Congratulations on your new appointment, you're now an electrician.' He planted himself down on the stool next to his brother. Lifting the lid of the Moka pot he said, 'Good, I need one.' He lifted a cup and poured himself a drink. 'Have we heard anything else from the Russians?'

Antonio cleared his throat, still looking across at Martini. 'We'll set up another meeting. See if we can come to an agreement.'

Martini nodded, looking over the rim of his cup at Antonio. He blew into the cup, then took another drink. He set the cup down, grabbed the key, and stood up. 'Right, I've somewhere to be.'

'Eamon.' Antonio called after him.

Martini stopped at the door and glanced back. 'We're here to help. If you need it.'

Martini nodded. 'I know. But for God's sake, Antonio, first set a meet with the Russians again.'

63

Agent Harper Black was the newest recruit welcomed into Greenwood's team. An eager thirty-three-year-old with bundles of potential, Black had come from a family of police officers. Her mother and father were both Senior Investigating Officers holding badges with the rank of Detective Chief Inspector. DCIs Black and Black had encouraged their daughter into the met. She grew up dreaming of becoming just like them, and after a brief stint in Afghanistan, she'd taken on the role. She eventually had the opportunity to come and work for the officers within British Intelligence who operated more in the shadows, did things off the books, and when necessary, as she was quickly beginning to learn, broke the law for the good of national security.

She had known it was important the moment she received an email from Greenwood asking her to come to her office. Few were invited there.

Her house was located at Number 8 Marsham Street, Westminster, with a fifteen hundred pound per month price tag. It was a mere fifteen minutes and one tube stop away from Vauxhall Cross. Reeling with excitement, she rushed home, showered and dressed in her best suit. She wanted to make the best impression, as if she were being interviewed for a promotion. And in a sense, she was.

Rushing back to HQ at Number 85 Albert Embankment, she checked herself over in the lift's mirror on her way up to the third floor. Her grey trouser suit was tidy and professional. Her brown hair was tied up in a bun, accentuating her smooth jaw line, clear skin and blue eyes. She stepped out of the lift and approached the door of Commander Falkner's old office, now occupied by a female half his age. *Agent Greenwood* was engraved into a stainless-steel plate at head height.

Black held her fist up, ready to knock, hoping that one day her name would be on the door. Taking a deep breath, she straightened her posture and knocked on the door.

'Come in.'

She opened the door. Greenwood was at her desk, on her laptop. 'You asked to see me, ma'am?'

Greenwood looked up. 'Harper, yes, come in.' She turned her attention back to her laptop and continued tapping on the keyboard.

Black closed the door and approached the desk.

'Have a seat.'

Black unbuttoned her suit jacket and sat.

'You've been working for us how long now?'

'Three and a half years, ma'am.'

'You've asked for more responsibility, on more than one occasion, is that correct?'

'That's right.' She crossed her legs and tried to hold back a smile.

'Well, today's your lucky day.' Greenwood sat back in her seat, interlinking her fingers. 'The job I've got for you, if we are successful, will be the biggest job either of us will ever come across.'

Black's face lit up.

'I've read your file. You're very ambitious. You're a good student and keen to improve. Your parents have had a good influence on you.'

'Thank you, ma'am. And yes, they have.'

'What do you know about Eamon Martini?'

'Until a few days ago, I'd never heard of him.' She paused mid-sentence, looking down. 'He brought the British government into disrepute, caused that big scandal?'

Greenwood nodded.

'He's half Italian, half Irish. He grew up in New York with his mother who was the last acting boss of the Martini crime family. At seventeen, Martini went to Belfast and got mixed up with the Provisional IRA, after our government planned to assassinate his father. His father and grandfather on the Irish side were leaders in the Irish Republican Movement.'

'Correct. And now there's a plot to assassinate the Prime Minister. Mr. Martini is the person hired to do the job.'

Black's eyes widened. She uncrossed her legs and sat forward in her seat, resting her forearms on her thighs.

'There are only a few people Martini would trust for a job like this. It has come to my attention that the Italian side of his family has started to muscle in on Russian territory in London. If Martini is in town, then I'm pretty sure he will have made contact with the Italians. Or at least tried to. There are only a few people in the area who would be able to get their hands on weapons at such short notice. I want you to pay them a visit. See if he's in the area.'

'What if I find out he has, but everyone seems to have developed amnesia?'

'Then you do what you have to in order to get the infor-mation from them.'

'Any means necessary?'

Greenwood nodded her head. 'You should be careful. Eamon Martini is an incredibly smart individual. He won't leave a trail, so we'll have to make one.' She went back on her laptop. 'I'll email you some documents the Americans and Italians have shared with us on the family members.'

'What about his Irish family?'

'That's trickier. Nobody wants to talk. But I'm flying to Belfast in the next hour to interrupt the Deputy First Minis-ter's dinner. He'll need to cough something up. You worry about his Italian family. I'll focus on the Irish.'

'Yes, ma'am.' Black stood up and buttoned her suit jacket.

'I'll be travelling soon, but you call me on my private number if you have anything. My number's in the email.'

Black stopped at the door and looked back. 'Yes, ma'am. Thank you.'

64

Strawberry Hill House was quiet for the time of the day. A few people were walking in the gardens, a golden retriever was chasing a tennis ball, and workers were preparing the gazebo for Churchman's book signing.

Martini parked the van in a bay allocated to contractors. He'd changed into the overalls before he set off. The hi-vis jacket was an added feature that made him look like a legit contractor, playing the health and safety game to a tee.

The time had just gone four in the afternoon, and the sun wasn't going to be up for much longer. He could hear the distant rumble of lawnmowers racing through the gardens, trimmers buzzing like a swarm of wasps. The eyes of the world would be on the estate for the security meeting between the US and the UK. The controversial book signing of the former PM's book was perhaps an overly dramatic way to carry out the pretend hit, but it would certainly have the desired effect. The book was about Churchman's role in bringing together the Irish peace process, but also about how he'd sent the British troops over to Afghanistan and

Iraq, along with their American allies. If Ahmad Jaleel wanted to cause a global crisis, then what Martini was planning would deliver exactly that.

Martini pulled his woollen hat on and grabbed his toolbox, making his way towards the entrance. Ascending the steps, he entered the foyer and approached the reception. It was a different receptionist from his last visit. Good. His accent was diluted, but still, that of a New Yorker, distinguishable in England. The lady smiled at him as he approached.

He smiled back and said, 'I'm here to carry out some checks on the lighting.'

She pulled a blue clipboard out from beneath the reception. 'Can you just fill in the contractor's signing-in sheet, please?' She handed it across the desk. 'Do you know where you're going? Or do you need me to call the manager?'

'I'm fine, thanks.' He filled in the sheet. He noticed Falkner had signed in and out just after one in the afternoon. He'd only been there for an hour.

He handed the clipboard back to the receptionist. 'Thanks.' He lifted his toolbox and made his way towards the corridor that led further into the building.

He took the lift to the top floor. He knew that if Falkner suspected he was to stage the attack here, he'd be looking for the best vantage point from which to fire the shot. The roof was the most likely place from which to take the shot, but also the most obvious.

And obvious was stupid.

The cold bite of the wind felt like it almost ripped the skin off his face as he gained access to the roof. He was blue before he reached the edge. He looked down on the grounds. The garden was still being set up – rows of bright white chairs were being placed on the neatly trimmed grass. The gazebo had been erected. His phone went off during his scan of the property.

He set the toolbox down, fished it out of his pocket, and quickly answered. 'Hello.'

'Eamon Martini, I thought you were dead.' The voice had a broad Belfast accent – one he hadn't heard in years.

'Mr. Meehan. Or should I say, Deputy First Minister? It's been a long time.'

'It appears that you've started to make the Brits a bit nervous again. What are you up to?'

Martini sniggered. 'Come on, Declan – you know it's best to not waste your breath asking questions that aren't going to be answered.'

'According to British Intelligence, you've planned an attack on the Prime Minister.' His tone lowered. 'I don't give a shit about what you're doing, Eamon. You know I have no love for the bastards...'

'But?'

'But make sure you don't drag the republican movement into it. We've done a lot of work bringing the war to an end . We wouldn't want anything to upset that.'

'Nothing leads back to Belfast.'

There was a momentary silence. 'You should come home for a break, kid. It'd be good to crack open a bottle or two with you.' Meehan's voice lightened. 'I remember when you fingered that piece of shit Bianco. You were just a wet-behind-the-ears kid in comparison to the rest of the leaders of the movement. They hated that such a youngster had become the brains of the organisation.'

The rain started to move in. 'I've got to go, Declan.'

'Take care of yourself, Eamon.'

'You, too.' Martini ended the call. He looked over the edge again. 'This would be the perfect shot, but Falkner knows that.'

65

Harper Black pulled up around the corner from Club Mediterranean, still counting her blessings that she got the opportunity to work directly with Greenwood. She knew that Greenwood was now dealing directly with the Prime Minister, and now she was dealing directly with her. She felt a tingle of excitement make its way up her spine.

Sitting in the car with the engine running, she opened the email Greenwood had sent her. Saving her number to her phone, she scanned through the email again. According to intel from the Italians, the business was being operated by Antonio and Leonardo Martini. The two had set up the businesses and were running a small crew of fellow Italians who'd followed them to England, as well as a handful of locals. In addition to drugs, weapons, and prostitution, they were also making money from extortion and were feeding a healthy six-figure sum per month back to Milan where older brothers Paolo and Pietro were said to be running the family empire, taking the reins from the old country. She looked at the photos of the two local brothers, familiarising herself with them.

Shutting the engine off, she reached into the back seat of the S Class Mercedes for her jacket. She got out and made her way across the street, rounding the corner to the outside of the club. As she approached, her phone buzzed in her pocket. She stopped and opened the message.

Just on my way to the plane now. I'll be in Belfast in the next couple of hours. Keep me updated. And watch your back. Greenwood.

She grinned, feeling the excitement begin to bubble up again, but quickly forced it back down. She pocketed the phone as she pulled the door open, the music and atmosphere spilling out onto the cold street. The overpowering stench of beer and flavoured smoke assaulted her sense of smell as she passed the smoking room. She headed straight to the bar. A couple in their mid-twenties were locked in an intimate embrace, the lady behind the bar looking at them with a less than approving expression; she turned her attention to Black as she approached.

Black offered her a polite, laissez-faire smile. 'Can I have a bottle of Coke, please?'

'Sure.' The lady turned and reached down into the fridge. 'Anything else?'

'Just wondering if anything is happening in here in the next few days? I'm planning a surprise birthday party for my brother-in-law, and I heard this place is quite good.'

'What age is he?'

'He'll be thirty.'

She pulled the lid off the bottle and handed it across the bar. 'Two forty, please.'

Black flashed her card.

The lady lifted the card machine next to the till. 'What kind of party are you thinking of? Dancers? Food supplied? Music?'

Black took a sip of her drink. 'Haven't really thought about it that much. We just want somewhere to get shit-faced.' She laughed.

The lady smiled and handed the card back. 'I can send the manager out to talk to you if you prefer? They usually deal with the business. I don't get a commission for bringing in more revenue, so you're better off speaking to them.' She sounded resentful.

'Sure, that's fine.'

She gestured towards the seating area at the other end of the room. 'Have a seat and I'll see if he's free now.'

'Thanks.' Black sat down, taking a few deep breaths to calm herself. Martini could walk in at any moment and she'd be face to face with, as Greenwood said, the biggest catch they'd ever make.

She spent the next few minutes on her phone, flicking through her Facebook news feed. As she gazed at photos of her mother and father, she realised how proud they'd be if she were to catch someone this big. Her attention was dragged away from the phone as a shadow was cast over her.

'You're interested in a party, is that right?' Antonio Martini stood before her, smiling widely.

She nodded. 'A surprise party for my brother-in-law's thirtieth.'

'Come join me outside. I can't hear myself think in here.'

She stood up.

'Antonio Martini, I own the place. What's your name?'

'Jessica Dickson.' Black offered her hand across to Antonio and followed him towards the outside seating area.

The door closed behind them and the music faded. The distant hum of car engines going up and down the street made it easier for them to talk.

'So, Jessica, are you interested in renting out a room for this party?'

'Depends on the cost. What else do you offer?'

'We can supply you with girls for entertainment, any ethnicity, we have...' He trailed off, his eyes narrowing, looking directly over her shoulder.

Black turned. A lady was approaching them, not looking the slightest bit concerned that she was interrupting a private conversation.

'Have you seen Eamon?' The lady was quick to ask. Her accent was Irish, diluted, but Black could still tell she was from Belfast.

'Can't you see that I'm in the middle of something here?' He gazed apologetically at Black. 'Sorry about this.'

She shook her head. 'No problem.'

'Can I have a word? In private?' The lady asked.

Black knew that she'd just gotten lucky and that this was going to lead somewhere.

Antonio stood up. 'Excuse me a moment.'

Black stood, too. 'It's fine, I have to go now anyway. Do you have a number I can contact you on?'

'Just the business number.' Antonio sounded rushed.

'I'll come back another time.' Black finished her Coke and stepped around the lady who was growing ever more impatient. She pulled her phone out the second she was out of sight and called Greenwood. She was immediately directed to voicemail. She sent a text.

I've just had a sit down with Antonio Martini and a lady with a Belfast accent interrupted, demanding to know where Eamon was. Who is this lady?

66

Joint Helicopter Command Flying Station, or JHC FS for short, adjoining Aldergrove's Belfast International Airport, was located eighteen miles northwest of Belfast and housed the Thirty-Eighth Regiment of the British army along with units of the Army Air Corps. Greenwood stepped off the RAF Voyager, chilled to the bone and frowning at the text message she had just received from Black about the mystery lady. She was welcomed by both the freezing air and MI5 Agent Malcolm Stephens. who was there to act as her transport.

AGENT STEPHENS WAS A MIDDLE-AGED MAN, about five foot six inches tall, with a waistline that gave off the impression that he didn't get enough exercise, and a messy hairstyle that led one to believe that he didn't have much motivation to make himself look good. Noticing no wedding ring on his finger, Greenwood assumed that he was a happily single man with nobody to make an effort for.

'Agent Greenwood.' He greeted her with a smile. 'I

haven't seen you for a long time. Congratulations on your promotion.'

'Thanks, Malcolm.' She offered her hand to him as she slid into the rear of the SUV. 'How's life in Belfast?'

'Same as always: politically entertaining.' He joked, running his hand through his greasy, chin-length grey hair.

He returned to the driver's seat and started the engine, guiding the vehicle towards the gate. After a quick nod to the guards, the barrier was raised. He looked at Greenwood in the rear-view mirror. 'Straight to Stormont?'

'Please.' She took off her jacket and fastened her seat-belt, her laptop case gripped tightly in her hand. She opened Black's text again. She knew that if anybody had more information about Martini and his past life, it would be the man who she was on her way to see. 'I hear the Deputy First Minister practically lives at Stormont now.' She was half stating, half asking.

'Ever since he was appointed Deputy King of the Hill, he's taken his job seriously. Putting his position before everything else, including his family.'

Greenwood grunted.

'Meehan's always been a man who cared more about the people, than his own people.' Greenwood's phone rang. It was Falkner. She answered it, a grin on her face. 'Don't you know the meaning of retirement?'

'Not when Martini's still on the scene.' Falkner was quick to reply. 'I hear you've gone over to Belfast.'

'I have. Just been picked up at RAF Aldergrove by one of your old drivers. I'm on my way to speak with Declan Meehan. We're running out of time.'

'He'll not say a word,' Falkner said with contempt. 'He's a die-hard republican and was one of the many whose ass Eamon Martini saved. He'll not talk.'

'He will if he doesn't want to lose his throne.'

'You've got nothing on him.'

'Nevertheless, I'm sure a threat that we have something on him will get him to talk. He's come a long way from the hard-lined republican on the streets of Belfast that he once was. He's become too comfortable. Civilised. And he won't want to spend the rest of his days in prison.'

67

King's Mill coffee shop was almost empty when Martini arrived at nine-fifteen. Just off the B1008 in the North Chelmsford village of Little Waltham, it had just enough discretion whilst remaining public. Ideal for a meet between Eamon Martini, once the most wanted man in Britain, and former Prime Minister Churchman.

Martini reverse parked the car in between a blue Ford Ranger pick-up and a black Harley Davidson. He shut the engine off and called Goodall.

'Eamon, what's your update?' She was quick to ask.

'I need you to make contact with West Middlesex Emergency Department. Bring them up to speed on what Churchman's doing. Make them aware that he'll be rushed to their hospital from Strawberry Hill House around midday by his driver. He needs to be kept away from public view until I get Enda. You need to contact BBC News and find out who their political correspondent is and bring them up to speed, too. Their story will be crucial in this. Schuster and Jaleel need to see a report on the TV that Churchman has been assassinated. Only then, will they release Enda.'

'This better work, Eamon. An eight-year-old boy's life is on the line.'

'Just you make sure the right people know what's going on.'

'Consider it done.'

He ended the call and sat for two minutes before a dark blue Mercedes Eqc estate pulled into the carpark, slowly moving into the parking bay on the opposite side of the Harley. Had he not been watching, he would have missed it; apart from the odd crunch of stones being eaten by the tyres, the electric vehicle glided in with complete silence.

Martini watched as the former PM got out of the rear, put his overcoat on, and made his way towards the shop's entrance.

Martini grabbed his phone and followed Churchman into the shop. Churchman was sitting in the first window booth to the right. Martini cast a glance around the shop as he approached the table. A lady in her mid-twenties was clearing the tables at the opposite end of the shop. A guy who looked to be in his early to mid-thirties was rinsing a mop in a bucket that was holding open a door to the disabled toilet open. A middle-aged lady wearing a black shirt in contrast to the blue shirts worn by the other two was at the coffee machine.

Martini slid into the booth facing Churchman. He cleared his throat. 'Thanks for meeting me.'

'I'm not doing it for you, Martini. I'm doing it because a man I respect needs my help, and a young boy's life is at stake.'

'Fair enough.' Martini accepted the animosity and moved on. 'So, you're on board?'

Churchman looked at Martini. He was now in his late fifties. He had been a young Prime Minister when he was elected in ninety-seven, but the stress of the job had taken its toll. He was slightly heavier now than he had been in office during his role as PM. His hair had whitened and receded. His brown eyes still had that ability to bore into someone, putting people on the spot. 'How's it going to work?'

Martini sat forward, resting his forearms on the table. 'You carry on as normal. The way you've planned your day will be just as scheduled. The action needs to be caught on camera for maximum impact. Schuster and Jaleel will believe it more if the world sees it.'

'So, at Strawberry Hill House?'

He nodded. 'Your driver must know the importance of this being realistic. It must be believable. Schuster and Jaleel will know if the driver is acting. But the only people who can know this is staged is yourself, your driver and your wife. Make sure she doesn't take part in any interviews. Televised or otherwise.'

'How long until you get the boy back?'

'The moment after I pull the trigger, I'll be travelling to Berlin for the handover. So less than twenty-four hours. But don't do anything until you've been called – by me.' He pulled a bag out of his inner coat pocket and slid it across the table.

'What's this?'

'Real effect blood. You just burst the capsule and it releases the liquid out with the same effect as a real bullet. I'm going to fire two shots. One headshot and one in the chest.'

'Christ, I can't believe I'm putting my life in the hands of the most wanted man in Britain.'

Martini ignored the comment. 'I'm a good shot. I'll take the shots once your vehicle stops at the security gates.

Remain very still. The shot will come through the window, into the seat, and few inches from your head. At the moment of impact, squeeze the rubber mechanism on the end of the blood tube and the blood will be sprayed over the window just like a real shot. I will then fire a second shot onto the seat a few inches to your other side. You squeeze the mechanism again and the blood will spill over your chest. There are instructions in the bag on how to fit the capsules to different parts of the body.' Martini sat back in his seat. 'Any questions?'

'Once the shots have been fired, and I'm supposedly dead, what do we do?'

'Your driver needs to rush you to West Middlesex Hospital where you will be dead on arrival.'

'The staff at the hospital will obviously know I'm not dead.'

'Don't worry about that. People in the CIA are informing the staff at the emergency department. Those on the rota to work tomorrow will know what's going on. They will rush you to a quiet room where you can get changed. You will be kept there until you receive my call. Anything else?'

'Just don't fuck this up, Martini.'

'I'll call you when the boy's safe.' He stood up and left.

68

Martini arrived back at Antonio's house shortly after ten-thirty. Apart from the outer perimeter, the grounds were cast in total darkness. The seven-feet-high white wall surrounding the grounds was lit up by evenly spaced, blue lights. He parked the vehicle next to the others. He could hear music coming from the back garden. Following the noise, he found Antonio and three other men around the same age, accompanied by four women.

The energy was good, perhaps aided by Antonio's usual debauchery.

One of the girls looked across the yard as Martini approached, still in his overalls. She got up off the lap of the guy she'd been dancing for. 'I love a guy who's not afraid to get his hands dirty.' She strutted towards him, slightly unsteady in her walk, her three-inch heels perhaps not the best choice of footwear considering the amount of alcohol and drugs Antonio was known to dish out at a party. Her leather miniskirt wasn't much more than a belt. Her matching bra just about shielded her breasts from view, smatterings of white powder left in the crease.

'That man's never got his hands dirty in his life,' Antonio joked, throwing one of the other girls off his lap. He struggled to his feet, staggering towards Martini. 'I need to have a word with you.' He slurred in Italian. 'About your sister.' He cocked his head in the direction of the house.

Martini smiled at the girl, then followed his cousin towards the patio doors.

'Make sure you come back,' she called out to him.

Antonio led them into the kitchen.

'What about Elizabeth?' Martini asked. He took off the overalls and smoothed out the worn jeans beneath. 'What has she done?'

Antonio sat down on one of the stools, swaying from side to side. 'She came to the club earlier, demanding to know what you're up to. She was ready to tear lumps out of me, the crazy bitch.'

'Well, it wouldn't be hard for you to wind someone up, now would it, Antonio?'

'Whatever, Eamon. But I never antagonised her. And she was being serious.'

Martini sat down facing him. 'Okay,' he sighed. 'What did she say?'

'She said that if she finds out the reason you're in England is because of us, she will personally put me, Leonardo, and the Apostles six-feet under.' He pulled a plastic zip-lock bag of cocaine from his shirt pocket, tipping some onto the table. Pulling his phone out, he flipped the case open and removed his driver's licence, chopping through the powder and sorting it into neat lines. He offered some to Martini.

Martini shook his head. 'I'm alright. And you need to go easy on that shit, as well.'

'Take it easy, Eamon.' He took a ten-pound note from his

back pocket and rolled it up. 'What the hell are you doing in England that's so bad that your sister threatens to take all of us out?'

'I'm going after the former Prime Minister.'

Antonio began snorting a line, stopping halfway across. He looked up at him. 'What?'

'You heard me.'

He wiped his nose with the back of his hand and set the roll down. 'Eamon, I know you've got balls, but you're not stupid. You're supposed to be the brains of the family. Heir to the Martini throne.' His last few words were spoken with a tinge of resentment.

One of the girls came running into the kitchen.

'Claire, give us a minute, sweetheart!' Antonio shouted. Although his words were sweet, his tone was deadly.

She froze in her tracks and hightailed it back to the garden.

Antonio studied Martini. He shook his head, a smile stretching across his face. 'You've got a death wish?'

Martini shook his head.

'Then what?'

'I don't have any other choice,' Martini replied with a small sigh. 'Some very nasty people have kidnapped an innocent kid, and they'll kill him if I don't do it.'

Antonio's face hardened. 'Eamon – you're going to need help. A world leader? Leonardo and I will help you. I'll make a call back to Milan. We'll have the Apostles over here tomorrow.'

'See your reaction? This is exactly the reason I shouldn't have told you. I know this is a dangerous job. But you have to believe I'll be fine.'

'Eamon, you're family. We stick together. You can trust us.'

'I know I can. But there's nothing you can do. You know I work better on my own. The bastards have kidnapped a child. I need to do this...on my own.'

'When's all this happening?'

'Tomorrow.'

'Christ.' Antonio blessed himself. 'So, you weren't joking when you said to look out for the news.'

Martini shook his head and stood up. 'I'm going for a shower and then going to try and get some sleep. I'll be off early in the morning.'

Antonio stood up off the stool, holding the side of the island to balance himself. He pulled Martini in for a hug. 'I know we haven't seen eye to eye in the past, but when I saw you the other day, I was happier than I'd felt in a long time. You make me proud to be a Martini, Eamon.'

Martini created some distance between the two of them. 'Don't speak about me like I'm dead. I'm not dead. And I'm not going to die. I don't want to be in this position. But I know if this kid is to live, I'll have to be the one that saves him.' He slapped Antonio affectionately on the shoulder. 'I'll see you in a few days. And less of the farewell bullshit.'

'Take whatever you need.'

'Grazie.'

69

Northern Ireland's Deputy First Minister Declan Meehan was at his desk, eating King Prawn Chow Mein from Yen's Chinese House, just a five-minute walk up the Newtownards Road. His mouth was still full when a knock sounded at the door. He quickly swallowed, washing the food down with some water. 'Come in!' he shouted, filling his fork again.

Greenwood opened the door and stepped in, marching straight across the office and planting herself down opposite his desk. 'Don't you have a home to go to?' she asked.

He set his fork down and wiped his mouth with a napkin. 'God, you really want to get your hands on Eamon, don't you?' He set the napkin down and lifted his cup of tea. 'I hope you didn't come all this way for more information. I told you on the phone that I don't know where he is. I haven't spoken to him in years.'

'I know, I believe you. But I know that you know who he'll be in contact with and I want you to help me find him.'

'I'm sorry, but your journey's been a waste of time, Agent Greenwood.'

'You realise that if Martini's successful, if he manages to

carry out a successful attack on the Prime Minister, our institutions will be in chaos. It'll be catastrophic for your cosy little office over here.'

'Get to the point.' He sighed.

'I want you to reach out to him. Try to find out who he's been in contact with.' Meehan went to speak, but she put her hand up and cut him off. 'Don't bother. I know you still roll in those circles. The Provisional IRA has long been stood down, but we both know your weapons were not all decommissioned. I don't give a shit about that. I want to know who has access to the firearms. I just want to know who he plans on getting the weapons from that are capable of attacking Number Ten Downing Street.'

'You think he's going to attack the Prime Minister in her own home?'

'You tell me – does he have the capacity to do so?'

Meehan didn't reply.

'My former boss seems to think he's capable.'

'Falkner?' Meehan laughed. 'He still not dead?'

Her phone buzzed. It was another text from Black.

Ma'am, I've followed the lady with the Belfast accent who was asking about Martini. I've got the make and model of her vehicle, along with the registration. I'm getting her details now.

Greenwood set the phone down on the desk. 'Does Martini have any family in London?'

'Eamon has always kept his life very private. His old man was just as clever – people thought he was a paranoid bastard. He could have family over there. Anything's possible with Eamon.' She studied him, trying to assess his truthfulness.

'As I said, if this goes ahead, you lose everything you've worked for, and the blame will be laid squarely at the door of the IRA. That means British troops on the streets of

Belfast again. House raids, a collapse in Stormont, and pretty much an end to the Good Friday Agreement.' She stood up. 'Good evening, Mr. Meehan.' She lifted her phone off his desk and made her way towards the door.

'Hold on a second.' Meehan called across the room. He stood up and approached her. 'We had a stash of IRA weapons not far from London. But the person who had been tasked with looking after them hasn't been heard from in years. I suspect he's dead.'

'Who is it?'

'Raymond Greer.'

'You mean James Greer?'

'They're brothers. James was a unit commander in the IRA throughout most of the war and was, alongside Eamon's father, in charge of the movement of weapons. If anyone knows about the old stash, it'll be James' brother Raymond. But good luck trying to find him. As I said, I wouldn't be surprised if he were dead.'

'Thanks for your help, Mr. Meehan.' Greenwood offered her hand to him. He begrudgingly accepted.

She left the office. Making her way back down the steps of Stormont, towards the car, she called Falkner. He answered almost immediately. 'You know anything about Raymond Greer, brother of James? Apparently, Raymond was given weapons to keep in the London area.'

'God. That's a name I haven't heard in a long time.' Falkner grunted. 'Wouldn't surprise me if that piece of shit was involved in something like this.' He coughed and cleared his throat. 'Is that the name you got from Meehan?'

She pulled the car door open and got in. The vehicle took off. 'I eventually got something out of him. I was halfway out the door of his office when he decided he had something for me.'

Falkner laughed. 'He's getting old now, you see. Nothing's worth going to prison for.'

Greenwood received another call. *Agent Black* flashed across the screen. 'I've got to go. My shining new star is calling.' She ended the call with Falkner and answered Black. 'Harper?'

'This lady's smart, ma'am. She's changed cars a few times, and is still moving around.'

'If we need her, we can squeeze the information out of the Italians.' Greenwood lowered the window, letting the cool air in to circulate. 'I want you to get back to the office and look up brothers Raymond and James Greer. Collect everything you have on them. Any addresses, associates, and anything else you think might lead us to this son of a bitch. I want him and we're going to get him.'

'Yes, ma'am.'

She ended the call. 'Take me back to RAF Aldergrove. I need to be back in London.'

'Busy lady.'

'God, you don't know the half of it.'

70

Martini's alarm woke him at four-thirty the next morning. He'd left the window open just a crack, and could hear voices in the garden. 'Christ, do they ever stop?' he mumbled. He rolled over to his left and raised himself up on his elbow, the light of his phone illuminating the surface of the bedside cabinet. He'd received a text message from Page.

Eamon, Agent Greenwood has hired an eager-to-impress young hotshot agent to help track you down. She was in the office a couple of hours ago looking up Raymond and James Greer.

He sighed and replied to the text.

Thanks. Make sure Lizzy's okay, and tell her I'm safe. She's got nothing to worry about.

'Don't need her returning to the club and tearing Antonio a new asshole.' Despite the situation, he managed to find a slither of humour in the thought.

He set the phone down, sat up and swung his legs off the bed, his bare feet sinking into the soft carpet. He got up and approached the window. Antonio's male guests were asleep on the sun loungers. The girls were in the pool, naked. Antonio was sitting at the garden table, glued to his laptop, appearing more concerned with whatever was on the screen than the topless women in the pool. He had them on tap anyway, so it wasn't as if he'd miss out.

Martini fought his instinct to go and join them for a dip. But one of his oldest friends was in White House worried about his grandson, and he needed to stay focussed. Instead, he went for a shower to get ready for the day. The only thing on his mind was getting Enda back.

71

By five-thirty, Martini had showered, shaved and dressed in one of the many suits he found in the wardrobe. Standing in front of the full-length mirror, he could only admire Antonio's taste. Italian fabric – a suit that almost felt form-fitted. He studied his appearance, thinking that if today was going to be a day that would go down in history, a globally recognised event that he would be responsible for, then he sure as hell was going to look good doing it. The slim-fit navy suit and brown shoes made him look like a man off for a job interview, not an assassin about to carry out a hit on the former British Prime Minister.

He went down to the kitchen, prepared the Moka, and placed it on the hob. He checked BBC News Weather. The forecast said that there would be a cold start to the day, but it was going to be bright and most importantly, dry, with little breeze. When the pot steamed, he poured the coffee and made his way out of the house. He left the van. It had served its purpose. He took the grey Range Rover that was parked next to Antonio's collection of Italian supercars.

His phone buzzed as he was exiting the driveway,

alerting him to an update from BBC News. He pulled into the side of the road, braked and put the car into neutral. He opened the report. It was a story about the meeting to be held at Strawberry Hill House. The Americans had been greeted by Prime Minister Pears at Number Ten and were due to first have breakfast before making their way to the stately home for the meeting. Heightened security meant that the location was kept from the public. He closed the report and called James Greer.

After the call rang a few times, his old friend, now foe answered. 'You know what time it is?' Greer groaned.

'Just letting you know everything's on track for the day. Keep an eye on the news. Former Prime Minister Church-man's book signing is going to be remembered in the world of literature for a long time.'

'Best of luck, Eamon.'

Martini ended the call and took off.

72

Black had been up all night, going through documents on all the key players of the Provisional IRA. Martini's father – how he'd fallen in love with the daughter of a New York mafia boss and secretly had Eamon. Martini's father was one of two people responsible for negotiating weapons for the IRA, both in America and other parts of the world. James Greer was the other. The current location of Damien Cleary Jnr. was unknown.

'Excuse me. I'm looking for Agent Greenwood. Have you seen her?' Paddy Lyttle was stood at the door of Black's office.

'Who are you?' she was quick to ask.

'Paddy Lyttle. I'm here to help her catch that son of a bitch, Martini. And you are?'

'Agent Harper Black. Agent Greenwood's brought me in on it.'

'Any luck?' Lyttle invited himself further into the office and sat down on a chair next to the window.

'I paid a visit to a club operated by Martini's family, hoping that the Italian side could lead me somewhere.

While I was talking to Antonio Martini, Eamon Martini's cousin, we were interrupted by a lady with a Belfast accent. She looked around middle to late forties, and was demanding to talk to the Italian about where *Eamon* was. Referring to him as Eamon is very personal. Perhaps someone who knows him intimately.'

'He has a sister. I bet it's her.' He pulled his phone out of his pocket.

'Who are you calling?'

'Falkner.'

'Commander Falkner has retired.'

'I know he has, but he knows more about Eamon Martini than most.'

'Even more than you?' Greenwood asked from the doorway. She stepped inside, looking at Black. 'Anything?'

Black shook her head. 'I've been up all night searching for something.'

She glanced at Lyttle. 'Who are you calling?'

Lyttle looked up at her. 'Your old boss.' He put his phone on loudspeaker and set it down on the desk.

'I'm beginning to wish we'd never come into contact again,' Falkner complained.

Greenwood walked closer to the phone. Sitting on the edge of the desk, she said, 'Stop complaining, you grumpy old bastard. Unless you want Martini to get away.'

He didn't respond, but they could hear shuffling in the background. 'What are you calling me for?'

Black took over. 'Commander Falkner, Agent Harper Black here. I wonder if you know whether there's a lady in Martini's life living in London, with a Belfast accent?'

More shuffling came from the other end. Falkner's voice returned, this time sounding louder and clearer. 'Eamon

Martini has family in London, Belfast, and of course – New York.'

'James – Agent Black here said that she was aged around mid-forties, and with the Belfast accent.' Lyttle added.

Black continued. 'Porcelain skin, piercing blue eyes – ones that look like contacts.'

'Cleary's eyes,' Lyttle said.

'And Martini's,' Falkner added.

'Commander – she'd interrupted me when I was chatting to Antonio Martini. I went there posing as a member of the public wanting to book a party.'

'Did you follow the girl?' Falkner was quick to ask.

'I did, but she covered her tracks many times. She must have changed cars a half dozen times before eventually disappearing into the London traffic.'

'She knew you were following her then,' Greenwood said, 'Harper, I want you to get back to the club. Get any CCTV footage of her, and we'll run it through the system. See if facial recognition picks anything up.' She stood up off the desk. 'I'm going for a shower, need to freshen up.'

73

Black got to the club just as it was opening for the day. She sat in her Mercedes, watching as a young lady, perhaps no older than twenty, lifted the shutters and quickly swept the front of the shop before going back inside. Black glanced at herself in the mirror, her grey eyes had red rings around them. She'd been up all night and was starting to feel drowsy. All the coffee in London wouldn't be enough to liven her up. But the opportunity of a lifetime was sitting right in front of her, and she was not about to let it pass her. She rinsed her mouth with a cap full of mouthwash and got out, spitting it out into the drain next to her car's front tyre.

Lifting her suit jacket from the back seat, she put it on, welcoming the warmth it brought amidst the chill.

She entered the shop, the radio playing gently throughout the room, and approached the desk.

'Morning,' the lady said, continuing to polish the windows of the front display. 'Would you like the breakfast menu?'

'Morning,' Black replied, scanning the area. 'No, thank you. I'm investigating a crime that took place just out on the street last night. I wanted to check your CCTV from yesterday if I could?'

The lady stopped what she was doing, set the cloth down, and looked at her with narrowed eyes. 'Do you have any ID?'

She flashed her badge.

She looked at it. 'Secret Intelligence Service, MI6?'

'We believe the incident that took place was related to ongoing terrorist activity coming in from the continent. MI5 are following up on a few other leads, but I've offered to help.' She tried to joke. 'The people in the met don't want anything to do with it when there's a mention of the big T-word.'

The lady nodded, but her expression didn't look at all sure. 'Okay, go and have a seat, I'll go make a copy for you. Any specific times you want?'

'From four in the afternoon to midnight.' She smiled at her. 'Thanks a million.' She went and sat down. She pulled her phone out and was about to call Greenwood with an update when she was interrupted.

Paddy Lyttle sat down on the seat next to her. 'You're keen, aren't you?'

Black looked slightly taken aback by the comment. 'What?'

'You do realise that when she checks the footage, she'll see you on it, talking to Antonio Martini.'

She swore under her breath. Jumping up off the seat, she made her way towards the office the lady had disappeared into. She peered through the window, she was at the desktop computer, logging into the CCTV. She opened the door and walked in.

Instinctively, the lady's head swung around. 'Sorry, but only members of staff can be in here.'

'I'm sorry, but my boss has just arrived. He's told me that I need to be here when the footage is being viewed, so that it can't be tampered with.' She walked further into the office. 'Not that I don't trust you, but you must understand. It's a serious crime and people may try to cover it up.'

'Okay, well, how about you let me go and finish opening the shop and you can make the copy.' The lady stood up. 'I've just logged in. Just wait a second for the thing to wake up.'

'Great, thank you.' Black took her seat. It took about thirty seconds for it to do anything. She selected the last eighteen hours and recorded it onto her pen drive. She quickly deleted the footage with her in it and left the office. She walked around to the customer's side of the counter and smiled at the lady. 'Thanks for your help.'

She smiled back. 'Hope you've found what you need.'

Lyttle got up off his seat, with two coffees to go, and followed Black outside. 'Here.' He handed her one of the drinks. 'You look like you could do with one.'

'Thanks.' She took a sip of the coffee and made her way towards the driver's door. 'Where's your car?'

He approached the passenger door. 'It can stay where I've left it. I'll travel with you back to HQ. I want to look at what you've got.' He pulled the passenger door open and got in. He waited for Black to take her seat, then extended his hand. 'Let's see the footage.'

Black put the key in the ignition and started the engine. She fished the pen drive out of her pocket and handed it over.

'Where's your computer?' He looked around the back seat, seeing the laptop bag on the floor behind the driver's seat.

Black took another drink of her coffee, and slid it into

the cup holder on the central unit. Putting the car in drive, she took off back the way she came.

Lyttle turned on the laptop. 'What's the password?'

'BritishIntel8888.'

He accessed the desktop and inserted the drive. He put the car's radio on while waiting. Radio One's half-hour news report was discussing the arrival of the US heads of state, and how the discussions between the Americans and the British was going to be mutually beneficial in the fight against Islamic extremism in England. So far, the threat from extremists had been much less severe in the US, but it was ultimately going to be what the enemies of the western world would be aiming for. 'Biggest mistake, going over there,' he mumbled. 'They'd created a whole new generation of hate towards us westerners.' An icon popped up; he clicked on it, opened the contents, and clicked on the video. 'What time did you see her?'

'Around seven in the evening,' she said, pulling up to a set of traffic lights, hungrily reaching down for another drink of the coffee.

He scanned the video, working backward. The entire day flashed by in quick reversal. 'Here we go.' He slowed down to normal speed, then to slow motion. He paused, watching as the lady came into view. His eyes followed her as she approached the table where Black and Antonio Martini had been sitting. He paused the video and zoomed in. 'Christ.'

'Christ is good news, right?'

He nodded and pulled his phone out of his pocket, quickly calling Greenwood.

The call was answered immediately.

'What have you got, Paddy?'

'I'm looking at the footage outside Club Mediterranean.'

He glanced at Black, then back at the screen. 'The lady that demanded to speak with Antonio Martini is Eamon Martini's long-lost sister.'

'How sure are you?' Greenwood pressed.

'I'd bet my life on it.' He scratched his head, deep in thought. 'But I've seen her somewhere else recently.'

'Maybe you just thought it was her,' Greenwood said.

'No. It's her. She was wearing the same jumper she's wearing in this video.'

'Just get back to the office and we'll run it through the system to see what comes up. Send an image across to Belfast, see if anyone in the PSNI can put a name to the face. I'm going to meet with the PM and the Americans. See you both back at the office.' She ended the call.

74

Martini got to Raymond Greer's house shortly after eight in the morning. Greer was just making his way back to the house from what looked like a morning stroll with the dog. He had a cane in one hand, and a plastic shopping bag in the other. He turned to see who was approaching, his expression softening when his eyes landed on Martini.

As the Range Rover got within earshot, Greer shouted. 'For fuck sake, Eamon. You trying to give me a heart attack?'

Martini smirked as he drove past, guiding the vehicle carefully along the driveway towards the weapons dump. He got out of the SUV and opened the boot. 'You out keeping yourself fit, old man?'

'More of a case that I'll never hear the end of it from this one if I don't, so better get it out of the way. Then the rest of the day's mine to do whatever I want.'

Martini took his overcoat and suit jacket off, then swiftly unbuttoned and removed his shirt.

'You decided you'd prefer to wear a t-shirt today, then?'

Martini smirked and grabbed a white padded vest from the back seat of the car. 'Ultra-covert vest, unnoticeable under a shirt.' He quickly pulled the vest over his head and fastened it to his torso, then put his shirt back on.

'You haven't changed your mind then?'

He pulled his suit jacket and coat back on again and approached the hatch door to the weapons dump. 'Not yet.'

'How about breakfast with an old friend before you go and set the bloody world on fire?'

'If you're talking about an English breakfast, then count me in.' He lifted the door, peering down into the store.

'Do what you've got to do, then come in.' Greer made his way towards the house, the dog following closely behind.

Martini descended the steps into the store, his eyes tiny slits, swatting the airborne dust particles out of his face. As he reached the last step, his eyes landed on exactly what he wanted for the job. The first weapon he'd learned to fire. The Barrett M82 semi-automatic assault rifle. He'd mastered this weapon training high in the green hills of Donegal and Galway – Ireland's picturesque west coast. It was then that he'd been quickly recognised by his father, as not only an intelligence gatherer, but an excellent marksman. With the Barrett, he'd stopped many loyalist paramilitaries from attacking Catholic homes in the early and mid-nineties up until the ninety-eight Good Friday Agreement when peace was established. Then in 2002, he'd taken up the weapon again in the dusty mountains of Afghanistan, picking off Taliban fighters with the ease of picking dog hairs off his jacket.

Grabbing one ten-round, fully loaded magazine and a bipod, he made his way back up the steps and over to the vehicle. Laying the equipment down flat on the floor of the boot, he covered them with a green sleeping bag. Making his way to the house, he called Leonardo.

'Eamon, I was wondering when I'd hear from you.'

'Can you be ready to take me up into the air for my return flight in the next couple of hours?'

'Of course. Anything you need.'

'Call the Apostles and have them on standby.'

'Of course.'

'You've flown to Germany before, right?'

'Yes, why?'

'Don't worry, I'll explain it all later.' He ended the call and entered the kitchen. The smell of bacon that had just begun to sizzle on the pan was making his mouth salivate.

75

Black and Lyttle arrived back at the SIS headquarters at Vauxhall Cross. Detective Chief Superintendent Ivan Shanks of the PSNI's Legacy Investigation Branch in Belfast was now trying to cross-reference the images of the lady with anyone they had on file. The LIB was set up in 2015, as part of Chief Constable Martin Ford's investigation regarding the past, and how the security forces would deal with the legacy of the Troubles. Neither Black nor Lyttle had faith in the LIB picking anything up, but as Greenwood said, if something were to go the wrong way, then they had to be seen as having exhausted all avenues.

Falkner arrived at HQ just as Black had sat down at her desk and switched on her computer. 'You pair are making me give some serious consideration to coming back to work again.' He strolled around the desk. 'What have you got?' He took his glasses case out of his inner coat pocket. 'Who's the pretty lady?'

'That's Martini's sister,' Lyttle said. 'She's the one that visited the Italian's club yesterday, demanding to know where *Eamon* was.'

Falkner looked closer at the image. 'I'd swear I've seen her before somewhere, but I'll be damned if I know where.'

'I agree,' Lyttle replied, shaking his head. 'It's going to bug the hell out of me.'

'Excuse me, gents,' Page said from the door. 'Is Agent Greenwood ready to go to Number Ten yet?' He strolled into the office, hands in his pockets. 'You all look engrossed.'

'Victoria's already left, kid,' Falkner said. 'She had to rush off a bit earlier this morning.' He looked over at him. 'Karl...you've been around here for as long as I can remember. Do you recognise this lady?'

Page stepped around the desk, joining them all. He looked closely, his eyes widening as who was in the image. 'That's Club Mediterranean, run by Eamon Martini's Italian family, isn't it?'

'Yes, and this lady's his sister,' Lyttle said. 'If I can't catch Martini, then this little bitch will do nicely as a ransom.'

'Really?' Page grunted in mock agreement, then straightened himself up as the rest remained hunched over the screen. Black adjusted the image, zooming in slightly. Lyttle and Falkner both studied the woman closer. Page took one step back. Reaching behind him, he lifted a metal bookend from the shelf on the wall and clocked Lyttle first, sending him to the ground, quickly following up with Falkner, sending the commander tumbling to the floor next to Lyttle.

Before Black had a chance to react, the bookend went sailing for her, knocking her off her chair, but not hard enough to knock her out. She was disorientated, but still able to act in response to what was going on.

She pulled out her Walther P99, but before she had time to aim, Page rushed in and wrestled the pistol from her. A silencer was already fitted. He pointed the gun at Black's forehead. 'Unless you want one of your own bullets between your eyes, you won't make a sound.' He stood up and ordered Black across the room towards the radiator. He rushed across the office and closed the door, locking it, then closed the blind on the only window. He ordered her to pull Falkner's and Lyttle's shoes off and remove the laces. He then ordered her to do the same with Falkner's tie.

Page snatched a roll of tape from the middle drawer of the desk, and wrapped her mouth closed. Lyttle was starting to come around. Page crouched down and whacked him on the side of the head again, this time with the butt of the Walther. Once the three were bound and gagged, he took Black's office key and locked the door on his way out.

On his way down to the car, he pulled his phone out and called his wife. She didn't answer so he left her a voicemail. 'Lizzy, we've been made. I've just left Commander Falkner and two others bound in an office in MI6 HQ. Get the hell away from the house and don't talk to anyone. Do as I say, please. And don't go near the Italians, they have footage of you there yesterday asking about Eamon.' He ended the call and walked briskly, but not too obvious, towards his car.

76

Greenwood was standing in the Prime Minister's office waiting to meet her American counterpart and Prime Minister Pears. She glanced out the window, wondering where the attack was going to come from. After the Provisional IRA had mortar bombed Number Ten during the Troubles, an attack that almost took out the entire cabinet, including the Prime Minister at the time, security around the place had been ramped up. The windows and doors had been reinforced, and the streets outside the building had since been lined with guarded gates. Since the Provos' near miss, the place was as guarded as Buckingham Palace.

'Where are you, Mr. Martini?' she wondered out loud. She went to the PM's self-serving drinks facilities and made herself a latte, then sat down and browsed through her emails. One had come from the former Prime Minister, telling her that he expected to have top-notch security at his book signing today. He also said that he was keen to speak with her about the current security situation in the UK. As she closed the message, Prime Minister Pears arrived with the Director of the United States Secret Service, Frank Dott.

Pears spoke. 'Frank Dott, meet Victoria Greenwood. She has recently taken over from Commander Falkner.'

Greenwood stood up and offered her hand to Dott. 'Pleased to meet you.'

'Pleasure's all mine, Agent Greenwood. The Prime Minister has told me great things.'

She sat back down, Dott took the seat next to her, the Prime Minister carried on talking while making a drink. 'So, I've quickly briefed Frank here on the Martini situation.' She cast a quick glance over her shoulder, addressing the two, whilst operating the coffee machine. 'Are we any closer to getting him?'

Greenwood glanced at Dott, then over to the PM. 'No, ma'am, but...'

Dott quickly interrupted. 'Excuse me, Agent Green-wood, but I think it's important that you do everything in your power to bring Eamon Martini in. He's a man the US government would also like to get their hands on.'

Greenwood took a drink from her coffee. 'And why is Eamon Martini of such interest to the US government? I believe it was not that long ago he was President Sherran's chief of security. He'd also turned down the role you're currently in, before doing...whatever it is he does now.'

'I'm afraid that's classified.'

Greenwood smiled, shaking her head. 'Don't give me that bullshit.' She crossed her legs and set her cup down on the desk next to her, turning her body towards Dott. 'If you know anything about Martini, anything that can help us get him, then you need to forget the need-to-know crap and just say it. We're supposed to be allies.'

The PM approached them, handing Dott his coffee, then sat on the edge of her desk. 'We need him dead, as soon as possible.'

Greenwood nodded her head, taking a drink of her coffee.

Dott took over. 'Eamon Martini knows things about both the British and US governments that could strip away any faith in our democracy.' He took a sip of the coffee. 'Nice coffee.' He continued. 'He knows more about our operations than anyone in the last twenty years. If he were to develop loose lips, he'd sink both American and British ships and we'd all be left red-faced.'

Greenwood looked at the PM.

'I think it's best for everyone that he disappears.'

'Ma'am, I know it was I who first mentioned the idea of silencing Martini, and I have no problem in putting a bullet in his head, but after looking through everything we have on him, I just think it would be better if we were to bring him in and find out what he has. Any fool can fire a bullet into someone's skull.'

'He's got dirt on all of us,' Dott said. 'He knows our greatest secrets.'

Greenwood wasn't sure about what she was hearing. But she wasn't about to start arguing with her boss. 'Very well.' Her phone started to ring. She looked at it. 'I've got to take this, it's Black.' She stood up and left the office. Closing the door behind her, she answered. 'What have you got for me?'

'Ma'am, we've just been attacked by your driver. He got away.'

'What? Why?'

'The moment he looked at the footage of Martini's sister, he took us by surprise. Me, Commander Falkner and Mr. Lyttle.'

'Okay, I'm on my way.' She hung up and quickly updated the PM.

Dott called Greenwood back, just as she was leaving.

'Ms. Greenwood, I have a team of eight Secret Service personnel with me on this trip. I'll be sending four of them with you. Just to help out on capturing Martini. They know him more than any intelligence we combine; he recruited half of them into their posts.'

Greenwood looked at the PM, then at Dott. 'I'm sorry, Mr. Dott, but I can handle this myself. I don't know who this team is, but they'll be better staying with you.' She rushed towards the door.

'Victoria,' the Prime Minister shouted. 'This could get very messy. You might need their help.'

'I've got to get back to HQ now.' She looked at Dott. 'If your team can keep up with me, fine, but I'm not waiting around.'

77

Martini sat across the kitchen table from Raymond, watching as the old man divided the sausages, bacon, eggs, soda bread, and potato bread out evenly between the two of them.

Martini made himself useful by pouring the tea. 'It's been a long time since I've sat with an old friend and shared a meal like this.'

Raymond smiled. 'It's good to have company.' He looked at the dog, who sat bolt upright to attention. He cut one of the sausages and tossed half towards it. The dog caught it, swallowed it, and was waiting for more. 'That's all you're getting.' He looked at Martini. 'So, what happens after this?'

'What do you mean?'

'Where are you going after the attack?'

'Leonardo's helping to get me out of the country. The Apostles will then collect me from the European side, and I'll make my way back to Germany where I finish this job and move on.'

Raymond pierced a sausage with his fork and dipped it into the egg yolk, a flow of thick yellow liquid running out over the white, like a volcano spewing lava. 'Do you need help?'

Martini looked at him curiously. 'You've managed to live to this old age and not fire one bullet in the name of Irish freedom. Now, when the war's long over, you want some action?' he asked humorously.

'Perhaps it's because I'm getting old. Coming to the end of my life and looking back, wishing I'd done more.'

Martini looked at him thoughtfully for a moment as he chewed a piece of bread. 'You've done a lot by holding weapons.'

'Our James always wanted me to have more involvement in it all.'

'Well, it's too late for that.' Martini's phone went off. He looked at it. It was Page. He quickly answered. 'Karl?'

'Eamon, the bastards have footage of Lizzy visiting Antonio yesterday. It's only a matter of time before they catch up to you. They're looking into James and Raymond Greer. I'd advise you to forget the job and just get the hell out of the country.'

Martini shook his head. 'That's not an option.'

'I've left Falkner, Lyttle, and some agent handcuffed at HQ. But that'll not last long. Greenwood will eventually walk in and find them. She's in a meeting now with the PM and the American Defence Secretary.'

'Fuck.' His eyes scanned the room and landed on Raymond. He noticed that he was discreetly looking at his phone on the edge of the table, when he noticed Martini look at him, his eyes reacted. Martini didn't like the reaction, like a deer caught in the headlights. What was going on?

'Okay, take my sister and get away. I'll call you later.' Martini cleared his throat and looked at Raymond. He glanced curiously back at him.

'Problems, kid?'

Martini smiled. 'It looks like they're starting to pile up.' He lifted a bacon rasher and dipped it into the egg yolk.

'Like I said, Eamon. You've only got to ask for help.' Raymond continued with his breakfast.

'Thanks.' He lifted his tea and took a drink. 'So, who's the recording for?'

Raymond's head shot up, instinctively looking towards his phone that was still recording.

Martini jumped up from his seat, but Raymond produced a silver Dessert Eagle .50 from his lap before he could act.

He raised his hands, shaking his head. 'What have you got to gain by handing me over?'

'I've received a call from Declan Meehan. He told me that the Brits have paid him a visit and are threatening to hold him responsible for anything that you do.' He pointed the gun at Martini's head and beckoned him to come closer, then spun him around. 'I can't let you go, Eamon. The police are on their way.'

'You're handing me over to the Brits? You know they want me dead, right?'

'Better your death than anyone else's, kid.'

'A boy's life is at stake, Raymond. I'm the only one that can save him.'

Martini, with his back to Raymond, took two steps back until he felt the cold metal against the back of his head. Seeing himself in the reflection of the kitchen window, he watched as Raymond reached for the phone. The moment Martini saw the back of Raymond's head, he swerved his head away from Raymond's aim, spun around and snatched the pistol. Raymond stumbled back.

'Eamon, please. I'm an old man, I don't have long left to live. I...'

Martini lowered his aim and shot Raymond once in each knee, he fell to the ground screaming. Grabbing Raymond's phone, he pocketed it with his own. He ran out the door, leaped into the Range Rover, started the engine and left.

78

Greenwood rushed into Black's office. They were all being attended to by first aiders. 'For God's sake.' She sighed. She checked her phone, three missed calls – all from Declan Meehan. 'Are you three okay?'

'We're fine, just more surprised than anything else,' Black said.

Greenwood left the room and returned Meehan's call. He answered almost immediately. 'Have you remembered something?'

'Eamon Martini's been given access to the Provos' stash of arms at Raymond Greer's farm.'

'And does Raymond know what Martini's planning?'

'He's being escorted by his Italian cousin Leonardo to mainland Europe via air taxi once he's finished the job.' Meehan spoke humorously. 'These bloody Italians live some life – aircrafts and all sorts.'

'What about the location of the attack?'

'He didn't say.'

'Send me the location of the weapons dump. I need to get there, now.'

'I'll text you the location. But it might be too late if Martini's already collected the weapons. You'll not find him there.'

'Christ! How can I not get ahead of this bastard! Where will he be running to?'

'Back to where it started – Berlin.'

Greenwood ended the call and rushed back into the office. 'Are you three able to accompany me? I've got the location of a weapons dump Martini's collecting from.'

Black stood up, swaying slightly. 'As long as I can still walk, I'm with you, ma'am.'

'Let's go.'

79

At eleven-thirty, Martini was just one mile away from Strawberry Hill House. His phone had been ringing constantly since he'd set off from Raymond's house, and it was the last ring that caused him to finally pull over and answer. He lifted the phone that was charging through the USB port. It was President Sheeran.

'Bill, I'm about to pull the trigger and make my way back to Berlin. This evening I'll have Enda on a flight back to Washington.'

'We've gone right down to the wire with this one, Eamon. Teresa's tried everything to find Enda's location. She's got nothing from Dott's phone, he must have changed it. I wish I wasn't saying this, but it looks like you'll have to pull the trigger. She has picked up on something else. Robert Carter, former CIA Director, who'd stepped down due to apparent illness last year, has been spending a lot of time with Dott over the last few months. Carter has received enough money to extend his sick leave, indefinitely. The FBI has seized his personal computer from his home in Virginia. They've found evidence on his hard drive of him accessing encrypted data from the Pentagon after he'd stood down. Around the same time, his bank account has been used in purchasing some of life's little pleasures, including a superyacht called Quantum of Solace, which is currently moored in Monaco.'

Martini shook his head. 'Very James Bond of him. He sold the intel to Schuster?'

'Looks like it.'

'Have you brought him in?'

'Can't find him. The bastard's been travelling Europe the past six months.'

'Didn't want to be around when the FBI came knocking on the door.'

'Regarding him and Dott – I don't want the bastards brought in, Eamon. They've attacked my family...'

'Leave them to me, Bill.' Martini hung up and called Leonardo.

His cousin answered almost immediately. 'Eamon, are you okay?'

'How fast can you get to Strawberry Hill House?'

'Never heard of the place.'

'I'll text you the address. It's about a twenty-minute drive from the club. I need you to drop everything and come right away, can you do that?'

'Si.'

'Can you bring the van I borrowed last night? I left it at Antonio's.'

'Of course.'

'Good. Come in that.' He ended the call and sent the text with the address.

He knew the range on the rifle. He knew that he was a good shot. He knew he'd have no problem hitting the intended target he was aiming for. He only hoped the former PM had enough faith in him. Martini was under a tremendous amount of pressure, not from the shot, but from the realisation that he was putting as much faith in Churchman as the former PM was putting in him. If Churchman were to chicken out at the last moment, it would be his brains all over the car and not the capsules of fake blood. But what else could he do? He could only control so much. The rest would boil down to that one thing: faith.

Twenty minutes later, Leonardo arrived in the van.

Martini was parked a half-mile past the entrance to the estate, down a narrow single-track lane that led down into an old house that looked deserted. He got out and greeted his cousin. 'I don't know who's heard about the plan, but the wrong people now know, that's for sure.'

'What do you need?'

'I need you to come with me to Berlin. We fly there, instead of the original.' He passed Leonardo and made his way towards the side door of the van. He opened the door, reached in, and grabbed the cordless drill and box of drill bits. He closed the door and walked back to his cousin. 'There's a hostage situation in Berlin and nobody knows about it except a handful of people.' He looked at him, glaring into his eyes. 'I'm involving you because out of a choice between you and Antonio, you're the one that will listen and do *exactly* as I say.'

Leonardo looked confused. 'Okay, so what are we doing?'

'A German billionaire, with links to the Taliban, has tasked me to take out former Prime Minister Churchman. And if I don't, they're going to kill the US President's grandson.'

'What? The US President? What the fuck do you have to do with the US President, Eamon?'

'A lot more than you can imagine. But now's not the time to go into it.'

'So, you're going to carry out this hit?'

'No, but the kidnappers need to believe that the job's been done. At least long enough for me to get the kid back.'

'How do you plan on doing that? Christ, Eamon, I know you're good, but this is heavy stuff.'

Martini forced a smile, at least to promote confidence; inside his nerves were all over the place. 'Welcome to my world. I need you to be my eyes at the end of the road you've just driven along. The target I'm aiming for will be driving past in a grey Rolls Royce. Call me the moment you see the car. That should give me twenty or thirty seconds to prepare the shot. Then I'll meet you back at the airfield, where we'll get the hell out of here.'

Leonardo, for the first time in all the years Martini had known him, looked unsure – frightened even.

Martini put his hand on his shoulder. 'Look, you trust me, don't you?'

'You know I do, Eamon.'

'Don't worry. Nothing will come back on you. I promise.' He checked his phone. The time was twenty minutes to twelve. 'Just get me to Berlin and I can take care of these bastards.' His phone went off. It was James Greer. He looked at Leonardo. 'Go, I'll see you at the bird in one hour. The moment you make the call to me, get out of here and don't be spotted. I'll see you soon.' He answered the call and walked away. 'Jim.'

'Any updates?' Greer said.

'I'm minutes away from the hit.' He made his way back to the Range Rover. 'I'll call you when it's done. Be at the house when I come back, with the kid. I won't be waiting around.' He ended the call and opened the boot. Uncovering the weapon, he lifted it and positioned it. Lifting the drill, he fitted a drill bit and drilled a four-inch-thick hole in the back door, level with the barrel as it rested in the tripod. He folded down the rear seats, creating more space for himself. He positioned himself like a sniper in the grass. He lay there in silence. His phone stood up, the screen looking right at him. The minutes seemed to go on forever.

The time was two minutes past twelve when the phone rang. *Leonardo* flashed across the screen. He answered. 'Leonardo.'

'Grey Rolls Royce has just driven past. Heading in your direction.'

'I'll see you soon.' He ended the call. Gripping the weapon, he looked through the scope. He could feel his heart beating against the carpet of the SUV's cold floor. He became aware of his pulse, everywhere. In his ears, on his neck, even on his wrist. He closed his eyes and took a few deep breaths, slowing down his heartrate. He opened his eyes again, looking through the lens. The car was heading directly towards him. The driver was busy talking, perhaps trying to calm the former PM's nerves. Churchman knew what was coming. His face reflected it. As the vehicle stopped at the security checkpoint, the former PM closed his eyes. From what Martini could mouth read, he looked as if he were in silent prayer. Martini's finger gripped the trigger, he inhaled, held his breath, then took the shot. The window of the Rolls Royce was sprayed in blood, Churchman slumped to the side. Martini fired the second shot, straight into the seat next to Churchman's shoulder, more blood spraying the interior. There was frantic shouting from the security guards as they ran towards the car. The Rolls charged forward, shattering the access barrier. The driver made a U-turn and raced out of the grounds again, just as planned. The clock was now ticking to get Enda back. Leaving the weapon where it sat, he climbed into the driver's seat and took off, not even checking what was behind him. His only focus now was getting to Berlin.

80

Greenwood was on her way to the weapons dump at Raymond Greer's farm when her phone rang. It was Falkner. 'Commander.'

'He's carried out the hit.'

'What?'

'Former Prime Minister Churchman, who had high hopes of becoming a bestselling author.'

'Christ.' She looked at Black. 'Harper, change of plans, get us to RAF Brize Norton. We need to get to Berlin. Now!'

'Why are you going back there?' Falkner asked.

'I need you to find out who in Berlin would have the money to employ someone with Martini's credentials; and would also want Churchman dead.'

'You've become my boss, now?' Falkner spoke humorously.

'Just do it!' She ended the call and called the Prime Minister. At the same time, she flicked between the radio stations until she landed on Radio One. A news update talking about scenes at Strawberry Hill House.

Prime Minister Pears answered. 'Victoria, you've heard?'

'He's already attacked. He's on his way back to Berlin to the person who's employed him to carry out the hit.'

'Victoria?'

'Yes, ma'am?'

'Do whatever you must to put this bastard down. Do you understand? This bastard has just attacked the heart of our democracy and needs to pay for it. Do you understand?'

'Yes, ma'am.'

'Send me your location the second you know where he is.'

Greenwood ended the call and looked at Black. 'Step on it.'

81

Martini got to the plane and was glad to see his cousin was there waiting for him. Leonardo looked less confident than usual, forcing a smile as Martini coasted the vehicle to an eventual stop. He grabbed his phone from the cradle on the window, and shut the engine off.

'Got the job done I hear!' Leonardo shouted over the noise of the plane, glancing down at his phone. 'Antonio's asking what the hell's going to happen now?'

Martini ran to the back of the Range Rover, opened the boot, and lifted a can of petrol. He emptied the contents all over the cream leather interior. 'I'll call Antonio when we've finished.' Pulling a lighter from his pocket, he lit it and smashed it on the interior dashboard, sending the entire vehicle up in flames. 'Let's go.'

They ran towards the aircraft and got in.

As Martini buckled himself in, his phone went off. It was his sister. 'Lizzy. Are you both away safely?'

'Eamon, tell me you didn't just assassinate former Prime Minister Churchman?'

'I've never lied to you, sis.' He looked across at Leonardo, who'd gone slightly pale. 'I'll explain everything to you when I have a chance.'

'Eamon for *fuck* sake! They'll all be hunting you now. After all these years the heat had finally come off you, but now they'll send everyone after you again.'

Martini sighed.

'And now you've involved me and Karl?'

'Okay, you're right. I'm sorry. I've messed up, but I'll explain it all when I get a chance. I promise. I just need to get to Berlin. I'll call you back in a day or two when this is all over.' He ended the call just as the noise of the plane's engine started to drown out the sound of everything else. 'Christ, this better go to plan.' He looked out the window as the aircraft began to taxi them along the runway.

'I don't like it when you're nervous, Eamon!' Leonardo shouted. 'A man like you isn't supposed to get nervous.'

'I'm not nervous. Just regretful for involving so many other people in this. It could have been a lot cleaner.'

'The person you're working for – who is this guy?'

'One of the richest men in the world. He plays people, and life, like a fucking game of monopoly. But I'll soon make him regret it. Get us to Germany.' He closed his eyes and put his head back against the headrest.

82

They'd just stepped into the aircraft when Falkner called Greenwood's phone. 'Commander, what have you found?'

'There's only one man in the Berlin area that's got the kind of money to pay for Martini's services. Billionaire businessman, Ludwig Schuster.'

'And why'd you think he's the one that's hired Martini to attack the British? He's not just doing it out of fun, I'm sure.'

'According to intelligence, he's half Afghan. A strange mix, I know. His father was German, and his mother was an Afghan who'd left her family behind to marry the German.'

'So, the Afghani link to him is reason enough for him to want Churchman dead?'

'That alone would not have been a strong enough reason. But his cousin –Ahmad Jaleel – recently lost his entire family in a drone strike; on his wedding day. That might just be reason enough for his wealthy cousin to fork out some money to take out one of the people held responsible for turning the Middle East into a warzone. There's another link as well, and it reinforces how Schuster would employ Martini of all people. James Greer has been working with Schuster for the last couple of years.'

'Greer recommended Martini for the job, and had his brother Raymond waiting with old IRA weapons to aid him.' She looked at Black, shaking her head. 'Do you have Schuster's location?' She took her seat and buckled herself in.

'He lives just on the outskirts of Berlin. A huge estate, almost like a bloody golf club. Even has a nice landing area for anyone wishing to visit him by air.'

'That's great. Now we know where we're going.'

'Victoria, you need to be careful.'

She ended the call and briefed Black.

'Whoever said that money can't buy you everything?' Black said.

Greenwood looked at her phone as Falkner's text came through containing Schuster's address. 'This estate is where we'll either find Martini or the people who'd hired him.' She lifted her handbag and removed her pistol. The fourth-generation Glock 17 was the Austrian-born replacement to the old Browning 9mm. Checking the magazine had full capacity with 17 rounds, she put it back in again.

'You seem incredibly determined, ma'am,' Black said, making herself comfortable in her chair. 'More eager than I'd expect.'

'Martini is a man who's evaded capture by the authorities for an exceptionally long time. I'm not going to rest until I've put him down like the dog he is.'

'Sounds personal.'

'Not personal, just business. Eamon Martini is a man who's been at the top of two families that are so anti-government, they almost make Pablo Escobar look like a fucking saint. Bringing him down will be worth all the effort.'

'Seems to me you're better suited for fieldwork than taking old man Falkner's job.' Black smiled. 'With respect, ma'am.'

Greenwood took her coat off, pulled a black shoulder holster out of her bag and put it on then fitted the pistol. She put the coat back on again and said, 'Well, maybe I'll remain in the field for a while. I'll need to find a replacement for Falkner.'

'You could do his job, ma'am. That doesn't mean you have to sit on your ass all day in the office.'

'Perhaps.'

83

Schuster and Jaleel were both sitting in the back garden of the estate when Greer approached. The two were laughing, smiles stretched wide across their faces. They looked as if the celebrations had already started. Greer had just got off the phone and looked as pleased as the other two.

'I've just got off the phone to some friends in London.' Greer pulled a chair out and sat down. He lifted the Moka from the table and poured himself a coffee. 'He's got the job done.' He lifted the cup and blew into it, looking over the rim at Schuster and Jaleel. 'You've got your revenge.' He smiled. 'How does it feel to have avenged the deaths of so many loved ones?'

'It feels like we should be celebrating with more than coffee.' Jaleel stood up. 'I'll go and get something stronger. I know it's against my faith, but Allah will forgive me after what we've done.'

Schuster's face became more serious as his cousin left. He eyed Greer. 'Now that the job's done, will Martini walk away and forget this ever happened or will we need to put measures in place to make sure he doesn't come back again?'

Greer sighed. 'It's always a risk with Eamon.' He took another sip of the coffee then set the cup down, resting his forearms on the table. 'You know his family. Both sides love him. If he were to disappear, you'd have all of them after you. Both the Irish and the Italians. You could awaken a terribly angry beast if something were to happen to him. And that's not taking President Sheeran into consideration, he looks at Martini as a son.'

Schuster's phone alerted him that he'd received a text message. He lifted it and read it. 'Our babysitters have watched the news and know that the job's been done. They ask whether they should bring the boy for the handover.'

Greer studied him for a moment. 'You sound unsure.'

'I knew this moment would come, but now that it's arrived, something inside says that if we hand over our only bargaining chip, we'll have nothing else to use against him. Which is why I ask you, James – is Eamon Martini going to walk away, never to be heard of again, or will we need to go into hiding? If so, we keep the boy, knowing that he's not going to come after us until the boy's safe, or...'

'Or we just waste the both of them when they're here and make them both disappear.' Greer suggested. He looked across the garden as Jaleel made his way towards them, the innocent childlike expression of excitement plastered on his face. 'I hope he's been worth all the aggravation.'

Schuster sighed, watching as his cousin approached. 'I hope so, too.' He cleared his throat. 'I'm paying you quite handsomely, James. You know Martini better than anyone else here.'

'Respond to the text. Tell them to bring the boy here. When Martini comes, we'll decide. But that team of German

Special Forces you have guarding this property need to know something's coming, and they need to be fully prepared to earn the money you're paying them.'

'That's what they're for.'

Greer cleared his throat. 'But if you do this – you'll have to disappear, forever. Ludwig Schuster – the German billionaire, will have to die. You'll become a ghost. You'll have the US President after you when this is done. In fact, Ludwig, I think that it would be best if you start packing your bags now.'

'I don't run from anyone, Mr. Greer.' Schuster said, smiling at Jaleel as he approached the table, nursing a bottle of champagne and three glasses.

'Here we go, gentleman. A glass each.' Jaleel sat down, jamming a corkscrew into the top of the bottle. 'I can't believe that crazy man managed to pull it off. He is something else, this Eamon Martini.'

Greer grunted, looking across at Schuster. 'He is something else, that's for sure.'

84

Inspector Becker was standing in the queue of the Dirty Pig butchers, collecting some meat for dinner, when his phone vibrated in his pocket, sending a vibration down his leg. Three individual vibrations meant he'd received a text from someone work-related. He pulled the iPhone out of his pocket and thumbed in the four-digit passcode. It was a text from Greenwood, asking him to call her as soon as he could.

He exited the shop as he made the call. 'Agent Greenwood, how are you doing this fine day?'

'I've had better days,' she was quick to reply. 'I'm guessing from your tone that you haven't heard the news?'

'What news?'

'Eamon Martini has assassinated former British Prime Minister Churchman while he was on his way to the official release of his autobiography.'

Becker's eyes widened. 'So it was Churchman he was after, then.' He could hear a noise in the background coming from Greenwood's end. 'You're travelling?'

'I'm in the air now. On the way to Berlin. Intel suggests that Martini has been working for one of your locals, a

Ludwig Schuster, and that he's on his way there now to meet with him.'

Becker glanced around the high street, trying to contain his excitement. 'Catching Martini in bed with someone as powerful as Schuster would certainly be a story to tell. One that will be read by many people. This catch would make you famous.'

'That's not really what I care about, Inspector.' She lowered her tone. 'I'm more concerned about punishing the man responsible for leaving a lady widowed and two kids without a father.'

He cleared his throat. 'Yes, of course.' He made his way towards his car.

'Can I ask for your help getting to the Schuster estate?'

He quickly pulled his car door open and got in as the rain started. 'Of course. What time will you be arriving?'

'Within the next hour. I will call you when I arrive. And Inspector, you better keep this operation a secret. You don't know who's on Schuster's payroll.'

He ended the call and started the engine.

85

It was just after three-thirty in the afternoon when Leonardo landed the aircraft. Martini was awoken as it taxied on approach to a rusty old shed next to a derelict farmhouse located on the foothills of the Naturpark West-havelland. The land was owned by the Fischer family, one of the Martini family's associates in the German underworld. Transporting anything from drugs and weapons to illegal immigrants from Europe into England. A business model that had been quite lucrative to both parties – one of Antonio's better business moves. And despite attempting to go legit, the Martini family still found times when it needed to dip its toe back into that world. It appeared to be fortuitous under the circumstances. The airfield was a few miles away from the hub of German organised crime: Berlin; and the Schuster estate.

'We've got about thirty minutes to one hour of walking to do, Eamon. Probably would have been better to just land in this guy's estate?' Leonardo asked, as he shut the engine off.

'That's exactly what he'd be expecting.' Martini lifted a

black gym bag from behind his seat, along with his coat. He put the coat on, opened the door, and got out. It was freezing. 'You can go back to London. And don't say a thing to anyone, Leonardo.' He looked at his cousin. 'You've always been smart. Don't change that now.'

'Bullshit,' Leonardo said. He lifted his coat and disembarked from the other side. 'I'm coming with you.' He shut the door and crossed the nose of the aircraft, approaching Martini. 'You might need help, and we both know our mothers would be turning in their graves if they knew I'd allowed one of the family to go alone into a fight.' He buttoned his suit jacket closed. 'Besides, I might need you to help with the Russians back in London after this.'

Martini fixed Leonardo's coat collar that was sticking up then tapped him on the cheek. 'You can't afford my help.'

'You'll owe me when I stop your old ass from getting shot.'

He laughed.

'Should have brought my gym trainers. I really don't want a long hike in these shoes.'

'There's a hotel a mile down the road. We can grab something to drink and call a taxi.

86

Greenwood and Black stepped off the RAF aircraft at Berlin airport, thankful to have brought overcoats and an umbrella. The rain was heavy and the windchill was almost enough to give frostbite. Greenwood struggled to keep her balance as she disembarked, gripping the flimsy handrail tightly with her left hand. Black tried to open the umbrella, but the wind was too strong. Instead, they both drew their necks as far inside their coats as they could and ran across the runway towards the terminal.

As she stepped inside, Greenwood shook the droplets of rain out of her hair and took her coat off. 'Bloody weather.' She took a packet of tissues from her pocket. 'Here.' She handed Black a couple to dry her face before doing the same. 'You hungry?'

'Starving.'

'Good, we can get something warm inside us while we wait for Becker.'

Greenwood led the way through two sets of automatic doors displaying a sign in German reading *No Return Beyond This Point*. Her phone rang in her pocket, repeatedly. She wouldn't have answered had the sound not begun to annoy her. Falkner's name flashed across the screen.

'We've just landed. Waiting on Becker to get us from the airport.'

'The PM has agreed to send two of Dott's men across to Berlin with me. He wants Martini as much as we do and is willing to lend a hand.'

'With all due respect, Commander, you no longer work for British Intelligence, so why am I hearing this from you and not the PM directly?'

'I'll pretend you didn't say that, Victoria.' He sounded stunned. 'We're being flown over to Berlin via RAF. We'll be with you soon. Don't do anything until we arrive. Becker's been informed.'

She looked at Black, her jaw clenched. 'And what if we lose Martini while sitting around?'

'Becker has informed me that a German undercover is working for Schuster. They've said that Schuster has ordered the special package to be brought to his estate. It's part of the deal with Martini. The package is on its way, but still hasn't arrived. So, you've got time. Sit down, have some food, and entertain Becker. Or try to let Becker entertain you.' He was attempting to lighten the mood, but it wasn't working.

'I'll keep you posted.' She ended the call and stormed across the arrivals hall towards Burger King.

Black rushed to keep up, 'What was that all about?'

'An American who was brought over to attend the security meeting, has offered to help us.'

'And why is that such a bad thing? Surely it can't hurt to have extra hands?'

'We don't need help, and that obnoxious dick will just come over here and take over, like everyone else.' She slammed her handbag down on the nearest table, flinging her coat over the back of a seat. 'What would you like?'

'Burger and fries.' Black hung her jacket over her seat and sat down.

'Drink?'

'Diet Coke.'

Greenwood made her way towards the counter, joining a queue of six. The couple in front of her was young, perhaps mid-twenties. The girl was wearing a backpack with *Berlin University* stitched into the flap. The guy looked like a rugby player, big and muscular. He wore baggy shorts, flip-flops, and a white hoodie. The girl was telling the guy how she'd been thinking of going to Milan in the summer. He joked and asked what kind of work he would be qualified to do in Italy, highlighting the fact that the only spoken Italian he knew was ciao and pasta. She suggested he buy a car and become an Uber driver. That one word – driver struck Greenwood like a bolt of lightning. 'How could I have not known?' She thought out loud, taking a step closer to the counter. 'And how the hell did Falkner never realise anything was up with that guy? He'd been working for him all those years.' She unlocked her phone and looked at the last message she'd received from Page. It was a daily text he'd send her, wishing her a good night and that he'd see her in the morning. They were close. They'd worked well together. He seemed like such a genuine guy.

Just a great actor, putting it on all the time.

She sniggered and shook her head. Martini was a clever bastard.

Without realising what she was doing, she pressed the call icon by mistake, and was about to end the call when Page answered. Her heart jumped to her throat.

'I'm sorry this all came out like this, ma'am,' Page said, sounding sorrowful.

'Don't give me that,' she scoffed. 'I've got to hand it to you, you've deceived everyone. How'd nobody ever know you were tied to Martini?'

'That's a discussion for another time, ma'am. I've always respected you and genuinely loved working for you. So, for that, I'll give you a bit of advice: go back to London, accept Eamon Martini won, and just get on with your life. You don't want to end up like Falkner, spending the rest of your life chasing a ghost. You won't catch him, and if you do, trust me, you'll be the one that comes off worse for it.'

She sniggered. 'Trust? Not sure you know the meaning of the word.'

'I'm sorry you feel that way. I have to go. Take care and just go home. Berlin won't end well for you.' He ended the call.

She ordered the food and paced around as she waited. Fuming.

She watched Black fiddling on her phone as she approached the table. She set the tray down and asked, 'You're not working for Martini, too, are you?'

Black smirked and reached across the table, lifting her fries. She shook her head and said, 'I'm one of the good guys, don't worry.'

Greenwood took a fry from the box and took a bite. 'Yeah. So was Karl.'

87

During their forty-minute walk, Martini had booked a taxi, which was waiting for them when they arrived at the Alt Berlin – an historic tavern with an expansive beer garden which, due to the weather was empty. Leonardo had joked about going in for a few, but Martini had told him a drink might settle his nerves, but would undoubtedly be an unwise choice, given the fact they weren't in Berlin on holiday.

The Mercedes, operated by a Berlin based taxi firm: Taxiunternehmen, brought them to a house, shortening another fifty-minute walk down to ten minutes, the cab gave them a chance to warm up, which was as welcome as a bowl of vegetable soup. The property was a new build. Martini quickly exited the vehicle as Leonardo paid the 23 euro fare. The house looked empty, like nobody had settled in it yet. The driveway was still covered in dry cement and plaster, fragments of powder blowing around in the wind. A large orange cement mixer sat outside the double garage with a ton-bag full of builder's yellow sand. Martini approached the house. A row of five plant pots lined the front wall below the living room window. He lifted the third from the left, finding a key. He waited at the front door for Leonardo to catch up.

'Is this yours?' Leonardo said, walking up the driveway, his suit jacket draped over his shoulder.

'No. It belonged to Seamus and Mary O'Toole, old friends of my pop from Belfast. It was their ongoing project, a dream home they wanted to retire in.' He turned and inserted the key into the lock. Opening the door, he stepped inside. His chest tightened with the smell of emulsion. 'But they'll not get to enjoy it now – and the bastard that killed them is going to regret that.'

'What happened to them?' Leonardo closed the door, putting his jacket on. The house was cold enough for them to see their breath rising from their mouths.

Martini cleared his throat, leading the way into the kitchen, 'A mistake of mine cost them their lives.' Turning the lights on, he scanned the area. It was in immaculate condition. Almost too perfect.

'Died recently?' Leonardo made his way towards the fridge. He opened the door and found nothing but four bottles of water and as many cans of German lager.

'Murdered a few days ago because I'd walked back into their lives.'

'Maybe it's not such a good idea for us to be here then, Eamon.' Leonardo grabbed two cans and made his way across the kitchen, handing one to Martini, but he refused.

'Few people know this place exists. This was kind of their hidden gem. And we're only here for some protection.'

'And what – you thought you'd come here and stroll around a murdered couple's house? You're feeling nostalgic?' Leonardo cracked his can open. 'Come on, Eamon. You're the smart one in the family.'

Martini ignored him. 'As much as Seamus and Mary had tried to become normal members of society, moving away from the republican movement after the ceasefire, I know Seamus kept weapons for protection. All active members within the movement were given protection. Seamus and Mary never had any problems with the local law, despite being well-known active participants of the war at home. As long as they didn't attract any attention to themselves, German law enforcement left them alone.' He looked at the camera mounted to the wall in the corner of the room, above the door they'd just entered through. 'But Seamus was a paranoid bastard. There's CCTV all over the place. I want to know who's been here since they died.' He looked at Leonardo. 'Have a seat, we won't be here long.' He made his way towards the door that led out into the garden.

'I've found some Spaghetti Bolognaise in the cupboard. You go and explore the house if you like, but I'm starving. I'll feel much better with a warm Italian meal in my stomach.'

Martini stepped out into the back garden. The garden was big enough to house a football pitch, edged with hedgerows and flowerbeds. A summer house was to the right. He followed the cobbled path that snaked through the newly grown grass. The summer house had a complete glass front. He opened the door and stepped inside. A hunting rifle hung from the wall facing him. The room was small, cosy, and split in two. A kitchen to the right and a living area to the left, with an eight-seater dining table separating the two areas. He imagined that this was where Seamus would have spent a lot of his time. He had always been the type to be more comfortable in something smaller than a big, posh house.

A collection of CCTV monitors sat neatly in the corner of the room, sandwiched between the white sofa and the adjacent recliner. After saving the footage from the previous three days to his pen drive, he made his way back to the house.

Leonardo was frying mince in the pan while playing Andrea Bocelli on Spotify.

'Find anything interesting?'

Martini sat down at the table, pulling his laptop out of the bag. 'I'll let you know in a minute.' He opened the computer and powered it up, inserting the device into one of the USB ports along the left side. As he waited for the computer to boot, he called Greer.

Greer answered almost immediately. 'Eamon, where are you?' He sounded concerned. 'We're waiting for you.'

'I know you are. I'm just having Spaghetti Bolognaise, then I'll be at the estate.'

'What? Why don't you just come here? We can have the cook prepare something.'

'I'll be a couple of hours, at the most.' He ended the call. 'How would you fancy joining the German police?' He called across to Leonardo.

'Like I'd enjoy a bullet in the head,' Leonardo replied, stirring the sauce into the frying pan. Martini sniggered. He accessed the CCTV footage, setting it to the day Seamus and Mary were killed, and put it to high speed fast forward. They had had three visits to the house the evening they were killed: one by the police, one by Schuster, and one by Lyttle. That bastard Schuster never missed a trick.

'I want to play a little game,' Martini said. 'I'm going to record us both in here, sitting at the table, and keep it on repeat. We'll call the police and report a break-in, with some shots being fired. When the police come, we're switching places with them and taking their car. That'll get us into Schuster's estate without any real problems.'

'Just a quick question, Eamon. Why is the safe return of the president's grandson your responsibility? This is dangerous, and if we're caught, we're both fucked.'

Martini looked across the kitchen at his cousin. 'The president has been a close friend of our family – both the Martinis and the Clearys – since before we were born. He was supportive of the republican movement in Ireland. Back during the time of Bloody Sunday, he campaigned against the internment of Irish Catholics. He was close to my father. And I've been by his side long before he was president. He may be our president right now, but he's an old friend first.'

'Never knew that,' Leonardo said. 'Jesus.'

'Why do you think our family had been allowed to operate in America and elsewhere with such a high profile?'

He looked unsure of how to respond.

Martini looked at his phone. A BBC News alert on his phone read: *Former Prime Minister Churchman Pronounced Dead On Arrival To West Middlesex Emergency Department.* Prime Minister Pears had issued a statement saying this was an attack on a man who tried to bring peace and stability to the Middle East. She said that the new head of MI6 was currently following up leads on the suspect, but other than that, nothing else could be said at that time.

'There's something about Commander Falkner's replacement that bothers me. She's very smart.'

'You're not afraid of some British Agent outsmarting you, are you, Eamon?' Leonardo joked. 'A battle of wits with Eamon Martini is hardly going to end well for her.'

'Don't blow smoke up my ass.'

Leonardo laughed, bringing the steaming pot over to the table. 'No more talking about this bullshit. We'll have our dinner then go and finish the job.' He handed a plate over to Martini and began tipping spaghetti onto both of their plates. 'Buon appetito.'

88

Becker reached the Arrivals Terminal just as Greenwood and Black were leaving the food court, Black with a coffee to go. He stood at the exit, shivering in the cold with his over-coat wrapped tightly around him, the left side of his collar flicked up, blowing against his cheek.

'You look like you're not used to this weather,' Greenwood said, pulling her coat closed in the wind.

'Who can ever get used to this terrible weather?' He joked. 'My dream is to retire somewhere warmer. I hope sooner rather than later.' He turned and led them towards the carpark.

'It's good that you've got a sense of humour,' Greenwood said.

'In this line of work, it's important to have one, is it not? You could be dead at any moment. We may as well have a few laughs along the way.'

'I'm sorry, Inspector, but a man lies dead back in London. He woke up today thinking he was celebrating his life and what he did to make the world a safer place, now it's been cut short.'

'Mr. Churchman knew the risks he took.' Becker unlocked a black Audi Q7 and climbed into the driver's seat. 'And Mr. Martini knows the risks he has taken.' He started the engine. 'We have rats in our midst, I don't know if it's from your side or ours, so I'm afraid it'll just be us. If there are people in my office who I can't trust, I don't want them feeding information back to Mr. Martini, alerting him of what we're doing.' He put the SUV in drive and pulled away. 'What about the Americans?'

'Dott's agents?' Greenwood asked, lowering the window next to her. 'Screw them.'

'Your employer has left strict instructions that we are to wait for them.'

'Commander Falkner is no longer my superior. And I'll deal with him when I get back to London. Let's just get this guy before he disappears again, and we lose our chance of catching him. I want to be there when the son of a bitch arrives at Schuster's home.'

'Who's the young recruit in the back?' Becker glanced into the rear-view mirror.

'Agent Harper Black, sir,' Black said, looking at the Walther P99 clasped tightly in her grip.

'You look nervous, sweetie,' Becker said. He switched his gaze to Greenwood. 'You think it was wise to bring a kid to such a big event?'

'Less of the sweetie, old man.' Black was quick to respond. Greenwood burst into a fit of laughter. 'I'm no kid.'

'No offense, young lady,' Becker continued, 'But it's just that this is a dangerous game. You don't want to risk losing your life at such a young age.'

'Agent Black is the best of the best in British Intelligence.' Greenwood was quick to her defence. 'She's got as much skill as someone with twice the experience.'

Becker nodded, guiding the SUV along the road, building up speed. 'The fearlessness of youth. Yes, I can imagine.' He cast a glance back at Black. 'Keen to impress.'

'When I put a bullet in Eamon Martini, I'll soon show you how wet behind the ears I am.' She glared back at him in the mirror.

'How long until we get to the estate?' Greenwood said, changing the subject.

'Twenty minutes. But I suggest we get you both equipped slightly better before going. We don't know what we will be walking into. We'll need to have you both protected.' He looked across at Greenwood. 'Are you wearing body armour?'

'I'm sure you could assist us with that. But I don't plan on going into a fire-fight.'

'Come on, Victoria. You're going after one of the most notorious hired guns in the world. You expect him to not have a contingency plan for the contingency's contingency?'

'That's a lot of contingencies.' Black joked.

'That's Eamon Martini,' Becker replied. 'And I'm sorry, but if I'm going into a potentially volatile situation with you two, then I can't afford to have you both get hurt needlessly and slow me down.'

89

Martini set the CCTV at a thirty-minute recording loop. A repeating video of them sat at the table. Nothing too obvious in the shot that would give it away as a hoax. He made a call to the local police station, reporting a break-in and a lot of noise, including what sounded like gunfire. Police were on the way.

'Can't believe you're making me put on a cop's uniform.' Leonardo complained.

Martini smirked, leaning against the frame of the front door, the door slightly ajar. 'I'm not too happy about it either. But it's the best way for us to get in there without having to use force. He's got grounds security. A team of ex-German Special Forces, heavily armed.'

'Always the thinking man. Never one to use force.'

'We'll live longer this way.'

After a five-minute wait in silence, the flashing blue lights of a marked police vehicle danced across the ground where they both stood. Martini looked across at Leonardo. 'You pretend you've made the call when they come in, I'll appear behind them and we'll cuff them and leave them here.' He produced his pistol – a Desert Eagle .50. The sound of car doors closing was followed by the crunching of the officers' shoes off the gravel. Both were male. One was a few inches over six feet tall and thin. The one who had been driving was a few inches shorter, and more muscular.

'Is anyone here?' the driver shouted.

Martini looked at Leonardo, cocking his head, indicating for him to move.

'Yes,' Leonardo shouted back. Gritting his teeth, he hissed at Martini. 'I can't speak a lot of German.' He stood at the door, pulling it open further, allowing the officers to come in, their weapons drawn, but now aimed. The two followed Leonardo towards the living room. Martini pushed the door closed, with his pistol pointed at them. The slam of the door caused both officers to spin around.

'No sudden movements, gentlemen,' Martini said in German. 'Neither of you will be harmed. We just need your uniforms and your car.' He looked at Leonardo. 'Disarm them, then cuff them.'

Leonardo smirked as he approached the two. 'You're getting me into a lot more trouble than I would have wanted,' he mumbled in Italian.

'You had your chance to go back.'

Leonardo grabbed the taller of the two who tried to resist, but Martini reminded him that he was holding a weapon.

'You know what will happen to you for this?' The shorter officer said. 'You'll have the entire German police force after you.' He spoke to Martini, looking at him with suspicious eyes. 'Who are you?'

'He's the one who murdered the people that owned this place,' the other officer answered. 'Why else would he be here?'

'For what it's worth,' Martini said, 'I'm not the one who murdered Seamus and Mary O'Toole, but I can assure you, the person who's responsible for their deaths will be dealt with. Don't worry about that.'

Leonardo cuffed the taller one to the three-inch-thick copper piping that ran up from the ground, supplying water to the radiator; then did the same with the other officer. Taking the keys from the officer's pocket, he ran out of the house. 'I'm not wearing their smelly bloody uniform, but if they have a change of clothes...' he mumbled. He released the boot and pulled out two coats and two pairs of trousers, still in their plastic coverings. He slammed the boot closed and went back to the house, tossing a set of trousers and a jacket to Martini.

'Forget the trousers, the coats will do,' Martini said.

Leonardo tossed the key to Martini.

'You drive,' Martini said, tossing it back over.

'Leonardo Martini, driving a police vehicle.' He shook his head as he got to the door, pulling it open. He looked across the roof at his cousin. 'You tell anyone about this, and we'll have a problem.'

Martini smirked and got into the passenger seat. 'I've already sent texts to Antonio and the Apostles.'

90

Becker checked into the station. He grabbed three Stealth Pro bulletproof vests, and his issue Heckler & Kosh SFP9, then joined Greenwood and Black back in the car.

'Here, put these on.' He passed a vest to Black and handed the other across to Greenwood. 'Hopefully, we won't need them, but better safe than sorry.' He started the engine and put the car in gear. 'Let's go and put this son of a bitch down, once and for all.'

As the vehicle took off, Greenwood's phone rang. She looked at the screen, then shook her head. 'Fuck,' she said, 'the PM.' She answered it with the window down, letting some air into the tense cabin. 'Ma'am?'

'Greenwood, you've spoken with Commander Falkner?' She sounded angry, and Greenwood knew why.

'You mean have I spoken to the man who retired from the job and left me in charge?' She waited for the PM's response, but nothing came. 'Yes, I've spoken to him.'

'Then why the hell is Falkner, Dott and a couple of Secret Service agents standing around like fools, left behind at the airport, while you're off trying to catch Martini?'

'Dott? He's a pen pusher, what the fuck's he doing here?'

'Dott served many years in the Secret Service as an agent before taking his current role. He's more than capable of helping us get Martini.'

'Ma'am, with all due respect, we both know the Americans will try to move in and take over. Martini is more valuable to them alive. Christ he's an ex-Secret Service agent himself. Having them around is a big mistake. This is our responsibility, and they're not getting involved.'

'This isn't a competition, Victoria,' Pears sighed, 'Do you understand what the word "Ally" means?'

'Martini has struck right at the heart of British democracy. A Prime Minister – former or current, it doesn't matter. This cannot go unchecked.'

The PM paused for a moment before answering. 'Don't bring me back bad news, Victoria. Falkner has vouched for you; don't disappoint. If the commander asks, I'll pretend I didn't reach you. Get it done. Now – my list of engagements has quadrupled following what's taken place this morning. I might be hard to reach for a while.'

'Have you seen the body?'

'What?'

'Churchman's body, ma'am, have you seen it?'

'Why's that important?'

'Just want to know what damage was done?'

'Well, according to the hospital, his face was beyond recognition.' She paused, then cleared her throat. 'The damage that's caused to a person from a sniper rifle.'

'Jesus. Poor bastard.'

'Just get him, Victoria.'

'Yes, ma'am.'

'And Victoria?'

'Ma'am?'

'Take care and bring yourself back here in one piece.'

She looked across the car at Becker, then back at Black who was fastening the straps on her vest. 'Ma'am.' She ended the call.

Becker cast a glance at her as she lowered the phone from her ear. 'What did your PM have to say?'

'Get the bastard.'

'We'll get him,' Black said, finishing up the last button of her blouse. She re-dressed the shoulder holster and removed the P99. Releasing the magazine, she glanced up at Becker in the rear-view mirror and forced it back in again with a satisfying click.

91

Ludwig Schuster was standing in his driveway admiring his car collection when the sound of the estate gates opening snatched his attention. A blue Sprinter van approached.

Greer and Jaleel joined Schuster as the van pulled up beside them. A man wearing a black leather jacket, navy jeans and brown boots emerged from the driver's side; he had a plain black cap pulled down, shielding his eyes. A lady dressed similar to the driver, minus the hat, emerged from the passenger side. Both looked between mid-thirties, and fit. They walked with a straight, confident posture – like those in the military or similar position.

Schuster approached them. 'Any problems?'

'Apart from the situation on the boat, no,' the lady replied. She spoke with an American accent. 'We put the kid to sleep. After I shot Torres and Hawkins, he wouldn't stop crying. Needed to shut him up.' She pulled the sliding door open, reached in and dragged Enda Sheeran out. The kid was barely able to keep his eyes open, circled in red rings. Dry blood was caked around both nostrils, with two lines running down to his swollen lip. He moved without protest, as if he'd accepted that if he struggled, he'd get more of what he'd already been given.

'Get him inside,' Schuster said, 'Put him in the room next to the kitchen, and lock the door. Martini will be here soon.'

'Yes, sir.'

They brought the boy inside, without any protest from him. He looked weak; his legs ready to give way under him.

Greer addressed Schuster and Jaleel. 'My advice: hand the boy over and pray Martini just walks away from it today. You'll at least have a chance to run. I doubt he'll enter into a fire-fight with the kid around.'

'Or we take him out and not spend the rest of our lives looking over our shoulders,' Schuster replied.

'Fuck Mr. Martini,' Jaleel spoke mockingly, 'I will end his life. We will not run and hide from anyone.'

Greer sniggered. 'You? You already tried that, didn't you? Look how well that turned out. You're lucky you're still breathing after your little stunt in the garden the other night. Now shut the fuck up.'

'I will end your life, too, Irishman.'

'Enough!' Schuster shouted. 'I'm going to get washed up. He'll be here soon. I at least want to shake his hand for a job well done.' He made his way into the house, Greer and Jaleel close behind. 'Maybe he can still be bought.'

'I want to thank you, cousin, for doing this. I think perhaps now I can sleep knowing I have avenged the deaths of our family,' Jaleel said, tagging along behind Schuster like a grateful puppy dog.

Schuster didn't respond.

'Don't thank him yet,' Greer said.

92

Becker approached the gates of Schuster's estate. Pressing the buzzer, he got Schuster.

'Mr. Becker, how can I be of help?'

'Just a few questions if you don't mind, Ludwig.'

The gate began to open, and Becker guided the vehicle slowly up the driveway.

Greenwood looked at the armed guard watching them as they ascended the driveway. She turned to Black. 'You've wanted to be part of something big since you joined the agency. Well, now you're getting your chance.'

'Yes, ma'am,' Black said forcefully, as if she were trying to overcompensate for the anxiety she was feeling on the inside. She looked over her shoulder through the rear window, the guard was still watching.

Becker clearly picked up on her nervousness and said, 'You'll be okay, Ms. Black. By tomorrow, you'll be known as one of the people that brought down the man who's evaded British capture for too long.'

They approached the front of the house, passing a blue van, then parked alongside Schuster's car collection.

'That van looks a little out of place next to all those,' Greenwood said, eyeing up the line of cars. 'The things money can buy.' She got out of the car. Black and Becker did the same.

Becker waved towards the front door where Schuster had just stepped out onto the porch.

'You've brought guests?' Schuster shouted, wearing an overly enthusiastic smile.

Before Becker had a chance to respond, Greenwood said, 'We're here for a Mr. Martini. We believe that he's here. Or will be soon.'

'And you are?' Schuster asked, as he descended the steps of the porch.

'Agent Victoria Greenwood, MI6. I'm sure you've heard about the assassination of former British Prime Minister Churchman on the day of his book signing.'

'And why would you believe such a criminal would be coming here?'

The sound of a gunshot behind Greenwood caused her to spin around, Black had taken a shot to the left leg, then another to the right. She fell to the ground, fighting to get back to her feet and cursing Becker. Becker now had his gun pointed at Greenwood.

'It's amazing the kind of things money can buy, Agent Greenwood,' Schuster said. He looked at Becker. 'Get them inside. Put them in the storeroom with the boy.'

'Why not just kill them?' Becker asked.

'Dead hostages are useless hostages, Mr. Becker.' Schuster stood to the side, hands in his pockets. The lady that arrived in the van came to the front door, her male accomplice close on her heels. Schuster looked at them. 'You two, get this wounded lady inside and get her wounds tended to. I want the bleeding stopped.'

'Yes, sir,' the male said.

Becker pushed Greenwood up the steps and into the house.

Schuster slowly circled Black's blood on the driveway, shaking his head.

Jaleel came from around the rear of the house. 'What happened?'

Schuster looked up at his cousin. 'Get this blood cleaned up off my driveway. Fucking British agents, think they can stroll in here and get blood all over my property.' He made his way along the front of the house, towards the back garden.

Strolling across the garden to the seating area, he looked up at the sky and inhaled deeply. 'Come on, Mr. Martini. I'm waiting.' He approached the table and sat down. Lifting the lid of the coffee pot, he noticed that it was empty and shouted for Greer in the kitchen to bring him another pot. He checked his phone. Looking at the top story on World News, he was proud of the fact that he'd been responsible for the story. There was now a nationwide manhunt for the culprit. The former President of the United States of America, and close friend of Churchman, had expressed his sincere condolences, and hoped the perpetrator would soon be brought to justice.

'Yes,' Schuster said. 'And you're lucky we haven't sent Mr. Martini after you, too.'

93

Martini and Leonardo arrived at Schuster's home shortly after seven-thirty. It was a frosty night beneath the star-studded black canvas above, stretching as far as the eye could see. Leonardo stopped the car on the brow of the hill just one hundred yards short of the estate's imposing black gates. He looked across at Martini. 'Alright, Eamon – what's the plan?'

'We get to the gates, pretend to be honest members of the German police force until we get in. Then we catch them off guard, eliminate their security, and go from there.' He checked the Heckler and Koch which he'd taken off one of the officers. The weapon was fully loaded. 'You're armed?'

Leonardo nodded, flashing Martini the Heckler taken from the other officer. 'It's loaded.'

'You've got your own as a backup?'

Leonardo pulled his coat open, revealing his holstered Sig Saur with a suppressor fitted. 'Fully loaded.'

Martini reached into his holster and pulled out his Desert Eagle. He checked it was loaded, tightened the suppressor, and returned it to its cradle. He looked at

Leonardo, who was pulling on his hat, completing his German police uniform. 'This was never going to be a simple handover. And *they* know I know that. So, let's go and finish this. We get President Sheeran's grandson and get out of here again. In and out, fast, Leonardo. As I mentioned earlier, this guy's got ex-Special Forces as his estate security. Heavily armed. We take them out at the gate first. But we do it quietly, maintaining our cover until we can't.'

'How many guards does he have?'

'The other day he only had one guy on the gate.' He smirked.

Leonardo cleared his throat, his breathing deepening, his chest beginning to rise and fall.

Martini knew his cousin was nervous. Despite the fact that all the Martini family had experience in the New York Italian underworld, all had fired weapons and Leonardo, Paolo and Pietro had all served briefly in the US military; but only Eamon Martini had made a career out of combat, so he could understand the nerves Leonardo was experiencing. 'Or you can turn back. Wait for me somewhere. I go in by myself.'

'Forget it, Eamon. I said it earlier – we're family.' He put the car into gear and moved off. Approaching the gates, he lowered the window, reached out, and pressed the buzzer next to the external post box, calling for access.

After about thirty seconds, which felt more like thirty minutes, the gates slowly began to part.

The distant hum of a helicopter could be heard from the distance, a tiny dot cutting through the sky, approaching them from the west.

'I wonder if that's company for us?' Leonardo said, gesturing towards the chopper.

'No idea, but they might just think it's my arrival.'

Martini spoke quietly, making their way in through the gates.

The mansion sat up at the top of the hilled driveway, sitting like a king atop of his throne, perhaps the feeling Schuster had every time he arrived home. They were stopped by a security guard, putting out his giant, shovel of a hand, for them to stop. Leonardo stopped next to the guy as the gates closed behind them again, shutting out the world.

Martini noted that the guard was different from the one he had seen last time. He was dressed the same – black trousers, black shoes, white shirt, and black tie under a jacket, armed with an AK47 assault rifle. From the intimidating stare on his face, Martini doubted he'd be shy of firing the thing.

Leonardo lowered the window, and the guard approached his door, crouching down to speak with him. Martini discarded the Heckler and quickly produced his silenced Eagle, reached across Leonardo's chest, shooting the guard in the forehead. The guy was dead instantly. His eyes rolled into the back of his head, showing all white, blood shot out of the back of his head. The sound of it spilling on the ground was followed by his dead weight and the metallic clunk of his weapon.

Martini jumped out of the car, ran around to the driver's side, grabbed the guard's rifle, and passed it in through the driver's window to Leonardo. 'You see anyone other than an eight-year-old boy, you start firing right at them.' He crouched down, grabbed the dead man's ankles, and dragged him towards the security hut, pulling him inside and closing the door after him. He checked the CCTV monitors on the desk next to the door. Monitor three was showing Schuster and Greer in the back garden at the outdoor kitchen area. Monitor seven had Jaleel packing a suitcase in one of the bedrooms on the first floor. The chopper was still circling above. He quickly checked the shift rota pinned to the notice board on the wall, next to a collection of torches, keys, and hi-vis jackets. According to the rota, only one man was ever on shift, but four out of the twelve-man team were always on standby, a maximum of three minutes away from the sound of an alarm. Meaning once Schuster knew what was happening, they'd soon have some highly paid, highly trained guards coming for them. He couldn't risk exposing Enda to flying bullets, so it had to be done quietly.

He stepped outside and pulled the door closed, engaging the lock. He crossed the front of the car and jumped back into the passenger's seat.

'Take us right up to the front door.' He looked across at Leonardo. 'You alright?'

Leonardo looked at him. 'I'm good, stop worrying.'

He parked the car right outside the front door at the bottom of the porch steps.

'Anyone here is guilty of kidnapping or at least supporting the kidnapping of the boy. Shoot on first sight. Don't second guess it, just fucking shoot.'

They both got out, approaching the door.

The front door was open.

Martini entered first, looking over his shoulder, checking Leonardo was right behind him. They stepped inside. Martini closed the front door, scanning the area. He could hear Jaleel upstairs, crossing the hallway, the claps of his heels getting louder.

He came running down the stairs. 'That must be Martini in the chopper.' Getting to the bottom of the stairs, he took one look around at the two officers behind him.

'Wrong, Mr. Jaleel. Mr. Martini is right here.' Martini spoke mockingly, approaching him, the AK pointed at his head. He flipped the rifle around in his hand, clocking Jaleel across the head with the handle, dropping him to his knees. He interlocked his fingers into Jaleel's hair, right at the crown, and dragged him back up to feet, marching him across the entrance hall, through the kitchen, and out into the back garden. He pressed the barrel of the gun to Jaleel's back. 'Lead the way.'

Greer and Schuster were both in a fit of laugher at something, Greer was pointing up at the chopper in the sky, Schuster was looking down at the end of the garden towards the pool house, the chopper's landing pod just beyond it.

Fifty yards from them, Martini said, 'If you're expecting that to be me, guess again.'

Greer and Schuster both turned and stood up, Schuster knocking into the table and toppling his drink over. Greer looked like a rabbit caught in the headlights. Schuster was more composed, a smirk stretching across his face.

'I'm not here to waste time,' Martini said. He pushed Jaleel in front of him a couple of steps, then put a bullet in the back of his head. Schuster reached for a pistol that sat on the table, Martini took aim and put two in his chest and one in his head. His body fell to the ground, dead before it hit the grass.

Martini approached the table. Greer stood there, trying to swallow what looked like a tennis ball stuck in his throat.

'Leonardo, meet Ludwig Schuster, one of the wealthiest men in the world.' Martini gestured at Schuster's body. 'Or should I say, was.'

'Pleasure,' Leonardo spoke mockingly, standing over the corpse.

Martini looked at Greer. 'Take me to the kid, now.' He

looked at Leonardo and handed him the AK. 'Keep an eye on whoever's in that chopper. Don't forget that they think you're a cop. When they get close, point the AK at them. I'll be out in two seconds.'

'Just don't take too long.'

Martini grabbed Greer, pushing him ahead. 'Walk.' Greer did as he was told. 'You don't look surprised?'

Greer shook his head. 'With you, Eamon – nothing surprises me.' He sauntered, as if his life had been snatched from him, and he was simply going through the motions. A man accepting his fate. 'The president sent the right man, that's for sure.'

'It's funny how you had me almost believing for a moment that you were being forced into this. There isn't an ounce of remorse on your face. You have the face of a man who knows he's been caught, without even a hint of protest at your innocence. You make me sick. I once respected you. Thought you were like a brother to my father.'

'Mr. Above-It-All.' Greer sniggered. 'You were born with the wealth of your Italian family. You never needed to think about how you were going to make ends meet.'

'Don't forget about the political morality of my Irish family.' He joked as he pushed the Heckler into the back of Greer's head. They entered the kitchen, crossed the room to the door where Enda was being held. It was locked. Greer lifted a key off a hook on the wall and opened the door. Inside was a narrow eight by six-cell. No windows. There was a tiny vent in the top corner next to the plumbing. Enda Sheeran was handcuffed to the radiator. Martini recognised Greenwood from the reports on the TV, but didn't recognise the other female with her.

Greer glanced back at Martini. 'Here you go. We'll even throw in a couple of British agents, Eamon.'

Martini looked at Greer, then down at the two. What was going on?

'Eamon Martini – meet Agent Victoria Greenwood. She's supposed to be Commander Falkner's replacement. And the lady with a slight injury to her legs is Agent Harper Black.' He looked amused, glaring down at them. 'Ms. Greenwood – here is the man you came all the way to Germany to kill.' A smug grin stretched across his face, even when he had no way out. 'If you don't want her, then there's plenty of other people who would have a lot of fun with a hot piece of ass like that.'

Martini spun the pistol around and drove it into the back of Greer's head, he fell to the ground. 'Let them all go.' He spun the gun around again and waited for Greer to get back to his feet, then forced the barrel into the back of his head, forcing him further into the room.

Martini looked at the boy, who was trembling and sniffling, his eyes red and swollen. 'You okay, kid?'

The boy glanced up at Martini, nodding his head, but he didn't speak.

Martini looked at Greenwood then Black. 'What about you two?'

Greenwood nodded. 'We're fine.' She gazed at him, her eyes filling up like tiny glasses of water. She looked unsure of what was to come. 'So, you killed Churchman to save a boy? It's still murder.'

'Churchman's not dead.'

'What?'

'It was all a setup, so I could buy some time to get the kid back.' Martini nodded towards the lad who was now free. 'I was...'

'On your six!' Greenwood shouted, looking over his shoulder.

Martini heard the unmistakable crack of a pistol, then a burning sensation in his right shoulder. He spun around, dropping to his knee, firing a shot at a male approaching the doorway, hitting him in the chest, sending him falling backwards. Martini stood up, gripping his shoulder where warm blood was soaking up the sleeve, a trickle running down the outside of his arm, building up at his elbow then carrying on down to his hand. It was a flesh wound that would need tending to, but not life-threatening. He walked over to the man and put another round in his head, spraying the floor with blood and brain matter.

'Behind you.' Greenwood shouted. Martini spun around. Greer jabbed a knife towards his chest. Martini dropped his gun and caught Greer's wrist just a few inches from his heart. Greer was strong, he was pressing hard, forcing Martini back against the wall. Martini was losing strength in his right arm, he'd eventually weaken. Greer's face was just a few inches from Martini's; they both glared into the other's eyes. Martini could see his reflection in Greer's glazed eyes, he could smell coffee and cigarette smoke off Greer's breath. Both of their hands began to shake, each trying to overpower the other. Martini felt Greer began to weaken, too. Martini looked down at the blade, trembling uncontrollably in their grip, he pulled upwards, the point of the blade turning from his chest, pointing to the ceiling, then, with all the energy he could muster, forced it upwards into the centre of Greer's throat, right through the Adam's apple. His eyes rolled into the back of his head and his body jerked for a moment as he choked on his own blood. Martini pushed Greer away from him, grabbed his pistol, and put a bullet in his head. Greer's lifeless body fell against the wall and slid to the ground, leaving thick red streaks of blood on the white paint. The keys to the cuffs lay on the floor next to Enda who was curled up in a ball, trembling uncontrollably.

Martini grabbed the keys and looked down at Greenwood. She was looking back up at him, breathing deeply.

'So, you came here to put a bullet in my head?'

'Following orders,' she admitted.

He crouched down, looking straight into her eyes. He inserted the key into the cuff. 'Nice to meet you, Agent Greenwood.'

She shook her head. 'Nice to finally get my hands on you, Mr. Martini.'

'It appears I'm the one that's got my hands on you.' She didn't respond. He looked at Black. 'Now, we need to work together if we're to get out of here. We can do whatever we need to do after this. Can we at least cooperate until then? According to the security desk, we have a few minutes before the other guards roll in here. And they're heavily armed.' He stood up and tossed the cuffs on the ground, looking at the kid. 'Are you injured or can you at least keep up with us?'

Enda nodded. 'I can keep up.'

Martini looked at Black. 'We're going to have to carry you.'

They got her to her feet, both Greenwood and the boy acting as her crutch.

Martini turned and approached the door, peering out into the hallway. 'Let's go.' He looked back at Greenwood. 'Do you have a weapon?'

She pulled the knife that was plunged into Greer's throat and wiped the blood on his shirt. 'I do now.'

'Here, take this.' He handed her the Heckler and produced his Desert Eagle. 'Let's go. We get Leonardo then we go.' He led the way out through the door, then stopped, looking down at the kidnapper at his feet. 'I know this guy.'

'How?' Greenwood asked.

'He's fucking US Secret Service.'

'How can you be sure?'

'Because I was the head of President Sheeran's security and vetted him during his application. I was there when he was given the job to protect the president's daughter and Enda in Belfast.' He pulled out his phone and took a photo. 'We can run it through facial recognition. That'll ID him.'

'This isn't making any sense,' Greenwood said.

'I'll explain later.'

He looked across the large, open entrance. The sound of footsteps from upstairs could be heard along the hallway above their heads. Martini pointed his gun in the direction of the bottom few steps, which were the only stairs visible and not obstructed by one of the foundation walls. He approached the stairs, the steps becoming louder.

The female kidnapper stepped into his line of sight. Without seeing him, she swung herself around towards him on the last step, holding the banister as she spun, stepping her foot onto the hallway floor, her eyes finally landing on him, but too late for her to react. Her jaw dropped and she froze in one spot.

'Who put you up to this, Melissa?'

'Eamon, please,' she put her hands up.

'Who?' He shouted.

'Dott.'

'Why?'

'He wants the Oval Office, thought if the president caused a diplomatic disaster, he'd be impeached and deemed unfit for office.' She swallowed. 'He killed Robert Carter to make it look like the former CIA Director had set it up, leading POTUS to believe that it was him. With Robert Carter dead he wouldn't have been able to argue his innocence.'

'Carter's dead?'

'Died on his superyacht.' She smiled. 'At least he died in luxury. And it was a heart attack. No sign of foul play.'

He smiled falsely. 'Very smart.' He put a bullet in her head, then walked over to her, pulled his phone out, then took a photo. 'Bill will love to see this. Fucking traitors.'

They made their way through the kitchen towards the patio doors.

'Were you expecting helicopter support?' Martini asked as they stepped outside.

'Just some American Secret Service agents, sent by Frank Dott. Apparently, the Americans want you as much as we do.'

Martini stopped at the door and looked back at her. 'What Secret Service agents?'

'Never met them. They were in London protecting Dott. He's a bit of an arrogant twat.'

'Dott's a dead man walking.' He led the way out into the garden.

Falkner, flanked by two men in black suits, were approaching them from the chopper.

Leonardo looked across the garden at Martini. Seeing them struggling with Black, he shouted, 'Eamon, you need help?'

Martini shook his head.

Falkner, hearing Leonardo's call to Martini, pulled his weapon and pointed it at Leonardo. Martini fired a shot at Falkner, hitting him in the arm, causing him to drop his aim. He then fired three shots, the first and second hitting one of the suits, and the third hitting the other.

Martini ran towards Falkner. 'The next shot goes right through your head. Now drop the fucking gun!'

'Martini, what the...' Before Greenwood could say another word, Martini made a dive for her, pulling her to the ground, just as a collection of shots clacked off from the kitchen door, he took a hit on the upper left bicep. Three masked figures, dressed in German Special Forces uniform, had spilled out into the garden and were firing at will. Martini and Greenwood fired back, their pistols unlikely to win in this fight, but keeping them from coming any closer. 'Everyone get in that chopper!' he shouted, lifting his pistol with his right hand. 'We need to get this kid out of here.' He gripped his pistol, blood running down his left arm, forming a drip at the middle fingertip. 'Leonardo, give me the rifle, I'll hold them off while you get in the chopper.' He flipped the table on its side and took cover behind it.

The others rushed down the garden, past the pool house, towards the aircraft.

The furious roar of vehicles over-revving along the front driveway got louder, followed by the screech of tyres. The low thud of heavy doors slamming closed, came with a barrage of voices shouting, quickly followed by the thud of countless boots beating off the ground. Another eight masked figures came from everywhere, four from the side of the house and four emerging from the kitchen, scattering across the garden, armed with Heckler and Koch HK 416, assault rifles.

'Fuck this,' Martini shouted, firing a long burst before following the others to the chopper, ducking and weaving as bullets came from all directions.

Greenwood pushed Enda into the aircraft, then turned and pulled Black in. She then manhandled Falkner inside, and jumped in himself.

Leonardo stood firing shots into the garden, wating for Martini to catch up. They both jumped in and pulled the door closed.

'Get this thing in the fucking air,' Falkner shouted.

The aircraft went up, the nose pointed west and left the estate behind.

Martini pulled his shirt off, catching his breath. Greenwood wrapped a rag around his bicep and told him to keep the pressure on it. He was glaring across the cabin at Falkner, the commander glaring straight back.

'Eamon Martini,' Falkner said, shaking his head. 'You've caused bloody mayhem. Are you finally giving yourself up? Too tired to run any longer?'

Martini, gripping his wound, pulled his phone out of his pocket with his bloodied hand and made a call. It rang twice. 'Mr. President? I've got Enda.' He looked at the boy and handed the phone over. He glanced at Falkner and Greenwood. 'I'm one of the good guys.'

Falkner laughed. 'Good guys? You've spent your entire life on the wrong side of the law.'

'Let's not do this.'

'Yet, you took the job to kill Churchman,' Greenwood said.

'I've already told you – Churchman's alive. We had to fake his death to give me time to get the boy back.'

'You expect me to believe that?' Greenwood laughed.

'Don't give a shit whether you believe it or not. Only a select few people knew about the operation.' He looked at Greenwood. 'Not even Prime Minister Pears knew.'

'Why?'

'Because President Sheeran is losing faith in the people he should have been able to trust. Protecting his family failed because someone on the inside has betrayed that trust. And talking of which,' he looked at Falkner, 'Where's that piece of shit Dott?'

'Decided not to tag along, sent a couple of his Secret Service men, instead. Went his own way once we got to Berlin airport.'

Martini took the phone from Enda. 'Mr President, I'll call you back in a minute.' He ended the call and made another, handing the phone over to Greenwood, 'Churchman.'

She put the phone to her ear. 'Hello?' Her eyes scanned the cabin, jumping from Martini to Enda, then back to Martini. 'This is Agent Victoria Greenwood, MI6.' She paused for a moment, listening to someone speaking on the other end. Nodding her head, she looked back up at Martini. 'Yes, sir, he's here.' She handed the phone back over.

Martini took the device. 'Mr. Churchman, the boy's here. He's safe. I'm arranging for him to be brought back to the states. His grandfather's sending someone to fly us back to DC.' He paused for a moment then ended the call.

Falkner sighed. 'What happens now?'

'We're flying south, into Italy, where we will go our separate ways.'

Falkner sat there shaking his head with a clear expression of disbelief. He grunted. 'Eamon Martini.' He looked across at Greenwood. 'The one blemish of my career is just going to drop me and my replacement off somewhere and disappear into the sunset.'

Martini looked across at the kid. 'That's right, that's exactly what's going to happen. And we'll all just get on with the rest of our lives.'

94

One hour and forty-five minutes after they left Berlin, they were in Italy, just across the Swiss border. Two miles from Lake Como, was a private plot of land that the Martini's used for air-taxi in and out of the country. The Apostles – Pietro and Paolo Martini – stood next to their white Audi, watching the chopper land. A second vehicle, a silver Mercedes, approached the Audi. A middle-aged lady, tall and thin, with straight black hair and a bronze tan, got out of the rear and approached the Apostles, a brown medical bag clasped tightly in her hand.

Martini addressed Falkner and Black. 'The lady down there is Dr. Libro, a friend of the family. She will tend to your wounds, then you can make your way back to London.'

Falkner didn't speak. Instead, he shuffled in his seat, failing to maintain eye-contact with Martini.

Martini caught Greenwood's eye. She shook her head. 'Interesting man, Mr. Martini.'

'Call me Eamon.'

He looked out the window as the aircraft touched down, then allowed himself another glance at Falkner. 'Looks like we've both come close to getting the other.' He unbuckled his seat belt. 'Maybe in the next life, Commander.'

Again, Falkner remained silent.

Martini got up and approached the door as the aircraft made contact with the ground. He opened the door and got out.

The Apostles approached him. 'Eamon, are you okay?'

Martini nodded. 'I'll be fine.' He looked at Dr. Libro. 'Can you patch up the two injured in the chopper?'

She nodded and passed him, making her way towards the cabin, just as Enda and Leonardo got out. Greenwood was next to disembark, allowing more room for the doctor to work.

Enda didn't know where to look, but it appeared Martini was the only one he was comfortable enough to approach. 'When am I going home?'

'Your grandad has sent a plane to pick us up. We'll get on it soon and it'll take us back to Washington. Your mum will be there, too.'

He began stepping from side to side. 'I need the loo.'

Martini smiled. 'Paolo, can you take him inside and let him use the toilet?'

His cousin nodded.

Greenwood stood next to Martini, watching as Falkner and Black had their wounds seen to.

Martini couldn't ignore the fact he was standing face to face with Commander Falkner, the man who'd colluded with the UDA and UVF to kill innocent Catholics during the British army's war against the IRA, even conspiring to assassinate his father. But Enda's safety was the priority, he didn't need to be around anymore flying bullets.

'Eamon?' Pietro Martini snatched his cousin off the deep

thought train he was riding. 'Where's the American transport meeting you?'

'Let's make our way further south into Italy. The president knows where to pick us up from.'

He offered his hand to Greenwood.

After a momentary pause, she accepted. 'Why'd you save us? We were here to take you out. Not down, but out. By orders of the British government.'

'Well, it's a good thing your British government didn't get a chance to, isn't it?'

'But why? You could have left us there.'

Leonardo tapped Martini on the shoulder. 'Time to go, Eamon.'

Martini smiled at her. 'Guess that'll be a discussion for another day, Agent Greenwood.'

95

The next day, President Sheeran was sitting in the Oval Office waiting to see his grandson for the first time since he'd been taken. Niamh was sitting at the far end of the room on the sofa next to Goodall. POTUS had just poured his second glass of Irish whiskey when the door opened and there he was, fresh off Air Force One. Enda entered, Martini behind him.

'Enda!' his mother jumped up from the sofa and sprinted across the room, pulling him in for a hug.

'Thank God.' POTUS set the glass down on his desk and rushed towards them. Given his size and stature, lifted the lad in a bear-hug, Enda's feet dangling a couple of feet off the ground.

Martini walked around them and made his way towards the president's desk. He studied the flags on either side of the desk. To his left stood the flag of the United States of America, and on the right side stood the coat of arms, the Presidential flag with the quote "E Pluribus Unum" in the centre. 'Out of many, we become one,' he said to himself, translating from Latin to English.

'Good job, Martini,' Goodall said, approaching him. She looked at the dressing on his arm. 'Flesh wound?'

Martini nodded, turned to her and said, 'You did well, for what we had to work with. What about Dott?'

'Give me a couple of days, I'll find him.'

'Eamon, how can I ever repay you?' The president approached Martini, Niamh and Enda along with him, Niamh looking like she was fighting to keep it together.

Martini shook his head, his eyebrows almost touching. It almost looked as if POTUS had said something offensive. 'Just helping an old friend. How long have we known each other, sir?'

'Since you were a little shit of a teenager, running around New York with those Apostles and the other pair.'

Martini nodded. 'We've helped each other along the way. And those Apostles and other two helped me get Enda home.'

POTUS offered his hand to Martini. 'How'd it feel, to be face to face with old Commander Falkner?'

He shrugged. 'The past is the past.'

'What are your plans now?'

'A good shower and a change of clothes. Then I'll go looking for Dott.' He looked at Enda, then back at POTUS. 'You heard anything from him?'

POTUS shook his head. 'The FBI and CIA are using all available resources to find him.'

'Well, when they do, give me his location. I'll close this up for you.'

'I know you're not officially employed anymore, but I could use you around here, if you'd be interested? You'd be the man to run the basement?'

'Let me think about it.'

POTUS studied him for moment, his serious expression

softening, his mouth stretching into a smile. 'You need anything, you call me, Eamon. You got it?'

Martini slapped POTUS on the upper arm. 'Call me when you have Dott's location. He's not walking away from this.'

EPILOGUE

For Frank Dott, Berlin was too cold *and* too hot to stick around. Too hot to stay without being caught by those he was now running from, and too cold to ever maintain the all-year tan he'd grown accustomed to ever since his third ex-wife had introduced him to sunbeds in the run-up to their wedding. He'd migrated into southern Europe, stopping off in Skiathos. Part of the Sporades Archipelago – a group of Greek islands – Skiathos was known for its beaches, wooded terrain, eye-watering coastal drives and snorkelling, all of which Dott had treated himself to, meandering around the island like a man with all the time in the world.

The last few days on the island was a glimpse into the life he was about to enjoy. His financial worries from a life-long career on Uncle Sam's payroll were over, thanks to the late Ludwig Schuster. He'd just come out of a meeting with Dr Christopoulos, a world leading plastic surgeon who specialised in cosmetics, and was due to begin work on Dott's face tomorrow. Lip augmentation, rhinoplasty, blepharoplasty, otoplasty and a facelift would

alter his previous appearance, which would have otherwise been picked up by the unavoidable web of global
surveillance. His known identity would have been passed
on to the analysts back at the Pentagon and forwarded
onto POTUS. If that were to happen, there would only be
one outcome, and as he looked at the drink's menu on the
table before him, that name was staring right back at him,
like a pest, a stark reminder of who'd be coming after him:
Martini.

He was feeling lucky; on his second Margarita, and third
plate of complementary nuts while eyeing up the waitress
who was clearing up the twelve-seater table, previously
occupied by a hen party of rowdy Englishwomen. Dott had
watched the waitress for the last twenty minutes, noting
there was no engagement ring on her hand, and, given the
eye contact between the pair ever since he'd accentuated his
American intonation, along with the thick wad of euros he'd
produced at the bar, he was going to take her back to the sea
view apartment on the other side of the beach.

Seeing that he'd just finished his drink, she approached
his table. 'Would you like another?' She spoke in good
English. She was around five foot eight, slim, with legs that
extended a long way out from beneath her loose white
dress. Her skin was the same bronze colour as the table, and
her eyes were piercing green. Gorgeous was an understatement.

'What's your name?'

'Ariana.'

'Ariana, I'm Frank.'

'You're American?'

'Yes. Would you like to join me for a drink when you
finish?'

She smiled and pushed a strand of her shoulder length

black hair behind her left ear. 'I thought perhaps you were waiting for company.'

He shook his head. 'I'm in this country all alone. On business. Will you join me? These Margaritas are very good.'

She looked over her shoulder towards the bar, the barman was busy serving a group of three local men who'd just came in. She turned back to him, biting her lower lip. 'I finish in one hour. We can go somewhere else for a drink. But I don't like what you're drinking.' She nodded towards the menu. 'I'd prefer a Martini.' She turned and made her way back to the bar. He watched her, unable to decide whether he wanted to launch the table at her, or launch her on top of the table. Perhaps both.

EAMON MARTINI WAS RECLINING on one of the wooden loungers in a row of thirty on Koukounaries Beach. Located on the south eastern tip of Skiathos island, it was known as "sand heaven", bordered by the clear blue water of the Aegean Sea on one side, and the lush green forest leading into the village on the other. His Android rang, buried inside his New York Yankees baseball cap beneath the lounger. He reached under and retrieved it.

Director Goodall flashed across the screen.

He repositioned his sunglasses, which had slid down the sweaty bridge of his nose and answered. 'Director Goodall.'

'Eamon, President Sheeran has asked me for an update.'

'Had you called me in two hours from now, I'd have a different answer for you.'

'But you've found him?'

'He's in La Bussola, a little beach bar on the south of Skiathos. I can imagine he's on his third or fourth drink by now.'

'POTUS wants an update as soon as it's done.'

He ended the call and sat for another ten minutes.

His attention was grabbed by Dott's unmistakable accent coming from his left. Martini had positioned himself perfectly. Dott would have to pass him to get to his apartment. The block was a new build, nestled on the fringe of the beach just a mile up the stretch of sand. Martini continued to relax, soaking up the sun, listening as Dott got closer, telling his female companion how he was a developer on the island to purchase land to build some new properties, including a golf course. Martini allowed himself a slight grin as they cast a momentary shadow over him in passing, then sat up, watching as they got further away, staying on the beach as they made their way towards his apartment.

He waited until they were two hundred yards ahead before he got up, lifted his phone and his gym bag, stuffing the cap inside his pocket – a piece of Yankees merchandise would have been too much of a giveaway.

The only thing he needed was the silver Desert Eagle .50, with a suppressor screwed tightly into the muzzle, the magazine fully loaded with 9 rounds of .357 Magnum. One bullet was enough, but it was better to have more, just in case.

ARRIVING AT THE APARTMENT, Dott opened the door, de-activated the alarm, then took Ariana by the hand, slowly pulling her inside. He closed the door and kissed her, feeling her tongue swim around in his mouth.

She broke away, 'How about a drink first?'

'Of course.' He pointed towards the living room, 'Have a seat and I'll see what we've got in the fridge.' He made his way along the hallway into the kitchen. 'Make yourself comfortable,' he called out to her. He lifted a bottle of red wine out of the fridge, and grabbed two glasses from the cupboard.

He entered the living room, finding her standing at the patio doors, looking out to sea. He stood next to her, admiring the view. The sun caused a blinding reflection off the water. 'Nice view, isn't it?'

She nodded her head, 'I would love to live here.'

They both stood for a moment, both of their reflections appearing on the pane of glass they were looking through, then, a shock to them both, a third reflection appeared over Dott's shoulder. They both spun around.

Dott froze. Eamon Martini had a Desert Eagle pointed at his head.

'Martini, please, I can pay...'

Martini fired off one shot, the report nothing more than a low thud, hitting Dott between the eyes, spraying the window and walls with blood and brain matter. He was dead before he hit the ground.

Ariana gasped. Martini signalled with a finger on his lips. She understood, holding her cries behind her lips. He fished his phone out of his pocket and made a call. POTUS answered quickly. 'It's done, sir.'

YOU CAN REALLY HELP!

If you enjoyed this book, I would be extremely grateful if you could leave me a brief review. Reviews help my author career which I'm very passionate about growing. Especially being a new author, reviews are something that helps a tremendous amount. If you'd like to help, you can access the book's review page by clicking the following links. Just click on the link from the store you shopped from:

US STORE
UK STORE

FREE SAMPLE - ROYAL SCANDAL - PROLOGUE

Lismore Castle, Lismore, Co Waterford, Ireland, June, 1982

The Prince of Wales – George Albert Harold Arthur, also known as the Duke of York and Duke of Essex, the first son of Her Majesty the Queen of England and her husband His Royal Highness the Duke of Wessex. Heir apparent to the British throne, Prince George had fallen in love with Lismore Castle on his first visit as an eight-year-old child. He'd returned again and again, often feeling like he was spending more time in Ireland than in what should have become his kingdom a few hundred miles east across the Irish Sea.

Unfortunately, Prince George's life was to be steered in a completely different direction, etching his name into the history books not as the would-be King of England, but rather becoming the highest profile death between the period of 1968 and 1998, during the most recent Anglo-Irish conflict, raising tensions like never before between Britain and Ireland.

Built on the southern banks of the River Blackwater, the castle was just eighteen miles and thirty minutes drive from the East Irish coast and the choppy Irish Sea. Surrounded by walls armed with Cromwellian cannons, it had stood the test of time. Built in and around the year 1170, it had been owned by many of history's notability. Sir Walter Raleigh, who'd been known to influence the first English colonies of America, beginning in what is known today as North Carolina. Raleigh was also believed to have been the one who'd gifted the Emerald Isle with potatoes and tobacco; the Irish people grateful for one more than the other.

Many of humanity's greatest contributors had spent a night or two within its walls including: Cecil Beaton, Lucian Freud, Fred Astaire, and most notably – the 35th President of the United States: John F. Kennedy.

Prince George always felt the castle's history seeping through his bones when staying here. And this time was no different.

The morning of June 23rd had been mouth-wateringly beautiful. The sun shone through the windows in rays as if sent down by the powers above, and the birds chirped, singing the same old melody they sang every morning.

Prince George sat at his kitchen table, reading the newspaper – the Belfast Telegraph – while stirring the stainless-steel teapot, preparing to pour his first brew of the day. A creature of habit, Prince George or "Georgie" as he was known to those closest, had grown accustomed to the smell of the paper as it sat just inches from his nose, whilst appreciating his favourite brew of Yorkshire Tea.

Learning what had taken place in Belfast the previous day was all he could read. Folding the paper down, he left it on the table and got up, walking across the rustic kitchen, looking down onto the river. The sky was baby blue, the summer sun bore down on the land of the Emerald Isle, causing the grass to look greener, a blinding reflection to bounce off the river's surface.

He allowed himself a moment to enjoy the landscape, before reminding himself of what he'd just read. 'Bloody ashamed to call myself British,' he mumbled as he returned to the table, lifting the tea pot and filling his cup.

'Don't let your oul ma' hear you say that.' A voice came from the kitchen door; a thick Belfast accent.

Prince George looked around, seeing Damien Cleary Snr., Chief of Staff of the Provisional IRA closing the door behind him. Standing next to him was his son – Damien Jnr., rising star within the republican movement, IRA Intelligence Director and most wanted man in Britain. Behind Cleary was Martin Dornan, Operating Commander of the Falls Road Brigade.

'Jesus, Damien. I've told you before never to come here,' Prince George spat, speaking with his private English boarding school accent.

'Relax, nobody spotted us,' Cleary Snr. replied. He was in his late forties, had dark brown hair and piercing blue eyes. His stare was cold and intelligent. The weathered expression on his face was one of a man who'd spent the last ten years arming and directing a paramilitary organisation with a membership of twenty thousand strong within its ranks. Cleary Snr. was one of the first Catholics to be burned out of his home by the loyalist Ulster Volunteer Force, while local police – the Royal Ulster Constabulary cleared the way for the loyalists to do so. The Official IRA, who'd mounted mediocre attacks on the Northern Irish "Orange, pro-Protestant State" every decade since the country's partition in nineteen twenty-one, had failed to protect the Catholic community which saw eight people dead and almost two thousand Catholics in Belfast flee their homes. Bombay Street in West Belfast was where Cleary Snr. had grown up, which had been completely burned to the ground during the attacks. A refugee in his own country, Cleary Snr., like many other Catholics at the time, went to Dublin, held a meeting with the ruling army counsel of the OIRA and accused them of failing to protect the Catholics of the north. This led to the OIRA being overthrown, and like a phoenix rising out of the ashes, came the birth of the new, more ferocious Provisional IRA or known colloquially as "the Provos".

After the failure of the civil rights demonstrations of the sixties, the Provos were men and women, normal Catholics, who were tired of the way the failed, sectarian state had opposed their basic human rights. Diplomatic channels and peaceful marches, which Catholics had adopted from Dr King in the US, had resulted in the Stormont government and its armed forces reacting with violence instead of responding with dialogue. The peaceful approach got Catholics battered and arrested, the burning of Bombay Street and the other parts of Belfast were the result. They'd asked for equal rights. They'd marched for equal rights. The result: arrested and beaten.

Out of options, feeling the tight grip of the Stormont government around their throats silencing them, the Catholic scum, the second-class citizens, the Provos drew up its three-stage offensive against the Northern Irish government. First: defence of the Catholic community, second: retaliation for attacks on their community, and third: launching a guerrilla campaign against the British crown forces with the end goal of a thirty-two county Irish sovereignty.

Stepping further into the room, Cleary Snr. looked at the copy of the Belfast Telegraph which Prince George had been reading. 'Interesting read, isn't it?'

'How can you be sure you weren't followed?' the prince asked. Cleary ignored the question. Prince George looked at the paper. 'I see your boys had a busy day yesterday.'

'Three dead.' Cleary Snr. sat down at the table, across from the prince. Cleary Jnr. stood at the door. Dornan went back outside to wait in the car. 'This war isn't going to end well for any of us. I need you to give me something. We need to hit the Brits so hard that the British public demand the Tories pull them out.'

Prince George nervously brought his cup up to his lips, looking at Cleary over the rim of the white ceramic mug with the crest of the Worcestershire and Sherwood Foresters on the side.

Cleary Snr. cleared his throat. 'Look, Georgie – bombing commercial and military targets in London, Birmingham or anywhere else in England was not what we wanted. We don't want English people suffering because your boys won't leave here.'

'They're not *my* boys.'

'The cup you're holding would lead one to believe otherwise,' Cleary Jnr. said from the door. He looked like his father. The same dark hair, the same piercing blue eyes. His face appeared to have the same expression all the time, as if every muscle had been frozen. Like a stone-cold predator. He was intimidating – and very calculating.

'I've spent the last ten years serving the Crown. Little more than to please my family. But I've always disagreed with British methods. It was wrong to partition Ireland. You

Catholics never had a fucking hope in hell. I love Irish people. As much as my own.'

'That blue eyed, freckle faced Belfast girl didn't have anything to do with that, did she?' Cleary Jnr. said.

'Don't bring her into it, you fucking ass-hole!' Prince George shouted, glaring across the room, Cleary Jnr. glaring back at him. 'Who do you think you are?'

Cleary Jnr. stepped further into the kitchen, approaching the table, holding the prince's gaze with every step. 'You know who I am, Georgie. And I know who you are. Or should I say what you've been up to.'

'Damien, back away, son,' Cleary Snr. said. He looked back at the prince. 'He meant no harm. You know what you youngsters are like these days, very quick to fly off the handle.'

'I do,' the prince spat, still glaring at Cleary Jnr. 'Any more of those wise cracks and we'll be stepping outside.'

Cleary Jnr. didn't reply.

'You'd fallen in love with a lady whose father was part of the Official IRA. Now she's an intelligence officer for the Provos. You secretly became sympathetic to our cause and have used your family and connections in British defence to help the people of this country. For that, we're grateful.'

'What do you want, Cleary?' the prince asked with a sigh.

'Like I said, I want you to give me something. One major assault on the British Army that will send so many shock waves throughout Westminster that your prime minister pulls your boys out of here and we can get on with the job of unifying this troubled land.'

The prince grunted, then smirked. 'Sounds very poetic.'

'Our people are suffering,' Cleary Jnr. said, approaching the table again. 'You make another snide comment about that, and I'll snatch the life right out of you – do you understand?'

'You don't frighten me, mate.'

'The shame of what you've done would kill your family. And perhaps bring an end to the monarchy,' Cleary Snr. said.

Prince George looked at Cleary Snr., shaking his head.

'Look, I'm grateful for the intel you've fed to our organisation. But it's not getting us anywhere. We need more.'

'How about a bloody invitation to Sunday lunch with the Queen and my father?' he spoke sarcastically.

'That would be an awkward dinner. I don't think the conversation would flow very well.' Cleary Snr. stood up and walked to the counter. Grabbing himself a cup, he returned to the table and poured himself a cup of tea. 'Find out where there will be a large number of troops in one place. Somewhere many Brits will die, but away from the crowded streets of Belfast and Derry. We don't need any more innocent casualties.' He took a sip of his tea then stood up. Setting the cup down, he looked at his son. 'Let's go, Damien.'

They left through the kitchen door, out into the garden. A 1978 blue Ford Cortina sat idling in the driveway, Martin Dornan occupying the driver's seat.

Prince George stood at the kitchen sink, looking through the window, watching as the Ford got further away. He filled his cup with warm water and left it steeping in the sink.

'Fuck you, Cleary,' he said, turning and making his way towards the hall. He lifted the phone off the receiver and called his friend and mentor in the army – the man leading Operation Banner. The phone rang four times before there was an answer.

'Hello, Brigadier Whiteside speaking.'

'It's Georgie, Brigadier. How's life in the troubled city of Belfast.'

Whiteside laughed, his voice becoming less military and more friendly. 'You know what Belfast's like. One half of the population trying to kill us and the other half trying to be a part of us.'

'Better you than me.'

'How can I help you, Your Highness?'

'Less of the formalities, it's Georgie.'

'You'll one day be King of England, and you expect me to call you Georgie?'

The prince laughed. 'I'm growing tired of the idea already.' He cleared his throat. 'Reading the news in Belfast, I thought about you and our old days together in the early seventies. I thought perhaps we could meet up, old time's sake you know?'

'You're still on tour?'

'Fourth tour finished last month, hence, I'm enjoying the spectacular views of Lismore Castle.'

Whiteside grunted his understanding. 'I'll see you in two days.'

Prince George ended the call and went into the living room. Sitting down at his writing bureau he began writing in his journal.

After four and a half hours and one hundred and eight miles, Cleary's journey north via the M11 and M1 came to an end as the Ford pulled up alongside Cassidy's pub on North Belfast's Antrim Road.

Dornan put the car in neutral and lit a cigarette, watching as an armoured police Land Rover flew by, the blue light flashing on the roof. 'Wonder where those bastards are going,' Dornan said.

'God knows, as long as they're not interested in us, I don't care,' Cleary Snr. replied.

Dornan looked across at Cleary Jnr., 'We still on for tonight?'

Cleary Jnr. blew smoke out through the window then looked across at him. 'The operation goes ahead as planned. Call your men, make sure they're all ready to go.' He looked back at his father. 'You and I are meeting with the rest of the army council at eight this evening. The only topic on the table will be stepping up the attacks.'

'What about our boys inside?' Dornan asked. 'Those prison conditions are still fuckin' awful.'

Cleary Jnr. looked back out the window, watching a young boy, perhaps ten, kick a football against the wall of Cassidy's. His Celtic football kit was old and worn. 'That wee lad over there doesn't know what's going on around him. Wondering where his da' is.'

That's Davy Cassidy's wee lad,' Cleary Snr. said.

Dornan nodded. 'Doesn't know where his old man is.'

'Better he doesn't know,' Cleary Jnr. said.

'I wouldn't want my son knowing I was locked away in some concrete coffin either,' Snr. retorted.

'Well, like I said, that's what the meeting's going to be about tonight,' Cleary Jnr. flicked the cigarette butt out onto the road. Dornan got out and Cleary Jnr. took the driver's seat. He put the car in gear. 'I'll give you a ring later.'

Dornan lowered his head back in the window. He was five foot eight and wiry. He didn't look intimidating until you held his gaze, it was almost as if he was constantly trying to stare you out. His hair was light brown but went blond in the sunlight. His eyes were an uncommon shade of grey. He was Cleary Jnr's right-hand man and spent a lot of time overseas in the US purchasing weapons. 'Speak to you lads later.' He tapped on the roof of the car as Cleary Snr. got out of the back and took the front passenger's seat.

The Cortina pulled away from the kerb, heading further north along the Antrim Road.

Two days later, Prince George welcomed Brigadier Whiteside to his home.

'God you haven't changed, have you?' Whiteside said, approaching the prince who stood at the entrance to the castle.

Prince George was six foot three and thin. He'd been a cross-country runner, and his build reflected it. At twenty-nine, he looked like most royals in history – like he'd live until he was one hundred and five. He had hazelnut eyes and matching hair that was permanently combed into a solid side-shade, being held in place by some sort of gel. Even when not in public, the prince was dressed in a suit – charcoal tweed being his favourite. He offered a warm hand to his old friend and commander, patting him on the shoulder with the other. 'A life that consists of exercise and healthy diet will allow any man to age gracefully.' He stood to the side, allowing Whiteside to enter the house.

'You're only twenty-nine, sir, wait until you're my age.' He spoke mockingly. Whiteside was in his early fifties. He stood a few inches shorter than the prince and fifty pounds heavier, much of it being around the waist. He had pale blue eyes and receding black hair, with one-inch-thick black eyebrows that met in the middle.

Prince George laughed off the comment, closing the door as he followed him towards the kitchen.

Whiteside sat down at the table. 'How is the Queen? And your father?'

'They're well, thanks,' he said. He lifted the kettle, checking it was full, then put it on to boil. 'Tea or coffee?'

'Tea please,' Whiteside said.

Prince George sat down at the table, facing Whiteside. 'How's Belfast?'

'Explosive.'

He nodded. 'You think our boys are going to be on the streets for long?'

'God, I hope not, but who knows? These bastards are growing more sophisticated by the day.'

'I guess you can thank Gaddafi for that, not to mention the fucking Yanks. Always sympathising with their Irish cousins.' Prince George cleared his throat. 'I'd like to spend a day with the troops if I may?'

'Why? You've just retired from duty.'

'I just want to offer them support, perhaps a morale boost. They've taken a real tanking from the Provos these last few months, and with the new Tory leader being the menacing bitch that she is, it's not doing much for them.'

Whiteside laughed, nodding his head. 'She's definitely an acquired taste, and not one which many of our lads have managed to acquire yet.'

He nodded, 'I get the impression mummy doesn't like her very much, but of course – she's the person the British public voted for.'

'Well, I think she's upset as many English as she has Irish.' Whiteside laughed. 'But we'll just keep on doing the job we're paid to do.'

'I'm on the phone with mummy this evening, I'm going to suggest a visit from her and my father. I think some recognition from their Queen would hopefully give them the boost they need. It appears every time we take out a couple of theirs, the IRA get us back.'

Whiteside's expression turned more serious. 'Yes, it's a war nobody seems to be winning.' He cleared his throat. 'When are you thinking of visiting the troops?'

'Perhaps in the next couple of weeks, mid-July.'

'I'll organise something.'

'Make it a good gathering, the more the better.'

The kettle boiled.

Prince George got up and went to make the tea.

'Have you been up north across the border recently?'

'Only to Londonderry to visit her.' The prince grabbed two cups from the cupboard above the kettle.

'Has Her Majesty ever found out?'

'What, that I met, fell in love with and had children to a lady whose family's knee deep in the blood of British soldiers?' He sniggered as he brought a tray with the cups, sugar, milk, and a tea pot over to the table.

'Why'd you tell me then?'

He sat down, lifted the lid of the stainless-steel pot and began to stir, pressing the two teabags against the inside. 'You're my oldest friend. And we both know this is a war. She doesn't. Neither does the new PM. They see the Provisional IRA as a bunch of terrorists. They're fighting for their people. Christ, if I were born here, I perhaps would have called it *Derry* and fought on their side, too.' He closed the lid of the pot and poured the tea. 'But as it stands, I'm a Brit, and it is my duty to offer support to our lads.

The next day, Prince George stood at the doorway, watching as Whiteside's green Land Rover moved further and further down the driveway. He turned and walked back inside. Going straight to the phone, he produced Cleary Snr's telephone number that he'd written on the edge of the Belfast Telegraph's front page. He lifted the phone off the receiver, pressed it to his left ear and dialled. The moment the receiver started to ring in his ear, his heart started to race. He felt the blood rush in his right ear, his palms starting to sweat.

'Hello?'

'I need to meet you, Damien, I've got more for you.'

'Can you come to Belfast?'

'No, but I'm going to Londonderry...'

'You mean Derry?'

Prince George shook his head. 'Whatever. I'm visiting Grainne on the weekend...'

'Are you sure it's wise for you to go there?'

'Aine is now four years old, and I haven't seen her as much as I would have liked. I need to see her.'

'Okay, we'll meet at the Free Derry wall, midnight on Saturday.'

'See you then.' Prince George hung up and went into the living room. He sat down, crossed his legs and picked up a framed photograph of Aine, one of the twins. The other twin, James, was in London being raised as the first child of his farce of a marriage. His wife Janice, Duchess of York was happy to go along with the charade. Disappearing from the public for ten months, the story they had told was that she wanted to have the child out of the public eye, less stress for the child. Of course, he wasn't even hers. Grainne was left heartbroken. Aine would grow up in Derry believing she hadn't a twin brother, and James would grow up, heir apparent to the British throne, not realising he had a twin sister.

He looked at the Telegraph next to him, the front page was a scene of devastation in Belfast where six British troops had been ambushed by a handful of snipers on the Falls

Road. The heading said the Provisional IRA's death count of British troops was on the rise.

He felt a wave of guilt wash over him. 'May God forgive me.'

CHAPTER ONE

Milan, Italy, June 26th, Present Day

Stepping through the electronic exit doors of Milan Berg-
amo's arrivals terminal, Eamon Martini stood six foot tall
with a slim, athletic build. His youthful face, high-cheek-
bones, sun-kissed olive skin and piercing, intelligent blue
eyes made him look like a man much younger than his
thirty-nine years. When asked what his secret was, he often
joked that it was the Mediterranean blood, handed down by
his Italian ancestors; other times he directed the reason
towards his happy-go-lucky Irish bloodline. In truth, it was
his lifestyle. From a young boy, his mother, despite the
finances coming from New York's organised crime network,
had given her only son every chance at a happy, healthy life.
After spending his late teens in Belfast with his father –
Damien Cleary Jnr. – Martini had joined the US Marines,
becoming one of the first boots on the ground in
Afghanistan, before moving into Special Forces, then
removing his Green Beret and moving into the CIA's Special
Activities Centre. After working for the CIA, he'd gone into

the US Secret Service, leading the US president's personal security. His mind and body were his tools, and they'd remained well-oiled and sharp. This was the real reason why he looked ten years younger.

Standing in the shade, he set his leather laptop case down, standing it between his feet, and removed his tailored grey suit jacket, then loosened his black tie, allowing the morning breeze to kiss the sweat soaked skin below his shirt collar. Hanging his jacket over the top of his laptop case, he fished his Samsung Android from his trouser pocket, the vibrations of the device sending tickles down his thigh. He activated Bluetooth on his phone and connected the call to his ear-pods before inserting them into his ears.

'Ciao,' he said, re-positioning the left ear-pod as sweat inside his ear had caused it to dislodge.

'Mr Martini, you have arrived?' A deep voice spoke Italian in a local dialect.

'Just stepped off the plane.' He looked around, searching for the caller's vehicle. There were too many vehicles to land on, and none of them stood out.

'I'm just coming into the pickup area now.'

The call ended.

He stood watching a queue of fifteen passengers wait patiently to get aboard the coach with *Terravisione Milano Centrale* along the side in bold red letters. All of the commuters looked eager to get onboard and out of the oppressive summer sun.

His attention was quickly snatched away from the queue by the sound of a black Maserati Granturismo, roaring along the narrow pick up area.

Seeing the driver fill out every inch of the seat, dressed in a red shirt, donning black shades, Martini knew that was for him.

The front passenger was Donatello Bianco, a member of the crime family of the same name that had followed the Martini family from New York back to mainland Italy where more money could be made.

Martini made his way towards the car, approaching the passenger side; it was a three-door coupe. Bianco had to get out, pull his seat forward to allow Martini to climb into the back. Bianco was a couple of inches shorter than Martini and a few inches wider, but more round than muscular. He had grey, thinning hair, with a scar cutting through the temple. He offered Martini a civil nod, getting one in return.

'Welcome to Italy,' the driver said, smiling at Martini as he offered his hand. 'Paolo Bianco.'

'I know who you are, Paolo,' Martini responded, accepting his hand out of common courtesy. Looking at the man next to him on the back seat he said, 'Federico Bianco.'

'How've you been, Eamon?' Federico Bianco looked at Martini, his long thin face looked unwell. His black hair was shiny, with a greasy complexion. His navy suit and red tie looked like a poor choice, given the weather, but Martini wasn't going to start giving fashion tips, and or constructive criticism to a man known as a psychotic killer who'd been born into a family with too much power and no idea of the difference between right and wrong.

'Very well,' Martini said, trying to get himself comfortable in the back of the car. Donatello slid his seat back into place and got back in. 'Could you not have gone with a bigger car than this one?'

Federico laughed. 'Yes, my brother Paolo here likes these sports cars. They are nice, luxurious and fast, but they are not good for travelling in.'

'Unless you're five and a half feet tall,' Paolo joked, as he put the car in drive and took off. He looked across at Donatello. 'Where do we go now?'

'Let's grab some breakfast at the club,' Federico interrupted, craning his head forward between the two front seats. He pulled out a box of cigarettes. 'Are you hungry, Eamon?'

'I could eat,' Martini said, looking at his phone. The time was ten thirty-three in the morning. 'But perhaps we can get on with the job of why I'm here, you need help with a little problem. Let's get that sorted out first before I think of switching off and putting my feet up.'

'Breakfast is the most important meal of the day, my half Irish half Italian amico. We will eat first. Don't worry, there is plenty of time to discuss our business,' Donatello said. He took a cigarette off Federico and lowered the front passenger window.

Martini was offered a cigarette, but he refused. 'I gave them up a long time ago.'

'Good for you,' Federico said, resting one on his lip and lighting it. 'Me – I love smoking. I know it will kill me one day, but I'm going to die of something, right? At least this way it'll be from my own vices.'

'True.' Martini nodded, looking down at his phone. He'd received a text message from his cousin, Leonardo Martini, one of his four cousins, son of his mother's sister.

Eamon, where are you? I've tried to get a hold of you. I've spoken to the others. They say you've agreed to meet with the Bianco family. What are you doing?

Martini looked out the window, watching as the hedges, lampposts and passing cars went by in the opposite direction, thinking of what to reply.

I'll call you in a few days. Don't worry. What I'm doing with the Bianco family will benefit the Martini family as much as them. Stay safe, Leonardo and don't contact me again. I'll contact you. Eamon.

He switched his phone off and put it back into his pocket.

Federico looked across at him, then lowered his gaze to the pocket he'd just deposited the phone into. 'Problem, Eamon?'

He shook his head. 'Just my cousin worried about me.' He spoke humorously.

Paolo laughed as he slowed the vehicle, gradually coming to a stop behind a bin lorry. 'That's very sweet.' He spoke mockingly.

'In fact, he's more worried about your welfare than mine,' Martini was quick to say.

'And why is that?' He looked at Martini in the rear-view mirror, then across at his brother.

Federico sighed, flicking the cigarette out the window. 'Just drive, Paolo.' He looked at Martini. 'How confident are you that we can broker a deal with them?'

'The Camorra are known to be tough negotiators. But if our proposition is appealing enough, then I'm *very* confident we can have a deal set up which all parties can benefit from.' He cleared his throat. 'Besides, these sons of bitches have only recently branched out into the northern part of Italy. So, them moving up from the south is no different from New York Italians wanting to set up a shop in Italy again, just after a century long vacation to the states. About sixty billion euros pass through criminal hands every year in Milan alone. There's plenty to go around.'

'Always the diplomat,' Federico joked. 'Would you ever consider going into politics?'

He grunted in amusement. 'My father's side of the family spent their lives in one of the most politically charged cities in the world. The topic of politics usually leaves a bitter taste in our mouth.'

'Belfast is not like it was for your father's generation,' Federico said. 'Be the change you want to see in the world.'

'Quoting Ghandi?'

'He was a great man, a man of his people.'

'That I don't disagree with, but I'm no politician.' He wanted to change the subject. 'So, where are we going for breakfast?'

'Our family has a lovely little café and restaurant just outside Monza. A picturesque part of this beautiful country. There we can make you the finest breakfast from here to Ireland.'

'I'll be the judge of that,' Martini said. He looked at Paolo. 'Does the bloody air conditioning work in this thing? I'd hope so given the price tag on something like this.'

CHAPTER TWO

After a thirty-five-minute journey south west via the A4 and E64, the Maserati made its 4.7 litre presence known on Monza's Via G Marconi. They travelled along the dual carriageway for another three miles, passing the Vendesi Fratelli Manufacturing plant on the right-hand side, a Fiat dealership on the left and finally a cluster of high-rise apartments before turning right onto Via Sant'Alessandro, a more built-up area just a few miles from Monza's city centre. The road was narrow, with vehicles parked on either side. The area was built up with typical Italian styled houses, each being of a different design and colour. From yellow, to peach, to red, to cream. The speed limit was thirty kilometres per hour, but Paolo's heavy foot ignored the regulations, the car flying along the road until it reached the junction with Via Mogadiscio. Their destination was number twelve.

Nero e Bianco – Italian for Black and White – was a modern styled café. Hidden behind dense hedgerow, it gave less commercial effect and more of a relaxing, well-kept family garden vibe.

'Nice place,' Martini said, respectfully admiring the

business, giving credit where credit was due. Feeling grateful that the car had stopped and the two front doors had opened, he was quick to get out and stretch his legs. He noticed two middle-aged men in suits leaving the café, both looking over at them. 'I can smell police a mile off.' He watched as the two suits got into a grey Range Rover. As the driver took his jacket off, his white shirt was decorated by a brown leather holster, the stainless-steel pistol cradled inside caught in the blistering sunlight sent a reflection bouncing momentarily off Martini's eyes.

'Relax, they just come here because they like the food,' Federico said. He looked at Paolo who'd just got back behind the wheel, glaring at his phone. 'What are you doing?'

'We've got to go. We'll be back later.'

'What do you mean *we*?'

'I'm going with him,' Donatello said, getting back into the front passenger side.

Paolo pulled the door closed and looked at Martini as he lowered the window. 'Was nice to finally meet you.'

Martini nodded his head. 'Next time bring a bigger car.' He followed Federico towards the entrance.

A young lady no older than twenty was bringing the garden furniture outside, a black wooden chair in one hand and a white one in the other. She wore a black t-shirt with the café's name in bold white lettering across the chest. She smiled at Martini, following him with her eyes as he approached.

'Buongiorno,' he said.

She set the chairs down then pushed them beneath a black table and smiled, illuminating her already pretty face. 'Ciao, buongiorno.'

Federico stopped and held the door open for the girl and Martini. 'Eamon, this is my eldest daughter, Francesca.'

'Nice to meet you,' Martini said, as he stepped inside, the overwhelming smell of fresh coffee bringing with it a homely aroma.

They sat at the corner table, directly below a painting of local Formula One hero Stefano Libri who was stood next to the Ferrari that had won the local Grand Prix and overall championship for the past two years.

Martini admired the photo. 'It's about time an Italian was the driver of a Ferrari again, it's been too long.'

Federico looked at the painting. 'Yes. I remember when he was just a kid, used to have the hots for Francesca.' He looked back at his daughter who was cleaning the tables down.

Martini shook his head, 'Until he found out who her father was.'

Federico smiled and nodded, then a silence fell over them. He cleared his throat, 'Let's address the elephant in the room, shall we?'

'Our families have a history,' Martini said. 'Some of that history bloodier than any of us would have wanted.' He was referring to James Bianco, Federico's cousin. Born in Belfast and becoming a member of the Provisional IRA during the Troubles, James Bianco served under Martini's father, Damien Cleary Jnr. Bianco was Cleary Jnr's Intelligence Agent, but when the IRA became riddled with MI5 informants in the late nineteen seventies, Cleary Jnr. re-structured the Provos into smaller, four-man Active Service Units or ASUs, so that each solider in their four-man unit never came into contact with anyone else outside of their own ASU. Once the Provos were re-structured, being harder to infiltrate,

Cleary Jnr. tasked James Bianco to lead a group of IRA internal investigators that quickly earned themselves the name: "the nutting squad" as Bianco sniffed out the IRA's informers and executed them with a bullet in the head or nut – "nutting" them. While all this was going on, James Bianco was acting as a double agent, leading the IRA's nutting squad while informing MI5 and British Army Intelligence of IRA operations. It wasn't until the double agent reported back to his Bianco family in Italy and New York what he was doing, including a plan to assassinate Cleary Jnr., that the word of his work was fed back to the Martini family in New York. Seventeen-year-old Eamon Martini heard of the joint MI5 / British Army plan to assassinate his father in Belfast and set about concocting a plan to reverse the plot, resulting in James Bianco and high ranking officials within British defence being left red-faced. James Bianco met a gristly end by an elite squad of IRA hitmen and Martini became known as the lad who'd outsmarted British Intelligence.

Federico studied Martini for a moment. 'Yes, but as long as we know it's in the past, and we're here for a common goal, then our past can be left where it belongs: in the past.'

'It's important you understand that La Camorra is an enemy we shouldn't underestimate.'

'Which is why you're here: to use those negotiating skills.' Federico was interrupted as his daughter approached, carrying a tray with two cups, milk and a Moka pot. 'Grazie, Francesa.'

Martini smiled up at her, 'Grazie.'

'Any food?' she asked.

'Two breakfasts,' Federico said.

'And an orange juice, please,' Martini added.

'Eamon here is from Ireland,' Federico said. 'Well, his father's Irish.' He looked up at her then down at Martini.

'My daughter is fascinated by Irish culture and wants to go and study there.'

Martini nodded, 'It's a beautiful country. And safer now than it was in the past.'

'Now that the IRA is no longer fighting a guerrilla war with the British army.' She spoke as if reading from a textbook.

He cleared his throat. 'That's right.'

'You know, Francesca, Eamon here was known as the man who outsmarted the entire British Intelligence world, and at only the age of....' Federico looked at Martini.

'Seventeen, Federico,' Martini looked up at her again, feeling like he was on display. 'I was seventeen.'

'How did you do that?' Her eyes widened, looking like she was about to begin taking notes for an exam.

'It's a long story, maybe another time.' He smiled and cleared his throat, reaching for the Moka.

'Yes, of course,' she said. 'I'll bring the food over when it's ready.'

'Grazie.' Martini smiled at her as she walked away. Looking at Federico, as he poured the coffee. 'So, where has this meeting been set for tonight?'

'On neutral ground. Safer for us all. Not far from here.'

Martini handed a cup of coffee over to Federico then took one himself.

'Do you still have contacts within the Irish Republican Army?'

'I wouldn't call them contacts, but I'd be able to contact them. Although they're no longer fighting a political war, instead using the only skills they have to make a living.'

'Why didn't you bring them into your family?'

'A lot of them became global assassins, gifted at only one

thing: war, death, shooting and bombing.' He looked into his cup as he spoke, a tad distant for a second.

'They may come in handy one day if we ever needed extra help,' Federico said.

'I'm here only to help my cousins who want to continue to do business in Milan, that's all. I'm becoming less interested in this life and more interested in living a quieter existence. In peace.'

Federico laughed. 'I don't think you'd be able to live a quiet life, Eamon. What are you going to do, take up poetry?'

He smiled, nodding his head. 'Maybe. But after we've negotiated a truce with La Camorra and agreed on a mutually beneficial deal, then I'll be looking to take a long overdue holiday.' He looked over Federico's shoulder as Francesca came towards them, a plate in each arm. 'But now, my only interest is the food on this plate.'

'Buon appetitio,' she said, setting the plates down in front of them.

Just as they both got started into their breakfast, the noise of the Granturismo's engine roaring outside grew louder as it pulled up to the shop. The engine died out and a few seconds later, Paolo entered, shouting over to Francesca to bring him a coffee.

He sat down at their table.

Federico looked at his brother. 'Everything's okay?'

'There's been a fire at the location for tonight, apparently two kids were seen running away by a passer-by. I've spoken to Leonardo Pitrelli of La Camorra. They've changed the location to another place.'

Martini looked at Federico, then at Paolo. 'This is not happening. The meeting's location has been changed? Well, we're changing it again. Call them and tell them. I don't believe in coincidences.' He looked at the two brothers. Neither of them spoke. 'Come on, anyone can smell something dodgy. Whatever caused that fire had something to do with them wanting to change the location at the last minute. Tell them we meet at another place. Otherwise, the deal is off, and the negotiations leave this country with me.'

'Paolo, tell them we'll have the meet in Milano. City centre. Nice and public. Nowhere to be set up.'

'In fact, give me his number, I will call him now,' Martini said, sounding inconvenienced. 'One thing I don't like is to have my fuckin' time wasted. I didn't come all the way to Italy to be messed around.'

CHAPTER THREE

Via Paolo Sarpi, is known as Milan's epicentre for the Milanese Chinese community. Located in the city's eighth district, the street provides a range of services from silk and leather stores, hairdressers to libraries, travel agents to fashion boutiques. Having spoken to his cousins – Pietro and Paolo, Martini had found their new place to meet.

Café Americano was a fresh face in the city's Chinatown, wide-open front window, sat at the junction with Via Messina. It provided a panoramic view of the street, but more importantly it had a rear exit and an anonymous vehicle waiting to get away – if needed.

Martini knew his cousins needed him there to negotiate for them. Not because they couldn't deal with the situation themselves, but he had earned the respect of everyone with some leverage in the world of Italian organised crime, both in Europe and North America. He was not only gifted with his hands – a trained killer from his time fighting the Taliban in the US Special Forces, but he was also his family's best businessman for a generation. He'd learned to make positive connections with influential people on both sides of the law – often arguing that both sides were more often than not intertwined. He'd bought the Martini family their freedom and a chance to move away from criminality and go legit. He was both feared and respected. But he knew he wasn't invincible, which meant putting measures in place to make sure his life wasn't going to be cut short, like specific locations of meeting, with spare cars in case a quick getaway was needed.

They left the Maserati at Nero e Bianco. Paolo Bianco drove them to the meeting in a silver BMW. Martini occupied the back seat and Federico was in the front passenger seat. As the car pulled into the parking bay just outside Café Americano, Martini checked his phone was on vibrate.

Seeing Martini fumble around with his device, Federico asked, 'Problem?'

He shook his head. 'Just checking I haven't missed anything.' He craned his head around the driver's seat. 'Paolo, you stay in the car, keep the engine running. They'll think it's our only way of getting away and will overlook the car out the back.'

Paolo nodded and grunted his agreement.

Martini looked at Federico. 'Let's go.' He got out of the car and buttoned his suit jacket closed, scanning up and down the street. There was a steady footfall in the area. June in Milan: perhaps an even number of tourists and locals.

'Here, Eamon,' Federico said, as he rounded the front of the car, discreetly slipping a Sig Saur to Martini. 'Fully loaded.'

Martini took the weapon and slipped it down behind the rear of his waistband. 'Thanks.' He'd already instructed his cousins to leave him a weapon in the toilets, but Federico didn't need to know that.

Stepping into the café, Martini went straight to the

toilets. 'Grab a seat. I'm just checking we have no surprises waiting in there.'

The toilets were not split into male and female. Instead, there were two individual rooms with facilities in each to cater for one person at a time, of either sex. As instructed by Pietro, Martini entered the first room he came to from the shop and lifted the galvanized stainless steel cistern lid, noting the lid would be a handy weapon in itself. A water-tight plastic bag was taped to the inside of the lid. Inside it was a black Beretta Nano, a three-inch barrelled, four-inch-tall hand pistol that packed an eight shot, nine mm magazine, more than enough to get him out of a tight space. Opening the bag, Martini took the pistol out and replaced it with Federico's.

He'd more reason to distrust Federico than to trust him. Should he trust a weapon he'd been given by his associate in the kill-or-be-killed world he found himself in, or go with the one his cousin provided? It didn't take a genius to work that one out.

Hearing low voices coming from outside the toilets, emanating from the shop floor, he flushed the toilet, washed and dried his hands, then made his way back out.

As the door opened, he had all eyes in the shop on him. A man of similar age to Martini, was sitting at the table facing Bianco. His brown eyes were cold and calculating, watching Martini make his way across the shop floor. He never took his eyes off him. It was as if he'd been challenged to a staring contest. Martini, feeling relaxed and fully aware of the consequences of showing any sign of weakness in this world, held the guy's stare. The guy stood up and offered Martini his hand.

'I've heard a lot about you.' He was a few inches taller than Martini and just as athletic. In this world, being physical wasn't a requirement for being a leader or a boss, but this guy, being the leader or at least the one doing the talking for La Camorra, was physically acceptable. 'Marco Pagina.'

Martini shook Pagina's hand and they both sat down.

'Before we get started, let's get some coffee,' Federico said. But before anyone had a chance to reply, flashing red and blue lights illuminated the street outside.

'Boss, police!' One of Pagina's men shouted from the door, then disappeared into the street. The sound of car engines starting was mixed with the skids of screeching tyres and voices shouting stop. Martini sprang up off the chair, sending the four legs screeching behind him, then rushed towards the kitchen. He cut through the kitchen, out the evacuation door and into the rear of the building. He found himself in a fenced off area, lined with industrial bins, all chained together. Boxed in. He approached the back gate, it was also chained and padlocked. He pulled his gun out and went to shoot the lock but decided against it. Wiping his prints off the weapon, he dropped it into the blue bin. He then climbed on top, the plastic lid denting in under his weight and leapt over the fence out into the back pathway. Federico came right behind him.

'Who the fuck has set us up?' Federico shouted, as he followed Martini over the fence.

A blue Alpha Romero sat fifty yards to the right of them. Martini ran for the driver's door, Federico quickly taking the passenger's side. Martini found the key under the dirty old foot mat, started the engine and took off.

'That's what I want to know,' Martini said. 'Someone set us up, and we're going to get to the bottom of it.' He turned a sharp left onto the Via Aristotile Fioravanti, sped up for one hundred yards and then a right onto Via Aleardo Aleardi.

He cast a glance in the rear-view mirror, seeing two marked vehicles with "Polizia" across the bonnet, both in pursuit. The thunderous drum of a helicopter's propellors above was accompanied by a blinding search light. Looking at the fuel gauge, he sighed. They had a three-quarter-full tank.

'When I get my hands on the stronzo responsible for this, I'm going to chop them up,' Federico shouted, looking shifty in his seat, continually looking over his shoulder, through the window at their pursuers.

'If it was La Camorra that set us up, they've just given us their answer as to whether or not they're interested in peace.' Martini increased the distance between them and the two police vehicles, but not outrunning the chopper. 'Where's the closest nightclub?'

'You want to party now?' Federico laughed without humour.

'No, but we're not going to shake off that police heli-copter anytime soon. We need a crowded place. Somewhere we can blend in.'

Federico pulled his phone out. Looking through it, he said. 'The university is holding an event there this evening, one of the local musicians is doing a charity event out in the student's football stadium.'

'Where?'

'Keep going straight.' He made a call, putting the device to his ear. 'Paolo, where are you?' He paused for a moment. Martini could hear the tiny scratches of a voice coming through the other end. 'Okay, see you later.' He hung up. 'Paolo got away.'

As they approached a set of traffic lights, a leather-clad biker straddled a Honda CBR1000, the superbike idling at the stop line. Martini looked in the rear-view mirror. There was a couple of hundred yards from them and the police. He put the foot down, creating more distance, the car flew down the road. 'We're taking that bike, be ready to jump out.' He looked across at Federico. 'Give me your gun.' Federico obliged. 'Hold on.' Approaching the bike, he pulled the handbrake, sending the car into a skid. Turning the vehicle in front of the bike, he almost hit the traffic light. He had his gun pointed at the guy on the bike before the biker had a chance to do anything, but gasp at the stunt. 'Get off the bike.' Martini threw the door open and jumped out, the biker was about to take off when Martini fired a shot in the air. 'Get off the fucking bike!' The biker didn't resist. Martini jumped on and indicated for Federico follow him, but he'd already opened fire on the police. The helicopter circled them above. Another two police vehicles came from ahead and the two that had been in pursuit had caught up. 'Federico, get on the fucking...' Before he had a chance to finish, Federico took a shot in the chest by one of the officers, then a second, and a third. Martini spun off in the direction they were headed, the bike negotiating the roads with ease. He turned down a narrow alley and let the bike make easy work of the distance, eating it up in seconds. The helicopter was still overhead. As he emerged from the alley onto the Via Festa Del Perdono, he saw the sign for the university. Universita Degli Studi Di Milano, or known colloquially as: UniMi or Statale was swamped by a sea of people. With around sixty-thousand enrolled students, one of the largest universities in Europe was, at that time, hosting a substantial percentage of those on the register.

The thumps of the chopper's propellors from above hunted him down like a giant metallic eagle, giving chase to its prey, following him all the way to the campus. He entered the crowd: young men and women, drinking, singing and cheering; emulating that carefree attitude radiated by students the world over – every bit the opposite of Eamon Marini at the moment who was as serious as a heart attack. He needed to get inside and shake the pursuit.

Pulling up just short of the access barrier, people filtering through the metal detector, the closest security guard to him was a six-and-a-half-foot-tall black male, first admiring the bike, then admiring Martini's suit.

'Nice bike.' The guard spoke with an African accent. With Martini's experience around the world on various clandestine CIA missions, he'd guess Nigeria, or somewhere thereabouts.

'You can have it.' Martini tossed him the key. 'That'll pay for my access.'

The guard caught the key, initially taken off his stride, his line of sight jumping to the chopper up above that was now shining a light down on them. He quickly composed himself and looked at Martini. 'That's for you?' He indicated the bird in the sky.

'I don't have time to explain, my daughter is in there, and she's not well, I need to get in there, now,' he lied.

The second guard approached, standing a few inches shorter than his colleague, but still taller than Martini. He looked more Italian than African but just as defensive, just as serious. 'Is there a problem?'

'There will be if I don't get in there and find my daughter.' Martini took his driving licence out and handed it to the guard. The Italian guard looked at it. 'Eamon Martini.'

'You know the Martini family?'

'I do but I've never heard that family having someone with a stupid name like Eamon.' He tossed the card back.

Martini caught it and smiled, putting the licence back in his wallet. 'You'll be visited by the Apostles very soon.'

'I'm with the Bianco family, now you can fuck off.'

'Well, let me be the first to tell you, Paolo Bianco is a chicken-shit and his brother Federico was just shot dead by those police officers coming up this street.' The two guards looked over Martini's shoulder towards the sound of three police vehicles heading their direction.

'You're not getting in, now fuck off.' The African guard tossed the bike key back at Martini. Martini caught the key, and threw it back at the guy, hitting him in the eye, quickly following it up with a right hook to the jaw, jumping in the air, a ferocious arching swipe to the face, sending the guard into his partner. The Bianco member stepped out of the way as the African fell to the ground unconscious. The Italian grabbed Martini by the throat, but Martini head-butted him on the nose, side kicking him in the inner leg, collapsing the hinge joint. He fell to the ground, screaming in agony. A group of students all stood back, creating more distance between them and Martini as he ran in through the metal detectors, shoulder barging a drunken guy to his ass. The music got louder the closer he got to the inside; the deafening thud of the base caused every bone in his body to vibrate, trembling even the marrow in his bones.

Taking his jacket, tie, and waistcoat off, Martini threw them in the bin. He unbuttoned the top button of his shirt and followed the signs towards the rear of the campus. The exit to the car park was clearly signed in bright green, with a cloakroom next to it. He went to the cloakroom, indicated to the guy on the other side of the desk that he'd lost his ticket, but the long coat to the far left was his. Initially taken off guard, the guy eventually gave the coat over. Martini put it on and exited through the rear of the building.

The car park was full. He had the pick of many cars. He chose a black Audi A5, fast but not attention grabbingly so. Putting his elbow through the driver's window he accessed the vehicle and got in. Ripping the casing off the steering wheel, he hotwired the car. The petrol tank was only a quarter full, but that was enough to get him to where he needed to go.

Putting the car in first, he followed the one-way system, approaching the exit. The chopper was still circling above. As he exited the car park, he turned left onto Via Francesca Forza and kept within the inner-city limits, not wanting to attract attention. He drove straight for one mile, then turned right onto Via S. Damiano for fifty yards then a sharp right onto Via Mozart where the Apostles were the named proprietors of a family run restaurant. Pulling into the rear car park of the building, taking the now stolen car out of view, he shut the engine off and got out.

As he stepped inside La Casa Famiglia, he saw Pietro behind the counter taking a payment from a young couple. Pietro acknowledged his arrival and indicated for him to go into the back office.

'Un café lungo?' Martini asked for a coffee as he walked through the main seated area, towards the manager's office.

'Ciao, Uncle Eamon,' Maria Martini said, as she cleared one of the tables.

'Ciao, Maria.' He offered her a smile. On the surface he was cool and calm, but on the inside, he was full of rage; his heart racing, the blood gushing in his ears.

He stepped into the office, the other apostle, Paolo, was sitting on the edge of the desk, on the phone. As soon as Martini walked in, he told whoever it was on the other end he'd call them back, then abruptly ended the call.

'Eamon, what the hell happened?'

'That's what I'd like to know.' Martini took the coat off and sat down on the sofa beneath the window. 'Some bastard set us up.'

'If La Camorra want a fucking war,' Paolo shook his head, his nostrils flaring, 'they've fucking got one.'

Martini sat forward, resting his forearms on his thighs. 'Calm down, Paolo.' Pietro entered the office, a tray of drinks in his hand. 'We don't know if it was them or not.' He stood back up and walked to the window, looking out onto the street. 'Who was that you were talking on the phone to?'

'Leonardo, he just wanted to know if we'd heard anything about the meeting.'

Martini turned and grabbed one of the cups of coffee. 'Well now you know.' He blew on the coffee then took a sip, looking at Pietro. 'The meeting didn't go ahead.'

'You think it was the Bianco family?' Pietro asked.

Martini went back to his seat and sat down, shaking his head. 'Federico's dead and Paolo Bianco's too stupid to act alone.'

'So, what now?' Pietro asked.

Before Martini said another word, the door was kicked in. Three uniformed officers of the Polizia di Stato, (the state police) had their guns on each of them. Two plain clothes officers entered the room. One was a male around mid-forties. His smug grin was evident, he'd caught a big fish today. The other plain clothes was a female of around early thirties, successful enough to wear plain clothes, the way she took her job with textbook precision meant she was new to the post and still working to impress those who'd hired her. She was more interested in the Apostles, whereas the male was looking directly at Martini.

'Turn around and put your hands behind your back,' the male officer ordered.

Martini took another sip of his coffee then set the cup down, doing what he was told. 'What's the charge?'

'Just shut your mouth, before I slap you around this room.'

Martini laughed; his laughter being echoed by his two cousins.

'All of you shut up, before I make you all suffer on your journey to Ferroviaria.' The male officer spun Martini around. He pressed his pointed nose directly into Martini's face. 'You got something to say, tough guy?'

Martini tilted his head to the left and looked past the officer at Maria who stood at the door. Her expression of concern bothered him more than getting arrested. He looked at the male officer again. 'I do actually.' He looked at Maria again. 'Maria, keep our dinner in the oven, we'll be home in a couple of hours.'

Paolo and Pietro both laughed, none of them appearing worried about the situation they'd found themselves in. The Apostles were taken out first, leaving Martini in the office with the two plain clothes. The male officer looked back at his female colleague. 'Elisabetta, you know who this is?'

She shook her head.

'Eamon Martini.'

'The Irishman?'

'You've caught yourself a highly wanted man.'

Martini looked at his niece who was still stood at the door. 'Like I said, Maria, keep our dinner in the oven. We'll be back once this pair are out of a job.'

'Get moving, you cocky bastard.' The male officer grabbed him, dragging him in front to lead them out through the door.

Martini winked at Maria as he passed her. 'Don't look so worried.'